Pop Scars

BY **Charli Poe**

ISBNs:
979-8-9988585-0-5 (EPUB Edition)
979-8-9988585-1-2 (Paperback — Amazon KDP Edition)
979-8-9988585-2-9 (Paperback — Trade Edition)
979-8-9988585-3-6 (Hardcover — Trade Edition)
979-8-9988585-4-3 (Audiobook Edition)

Cover thanks to GetCovers.com

The typography in this book uses open-source fonts licensed under the SIL Open Font License, Version 1.1. Fonts used include: **Alike** (Eduardo Tunni) for body text; **Anton** (Vernon Adams) for title text; **Lexend** (Bonnie Shaver-Troup & Thomas Jockin) for front and back matter; **Antonio** (Vernon Adams, Pablo Impallari, & Andrés Torresi), **Roboto Mono** (Christian Robertson), and **Over the Rainbow** (Kimberly Geswein) for accent text.

First Published: June 2025

Published by Charli Poe under the *Liminoumenal* imprint
www.charlipoe.com

This book is dedicated to my siblings, my parents and my very good friends without whom I would be an entropic particle floating in the void of space.

Table of Contents

Prologue. Twenty–Seven Years Earlier (Approximately).

Rebecca sat in the dark, tracing the edge of her fingernail along the shallow grooves in the wood-grain floor. She shivered, breathing in a long, slow breath, straining her ears each time the house groaned, expecting to hear footsteps. Instead, she heard the whisper of blood rushing in her ears and imagined frightening things: her father frozen in bed, while her mother, lying beside him, slowly faded out of existence.

Rebecca's eyes stung. Focusing on the room around her, back upright and rigid, she became aware of herself in a new way. Her skin felt like a cold film stretched to its limits around the warm, pulsing body of someone else. Her thoughts were flitting about like hummingbirds, pausing only briefly to think about how she was thinking about herself thinking about herself.

Never before had she deliberately and without permission left her bed after climbing in for the night. It wasn't that she had been forbidden to leave by her parents or feared their wrath. She had never gotten out of bed because it never occurred to her that she might: her mother and dad had said it was time for bed, so it was time for bed. If she was hungry or thirsty or needed to use the bathroom, well, she was a big girl and she could wait until morning. At no other point in Rebecca Ziel's seven years, five months of life had she considered being somewhere other than where she expected and was expected to be. In fact, as far back as she could remember, she had never before felt so strongly about doing something that she was unable to do anything except follow her gut. So she left her bed and sat with her back flat against the front door.

Her mind went back to the large room down the hall. Her parents had always been what made things make sense. They were like the frame around a picture, keeping what was outside of it outside of it and protecting the family from the empty spaces outside. But empty spaces had begun leaking in, and while Rebecca didn't have the words to describe it, she had sensed a wrongness growing in her mother for some time.

It wasn't just that her mother didn't smile or laugh as much anymore, or that when she did, the laughter tended to come out like a cough: automatic and without feeling. That was part of it, but there was also the way she spoke to Dad, friends or people at the store. It sounded the same, but there was a separation between the words she used and the stiff way she stood or tilted her head. Rebecca didn't understand how or why everyone else could ignore something so obvious.

Without realizing she was doing so, or knowing exactly why, Rebecca found herself trying to sing more loudly and laugh more readily whenever in her mother's presence, as though pleasure were contagious and eventually her mother would become infected. Occasionally, very occasionally, it seemed to work. Alone in the dark, Rebecca remembered the time at the Raley's when she had sung along to the black guy in green: "What's cooler than eating poop ICE COLD!?"

Her mother had asked—one of her eyebrows cocked higher than the other in the mysterious way that only she knew how to do—"What did you say?" When Rebecca repeated the lyrics, finishing with the "Heyyyy-ah, ayyy-YA!" her mother was overcome with laughter, saying, "I don't think that's what he says!" For the rest of the trip, Rebecca basked in her mother's really for real joy. She hummed the song, hoping to hold on to the memory, the moment. When they returned home, her mother, still smiling, went on the family computer to search for the right words. She corrected Rebecca, laughing again. It was glorious.

Rebecca didn't understand the real words any more than the fake ones, but she liked the sound of the song and loved the sound of her mother's laughter. So, the following week, she tried singing it again, using the same wrong words that had made her mother laugh. That time, the song accomplished nothing.

The first time Rebecca voiced her concern had been in February after another of her mother's increased absences from the family dinners in the living room. Seated on the sofa, they would eat and watch one of the movies their dad rented for the occasion. Though her mother had never been enthusiastic about the tradition—had, in fact, complained frequently about too much time in front of the TV—it had always just been what the family did. Rebecca trembled when finally asking about the change, half-worried that the question itself might make things worse. Her dad tried his best to smile and told her that "Mommy isn't feeling well, but she'll be back next time." Sure enough, she was.

Four days later, she missed another meal, then another. Rather than ask again, Rebecca gradually accepted that the family dinners now included only her sister and their dad, even when her mother was present. Maybe, Rebecca thought, she, too, was getting too old for them.

In March, a month before her birthday, Rebecca had been preparing for a Saturday morning trip to the park with her sister, Erin, when she walked in on her mother seated on the toilet, quietly, almost imperceptibly sobbing. The young girl reached as high as she could, wrapping her arms around the woman's crooked neck. Her mother scooped Rebecca up into her lap, repeating again and again that she loved her and that she was sorry for making her sad. Rebecca insisted she wasn't sad and that she didn't want to cry, only barely avoiding tears. She never asked her mother why, and her mother never said, but thirty-five minutes later, when she and her sister were dropped off at the park, the thick smell of grassy soil swirling about in the air, her mother smiled with an empty pleasantness and a familiar, faraway look in her eyes.

In May, there was a brief period of increased affection toward Dad, and both he and Erin reacted as though things were back to normal. To Rebecca, however, the apparent contentment made the hairs on the back of her neck tickle. During this time, whenever her mother smiled, something about it reminded Rebecca of an old movie she'd seen of a chimp imprisoned behind glass grinning so hard that it had given her nightmares. She would turn away, fearing that she might see the same primitive fire in her mother's stare or see her with the same clenched fists. Rebecca wanted more than anything to flee the falsehood she was seeing. When her mother returned to her regular, withdrawn self a few weeks later, Rebecca was almost pleased to have things, if unpleasant, at least honest.

Finally, earlier in the week, Rebecca's mother started taking the sisters on daily trips to the thrift store down the street. She encouraged them to carefully consider their belongings and decide what they could give to people in need. The three of them walked through the permanently smudged and scuffed glass doors, through fluorescent gray aisles and sticky plastic floors that smelled of abandoned houses and old people to a too-hot back room where they disposed of their family's used articles of clothing, unused toys and broken but functional furniture and appliances. The peace radiating from the girls' mother as they left the pile told Rebecca that something had changed for good. Though the donations came from all of them, for every box of the girls' or their father's belongings, there were two of her mother's, and by Saturday, her mother was down to a single pair of shoes and only enough clothes to last a week or two without washing. To his credit, Dad had asked about the reduced wardrobe, and her mother had just shaken her head and said she didn't need or wear any of those clothes anyway, so why should they take up so much space? He'd gone quiet then, saying nothing until it was just him and the girls at dinner. And even then, all he talked about was the movie they were watching.

Rebecca's body jerked back into an awareness of the present, and she struggled to remain alert. Her eyes, mostly useless in this darkness, tried to convince her that they might safely close for only a moment, but knots of muscle in her chest and tummy told the young girl that her mother was planning to leave and had been planning to do so for a long time. It might not be for forever and always, but the departure was going to be any day now, and her mother didn't want to, or couldn't, talk about it with the girls or their dad. The fact that, when she peeked into the partially-opened hallway closet instead of washing her hands at dinner, she had seen a brown leather travel bag stuffed with her mother's clothes and wallet, as well as a toothbrush and toothpaste, made Rebecca believe that the day of departure had finally come. And so it was with this strange certainty that she slipped out of bed after her parents' door had shut for the night, hoping to God that she was being a baby and worrying about nothing.

Interrupting the quiet with its dull, aching creak, the door to her parents' room slowly opened. Rebecca heard the soft tap of her mother's bottom pressing down onto the hallway toilet seat. Maybe, she thought, her mother wasn't going to leave them after all. Something was going on, but it was a normal something that, though Rebecca might be too young to understand, would pass them by and be forgotten. She was worrying about nothing. But when her mother stood up, a lack of running water meant that she didn't flush or wash her hands. Rebecca heard the soft squeak of a leather strap being lifted by a breathless body from the hallway closet. Any remaining hope that Rebecca's instincts had been wrong fled her. She rose unsteadily to her feet, her legs numb and her body trembling in anticipation of whatever came next.

Helen, Rebecca's mother, stood there staring at her daughter. Her eyes shone with ambient moonlight, travel bag hanging from her shoulder, and she assessed the situation.

Unsure of how or why she knew—pale eyes peering into pale eyes—Rebecca understood with a certainty that the two of them were somehow connected, that her mother was experiencing the same twist in her stomach, the same cold prickle on her skin, the same light-headedness and burning cheeks: in that moment, mother and daughter were aware that what they had each hoped would not be waiting for them, though both had known it would be, was. In that moment, the two of them were one and the same.

Then Helen tried to smile, and she spoke softly. "Why aren't you in bed? It's late. You should be in bed."

"I'm sorry."

"Go to sleep." Helen bared her chimp teeth in an effort to reassure her daughter.

Rebecca shivered, but she didn't back down. "Where are you going, Mommy?" She tried to ignore the salt water–stinging in her sinuses.

"It's time for sleep. You're going to be too tired in the morning."

Rebecca wanted to remain there, to stop her mother from doing whatever it was she had decided to do. She wanted to call out to her father or to her sister, or to God, for God's sake. She wanted to cry. She wanted to outstretch her hands and freeze the family in time like a framed photograph, capturing them in their perfect moment. She wanted to try anything that would make her mother change her mind. But she couldn't. Her mother had told her to go back to bed, and though it was exactly where she didn't want to go, she was going to do it because it was the right thing to do. *Right?*

Besides, she knew—not in any way she could describe, but deep inside, since the moment she shared with her mother, she knew—that stopping her mother from leaving would not fix whatever was broken. There was no perfect moment to freeze in time, even if she could. Rebecca walked into the hallway toward her bedroom and stopped only to turn and ask if she could come, too, to wherever her mother was going.

For the first time in a long time, Helen's face softened. Her frozen eyes melted, spilling cold tears down her cheeks. Helen lifted her hand toward Rebecca.

For a moment, the moonlight burned like the sun, and they were together, and it was tomorrow morning and every morning after, and they were there at the dining room table, eating Frosted Flakes and Fruity Pebbles in milk. They were a family again, framed in a picture, the four of them, happy forever and always.

But Helen dropped her hand and shook her head, returning Rebecca's world to midnight. "Mommy has to go out for a little while. You take care of Erin, okay? And your Daddy; he's going to need you to help him, okay?"

Rebecca watched as her mother's eyes froze again, and her lips opened into the chimp smile as she turned away, walking out of the front door, and Rebecca went back to bed, telling herself she needed to do something to make things better, and knowing she could do nothing but try or pretend to sleep.

Chapter One. Thursday.

It was the second time that day that Rebecca set the flower-power, airline-approved rolling case atop her bed and unpacked the neatly rolled clothes. She held up several tops and questioned whether they were right for the trip. Her eyes wandered down to the culottes slowly unfurling on the duvet; would they chafe her thighs? Trying everything on again was the only way to be sure.

Tokyo was not like Sacramento; you were expected to use public transportation or to walk. She knew this. She needed to have clothes that could breathe and wouldn't cause problems in the late-June heat. She knew this. But she knew also that it was a city where the individual was meant to endure, even embody discomfort for the sake of those around them, where if you had to choose between being relaxed but standing out or being miserable but invisible, you'd better choose the latter and be grateful that everyone around you was doing likewise.

More than anything, Rebecca didn't want to look like a tourist. But as a 5-foot-9-inch woman, she stood out even at home, her thicket of fiery red hair prone to getting caught in everything from automatic doors to strangers' glasses. Her goal, then, was to minimize any attention she might attract. She planned to accomplish this with a full pack of hair bands, an unassuming yet comfortable wardrobe filled with grays, browns and blacks. Still, she couldn't shake the feeling that she'd miscalculate something.

Sydney, Rebecca's best friend since Thomas Jefferson Middle School, who was taking the trip to Tokyo with her, would be entertaining no such doubts. Sure, Sydney changed her mind about things. She'd swap an outfit last minute if she decided it didn't fit the mood she was going for. But she didn't dwell on those changes or feel like a loser for having made the wrong decision. And she certainly didn't consider the opinions of others when deciding whether to wear jeans versus slacks. It didn't matter what anyone else thought.

I'm being unfair. Rebecca paused as she repacked, silently correcting herself. Her friend might doubt the taste or wisdom of anyone who disagreed with her before doubting herself, but she was acquainted with both doubt and embarrassment. It's just that for Sydney, rather than front-loading her uncertainty like Rebecca did, hers was concentrated in later moments of self-reflection that came after the decisions had been made, the debates had been argued and the consequences had been endured. On evenings when her daughters were away with their friends or their dads—and it always happened on an evening that she was alone—Sydney would call up crying, and she'd ask Rebecca to drive the three hours down so they could commiserate and eat ice cream.

As grateful as Rebecca was that she didn't suffer from Sydney's history of bad decisions, she sometimes wondered if she wouldn't be better off being impulsive instead of falling into the same trap she almost always did: leaving her choices up to the clock so that when there was no time left to reevaluate her decisions, the decisions were made.

Rebecca swapped a final pair of skorts, rolling and placing them in the carry-on atop a carved cedar box of pencils and the new drawing pad she'd purchased two months earlier. These pencils and paper were the only luggage she never questioned. As a child, she'd loved the original illustrations for Alice's Adventures in Wonderland, and she had pestered her parents until they bought her a book full of John Tenniel's art. As she aged, she found evidence of his whimsy in all of her drawings, no matter how abstract or realistic. When she happened upon a drawing pad with a dog on the cover that might have jumped straight out of the looking glass, she purchased it before even realizing it would be ideal for the trip.

Whereas Sydney intention for the trip was to take the two of them through Shinjuku and Shibuya with hopes of experiencing the exotic lights, foods and nightlife of a foreign capital, Rebecca was more interested in the figures and faces, the trees and skylines, the shadows and shapes in everything that she would see. Where others might take a hundred pictures on their phones, she would select key times and places and sketch those moments from this once-in-a-lifetime experience for later appreciation. That was her way of capturing memories. It wasn't that she never took pictures on her phone, it was just that, unless a picture was properly lit and staged, it felt flat and showed too much to know what was important.

It was most probably a coincidence that, just as Rebecca's thoughts were on her phone, her phone rang. According to the display, the caller was Charles Sprock, owner of Halcyon Realty (and her boss). It was 11:25 in the morning, about seven hours before she intended to be at the airport. Rebecca was going to let the call go to voicemail. She had reminded him before leaving the previous day that she wouldn't be back in the office for just over two weeks. That he was calling anyway told her that either he had forgotten about the trip, or that he had gone into the office and determined some emergency or other justified his ignoring it.

In either case, she reasoned that whatever he was calling about was something she did not want to know, and she wasn't going to answer. She wasn't. But what if it was important, and there was no space left in her voicemail? Besides, Charles would chain call four to ten times before he even considered leaving a message, and that message would imply without stating that she was risking her job. Rebecca knew from experience that regretting decisions while employed beat getting yourself fired any day of the week. The sound of wind on the other line told her Charles was driving somewhere fast; knowing him, it was probably south to San Francisco or Los Angeles.

"Rebecca, I'm so glad I caught you. You won't believe your luck!" People in Charles's sphere were always getting lucky in ways they wouldn't believe. "I've got to meet up with some clients in L.A." He paused, providing her an opportunity to volunteer for whatever needed doing and save him from asking. Instead, she kept quiet and waited for him to continue. "And as you know, we're prepping the Sweet house for sale. It's a big deal. A big deal."

The words she wanted to say— *That's great, but you know I'm leaving for Japan in a few hours*—stuck in her throat and instead came out as "Uh huh."

"I'm going to need you to drop whatever I've got you working on and start that process right now. I should be back to take over in a couple of days, so you'll still be able to make the trip, right?" Rebecca's face tingled, like she'd been slapped.

"I need to be at the airport in six hours." She didn't question whether or not he had actually convinced himself that she had time for this job (did it really matter anymore?) but she knew that she had reserved the thirteen workdays well in advance, marking them on every calendar that he used and setting him daily reminders. Of course, he rarely checked his calendars, which is why she made sure to mention the trip in every weekly meeting for the past month. She couldn't remember now whether she had specified the exact departure time, but the information had most definitely been stated multiple times before then.

"That's...Well, hmm." Charles took a moment to think. "How about this." He paused: another opportunity for her to give up her time voluntarily. "How about I buy you a ticket for when I get back so we can get this whole thing going? Trust me, this is B*Sweet we're talking about! This is a once-in-a-lifetime opportunity. She was one of your heroes, right?"

Professionally known as B*Sweet (pronounced "be sweet"), Becky Sweet was born Becky White, but she adopted her mother's maiden name, Sweet, for the stage because of course she did. A former Mickey Mouse club member alongside Britney Spears and Ryan Gosling (who some said inspired the song 'Wanna'), she had, to Charles' credit, been a significant figure during Rebecca's early adolescence, but primarily because B*Sweet was a publicly motherless teenager and that inspired a feeling of kinship. Beyond that, however, Rebecca felt no more admiration toward B*Sweet than toward any of the other young pop stars who'd shepherded her into her teenage years; the time when she was, paradoxically, filled both with a need to be perfectly normal and a deep desire to be completely unique.

B*Sweet's style and, more significantly, her early maturity had helped Rebecca and her young friends define what becoming a woman actually meant. Of course, by the time Rebecca was 15, she could see that the B*Sweet on MTV had never been a real woman. That girl with the perfect face and body had, in fact, always been a product manufactured by faceless men in windowless rooms to be presented to young girls and slightly older boys as a way of selling CDs and skirts and single-use socks. In the years since Rebecca's adolescence, B*Sweet had only ever entered her consciousness when a new scandal or meltdown qualified as either deviant or pathetic enough to warrant attention on TV or TMZ. Never, however, not even as a tween girl, would she have identified any of her favorite musicians, including B*Sweet, as a hero.

"Sort of," she compromised.

"Right, I'm going to need you to stay in her house with the family while you get things ready for the listing. They're throwing a charity event there tonight, so you'll need to wear something nice. Black tie. Don't worry, I've already called them, they're expecting you. Chris White, or a man called Kyle, should meet you there. You can hide in the background, out of the way, doing whatever needs doing." He gave her an opening to respond, but Rebecca was caught in a mental loop, trying to reconcile two equally powerful, yet contradictory truths: she couldn't agree to do the job, but neither could she turn it down.

"Can you believe it!" Charles continued, "She's going to be there, in the house with you! It makes me sick that I'm going to miss it, but it should still be an exciting adventure! Wouldn't you say?"

At her silence, he added, "And wait until you see the house!" Rebecca had seen it. She started researching it two months earlier, less than an hour after Charles had mentioned the possibility of their listing it. "Would you believe it's great for drawing? I want to say it was in an architectural magazine." It had been: she'd purchased a physical copy of the magazine and given it to him, open to the article (which she marked clearly, in case he closed it). "In fact," Charles' voice lowered opportunistically, "I was hoping you might do some of your drawings of the property that we could use as part of the listing. Maybe even offer them to the buyer as an added bonus. Great, right? Along with the pictures you'll be taking, of course. And maybe clippings from the magazine, if you could find any of those."

While he might sometimes misrepresent the significance of things, Charles Sprock was not the sort to blow smoke about the facts. If he said B*Sweet was going to be there, she'd be there. And if he said he'd buy her the replacement ticket, he'd buy her the replacement ticket. He might even be willing to cover both the difference between Sydney's return ticket and the hotel fee so the two could still return together. But Charles Sprock was also the sort of person who would make plans without considering their impact on, you know, actual life. He'd buy the ticket, but something else would come up and it would be delayed again and again until everyone had forgotten why the tickets had been purchased in the first place.

"Thank you for doing this. It's really an emergency."

"Uh-huh." She was used to this sort of emergency and the collateral disappointment. Could she even call it disappointing if it was expected?

The worst part, really, was going to be telling Sydney that she was going to miss the first several days. This was assuming, of course, that something else didn't come up and cause her to miss it all, a possibility that was feeling increasingly probable. It wouldn't be any more of a surprise to her friend than the whole thing was to her, but Sydney, who lived closer to San Jose, had departed from that airport two hours earlier.

Sydney's flight included two layovers, but she was still expected to touch down about twelve hours before. Telling her now, mid-flight, was going to be awkward and uncomfortable, and it would give Sydney leverage whenever she wanted Rebecca to do something for her. The problem was, that leverage was deserved because, unlike Rebecca, Sydney was a single mother with two teenage daughters. She had worked hard to arrange for her own mother to watch over them while she was away.

At least, Rebecca thought, Tokyo was reputed to be safe enough to explore solo, even for a woman. Some of the initial night plans might need to be delayed or canceled, but that was always a risk. She considered not saying anything; she could always come up with an excuse when she didn't arrive at the airport, or she could say she didn't have a choice, which, when she thought about it, she really didn't. But, of course, any hopes of avoiding the talk were fantasies.

"Take the—" the line went silent.

"Hello?" Pulling the phone from her ear, Rebecca confirmed that the connection was still active, just on hold. Charles's voice returned to the speaker.

"I'm on another call. Grab the iPad and whatever paperwork when you leave the office. You know what you'll need. I have to go." He didn't hang up; instead, he ended the call by putting her back on hold. It was so very typical. At least, she mused, she had purchased the insurance that allowed her to cancel the ticket at the last minute. Planning for the worst rarely made life better, but it did, sometimes, make the disappointment easier to bear.

Chapter Two.

Pounding pop music radiated from Rebecca's white GTI, both in preparation for who she was going to meet and as a distraction from the voice in her head telling her she should have fought harder for the trip. She hadn't actually listened to any of B*Sweet's songs in years, but the music was working on both fronts. The drive from the offices in Downtown Sacramento to the estate in Granite Bay was mostly free of negative thoughts, and—as the chorus rose, and she sang along—it felt downright transcendental.

Overcome with nostalgia for what teenage Rebecca had expected her life to become, hazy images of what she might still achieve condensed in Rebecca's mind. Deeper still was the nagging thought that, perhaps, Charles was right, and the job was a legitimate opportunity. Maybe everyone saying life got better in your thirties was right, and this would be what started the change.

Maybe, in a fabulous twist of fate, the old mistakes and missed chances that so often played on repeat in her head might cease to be mere regrets, transforming into the valuable life lessons failures were always said to be. If she could hold on to that truth she felt in that moment, following those lessons to their logical conclusions, she might still become a version of herself that teenage Rebecca would respect.

As the surroundings shifted from urban to suburban, dusty Charles Sheeler clouds were replaced by luminous Maxfield Parrish tufts floating serenely above happier trees and more manicured lawns. House styles transitioned from generic to eclectic, and property lines from modest to generous, signaling an exponential increase in the residents' wealth. Even the summer air outside seemed to breeze cooler where the houses were further apart and grander, as though temperature itself could be convinced to shave off a few degrees in exchange for a cheeky bribe.

Listening to B*Sweet, Britney, Taylor and the other divas of her youth, Rebecca was filled with the uncanny feeling that she was entering an alternate reality, one where the past ten years of stagnation had been a surreal test she'd been given to ensure she would be mature enough to return to the life she was supposed to have. Although Rebecca's boss always had tales of celebrity acquaintances, she rarely visited those clients' homes, and she never spoke to them face-to-face. Confronted with the possibility of conversing with B*Sweet while under the influence of the star's own music, terrified her, but in a good way.

Rebecca passed a line of large white trucks parked on the main road as she approached the small forest that surrounded the Sweet house. Among mature native trees such as black oak and red willow was the occasional Japanese maple. These had all been planted in the area to obscure the properties from their neighbors and anyone who might be driving by. Across the street from the turnoff, a dark gray motorcycle and black Mercedes sat facing the Sweet's driveway entrance.

As she approached the cold metal code box, Rebecca turned down the music, ostensibly out of respect for the neighborhood, and entered the code. With the lack of mind-altering melodies, her optimism deflated, grounding her in reality. No matter who would be present, she was there to work, and she'd agreed to live at work, for the weekend, if not longer. Unconsciously, she slumped down in the car seat as though being an inch shorter would disguise the fact that she did not belong.

The black Mercedes pulled forward, crossing the road and trapping her between it and the slowly opening gate. A barrel-chested black man exited the car, a camera hanging from his shoulder like a military saber. He bent down, gripping the car door like a banister. Rebecca blinked, staring at the dollar sign tattooed between the thumb and forefinger of his right hand. She followed his arm up a strong shoulder to his friendly face, reflexively smiling in return. Nostrils full of his minty breath, she wanted to say something to move him, but what came out was, "Hello?"

He tilted his head toward the code box and said, "You're too late to be crew. And you're too early to be a guest. Who are you?"

Rebecca shook her head and stuttered, "No, I, um, I'm here for the house. I'm supposed to meet with the family about it. Did I do something wrong? I was given a code and told you all would know I was coming."

The man she'd initially assumed to be security personnel grinned wider. "I can't say one way or another; we're not party to the party. We were just wondering whether you might be here to meet Ms. Jenna Sweet?"

"Um, I don't know." A movement in the woods attracted Rebecca's attention from the man to a slender figure also wearing a camera on a strap about her shoulder. She was peering through the viewfinder of a second camera toward the obscured house. The lens barrel lowered a moment, and the Asian woman looked at Rebecca and the man before wandering deeper into the forest. Rebecca felt so naive; of course he wasn't security, wielding a camera like that. They were paparazzi, hunting for photos of the rich and famous. The open gate screeched, starting to close. Rebecca should already be inside, but the man's grip on her door held fast.

From a pouch at his waist, the man pulled out a plain white envelope. Onto it, he drew a dollar sign, followed by 'Bill Hicks,' and his phone number. "We're photographers." The man turned and motioned toward the Asian woman in the woods. "We're here to speak to her, Jenna. If your paths cross, can you give her our number? Let her know we're here." He waited for Rebecca to nod before returning to his car, snapping a picture of her license plate and backing out.

Rebecca re-entered the code and passed through the gate. The driveway leading to the main house was wider than the entire street that Rebecca lived on. It curved into a roundabout surrounding an island of grass and a sun-bleached fountain complete with naked cherubs aiming miniature bows from the tops of Grecian columns. In what would probably be considered the property's front yard, a group of brown men and women dressed tables and hung string lights in front of a partially-built stage.

Rebecca parked behind a candy apple red Tesla stopped along the curve of the driveway leading to the garage. She checked her phone: during the drive, Sydney would have landed at her first layover, and Rebecca assumed the several consecutive buzzes were her friend's response to the news that Rebecca couldn't make it. Reading those particular texts while driving would have been too emotionally draining, so she'd waited before confirming her suspicion. The delay had repurposed them from a stressful distraction to a welcome excuse to remain in her car for even a couple minutes longer.

Sydney had responded with the same crying face emojis Rebecca had used, followed by "Of course," and "Should I cancel too? I'm still in Seattle."

Rebecca hadn't even considered that possibility. She mulled it over, knowing that Sydney would not have purchased any insurance and would eat the entire cost, which was already more than a responsible adult should have spent. She could imagine Sydney doing it, not just flying back, but talking the airline into a refund. But it wasn't worth the risk. Rebecca began composing another apology, deleted it, and instead responded with, "Don't you dare! I should still be able to meet you there next week." She hoped that was true, sending the crossed fingers emoji, instantly regretting it. What if Sydney mistook that to mean she was lying? Thankfully, the conversation ended with a simple smiley face.

Rebecca composed herself; she needed to be in work mode. She reached into her backpack, extracting the padded green sleeve containing the iPad she used for work. She opened the Sweet Estate's plat map. The lot, in toto, was just under 3.5 acres, with the 9,200-square-foot main house facing west and abutting the southern stretch of forest. Along with the attached four-car garage, the main home extended approximately to the center of the property. The area where the stage and seating were being set up constituted the largest continuous stretch of open yard, almost an acre by itself, sitting at the northwest quadrant and separated from the Eastern portion of the yard by a driveway extension too new to appear on the map. The extension appeared to lead to the one-bedroom, one-bathroom guest house.

East of the guest house, between it and the main building, was an indoor pool house built entirely of glass. The final building on the lot was the three-bedroom, two-bath home that had supposedly been converted into a recording studio ten years earlier when the family founded *Knotty Bark Sound House* in order to distribute B*Sweet's music themselves. A forest surrounded the entire property on all sides. The north and south woods were shared with neighbors, while the eastern side became public land at the tree line.

Rebecca opened the Photos app and exited the car, testing different angles to determine which best showcased the façade's majesty. She was careful to frame out any people as best she could, but they were all over, and she could only capture so much with an iPad camera.

A fiercely-pointed gabled roof rose above the unreasonably tall pair of front doors. Mansard roofing extended from there, covering the remainder of the house, with a single fairy-tale-inspired turret rising from one corner. The mix of French

Provincial, Medieval and Classical styles gave the house a glamorous, if slightly mishmashed feeling. Rebecca couldn't help being impressed by the construction, but she made a mental note that it would appeal to someone more interested in flair and fashion than classical elegance.

Snapping low-contrast pictures of the lot, fountain and textured bay windows, all of which she would later improve in Photoshop, Rebecca advanced toward the entryway. As her foot landed on the bottom step, the rightmost door swung open, revealing the most beautiful man Rebecca had ever seen. The hint of crow's feet at the corners of his eyes and the gray stubble peppered almost too perfectly through his evenly-cut, barely-there chestnut beard were the only clues that the man in fitted gray jeans and a tailored wine-color shirt was older than, say, 24. And yet, even these signs of age somehow enhanced his impact. Around his neck, he wore a black silk scarf with red stitched letters in a difficult-to-read, ye olde English typeface as an ascot.

"Rebecca Ziel?" He extended his hand to welcome her. "Welcome, I'm KL." Her eyes were still transfixed on the scarf, and he showed her the letters, repeating his name. With effort, Rebecca eventually perceived a 'K' and an 'L.' As soon as she looked away, however, the letters were lost and had to be found again. He must be the Kyle that Charles had mentioned. KL's eyes darted from her face to her waist; theatrically, he placed his hand over his heart. "A backpack *and* a fanny pack," he said. "*Brave.*"

She stuffed the tablet into her armpit and accepted his immaculate hand. It was soft enough that, for a moment, she wanted to stand there petting it. The moment was short-lived, though, and she pulled her hand away, pointing to a sculpture on the architrave above the door. "Is that her?"

He glanced up to the relief, the one with an elegant, nearly-nude woman conspicuously meant to look like B*Sweet circa 2001, then turned around with a hint of annoyance, "Yes." He left the door open for her to walk in and close herself.

"Wow." The grandness of the entryway surpassed even the outside, with a rose-tinted marble floor that appeared to be actual marble and a large portrait of the family. At least four or five feet in height, the artwork showcased B*Sweet in her early-to-mid teens, with her sister appearing to be around 10, and their parents flanking the girls on either side. Given the ages, it had probably been painted around the time of the first album.

"Yeah, I know," the man replied. "It's a *lot.*"

A gaudy, gold-leafed wood bookshelf without books occupied the opposite wall beside a large, overly-ornate window. Rebecca fought against the natural urge to stare dumbly at luxury, snapping pictures of the room and moving close to casually examine the shelf's contents. Framed photographs displayed the smiling family over the years, revealing the girls' transitions from children into teenagers. In one, B*Sweet and her sister hugged their wheelchair-bound mother on opposite sides, while others presented the sisters and their father in more recent years. The shelf below showcased multiple awards, most of which Rebecca didn't recognize. Two, however, were topped with the unmistakable golden Gramophone. "Are these all hers?"

The man turned slowly. Without seeing what she was referencing, he grunted, distorting his expression like he was explaining something for the thousandth time. "Mm-hmm. Any questions, she'll tell you *all* about those. More than you care to know. Except for that one back there," he pointed at an orange blimp shadowed in the rear of the shelf. "That one is Jenna's Kids' Choice Award from sixteen or seventeen years ago. That's our *actor's* contribution to the collection." KL's condescending smirk felt like an invitation to mock B*Sweet's sister. Instinctively, Rebecca shivered. "The others, though, yes. All hers."

"Who's that?" The many years had done little to lessen the mellifluous voice that drifted down the staircase.

"Speak of the devil, and she will appear, as they say." His whisper became a lazy response to the pop diva's question. He cupped a hand to his mouth and called, "This is Rebecca *Ziel.* Ms. Ziel's here to prepare the house for sale."

If she hadn't already been standing there, B*Sweet's hesitation made it clear she wouldn't have bothered to introduce herself; Rebecca, it seemed, was just another intruder. However, adherence to formality forced a smile to her lips. She set down the stack of glossy one-sheets and blue Sharpie she had been carrying on the shelf beneath the trophies and politely spread her arms. Rebecca hesitated, juggling her belongings as B*Sweet swooped in with a hollow embrace. "Welcome," she said flatly.

Though her focus was on the items in her arms, hoping that she was keeping them safe, at this distance, Rebecca couldn't help noticing the precision hair and makeup work and the many cosmetic procedures that must have gone into maintaining the illusion of youth the pop star evoked. Underneath a slight puffiness, Rebecca could see the natural good looks that had originally enamored her to casting agents and the House of Mouse.

"I love the frieze above the door. It reminds me of an artist I like, though I'm not sure how you say his name: Tan-dash, villi?"

B*Sweet's face beamed at the recognition. "You know him?! I don't think anyone's ever recognized his work before. That's wild! Can you believe I got him to make it for me?" She stepped out onto the riser, admiring the fantastical reimagining of her bygone youth. The beautiful man rolled his eyes and tried not to snicker. Rebecca followed outside and looked up as B*Sweet continued: "He is actually a good friend. I know people like to say he's difficult, but he's just exact. *Exacting.* Beautiful art demands a singular vision, don't you think?"

"Of course, she knows *all* about that." The man's words stalled Rebecca's response.

"Go sit on a cactus!" B*Sweet flicked her fingers. "Actually, no. You know what? I'm thirsty; grab me a water." As he swiveled toward one of the cavernous hallways, she snapped. "No; one of the energy waters we have in the studio." Pursing his perfect lips, he considered an objection. Instead, he curtsied dramatically and exited through the front doors. "You have to just ignore KL. He is so stereotypical that I think he's probably offensive."

"Is he your butler?" Rebecca asked nervously.

B*Sweet's head fell back in laughter. "Oh GOD, no. He's my stylist. Has been for something like fifteen years now. He's good enough at his job—not the best I've had—but he's a terrible human being. Christopher insists I keep him as my guy. And because I currently don't get to make any decisions about my life," she raised her wrist, showing off what looked like a miniature white smartwatch without a face, "well, he's still here."

Rebecca, focusing on the bracelet, needed a few seconds before it clicked: "Christopher" was Chris White—B*Sweet's father. According to the internet, Chris had been the conservator of the B*Sweet estate for the past 7 years. Rebecca didn't believe the position gave him authority over who B*Sweet hired, nor did it explain why she'd kept KL for the eight years before that. Rebecca shook her head: better not to kick that particular hornet's nest. Instead, she asked about the electronic bracelet.

"It's my comings and goings and stayings at home," B*Sweet mused. Rebecca didn't understand. "It's GPS; I choose to wear this, so I'm not forced to wear an ankle monitor. Again." She added in a whisper, "This way, I can still sneak out on occasion," and winked.

Rebecca was lost for words. Not wanting silence, she said, "he mentioned your Grammys," then immediately turned red.

"Those," B*Sweet led them back to the oversized shelf, seemingly unperturbed by the mention, "those are old. Another of Christopher's decisions. He feels it somehow makes me seem more impressive to others than I am. I guess it looks good for publicity stills. It's for 'Mothers are Daughters.' 'Best Pop Solo Performance, 2014.'" B*Sweet's eyes twinkled. She ignored the other Grammy, instead reaching inside and pulling the Kid's Choice Award out from the shadow, positioning it beside the other trophies as though it was equally important. "This one is Jenna's, though. She won it for her Gilly Hawkins show on the Disney channel. Did you ever watch it?"

Rebecca was a couple of years too old to have watched The Impossible Gilly Hawkins unironically, but Erin's temporary fixation on the show meant she was certainly aware of it. She affirmed her loose familiarity with a polite smile and a nod.

"I was so proud of her for that. She's a great actress. Deserved an Emmy if you ask me. I wish KL would stop hiding it. I found it behind the fridge once. He's such an asshole." She shook her head and placed Jenna's award in front of the unmentioned Grammy. "So," she said, "you're a Becky, too."

Though she had never gone by that name, Rebecca nodded. "We have that in common. But I always felt connected to you because your mother. I lost mine at a young age, too. Mine left us, our family, but when yours passed, I don't know. I felt a little like I understood you, and that you could understand me." She added clumsily, "If we, you know, ever met."

The two swiveled to the portrait dominating the opposite wall. B*Sweet's mother had been beautiful, possibly more so than B*Sweet herself. She had died of ovarian cancer not long after the portrait had been painted.

"It's hard," she admitted. "Mothers provide the structure that lets us be free."

Rebecca nodded gravely. "That sounds—" she said. "Is it from..." she pointed at the Grammy B*Sweet had just shown off.

B*Sweet nodded, swatting away the recognition. "It was inspired by something Ann Patchett said." Rebecca shook her head, not recognizing the name, but guessing her to be an obscure singer.

Teary beads were forming at the edges of the singer's eyes. She carefully removed them. "No child should have to grow up without a mother. I'm sorry you had to feel that, too." She hugged Rebecca, with what seemed like actual emotion this time, and Rebecca hugged her back, uncertain about the propriety of embracing a client, but comforted by the connection.

"Okay, until you get back to me, all I'm doing is rewriting the same chapters over and over again." A new voice entered the room, followed by echoing footsteps. "Oh, I haven't met your new friend."

B*Sweet pulled out of the hug and extended her arm. "This is Caroline Invers. She's my biographer, but she's so much more than that." B*Sweet leaned in, "She used to write for Vanity Fair."

"They only published two of my articles and a single piece of fiction." Caroline swooped in, taking Rebecca in a surprise embrace. The hold was stiff, sterile and more than a little aggressive. She had a generically sweet aroma that Rebecca couldn't identify: bubblegum, maybe, or cotton candy. "A pleasure," Caroline said as she pulled away.

Rebecca resorted to a muffled "You too."

"I reached out to her after she wrote an amazing article about the situation with my dad for Rolling Stone. She is an incredible writer." B*Sweet scratched her nose and shifted away from them. "We've been working on my memoir for a while now," she explained.

"She's too kind," Caroline countered, speeding through her explanation. "Most of my work has only appeared online. If you've read any of my work, it was probably there. I rarely get anything in a major periodical. Speaking of the book, however," she shifted her focus back to B*Sweet, tastefully enunciating every word. "Have you gotten a chance to read the latest draft?"

"I don't, I didn't—which email did you send it to?" B*Sweet looked around the room.

Caroline stepped in front of B*Sweet. "The one only you can access."

Rebecca inched away from the talking women, backward toward the door, not wanting to be involved in what seemed like an ongoing conversation.

"Can you just send it to my main email? I don't remember the other passwords at the moment."

"I don't think sharing the current draft with that one is wise."

Rebecca backed into the soft but solid resistance of a man's body, and she yelped, jumping forward.

"Watch where you're going," the man growled. He was a tall, gel-haired man, probably in his late forties or early fifties, standing just outside the door. He pulled back his fist like he was about to punch her and sneered when Rebecca flinched. He relaxed and said, "Calm down, I'm joking."

"I'm sorry," Rebecca said.

"What are you doing here?!" B*Sweet shouted. Her voice sounded hurt, torn. "Why would you even be here?" She reached for the shelf, grabbing Jenna's orange award, wielding it like a weapon in case the man advanced.

The man's smile grew, and he said, "Nice to see you again, Sweetie pie. It's been a long time." He half-attempted a one-arm hug.

B*Sweet jumped behind Caroline, who stood with her chest out like an aggrieved rooster. Rebecca backed into a wall. B*Sweet shook with anger, then stamped. "Oh my God, Christopher, you asshole! Give me your cell." She traded Caroline the trophy for the phone. "I can't believe he would do this." As B*Sweet dialed, she shouted, "You are not welcome in this house! If you step one foot inside, I will call the police and tell them to bash your brains in!" She rushed up the steps. Caroline shoved the trophy back onto the shelf and followed B*Sweet out of the room.

"How could you do this?! You know, you—" Remnants of B*Sweet's shouted conversation were filling the space. "When are you coming back? This is urgent?"

The man looked almost proud at having prompted the outburst. He pursed his lips at the staircase B*Sweet and Caroline had just climbed, and he took a performative step inside. He looked at Rebecca and said, "She remembers me."

"She said—" Rebecca started.

"It's okay, we're old friends," he interrupted, invading further inside.

B*Sweet's echoing shouts became increasingly unintelligible the deeper she ventured into the house. Rebecca turned to see the man pick up the stack of glossy one-sheets B*Sweet had set onto the gilded shelf; it was a photograph of B*Sweet with "The Sweet Foundation" written in large lettering across the top. At the bottom of the page was smaller printed text as well as a flamboyant blue signature. The man spilled B*Sweet's stack of papers onto the floor. He stared at Rebecca, his lip half curled, seeing what she would do. Somewhere from the depths of the house, a door slammed. Rebecca knelt to collect the papers. She felt the man's arrogant eyes on her neck.

When she rose, cradling B*Sweet's glossies and her own belongings to her chest, the tall man was too close. She smelled his heavy cologne and the sour of alcohol drifting from his too-straight, too-white teeth, and she took a step backward. The rings on his fingers jangled when he stuck out his hand and introduced himself as "Ghosted, you've probably heard of me." She hadn't, and, with her arms full, she couldn't take his hands anyway. That seemed to irk him, and he walked quickly back to the door, cradling the leather jacket to his chest with his crossed arms. Stopping at the threshold, he said, "You won't need to tell Chris White I was here," he motioned toward the halls, still echoing B*Sweet's shrieks, "he'll know. But inform him I will be staying at the Exchange. Room 742. Tell him if he doesn't come, I will be back."

Chapter Three.

Rebecca's heart was pulsing like a helicopter blade. B*Sweet's voice was small, almost imperceptible, leaving the room in near silence. She hoped sorting the pages B*Sweet had left might help. Replacing the unscathed sheets on the shelf, she set those with bent corners in a new pile beside them. Still tense, Rebecca moved around the trophies, trying to arrange them as B*Sweet had. Struggling to focus, she couldn't make it look right, and she threw out her hands in frustration.

Stepping outside, she took a deep breath of fresh air, watching the obnoxious man, Ghosted, walk casually down the driveway until he reached a turn and was obscured by the trees. On the lawn, the staging, which had looked almost skeletally bare only a half hour earlier, was beginning to look like it had always been present. A video showcasing children running in a park played on the large screens flanking the sides of the stage. The workers were separated into two distinct groups: those focused on the construction and those watching whatever was most interesting—Ghosted, the video wall, or their busier coworkers. Near the tree line, away from the stage and tables, Rebecca discovered a bald man hurrying into the shadow of trees near the guest house. Maybe he was looking for a place to relieve himself.

Rebecca closed the door and fantasized for a full minute about driving away from the sprawling estate, never to return. Following that were visions of boarding a plane and watching the Japanese islands materialize through Pacific Ocean clouds. The level-headed part of her dismissed the fantasy. She'd already canceled the ticket. Like it or not, this was her job. If she could hold out for only a couple more days, she would be free of whatever drama this place and these people thrived on. Now empty, the foyer could be photographed without people. She focused then on work, slowing her breath and taking the pictures.

From the hallway KL had initially tried to travel for B*Sweet's water, the one Rebecca knew to lead into the large kitchen, a woman of roughly Rebecca's age walked in, a black porcelain cup of coffee held securely between the fingers of one hand. Rebecca recognized the woman as Jenna Sweet, B*Sweet's younger sister who—though never reaching B*Sweet's level of stardom—had continued acting on television (nothing recent enough for Rebecca to recognize her at first sight). She shared several facial characteristics with B*Sweet, and she was pretty, but Jenna lacked the uncanny prettiness of her sister or their mother, instead coming off as a slightly off-brand recreation. She also looked, somehow, a little older despite being almost ten years younger. Because the actress mostly stayed out of the tabloids, Rebecca didn't know much about her.

The younger Sweet scrutinized Rebecca and breathed across the surface of the coffee, displacing pillars of steam. "I take it that was Becky and Dad being Becky and Dad? Let me guess, she was complaining again about tonight's event, and he was gritting his teeth and quietly taking it because he knows it was idiotic to schedule it less than two weeks before she starts her residency in Vegas?" Before Rebecca could respond, Jenna extended her hand and said, "I'm Jenna Sweet. You're Rebecca Ziel. Here from Halcyon about the house. We expected you an hour ago."

"I'm sorry, I was in the middle of something else." She sighed. "That noise was your sister, but it was because there was a, um, man who showed up at the door. She was yelling at him. I don't know who he was, but I think he called himself 'Ghosted?' He left and gave me his roo—"

Jenna shook her head and issued a low, sardonic laugh. "Of course he did. It's hard to believe he could have been that ignorant."

Jenna, recognizing that Rebecca had no idea what was being discussed, said, "My father must have hired him for the new songs. You might know 'Ghosted' as James Logan. That's what he went by, back in the day." She touched her cheek, as if remembering. Then she looked at Rebecca, apparently seeing that she still didn't know who the man was. "He was a fantastic musician; he produced 'Open Secrets,' the song that defined my sister's sound. So, when the second album came along, the studio hired him to do all of it. That one was even bigger. Unfortunately, he was a garbage human being who sexually assaulted my sister when she was 17." Rebecca recalled reading something about that in the news, but all those stories about abused starlets and abusive producers sort of blended together. "Who would have thought that a 26-year-old guy who writes songs about teenage girls fantasizing about 26-year-old guys would turn out to be a predator, you know?"

Rebecca's mouth remained agape as Jenna strode to the gilded shelf, picking up the undamaged stack of one-sheets Rebecca had sorted. Seeing her Kid's Choice prominently displayed, she shook her head, scrunching her face, and she shoved the award to the back of the shelf where it had earlier sat. Turning back to Rebecca, she said bluntly, "So you're here to sell our childhood home." Jenna eyed her placidly, gauging the response. Rebecca turned away with a blush. "I suppose you'll want pictures for the listing. I'll show you around."

The long hallway between the foyer and the kitchen was a pleasing neutral blue with infrequent lighting that, along with the north-facing wall, meant that, at least in the afternoon, the passage was darker than it should be. Rebecca noted this among her suggestions for Charles to present to the client. The large white bidirectional door at the end of the hall was heavy and likely composed of a dense wood that could be sanded down for greater curb appeal.

"This is the kitchen," Jenna announced. The room contained multiple cooking stations, and it was spacious enough that she wondered why it wasn't being used for the day's event. A giant marble island sat beneath a commercial kitchen's worth of copper and cast-iron cookware hanging from the ceiling. Beside a walk-in pantry was a large fridge that droned an infrequent, low buzz that repeatedly drew Rebecca's eyes like a child's tongue to a loose tooth. "Annoying, right? I'll be replacing that soon." Rebecca took pictures, trying her best to avoid including Jenna, who made no effort to move out of the way. "You ready?"

Rebecca nodded.

"Since they're busy up front, I'll show you the studio out back. Unless you think buyers will be turned off by a music studio?" Rebecca's head shook slowly, uncertainly. "Good. I've got the key in my room." Jenna led them out of the kitchen and up some stairs. "The people you saw outside are setting up for an event our father set up showcasing the Sweet Foundation's 'good deeds.' He thinks his rich friends will be so impressed they'll donate to his cause." She shook her head. "It's Becky's foundation, but he's treating it as his own. He chooses what charities receive her money. It's like this," she waved around them. "Technically it's not even his house, it's Becky's. And my name is on the will, so he has no right to be doing anything with it." She cocked her head in thought. "But I'm sure you know all of that."

Rebecca didn't. "That sounds difficult," she said, not knowing what else to say. She peered out the window; talking to this family was difficult. Their lives were interesting in a novel way, but they were all so self-involved. And that wasn't even touching on the fact that B*Sweet and her sister, it seemed, didn't actually want to sell the property. Had Charles known that before he sent her? She doubted it, but regardless, she was there dealing with the fallout, and he was not.

Standing outside the game room which Jenna had opened moments before, Rebecca felt Jenna's expectant stare and quickly framed her shot. Because all the games—a billiard table, a dart board, several arcade cabinets, and more—were covered or turned off or both, a picture would be unusable for any listing, but she snapped it anyway and thanked Jenna, who grunted with a strange sense of humored satisfaction. Then they continued the tour.

"He simply lacks understanding of other people as other people; I'm sure you know the type," Jenna pointed nonchalantly as they passed quickly toward her destination. "They both do. It's like they exist in a world where it's just them. The rest of us are background actors who enter and leave the story solely for their personal growth. Do you know the feeling of sonder?" Rebecca didn't. "They have the opposite of that."

"Wow," Rebecca said.

"It is crazy that Dad wouldn't consider their past before hiring him back from the dead; that he wouldn't realize how much it would hurt Becky to have him produce her new album, but it also makes perfect sense. In his mind, it's supposed to be her comeback. It's supposed to tap into that nostalgia for the turn of the millennium that everyone is looking for right now. And to be fair, it does sound good. What I've heard, anyway. If Ghosted did produce it, he hasn't lost his ear."

She stopped at a closed door, and Rebecca admired the polished yellowheart wood and solid construction. Jenna stroked the knob with her fingertips. "Isn't it unfair that so many talented people are so evil? That those of us who have to work for everything we have are expected to just let them do their thing without complaint?" Jenna inserted a key and grappled the knob.

Inside was an unnervingly tidy yellow room. Multiple floating shelves supported dolls arranged by color and size. Rebecca couldn't be sure, but a few looked especially old and potentially valuable. Bookshelves across the other walls contained, perhaps, every movie and television DVD ever produced, which, upon closer inspection, appeared to be organized alphabetically and possibly by color. The bed was also immaculate, looking like it had been made minutes before by an obsessive hotel maid.

Rebecca took a step inside and was stopped from progressing further by Jenna's upturned hand. "That's okay," she said, "I can get it myself." Rebecca backed out of the room, eliciting a gracious smirk from her host. "Becky, on the other hand, doesn't realize how good she had it. Mom basically forced her own interest in music on her, which, of course, was a problem in its own right, but at least she got to spend time with her. Once Becky was in the Mouseketeers, Mom pushed her to know how to do everything or else she was going to be just another failed child actor. She prevented that from happening. *Mostly.*" Jenna unlocked a heavy-looking wooden cabinet and pulled out a squared black briefcase with number–code locks to retrieve a set of keys. Finding the one she wanted, she returned the remaining keys and the briefcase, locking them inside.

"This house is all we have left of our time with her, but Dad doesn't see that." Jenna looked ready to cry, but she controlled herself. "I'm forced to work three times as hard as they do, just to make sure that if worse ever does come to worst, we'll all be okay. All I can do is control my world as best as I can. Hopefully, they will learn for themselves before it's too late."

She led Rebecca down a long hallway toward the rear of the house. Rebecca snapped several pictures, stopping when she saw what she thought was a figure traipsing through the forest at the yard's edge. It brought to her mind the people she'd seen at the entrance. Rebecca lowered the tablet, but if anyone was there, they were too far under the trees to be seen.

When Jenna had seemingly run out of things to say, Rebecca felt obligated to fill the silence: "You both know, I think, better than me, certainly, what it is you deal with. Like any of us non-famous people, you have your life—there's moving around, your mom dying, going to school and being a kid—and on top of that, people like Ghosted. And then there's fans and paparazzi always following you. I can't imagine what it would be like to have every mistake I made played for an audience of millions. When I came in today and saw the people with cameras outside, it made me realize what I have." She gulped. They had asked for Jenna by name, and she hadn't yet said anything. "They asked for you, actually. A man and a woman." Rebecca barely avoided crashing into Jenna, who had stopped and was now looking at her. "I meant to say something earlier, but..."

"Who was it?" Jenna interrupted.

Rebecca reached into her pocket for the envelope. "He said his name was Dollar Bill Hicks. I didn't get the woman's name. He gave me this."

Jenna looked at her watch without really seeing the paper. "They're early. She's not even ready yet. I'm sorry to cut this short, but I must go." Jenna left her there.

"Sorry," Rebecca was trying to orient herself in the house and to the family. Talking to Jenna had made her think of her own sister, Erin. It had been a month, at least, since they'd spoken, she thought. Too long. Situating herself in a windowed nook, Rebecca dialed, subtly hoping her sister might not pick up. As expected, however, the dial tone clicked off before the second ring concluded, replaced with Erin's cheerful voice.

Chapter Four.

"RB! Long time!" Erin chirped.

"Hi, Erin. Sorry if I'm interrupting something important." It was always like this. Despite ending up back in their hometown and following in their father's footsteps to become a schoolteacher, Erin had always seemed more put together and accomplished to Rebecca. By 25, she had completed her four years in the Army, and, for the past year, she had been engaged to a man she met while serving. Rebecca didn't think they were pregnant yet, but it was only a matter of time. When that happened, Erin would be a wife and a mother (an honest-to-goodness adult!), while Rebecca would still be just...Rebecca.

It wasn't that she needed kids to feel complete, or even that she wanted them. Collectively, Rebecca had spent full years helping Sydney, who had gotten pregnant in high school. Bethany and Fern were good girls with a strong-willed mother, but caring for them had convinced Rebecca that motherhood wasn't for her. Despite that conviction, however, Rebecca wrestled with the suspicion that remaining childless was somehow both selfish and childish and that she could only ever be a distraction to real adults like Erin; consequently, she rarely called.

"Are you kidding? Brad's out of town for the weekend, and our first summer meeting isn't until Monday. All I've been doing the entire day is eating cereal and watching my neighbor's TV through his window. You wouldn't believe how bad his taste in shows is. Besides, Syd posted all about how you were canceling your trip to hang out with pop royalty. I want to know about that."

"It's not like that; I—. It wasn't my choice."

Erin's "Uh huh" stung like an accusation. "Okay, drama. But how messed up are they? Is it all drugs and crotch shots like they say online?"

"I mean, they're just, you know, people." Rebecca wasn't sure why she was being made to defend them.

"Is that right?" Again, Erin's tone implied disbelief. The perceived subtext, that Rebecca was avoiding some unpleasant truth, prickled her already stretched nerves.

Trying to think of something both benign and salacious enough to satisfy her sister's curiosity, Rebecca offered: "Well, they have a giant painting of the family in the style of John Singer Sargent..." she knew Erin wouldn't know the name, "...hanging in the foyer like they're royalty or something."

"You know I don't know who that is. They sound nuts."

"I don't know. I don't like calling anyone nuts. We're a little nuts."

"I wonder why that is," Erin replied sardonically.

"Yeah," Rebecca pictured their mother, forever the same age she'd been when she left, misplaced somewhere in the vacuum of time, and she hoped the woman was alive and well with people who loved her. "Besides, I shouldn't really talk about them. They're clients."

"There must be something other than a painting," Erin insisted. "Spill."

Rebecca was struggling; why wouldn't Erin take the hint? "I guess," she thought. "They do enjoy talking about themselves. And each other. There's a—they have a lot to say."

"Nuts," Erin repeated.

"That's not very nice." Caroline stepped evenly toward Rebecca, stopping at the end of the hall. She pulled a candy apple red vape mod from her lips, dropping it to her side. Clouds spilled from the lower right corner of her mouth, dissipating like smoke from a movie gun. "Considering she's on the phone with her therapist right now. Dr. Lane doesn't want me in there." She shook her head in exasperation and offered the vape. "Rich of her to worry about confidentiality."

"Is that her? Or her sister?" Erin asked. "Hello?"

Rebecca tried to respectfully wave away the offered vape. "No," Rebecca blurted into the receiver, "it's a friend of the family." Caroline coughed derisively at Rebecca's description. "It's my sister," Rebecca explained to the writer. Into the phone, she said, "I have to get back to work; love you."

"Love you." Erin hung up.

Caroline exhaled another frothy plume. She gave Rebecca a moment to compose herself before asking, "What is it you do, exactly? You're a realtor? You sell houses?"

Rebecca blushed. "No, I'm, uh, I work as a broker's assistant." Not wanting to make Charles look bad for sending her in his place, she added: "I've taken all the license courses; I, I just haven't taken the state exam yet."

"Why's that?" Caroline asked.

Rebecca didn't have a good answer. After taking all the necessary classes at Charles' suggestion, she chose not to pursue the license because real estate wasn't for her. And yet, here she was, three years later, classes no longer valid, still working for Halcyon Realty. She shrugged and simplified the answer: "It's not what I want to *do* do."

Caroline asked: "What do you want to *'do* do?'"

Rebecca shook her head: she didn't know. Since she was a child, drawing was the only activity that meant anything to her. Scraping a pencil against paper, smudging the fat lines of a charcoal sketch, these were as close as she came to a calling. Still, as far as she knew, there was no sustainable career in that, excluding the occasional freelance job.

It had been one such job where she first met Charles. He hired her to design his company's logo. Being the first job since high school to make active use of her art, she was unusually enthusiastic, willing to answer him at virtually any hour of the day and to change any detail. Her eagerness convinced him she would make the perfect assistant, which she kind of did. Art became again what it had been before: something she did when she had spare time. For work, she had to do what brought in actual money. What choice did she have?

"Ah, you're one of those." Caroline nodded, looking down at Rebecca knowingly. "You don't look at the impact your choices have, especially on yourself, do you?"

Rebecca stood there, stunned. If anything, she overthought her choices and how they would affect people. She deliberated over each decision extensively before making it and criticized herself endlessly afterward. Rebecca's heart fluttered. She didn't understand why she was being attacked.

"You're like a little Emma Bovary, going from place to place, doing whatever you like without considering the people you hurt, right? Have you ever read that: *Madame Bovary*?" Caroline's stare felt like a rusty microscope. "No, probably not. Too mundane. Too close to home? You're probably more of a TikTok gal." The way Caroline pronounced her 't's, they snapped like fireworks. She twirled the red vape above her temple like a baton. She seemed to notice Rebecca's distress and offered: "I'm not being mean. Many people live empty lives and require superficiality to protect yourself from the trauma of reality. We all have our weaknesses. There's no shame if that's yours."

"You better be careful. Caroline is *rabid* with literary references." KL emerged from a nearby bedroom. "If she foams at the mouth and rattles off Jonathan Franzen quotes, run!" He sipped from a can of caffeinated water and said, "Thankfully, other than occasionally punching you in the face, she's all bark. *Mostly.*"

"Screw you. Becky's in her room talking to Bridgette about, amongst other things, this woman's efforts to sell her home." Caroline pointed to Rebecca. "This whole experience is incredibly upsetting to her. If you truly were the Mama Sweet you wish you were, you'd want to know why this woman is doing what she's doing. Whether this is her normal?" She confronted Rebecca, asking, "Is it? Are you like a repo man? You go around selling a person's house when she's most vulnerable?"

KL sneered. "Don't play ignorant. Or innocent. We both know Ms. Ziel has *nothing* to do with what's happening."

Caroline expectorated a dirty word toward KL and exhaled another heavy cloud. "Pardon me, 'Ms. Ziel.' KL doesn't understand nuance, and so it's pointless to engage him in constructive conversation. I'm sure you are able to understand this is just my curiosity as a writer. Sure, I'm worried about my friend, but I'm also interested in what makes you tick." Again, she put such force into the 't' in 'tick' that it crackled like a gunshot. Caroline's lips curled in a smile, but her eyes remained vacant. She brushed past Rebecca and KL, disappearing down the hall.

KL asked, "Are you okay?" His eyes danced between Caroline's departing figure and Rebecca. "Don't worry about her. She's a hack writer whose best work is written in promises across her patron's ego. She's only angry because she was promised the guest house as payment for the book they're working on, and the trust recently refused to accept the agreement."

"What do you mean?" Rebecca asked. Rebecca followed KL into the room he'd emerged from.

Diaphanous white curtains occluded windowed balcony doors, limning the largely brown room in a layer of soft light. Silk sheets lain in rumpled piles on the unmade bed shifted discreetly while loose papers danced across the sprawling mahogany desk in time with the raspy rhythm of the air conditioner fan. KL began dressing the bed. The air displaced by the sheets smelled of vanilla and coconut with a hint of old sweat. Rebecca set her belongings in the opposite corner to help him tuck.

He answered: "B*Sweet was in an especially manic mood and, as I've heard, she told Caroline that after the memoir is published—in addition to whatever backend deal they've arranged—she gains ownership of the guest house. Not complete ownership, of course, only until she dies."

"A life estate?" Rebecca asked.

KL nodded, "That sounds right. Fortunately, the conservator of her trust determined the arrangement couldn't be reasonably honored."

"Chris White, you mean" Rebecca clarified.

KL shrugged; "It wasn't in her best interest."

Or, Rebecca thought to herself, *they'd be losing out on millions if they tried to sell with a life estate hanging over the property.*

She watched KL brush smooth the surface of the bed. She wanted to help, but her eye was drawn again to the calligraphed ascot around his neck. Before she realized it, he had stopped and was eyeing her in return. She blushed and immediately picked up a couple of shirts from the ground, tossing them into a dark red hamper in the bathroom. KL removed the black scarf and foppishly draped it over his wrist, approaching her to show it off.

"I see you staring at it," he said, "and I can't blame you. It *does* look amazing on me."

"May I touch it?"

"I didn't take it off because I was *choking*," he quipped. Rebecca traced her fingertips across the shimmering black silk. "It's one of a kind. We holidayed in Italy when I was 11. My sister and I and our parents, we each received one from an apprentice tailor. I watched him stitch every initial: KL, EL, BL and GL. Most people can't see the difference, but," he pointed at a little flourish on what Rebecca thought was the 'K.' No, the 'L' "They're there if you look closely."

KL flitted the fabric around like a cat toy before wrapping it back around his throat and tying it in a single smooth motion. "There was an eroticism to the way the tailor used his fingers that I didn't understand at the time, but which I felt." Rebecca was growing red and warm. KL said, "I'll wear this until the day I die. It's always brought me luck. I was wearing it during my first-ever kiss.... With the *tailor.*" Entering a walk-in closet the size of an apartment, he mused, "His fingers were good for things *other* than threading needles." He winked in a way that made Rebecca a little nauseous.

KL was still wearing a dirty grin when he exited the closet, his arms overflowing with suit components. He mixed the jackets, shirts and pants, all much too large for him, in different combinations on the freshly-made bed. "The girls," he said, changing the subject, "they refuse to acknowledge what Chris does for them. They paint him as some kind of *villain*, but he's just a man trying his best to ensure his daughters' success, trying to keep the machine running. He hardly sleeps for worry about their well-being. Does this look like the lair of an *evil mastermind?*" KL sighed. "What do you think?" He had placed a black tie and lavender shirt inside a dark, steel gray suit jacket. Rebecca nodded.

KL hmm-ed with satisfaction and said, "I know you know she's been fighting for control of her finances. You might even think she should have it." He probed her eyes, nodding with a humph. In reality, Rebecca didn't have a strong opinion one way or another. Based on what she'd seen, however, what was happening in the Sweet household felt exploitative and immoral.

"Whatever, you're entitled to your opinion," he finished. "What you and your friends online might *not* know, however, is *why* her rights were restricted in the first place."

"According to the news, she went psychotic when her daughter died during childbirth," she answered.

KL nodded, releasing a weary sigh. "She did. It was hard for her. Hard for *all* of us. But that was *ten years ago*, Chris didn't insist on the conservatorship until three years later. Why do you think that is?"

Rebecca was absently tidying the desk, sorting financial documents from personal letters and pens from letter openers. She shrugged.

"Because," KL said, "seven years ago *she* tried to give all her money to her insane ex-husband. He swore their baby was alive, that it had been swapped with another family's child. It was *sick*. He convinced her the conspiracy went all the way to the White House. He promised that if she gave him enough money, he'd find the child and bring the conspirators to justice." KL's eyes darkened. "She sued the city, and was trying to exhume the casket when Chris stepped in. He upped her meds and froze her accounts, all for her *own* protection. And, even then, he didn't file for conservatorship." KL paused in the closet door. "Not until Simon Cowell. Do you remember that?"

"Yeah," Rebecca nodded. She was thinking about how B*Sweet's psychosis hadn't been enough. It wasn't until money was at risk that the conservatorship had been enacted.

B*Sweet had crashed into Simon Cowell's driveway gate three times before the car died and the police came. Somehow, it had been reported as an accidental collision, a freak accident. Rumors related it to a breakdown in discussions about co-hosting one of Cowell's talent shows, but anytime anyone online talked about it, B*Sweet's drug use was brought up. A brief hospitalization followed.

"The two of them were on enough coke to fill a snow globe, and they drove *nonstop* to Beverly Hills in a rental car. Cowell demanded protection. *That* was when Chris finally took it to the courts." KL looked Rebecca in the eyes, dead serious, concerned even. "If you knew *half* the messed-up *nonsense* that goes on inside her head, you'd realize she *needs* someone looking after her. At least with Chris, it's a man who loves her."

"I'm sorry, I didn't know."

"I swear," he smirked, "if you say you're sorry *one* more time, I'm going to have to shoot someone. You take *everything* so seriously," he said. "You're a lot like my sister in that way." He laughed. "I'm constantly reminding her that there's only so much a person can control. When you try to do everything for everyone, you end up with a lot of mess, a lot of stress and nothing to show for it. And who is it that has to clean up after you?" He laughed again, pointing at himself.

Rebecca did the only things she could think of: apologize and get back to work. Picking up the iPad, she framed up pictures of the cleaned room, capturing the made bed, windows and tidied desk.

"What do you think you're *doing*?!" KL rushed her, snatching the camera from her hands. "There is still a *man* living in this room. At least wait until he's out of the picture." KL deleted the images she'd taken of the desk before beginning his examination of the others. "You should probably let me go through these. The family has a certain *aesthetic.*" KL pronounced the 'TH' in 'aesthetic.'

"We get client approval for any images we use," she said, holding her hand out expectantly. "We delete the rest." She hated confrontation, but he was forcing her hand.

He returned the tablet and, as she tucked it back into its green sleeve, and that into her backpack, KL said, "You are a serious one."

Rebecca knew he was right. She was the serious sister, the serious friend. She only wished all that seriousness actually did something for her. It was nearly evening; she hadn't slept the night before, because she was supposed to have an entire flight for that.

"I'm sorry, I need to rest a bit before the event. Can you point me to my room?"

"Of course." KL walked her down several halls and up another flight of stairs to the smaller third floor, stopping in front of a more homely-looking door. "Here's the guest bedroom. Call me if you need *anything.*"

Chapter Five.

The 'guest' bedroom was for guests in name only. A narrow bed sat beneath a small window. Across from it, an armoire and a vanity desk were shrouded in heavy beige dust covers that gave them the appearance of ghosts who'd been mauled to death by boredom. Rebecca set her small backpack and belongings on the foot of the bed, surveying what was meant to be her private abode for the next few days. She stabbed the thin memory foam mattress with her fingers; it wouldn't be any worse than sleeping on the office sofa.

From her bag, she pulled out the shapeless forest green jacquard dress and black satin heels she'd brought for the event. Originally purchased for a cousin's wedding—and worn a handful of times since—it was the fanciest dress in her closet. Lifting the drop cloth from the vanity desk, she held the dress to her body and examined herself; it wasn't showy, but she still liked the way it looked on her. She covered the chair with her dress and looked out the window.

The view from the room looked how she imagined the view from a villa in Italy might look: beyond the tall, green forest, Folsom Lake glistened invitingly in the late-afternoon sun, reflecting the cool blue sky. She'd seen nearly identical compositions when peering out the windows on the second floor, but alone in the house for the first time that day, she was finally free to sit and absorb the scene. The sloped ceiling of the top floor also imbued the setting with a sort of cinematic nostalgia, like the view looking down on a childhood street from a grandparent's attic window in a movie from the 1990s.

Resonant music had begun filtering across the grounds, and she could make out the same inoffensive pop songs that played every event or industry get-together she'd ever attended. Almost certainly, the DJ was a middle-aged white man with a paunch and a soul patch. The pool house, a cube of glass panes jutting from the flat green yard like a piece of modern art, vibrated with the music, sending random rays of sun across the yard. Whether it was the beauty of the scene or the day's emotions in search of release, Rebecca needed to draw what she saw.

Removing the old pad and a pencil pouch from her backpack, she outlined the scene quickly with her trusty 2B, starting with slow, steady lines. Before long, she was earnestly gripping the remaining nub of the 6B, shading the bushes and trees that occluded the house from outside eyes. She paused, again noticing a human figure creeping into the trees, peering cautiously toward the main house.

From on high, she couldn't tell for certain whether it was the same man she'd earlier seen running past the stage into the woods; it almost certainly wasn't either of the paparazzi encountered at the entrance, however. She set the drawing pad and pencils onto the vanity and took out the iPad, hoping its zoom could capture details her eyes were missing. Tapping open the camera, she pushed in on the image, capturing him in bursts before he receded into the trees. She froze. He was looking at her; she was sure of it. Without shifting his gaze, he backed into the woods, falling into shadow.

Appraising the pictures, Rebecca decided that it was indeed the man she'd seen earlier. He had a long, angular face, and though the expanded zoom blurred the image, she could make out what looked like a thick, apparently well-groomed mustache.

"You're good!"

Rebecca nearly peed her pants. Correction: she peed a little. Relaxed, B*Sweet stood in the doorway, idly flipping through Rebecca's sketchbook. Her mere presence enlivened the room, and

Rebecca walked to her, curious about which picture had drawn her in.

"I didn't mean to startle you." B*Sweet said languorously. A slack smile stuck to her soft face. "I came to apologize about earlier. I saw your drawing, and, well, you're good." She put her hand to her forehead and laughed. "But you know that. You drew it." She showed Rebecca the page she'd been examining: it was the initial draft of a sketch offered to Sydney's eldest daughter as a senior yearbook portrait. Rebecca nodded in lieu of thanks. "I assumed everyone just used their computers these days. I didn't know people still used pencil on paper, but these are...beautiful. Do you think you could draw me like this?"

Rebecca nodded. She gestured to the pad and said, "I prefer the physicality of paper." She showed off the layer of graphite coating the bottom of her hand, grinning with, against her will, a gentle pride. "I don't know why, but I like the feeling and the smell. All of it, really."

"That's so you." B*Sweet set down the pad, lifted the sheet beneath it, and joined Rebecca at the window. She handed over the glossy page, where, above her signature, she had written in blue: 'To another daughter without a mother.'

"I'm sorry I jumped when you came in. I was watching a man creeping in your woods."

B*Sweet tapped the autographed paper. "Oh, there's all sorts here today. It was probably one of the workers. Which leads me to why I'm here. This thing is about to start. You should come. That paper will let security know you're invited."

Noticing Rebecca's iPad, B*Sweet placed the drawings on the bed and held out her hand. "You've been taking pictures of the house today, yeah?"

Rebecca's nod became a shake: "Yup. But they're not ready; I usually do a little prep work on them before they go out." B*Sweet's hand lingered expectantly. Rebecca, uncomfortable but obedient, handed it over.

"That's because you're an artist; you care about the detai— ooh, this one's nice!" Rebecca craned her neck to view a shot of the entryway and the warm rays visibly spilling in from the windows.

"I won't show that one, due to the personal nature of the painting." Though Rebecca liked the image, its contents were too personal to show publicly. She should have already deleted it, but this whole experience felt like it was going to be one of those that she'd remember later like a sort of dream, and she wanted evidence that it had actually happened.

B*Sweet zoomed into the portrait, singling out her father. "He's willing to let it all go. For what? To Christopher—" She let the tablet dangle at her side. "This is all just money. Jenna and I, we're just dollar signs to him. If I were to die right now," she snapped her fingers, "the life insurance would ensure that he didn't even notice I was gone until he ran through it. Dr. Lane would like hearing me say that, but," conspiratorially, B*Sweet leaned in, "she doesn't need to know everything, right?"

"Even Jenna," she swiped to the painted face of her kid sister, "she always was a better actress than me. Unbelievably good. Like Dad, though, she can't see past the money. I trust her with my life, but she's been on such a slippery path these last few years." Becky shifted focus to her mother's face. "We were a real family, once upon a time. I miss that. Being kids, working in those stupid movies together, Mom smiling at the video village. Just outside our eyelines." B*Sweet swept a tear from the corner of her eye: "She wasn't perfect, but she was a good mom. I wasn't the perfect daughter, and I've never been the best sister, but I tried." Her voice lowered, thickening with emotion. "I always thought I'd be a good mom like she was to us." B*Sweet continued swiping through the images, moving back to a previous one and pausing a few seconds to appreciate it, but generally moving through them without looking at them. She froze when she reached the attempted close-ups of the man in the foliage. She tapped the screen, "Wait, this is who you saw just now?" Rebecca nodded. The image rubber-banded several times as she tried zooming beyond the device's limits.

"I thought you said it was one of the workers." Her voice sharpened. B*Sweet abruptly returned the iPad and pointed to the trees. "He was there?" Rebecca nodded.

Becky took out her phone and stared at the blank screen, biting her lip. Without warning, she said, "Thanks, I'll let security know. I need to get ready for the party." And she was gone.

Rebecca returned the iPad to the neon green padded sleeve and placed it back inside her pack. Then she turned to the window, straining to see within the shadows under the trees the second man that day to whom B*Sweet had reacted. But under the trees she saw nothing. Only darkness.

Chapter Six.

Rebecca, in her green dress, waited at the exit door. The dress felt suddenly cheap and inappropriate, like walking into an office in cutoff jeans; its stiff shoulder straps weren't helping. Her hand hovered unsteadily about the doorknob for a moment, grappling it open before her brain had time to turn her around. The world beyond was a black curtain, rustling in the light wind, an omen to turn back and work.

Above the black partition, the sky was blue and open; a flock of birds flew in formation away from a growing mass of dark clouds. In her hand, the glossy image of a 27-year-old B*Sweet posing with a child felt like a burden. It was a personal invitation from the most honored attendee; how could she decline? At the bottom of the sheet, beneath B*Sweet's blue Sharpie signature, was a list of three organizations being supported by the fundraiser: The Galaxy School, UFU and the Aegis Clinic. Rebecca flipped the one-sheet, reading about them on the back.

Despite the name, the Galaxy School in Fairfield was more of a group home for children with developmental delays and dual diagnoses. It did provide educational services, but its primary function was to "graciously and with the utmost dignity and respect" offer the children a home until they were old enough to be sent to an assisted living facility, usually (*and conveniently*, Rebecca suspected) in their early teenage years. The video she'd seen playing on the video wall during rehearsals had almost certainly been of that school.

UFU, or Underwear for the Unhoused, in addition to doing what they said on the tin, provided outerwear for the unhoused. The non-profit also offered rehousing grant assistance, on-site job training, childcare assistance and rehabilitation for those struggling with drug addiction and related issues. They had recently gone international, with operations abroad "focusing initially on providing care for vulnerable young women facing homelessness."

The Aegis Clinic was an independent wellness center that specialized in treating personality and emotional disorders, especially Treatment-Resistant Depression. Dr. Bridgette Lane operated the clinic and advertised on the one-sheet as "B*Sweet's personal therapist for the past 20 years."

Chris White and Jenna Sweet were scheduled to speak, along with representatives from each organization, with appearances of select kids from the school and patients from Dr. Lane's clinic. Most impressively, the event would be closed out by a brand-new song from B*Sweet herself.

Rather than pass through the curtain to the crowd beyond, Rebecca followed nearby voices to navigate the fabric labyrinth.

"Thank you for inviting us," the first voice said.

"No, we're grateful to you. This is important work you're doing," the second, emotional voice volleyed. "You are providing more than surface-level help, and we are proud to support your cause."

Rebecca rounded a corner, seeing first B*Sweet dozing on a metal chair, resting her head on the uncushioned back. Beyond was the small stage, and, standing in front of it were two men. The first was tall and slender with short-cut white hair; his back was to Rebecca, so she could not see his face. His conversation partner was a much larger man. At least six-and-a-half or seven feet tall and weighing north of 300 pounds, the goliath smiled broadly and nodded excessively. KL sidled up to him, attempting to slide his fingers into the large man's hand, which was pulled away in annoyance. KL crossed his arms, listening with a strained smile.

Rebecca vaguely recognized the man's round face, but she couldn't put a name to it. His clothes, though—dark steel gray outerwear with black tie—identified him as Chris White, the family patriarch. Minus the lavender shirt, he was wearing the suit KL had earlier laid out on the bed. Though she had been slightly shocked by the size of the clothes as they lay on the bed, she hadn't adequately imagined the largeness of the man who could wear them.

Chris White shook the white-haired man's hand and showed him through the curtain.

"What's so important?" Chris grumbled. KL looked down, clearly ashamed, and Chris White's expression softened. He offered his hand to KL, who accepted and kissed it, pulling KL into a brief hug. "What happened?"

"The meetings with the reality show people ran late," KL said. She's doing her best to get here quickly."

"She will be late, or she won't make it at all?" Chris stepped out of the embrace, maintaining a grip on KL's hand, which had begun turning purple. "Say what you mean." He pulled away, his face a nascent red.

KL slumped like a scolded child. "It's possible she makes it. But—" He shook his head.

Chris White clenched his fist, slamming it against his thigh with a fleshy thump. "I single-handedly plucked her practice from nothing; you must tell her this. Bridgette would be a nobody in Orangevale without me. And this family. Half the reason we're doing the whole bloody function is to raise money for her clinic, and this is how she repays us?"

"The show will be a good thing for us. She's trying—"

Chris cut him off. "I hate when you act as her apologist. Ifs and tomorrows do nothing to fix an empty stage. I don't need you to explain her actions. I need you to solve the problem."

"That's what I mean. The fact the meeting went overlong is *good*," KL suggested. "TwoSweet is paying for the show, so Becky is an *EP*. If the show goes into syndication, you're talking *major* residuals." Chris White was still angry, but his eyebrows rose in consideration; he was listening. "Besides, we have several of her patients on the premises, I've spoken to them all, and their stories are great. It's probably more effective to let them speak for themselves, anyway," KL said, encouraged by Chris White's reaction, "to give your guests a *narrative* rather than details."

A light, tinkling laugh told Rebecca that B*Sweet was not actually asleep. She was watching the exchange between KL and Chris with an incurious amusement. Her body, overly relaxed and contorted, was practically melting into the chair, though a lazy smile implied no discomfort or, at least, no awareness of it. She weakly lifted her hand and closed all fingers but the middle one.

"Do something about this," Chris demanded, thrusting his hand at his daughter. "She's on in one hour. She's doing this to punish me." The music died down, and he ascended the stairs. His demeanor transformed on stage; beaming magnanimously, he welcomed the audience to the event.

KL caressed Becky with the back of his hand and bent down to whisper something to her. She shoved at his shoulder, barely moving him.

"I'll be right back with your Red Bull and Ritalin," he said, freezing upon seeing Rebecca in his path. Looking like he wanted to ask her how much she'd heard, KL adopted a controlled stance and said, "Hello again. Are you lost?"

Rebecca shook her head. "Sorry, no, I—" she couldn't finish. Something about the way Chris White was treating KL triggered memories of Sydney when she'd dated abusive men. Rebecca had comforted her friend through cycles of flooding and withholding affection, of Sydney being blamed for her boyfriend's actions. "Are you okay?" She pointed to Chris on the stage. "He seemed angry. Violent, maybe?"

KL smiled and nodded. "Oh, he's got a lot on his mind. I'm fit and fine as ever."

"And her?" Rebecca asked, pointing to B*Sweet, who, an hour before, had seemed a little fatigued, maybe, but nowhere near tired enough to collapse on the chair as she currently was. In online tabloid videos of B*Sweet slurring her speech or struggling to stay upright, Rebecca could view the scene with a detached objectivity: she could turn the video off and turn away. Standing in front of the doped-up singer, seeing her draped over the chair like a human blanket, Rebecca couldn't pretend that the woman in front of her was anything but a real person in pain.

"Oh, she's like this," KL said dismissively. "It's, you know, new meds. And old meds. And more meds. She loves her pills is my point."

"You love pills," B*Sweet said quietly. She laughed to herself.

KL rolled his eyes as he took Rebecca's arm. She sensed concern somewhere deep in his unwavering stare. "Why don't I get you to a table?" He pulled her through the fabric.

KL summoned a woman in head-to-toe black. He instructed her to, "Take Ms. Ziel to an empty seat. Make sure she's fed," and disappeared behind the drape. The woman led her roundabout to a table at the other side. Excluding a sole vacancy, the table was full of young women and one man in their late teens or twenties, all of whom looked like they belonged in a hip, cool clothing ad. The name card in front of the seat she'd been given identified "Dr. Bridgette Lane," B*Sweet's therapist.

Seated opposite Rebecca, the man and one of the girls welcomed her to the table, calling her "Doctor" and erupting in giggles as they hid their laughing faces in their hands. Rebecca turned red and flipped the name card face down. A girl beside them slapped their elbows and mouthed "Sorry," to Rebecca.

Rebecca quietly replied, "That's okay; sorry," then turned to watch the same video of kids running that had played earlier.

Meanwhile, the girl in the seat next to Rebecca was reaching under the tablecloth to the ground, feeling around her feet. The girl stood and trotted over to one of the servers carrying a pile of empty plates.

Even in the best of times, Rebecca didn't like spending time with people in their early twenties; it made her feel old, even more so than being around children. With kids, it was almost like interacting with a different species, or—she felt guilty for thinking it—unusually intelligent pets.

But these people were technically old enough to have meaningful jobs and were thinner and cooler than Rebecca or her friends had ever been. Being around them was like being reminded yet again about both what she couldn't be anymore and, let's face it, what she never was in the first place. It was the ultimate expression of the feeling that she was being slowly erased from relevance.

The server who had seated her presented Rebecca with a black plate and utensils. She smiled curtly and asked if the water needed to be refilled; Rebecca shook her head. She poked at the chicken fillet and speared an asparagus stalk, bringing it to her mouth. Given the droop, it tasted better than she'd expected, but it was no longer hot.

"Excuse me." Rebecca looked up, expecting the waitress. Instead, it was the girl who had been sitting next to her. "Do you mind if I look there?" She was pointing to Rebecca's seat. Rebecca stood, and the young woman undid the bow knot that affixed the cushion to the chair. The girl checked underneath the cushion, then replaced it, leaving it untied. She bent and looked under the table where Rebecca's legs had just been. Rebecca watched, debating internally whether she could leave immediately or would need to wait for an opening. She decided to wait until she could verbally excuse herself to one of the—she thought of them as 'kids' which only made her feel older.

"Can I help you with something?" Rebecca asked when the search didn't stop.

The woman, down on hands and knees, lifted her eyes to Rebecca and said, "No, sorry, I have a—" she scrunched her face and considered. "It's like a tablet, but it's e-ink, so it's supposably better for the environment. It's called a 'D-Note.'" The woman carried in her voice the slight desperation of a teenager explaining something to an adult that they would never understand. "I put it down somewhere, and I can't seem to find it anywhere. It's got all my notes on it. For everything, not just this."

"Supposedly," Rebecca corrected quietly.

"Huh?" The girl stood up and introduced herself: "I'm Lucy. No, sorry, I'm Kelli. God, I love your hair." To Rebecca's chagrin, she touched it without asking, rubbing the strands between her thumb and forefinger. "I'm one of Dr. Lane's patients. I used to be. We all are." She swept her hand to include the others at the table. "She helped me at her clinic. With my depression. They were some prett-yyy tough times," she said, her eyes aimed straight up, examining the sky. Rebecca turned to see what she was looking at, but, other than a few dark clouds out by the mountains, the sky was clear. After finally sitting, Kelli (or Lucy?) looked under her plate and napkin in a last-ditch effort to find her missing D-Note.

Rebecca sat, too. She covertly checked under her own plate and placemat, just in case, finding nothing.

Distracting from the monotone presentation of the woman onstage, someone shouted, "GILLY!"

Some in the audience laughed, others, including Rebecca, scanned the crowd in search of the catcaller. The man at Rebecca's table whooped and clapped at the call, but his attention was on a list written on a white envelope being passed around the table. "This one says he does headshots," said the girl next to him, pointing at a name.

Rebecca looked up to see KL making a beeline for her from backstage. He snatched her plate, handing it to a nearby attendant. "I'm sorry for the trouble, but will you come with me?" Restoring the doctor's name card and sweeping nonexistent crumbs from the placemat, he led Rebecca away from the table. "That was a reserved seat. She shouldn't have placed you there."

As they searched for an empty seat, Jenna Sweet took the stage, inviting everyone to applaud Marjorie Heinz. The director of Galaxy School had just finished speaking and was returning to a table with two other women and four kids. Jenna continued, saying how sincerely proud she and her sister were to pledge a portion of profits from their Two Sweet wines to the laudable organizations there today.

Someone shouted again, "Gilly, I love you!" Rebecca heard the sound of crashing glass or porcelain. A man charged the stage, launching himself at Jenna.

KL left Rebecca, running toward the stage, while a tall man from the front row of tables tackled the interloper before he could reach his target. Rebecca stood there, unsure of what she'd just seen, with about fifty other people equally uncertain. The guest who'd defended Jenna handed the man off to two security guards, then returned to the stage to check on her.

Gradually, everyone returned to their seats, including the hero. Everyone except Rebecca who still didn't have one. KL was gone and she decided she was done waiting. There was too much to do to waste her time being shuttled from table to table. She moved toward the main house, maneuvering through the crowd while Jenna continued her speech as though nothing had happened.

"Thank you all." Jenna cleared a crack from her voice. "I'm grateful to you all today. Despite the gaps, we are fortunate. Outside, protection often comes too late, not only for women attacked on the street, but for the disturbed men who need support and direction. When we show the most vulnerable in society that we care, we give them a society to care for. That is why I am honored to introduce the President of You-Few, Underwear for the Unhoused. Their new mission statement expands beyond providing clean clothes and warm food to providing tool sets for total human wellness. Ladies and gentlemen, Xander Berman." The attendees rose to their feet, applauding as Jenna hugged the lean man with white hair Rebecca had seen talking to Chris backstage. Before the man could ask everyone to sit, B*Sweet's slushy voice exploded from the speakers. Rebecca listened from the door to the house.

"Ladies and gentlemen," her words were slurred, but B*Sweet sounded more alert than she had earlier. "I'm sorry to disappoint you, but the song I planned to share is *defiled*. Like I was. So, I took that song—and album—and destroyed every copy—" There was a whoosh and a whine from the speakers as someone intervened backstage. Rebecca heard the muffled cries of "Stop, no. Let me finish!" but the microphone had been cut. No one else spoke.

Chapter Seven.

Rebecca was tired. Paperwork was always tedious, but paperwork for a high-value client, as Charles called them, was inevitably worse. The problem was that that brand of consumer knew too much to accept mistakes as unavoidable, but they took too much for granted to accept their share of the responsibility. Whether because they believed the answer obvious, or felt too busy to be bothered, when problems did arise, it generally came from the client's unwillingness to communicate some detail. They believed their money was the alpha and the omega of the transaction and nothing else should be required of them.

Everything is an exchange, she thought. *Everything.* It was so entwined in all aspects of life that it rarely consciously registered. It just happened, like breathing or blinking or hating a driver who cuts you off. For most people, considering the instruments of exchange—the assumptions inherent in evaluating what a person wants, the faith exercised in trusting a currency, and the closed-eye blindness that ignores the exploited peoples and exploitative systems inherent in the simplest of exchanges—was not merely difficult, it was repulsive.

The average person didn't think about the mechanical or software engineering that went into rigging a vending machine any more than they considered the fabrication of the candy bar inside it, or the candy bar's wrapper. The coin they slipped into the slot was not even a coin to them; it was a sensation held between fingertips: an abstraction of an abstraction. It was long ago disconnected from the precious metals that made it, the slaves who mined it, and the mint that shaped it. The elements of exchange had been reduced to means to an end. When a person reached into the delivery tray and pulled out their purchased Snickers bar, their participation in the process felt just as natural as a bee gathering pollen from the stamen of a flower.

Among these hidden elements of exchange was the vast amount of legalese-infused paperwork haunting the modern real estate agent. If, to complete a form, the agent needed information that a high-value client refused to give, or discovered something amiss on the title, the agent was always the incompetent one, it was never the owners themselves. It was under these oppressive expectations that Rebecca completed her first day of lodging with the Sweets.

The music outside had died down around 8 p.m., so she was only that evening able to begin in earnest the paperwork that Charles Sprock, realistically, should have started, if not completed, weeks before. She understood why he hadn't: there is information that people just assume should be obvious, that they shouldn't have to know themselves, let alone need to communicate to others, and acquiring this information from people can be stupidly difficult. The late call to Charles in LA—"things are going great down here, there's a ton of interest"—had helped her answer some questions, but there remained a great deal more to discover and to do over the coming days.

She set down her work around midnight, finally acknowledging after reading the same page for the tenth time in a row that she was too tired to continue. Unfortunately, a chaotic melody had begun pulsating from the pool house around 11:30. The irregular sounds prevented her from falling asleep, inciting, instead, racing thoughts that kept pace with the rhythms of what she assumed to be an after party of some sort. Her body tossed about for another thirty minutes until exhaustion took control, plummeting her into an unrestful sleep, dreaming that she was unable to find the paperwork necessary to board the airplane taking her home. "Hey," a flight attendant was tapping her shoulder. "Hey, Rebecca."

Instantly awake, her heart drumming like a terrified rabbit's, Rebecca's eyes adjusted to the moonlit dark of the room. The woman standing over her was either the flight attendant from her dream or B*Sweet. Neither seemed more or less plausible than the other. A languid "I'm sorry," slipped from Rebecca's lips, eliciting laughter from the shape. She didn't know why she'd been awakened, but she felt certain both that it was deserved, and that she was unprepared for it.

Rebecca's body relaxed, eager to pass back into sleep. Her head and back lay heavy on the mattress, as her eyelids dropped steadily over her eyes. "B*Sweet. I don't think I'm fully here. Maybe you can come back in the morning. I'm sorry," she slurred, and her consciousness slipped away. B*Sweet sniggered and pulled her out of the bed, splitting finally the spidersilk connection between dream and consciousness. "I'm not dressed," she protested, clothed in the pajama pants and t-shirt she wore whenever she slept away from home.

"You're fine. Come on." Rebecca followed her dreamily from the room, stumbling with eyes half closed, through dimly-lit hallways and shadowy stairwells, transfixed by B*Sweet's hypnotically swinging hoop earrings.

"Please, call me Becky. B*Sweet is who I was." Her fingertips were cold and soft, simultaneously gentle and firm as they grasped Rebecca's hand, guiding her through the house. The two of them exited through the kitchen door, their bare feet prickling on the cool, recently-watered grass as they approached the source of the music.

Caroline, in the pool house, poured drinks. B*Sweet—*Becky,* Rebecca corrected herself, *she wants to be called Becky*—took Rebecca's other hand to dance and sway with her in time to the music, trying to rouse her to awareness. The wind was blustery and warm but mixed with strands of chill, heralding a storm, and it pushed against them, encouraging the dance. Rebecca followed the movements with neither thought nor emotion, her skin coating with a chlorinated syrup from the hot humidity emanating from the pool house. Hard as she tried, Rebecca could not quite convince herself that she wasn't still lost in a dream.

"I was a real bitch today. I need to express that to you." Becky spoke with the same sweetly-sad smile Rebecca had seen on too many faces of late. Sometimes, Rebecca even saw it on her own face, when she caught her reflection unawares. Becky said, "It wasn't fair for me to take out my frustrations on you. I want you to know I know that."

"Thank you," Rebecca was taken aback.

"It's just, so much is going on at the moment. I will be performing in Vegas until the end of the year. It feels like a chance at something new." Becky's movements slowed as she grew introspective. "First you come. No, I know, it's not you. Then there was the fundraiser today, and that..." her hands tensed, unintentionally squeezing Rebecca's. "...*thing* James Logan, Ghosted, whatever he calls himself now. He comes to my house. It's bad enough he had his claws on my album at all, but for him to come here is unconscionable."

Caroline joined them outside, carrying two drinks and an irritated smile. "You look like you could use this." She handed one of the drinks to Becky, who shot it in one, choking back a cough.

"No, thank you," Rebecca declined. Caroline shrugged, wiping her nose, and sipped from the offered glass. "Did you really do what you said today? Did you destroy it?" Rebecca asked.

Becky's face exploded in a mischievous grin. She nodded. "Every local copy, every cloud backup, every share link canceled and promotional thumb drive snapped in two. All of it." She stared thoughtfully, swapping her empty glass for Caroline's half-full one. "There are bound to be a few early copies of the title track that we sent out remaining, but that's it."

They walked into the pool house. Caroline lit a joint. She hit and handed it to Becky butt-first. Becky breathed in and held. As she exhaled, she gave the joint to Rebecca and said robotically, "Back for more."

Rebecca accepted the cigarette and inhaled superficially before returning it. Becky accepted it with a snort and passed it back to Caroline. She said with a quizzical expression, "You complete the circle."

"Sorry, I thought you said you wanted more."

Becky laughed and looked at Caroline, whose mouth curled in mild amusement. "Back *four* More. Like the *number.* It's the title track of my new album. My old, new album." She pouted.

Becky danced to the back of the bar. She sat beside Caroline, resting her head on her friend's shoulder; Caroline, in return, set the still-burning cigarette into a sparkling ashtray that might have been either a lotus or a vagina. She rested her head onto Becky's. Becky stroked Caroline's cheek. "There was always something about the sound of the new music that I didn't like, even though everyone else kept trying to convince me that it was great. They're pleasant enough melodies, but they're, I don't know, *vacuous."* Becky pulled away from Caroline, "I said that, didn't I? I said that."

Caroline wiped the sniffle from her nose and nodded. "Mmm-hmm," she sounded. Her jaw was tight; she was clenching her teeth. Rebecca thought Caroline looked annoyed, and she wanted to slip away, back up to bed, but Becky seemed obliviously happy to be with the two of them. She returned to Rebecca, wrapping her arm around her, keeping her there.

"Yeah, even you, I'm sure. You're untainted by all this. A neutral third party. I'm sure you'd hear it and know immediately it was wrong."

"I just can't with this." Caroline shot up, moving to the door. She turned around. "What is this? Who is this? What are you doing?" Caroline appeared authentically bewildered. "I'm pleased as punch that you made a new friend. I'm just confused about why she's here. You said we were going to relax a little first, maybe sniff a couple daisies, but ultimately, I thought we are here to write. What am I missing?"

Becky walked to Caroline and took her hands. "I can see you're upset." She straightened her expression; Caroline wasn't buying it. "I'm serious; I want to read the new stuff, to work on it with you. But I need to relax first. You don't understand the pressure."

Caroline pulled away, exiting the glass house.

"I'm sorry. I'll leave," Rebecca said and made for the door, but Becky stepped between them.

"No, stay." She followed Caroline outside. Rebecca just stood there, hot, sweaty and frozen. Becky implored her friend: "Care. Stop. Tonight is for celebrating with friends. Please. Let's get through tonight and work on it in the morning."

"Like we did yesterday? Or Monday night? Oh, that's right, you were busy rehearsing for today yesterday, and we went out on Monday."

"I needed the—"

"Stop." Caroline stopped her. "If you don't want to do this, okay, we can stop. I will return the hours of recordings and notes I've taken of your rambling stories. I won't use any of it. But..." she shoved her finger at Becky's face, "...my research, that I've done independently, that's mine. I'm trying to give you the benefit of the doubt, but you don't even do what you promised."

Becky protested, "I handled it. I told you it's yours, I just need—"

"Yeah, you keep saying that, and I keep falling for it. But, nuh-uh, not anymore. This book will come out, with or without you." She shoved Becky to the ground.

Rebecca was snapped out of her paralysis by three bright flashes from under the trees. She trotted over to the quarreling women. "I'm leaving," she pleaded, "you can work on what you need to work on. I have my own things I need to do!"

Caroline was frantically rubbing her face. She pulled her hands down to reveal the frighteningly calm expression directed at Rebecca. "No, that's all right. You stay with your new best friend." She motioned to the woods where another light flashed. "And all the creeps with cameras who follow her everywhere. I, yeah, I think I'm going to leave." She turned toward the driveway.

"Care, I need you." Caroline stopped, keeping her back turned to them. Becky sobbed, "I'm sorry about all of this. Both of you. I wish I had a normal life where we could just be here and talk like normal friends. I think after this thing in Vegas, I'm going to try that. I'm going to try to live a normal life."

"As if you could." Caroline turned and stated categorically, "You're B*Sweet. You can perform for 75,000 people in a stadium, but you couldn't handle normal if you tried. It's all people like her and me out there; you might think that's what you want, but in your heart, you'd go crazy." Caroline shut the door. The red car peeled down the driveway.

Rebecca helped the singer to her feet. Becky wore a fragile smile. "Don't think badly of her, all right? She's been working on this book with us for a while. After she and Jenna fought about things, it was just me, and I'm not as responsive to these sorts of things as I should be. She's feeling abandoned, and why shouldn't she." Rebecca followed Becky's slow walk into the pool house.

Becky ducked behind the bar and searched through what sounded like quite a collection of plastic pill bottles. She pulled multiple orange and clear containers onto the bar and spilled out a multi-colored pile.

"Are you two okay? I'm sorry, I didn't mean to—"

Becky laughed and rounded the bar, wrapping an arm around Rebecca. "Really, it's okay. We love each other. She just wants a place to feel at home and I—sometimes, I make it hard for people. She'll be back, and we'll take something. Then we'll talk it out and ugly cry and make up like we always do."

Becky took a capsule from the bar top and tossed it into her mouth. She offered one to Rebecca, who declined. "It's just a Xanax. Trust me, you could probably use one after all that. After everything you've been through today. Me, too." Rebecca again shook her head, and Becky bit the tablet in two, swallowing one half. She shoved the remaining piece into Rebecca's hand with a sense of urgency.

Rebecca reluctantly held the moist medication in her fingertips, regarding it uncertainly. "It's only half; it'll help you calm down and sleep. Please, for me. It'll make me feel better knowing you're not cycling." Rebecca placed the pill into her mouth and let it sit on her tongue for a second before swallowing it. Becky smiled, "to all the Beckys who have been put through the wringer in this world." It felt like a toast, and Rebecca raised her hand as though she were holding a wine glass, instantly feeling like a goof. Becky pulled her by her arm out onto the still summer-warm concrete, and they sat down in sync, stretching their feet onto the grass.

Rebecca dug her toes into the wet blades, the pricks on her soles a sort of sensual mirror to the pricks of light from the stars above. She yawned. There was another camera flash from the trees. Or maybe it was Caroline's headlights peeking through as she turned.

"They really have no boundaries, those zombies with their cameras." She flipped off the area from which the flash had come. "I'd moon 'em, but that would be giving them free content. I'm done with them, I'm done with James Logan, I'm done with anyone who brings me down. They're out of my life for good. They smell pain and vulnerability like blood, and they scratch, and they bite, and they come for you at your worst times." She fell silent, stretching her slender legs.

"I was pregnant once," Becky said finally. "I named her Miriam Zosia White." She seemed to be staring at herself in the glass wall. "Miriam was my mom's name. I had a home birth," Becky sobbed again. "Her heart wasn't right and her...she had so many problems. They rushed her to the hospital, but—" She didn't need to finish. Even if the story hadn't been visualized on the national news with a tiny casket, Rebecca could have figured it out.

Becky took a shot of something, then wiped away her tears, careful to avoid mussing her mascara. "Those ghouls, the paparazzi," she continued, "they were at the hospital, waiting for me. They asked me how I felt. How do you think I felt? They knew she was dead before I did." Rebecca grabbed Becky's hand and squeezed. She had no words she could offer, only human contact.

"I don't know if you've ever carried a child, but you actually get to know them, their personality. You can see who they're going to become. I could tell she would be strong-willed and wise. Zosia means wise." They remained quiet, lying on the ground. Neither knew what to say and they were okay with that.

"There's so much beauty, don't you think?" Becky broke the silence and Rebecca felt it like a bubble bursting. "The world conspires to keep it from us, and when they allow you to glimpse it, it's pre-packaged in those plastic product cases you can never quite open without slicing your hand." She struggled to make a box shape with her hands. "And then when you're confronted with it, with unmodified, organic, true beauty, it's kind of unbearable. It's overwhelming, I think, because we're so used to the small concentrations they let us have that our senses don't know what to do with the real thing." The erstwhile teenage icon thrust her hand at the sky, swirling it under the stars. The cool, light breeze and the mist escaping from the open pool room deposited dew drops on her arm, which, when they caught the light, gave Rebecca the impression that the universe had settled on Becky Sweet's spray-tan skin.

"I'm supposed to be in Japan right now." Rebecca heard the words as though they were coming from someone else. For the first time, she accepted that she wasn't merely disappointed by the cancellation, she was angry.

"You should go," Becky said simply. "Right now. If my father wants this sale to go through, it'll happen either way." She stood, offering Rebecca a hand to pull herself up. "Really, I'm not joking. I love it there."

For a moment, it felt like she could do just that: that she could simply stand up and leave. But even in her buzzed state, Rebecca knew: people like B*Sweet could fly to another country at a moment's notice; people like Rebecca had to plan for a trip to Target.

Rebecca fixed her eyes on the GPS monitor around the pop star's wrist; she flushed with shame. This woman couldn't up and leave any more than she could: her father controlled her finances, the courts controlled her comings and goings, and her past choices controlled her future options. She could not make a move too reminiscent of her earlier career without being called derivative, and she could not try something too new without being called desperate.

"I know I'm supposed to be angry at you because you're selling my house." She smiled at Rebecca and explained: "It does bother me, but, to be honest, this is not my home." She shook her head. "For Christopher, it's an asset. For Jenna, it's where she grew up. For me," she looked at the main house with a stony stare, "it's a tomb. It's where my mother died. Even Caroline has more reason to stay than I do." Becky closed her eyes; she sniffled. "For me, home was always the house from before we moved to Orlando. Before Jenna, when we were a normal family living in West Sac."

Becky lowered herself back to the ground, laying her head on the warm concrete, hands sweeping through space. Rebecca's body relaxed, her eyelids growing heavier and harder to keep open. "Sometimes I imagine living in that house with my own family, like a normal person. If none of this had happened, who would I be?" She hummed something Rebecca didn't recognize, her vocals becoming deep and sonorous, a product of her practiced diaphragm. The melody swirled through the air, landing on Rebecca in the inky drops of a forgotten dream.

Chapter Eight. Friday.

Darkness. And in the darkness, muffled voices. A voice screeched: "Give me that!"

Rebecca felt like she was swimming through her unconsciousness, striving for light, any light. The blackness clung to her. She was wet and cold.

Though there was no visible light when Rebecca's eyes opened, compared to the absolute void of sleep, even the dimness was painfully bright. She blinked her eyes to adjust them; it remained dark. Thinking she had slept through the day, she was seized with panic.

Rebecca was lying atop an unfamiliar blanket on an unfamiliar bed in an unfamiliar room. She winced; there was an unfamiliar pounding in her head. She sat up too quickly and, along with waves of nausea, pieces of the previous night materialized and faded in front of her like flash burns: B*Sweet woke her; she was summoned to the pool house; there was a confrontation with Caroline, and a heart-to-heart under the stars. Was she actually friends with a former pop star, or had that all been a dream?

When the worst of the migraine subsided, she stood, a layer of something coating her heels. Stumbling on tiptoes to the wall, she flipped the light switch and looked at her feet; her heels and ankles were covered in mud, some of which had dried and begun to slough off in clumps. Some had even broken off in the bed as she slept. Bending slowly to collect the chunks of dirt she'd trailed from the bed, she examined the room. It was sparsely furnished with a silver-gray office chair beside a small desk topped by a cup of pens and a thin, white computer cable. The sky outside was dark, blanketed in thick, black clouds. Thunder bellowed, but a thin ray of sunlight pierced through just long enough to assure her that she still had time to make the day count for something.

After picking up and sweeping every bit of the dried mud into the empty and bagless trash bucket from beneath the desk, Rebecca looked around for her phone. The search left her light-headed, and she fell onto the bed in a partially controlled drop. She regained her composure, continuing the search for her phone. It was nowhere.

Exiting the bedroom, she braced herself, first, against the wall, and then against the countertop between the kitchen and living room. She was hit with another wave of nausea. Hand clamped over her mouth, she stumbled to the sink and retched. A viscous strand of foamy saliva extended from her chin to the drain. What had she done after joining Becky at the pool house? She located a roll of paper towels to clean her face, but discovered the kitchen wastebasket, like the one in the bedroom, lacked a plastic liner. She balled up the soiled napkin and shoved it into her pocket, as she exited the house.

Once outside, she knew she was in Caroline's guest house. All evidence of the previous day's fundraiser had been removed, and the unexpected emptiness of the yard gave Rebecca a sort of vertigo. She bent forward. Scattered sprinkles collected on her hair and the exposed parts of her neck. The tiny raindrops coalesced into small streams that dripped down her face, bringing with them a sense of relief. Lowering herself into the grass, an image from the previous night (probably) of Becky placing pill bottles on the pool house bar played in her mind like a scratchy film projector. Maybe among the myriad of questionable medications was one she could take to alleviate the pressure in her head.

Hot, thick humidity assaulted her when she entered the pool house. She searched the bar for pills but found nothing, not even alcohol. Someone had apparently removed all traces of the previous night's party. With bloodshot eyes, she scanned the room, but all that caught her attention was a bright green amorphous object floating in the water.

Hearing a creak, Rebecca jumped: KL was standing in the doorway. "I was watching you stumble around out here. You looked cold. *Try* and tell me you wouldn't kill for a coffee." Steam rose from the black surface.

"Thank you." She stepped outside to join him, the cool, misty morning refreshing her skin. A cautious sip confirmed the black coffee was not too hot, and she downed it. Warm relief spread through her body. Rebecca could have hugged him.

"Did you sleep all right?" he asked.

"I think so, I don't know. I was in there." Rebecca pointed toward Caroline's house.

KL nodded. "You were spread out on the grass over there. I'm not as strong as I look, so I took you to the nearest bed." He pointed to the same guest house. "Caroline's car was gone, so I figured she was out for the night. And if she wasn't, too bad, it's not her house."

Rebecca flushed with embarrassment. What happened that KL had to physically carry her to bed? And why couldn't she remember anything? Milquetoast as she was, she didn't think she had ever blacked out before. "I'm sorry I made you do that," she said, feeling like he was judging her for something she didn't remember doing. Maybe it was projection. The cold wind buffeted them, a new discomfort to add to the existing ones. The coffee mug with which she had been warming her hands was empty and quickly losing all lingering warmth. "Can we go inside?"

KL held the door open for Rebecca and shut it behind them. Jenna was inside, sitting at a tall breakfast table, drinking from a Peet's cup and eating spinach while typing into her phone. Entering the warm, dry room, Rebecca immediately began to feel better.

"It sounds like you were busy last night," Jenna said without looking up from her screen. KL ignored her, directing Rebecca to the stairs.

Rebecca needed the Motrin, but it was in her backpack, and the backpack was not where she left it. She scoured the room, eventually finding it splayed on the floor, crumpled between the open door and the wall. Inside she located the pain reliever, but finding that also let her know that the iPad and its case were missing. As she shifted to looking for them, ignoring the disorienting waves crashing onto the front of her skull with every heartbeat, she tried to also recall faded memories from the night before, hoping to summon the moment that she moved the tablet and where it had ended up.

It wasn't on or in the bedsheets, nor anywhere under the bed. She checked the table and windowsill but found only her phone. Did she return to her room and grab it sometime during the previous night's fugue state? In the soft gray light of the morning, her head pulsing with leftover consequences, it seemed possible.

Then she remembered the green object she'd barely noticed floating in the pool, and she sprinted down the stairs and outside, nearly slipping on the wet grass. She prayed that she wasn't going to owe Charles a new iPad. She pulled the green thing toward her with a pool net, confirming it to be the empty carry case. She didn't see anything else in the pool, which meant, in an instance of good bad luck, the electronic device hadn't been submerged. When Rebecca was convinced there was nowhere else in the pool house she could look, she returned to Caroline's guesthouse and began looking in there.

She had checked all obvious surfaces before leaving the first time, so she switched to searching the less probable locations. Maybe a week's worth of clothes hung in the wardrobe, and a few shoes, but nothing else. Next to it, she found a single travel case with, maybe, another few days' worth of clothes. Under the bed was a soft laptop case emblazoned with a prominent 'VF' logo. She felt inside and found an open letter addressed to B*Sweet, but nothing else. She set the case on the desk and peeked into the bathroom, finding only hotel toiletries. The same was true of the kitchen and living room.

"Did you lose something?" KL was standing on the guest driveway, holding an open umbrella. He offered it to Rebecca and opened one for himself.

Rebecca nodded and showed him the soggy green sleeve, explaining that she was missing her work iPad, the one he'd seen her using the previous day.

"You're sure it's not in your room?" he asked. Rebecca nodded; she'd looked everywhere. "Why don't you go inside and keep warm. Focus on feeling better. I'll look out here." But Rebecca needed files on the device; she didn't want to have to start over. She couldn't think about anything else while it was missing. She was responsible for it, after all.

As KL spiraled outward across the lawn, Rebecca looked around where she thought she and Becky had bonded on the grass. Almost immediately, she spotted a thin glass rectangle on the pool pump enclosure that she hadn't noticed earlier. It was always the same: the moment someone else got involved, problems solved themselves. On closer inspection, however, it wasn't her work iPad. It was the same size as hers, but this was made of molded white plastic and had the word 'D-Note' printed above the screen. She turned it over, revealing on the case a mess of film and theater stickers on which was one of those "Hi, I'm" employee stickers for the Hornet bookstore. "Lucy P." was written by hand above the printed "I give good read." It was the electronic notebook Dr. Lane's patient had been looking for at the fundraiser. Rebecca set it beside the drying green sleeve in the pool house and continued her search.

Between the two buildings, she found a patch of flattened grass, about the size of a body. It had to be where KL had found her. It was well away from where she had remembered being. Two long drag marks cut through the blades, leading toward a second, smaller impression—as though he'd set her down before trying again. But something was off. The tracks pointed east, toward the studio. She followed the trails until they, too, ended.

Listening to the rain tapping the plastic of the umbrella, she surveyed the lawn, beginning to feel that the endeavor was hopeless. Her heart trembled violently: there, in the shadow of the woods, she spotted a figure huddled low to the ground. "Hey!" She called out, hoping to simultaneously announce herself to the lurker and attract KL in case it was the strange man she'd seen from the window.

"Hello?" Rebecca approached carefully, finally recognizing the red button-up top Caroline had been wearing the night before. She shivered involuntarily. "Caroline?" Rebecca's voice barely registered over the rain. "Are you okay?" KL rushed past, lifting Caroline's slumped head.

"She's not anything anymore," he said, kneeling beside the body, fingers on the woman's pale throat. Congealed vomit glued the dead woman's hair to her face. In the lifeless eyes, Rebecca saw reflections of herself and KL and of the colorless sky.

Chapter Nine.

Rebecca's leg bounced, unintentionally keeping time with the machine-gun patter of rain on the windows. The constant drumming of her heel stopped only to listen for meaningful sounds outside the room or during occasional interactions with Becky's psychiatrist, Dr. Bridgette Lane. One of the many rooms in the house was reserved for Dr. Lane during particularly challenging periods in Becky's life. The present was one such period. Her doctor had arrived sometime late in the evening or during the night ready to talk, but Becky had not yet been in to see her.

Just outside Rebecca's view of the window, the lone officer on site was keeping watch of the scene, until support got there. He had instructed everyone to remain in the room wherein Rebecca and Dr. Lane sat. Despite the order, Jenna and KL departed almost immediately after he did. Jenna said she needed to find and retrieve Becky while KL called to check on Chris, who was in a meeting. Their conversation had grown heated, and KL, showing the barest bits of red in his cheeks, excused himself, wandering toward the kitchen.

"It's about mindfulness," Dr. Lane said, interrupting another bout of leg shakes. Her attempts to comfort Rebecca thus far, though saturated with encouragement, felt more like poorly-hidden irritation. Each time she looked over with compassion or gently tapped Rebecca's chair, the movement stopped for a minute, but only a minute.

Then the doctor own leg began to shake. Rebecca initially interpreted the movement as passive aggression, but the doctor appeared too absorbed in the gathering emergency vehicles outside to fake nervousness. Rebecca's rhythm joined with the doctor's as she, too, watched the newly-arrived lawmen approach the one who had arrived first. Dr. Lane's leg slowed to a stop, and Rebecca's—unconsciously following her—did likewise. The doctor was smiling when Rebecca looked at her; she realized both their legs had remained still for a while. "Sometimes," the doctor said, "all it takes is to know that we're not alone in our anxiety."

Rebecca was grateful for the peace, but she felt played. Her face must have made that apparent. The doctor clarified: "I am nervous too. Though I typically manifest in other ways, every so often, the legs go wild. This, what's happening today, it's a lot. You know, I spoke to Deepak Chopra last year, at a retreat in Sicily. Have you ever been?"

Rebecca shook her head weakly.

Dr. Lane said, "Well, I hadn't been there since I was a girl; it's gorgeous. Better now, if anything. Deepak taught me his *personal* techniques for managing anxiety through mindfulness. Without that, I'd be a mess."

She pursed her lips in a mild smirk, appearing as far from anxious as humanly possible. "If you could read my thoughts right now, I really think you'd see we're not so different. I'm able to be mindful 90% of the time, but, sometimes, even I lose myself." She stretched her hand to Rebecca and asked, "Will you try breathing with me? I think it would help me with my nerves." Rebecca tried following the woman's measured breaths. Her heart rate slowed. Soon enough, even the nervous vibration she felt in her motionless leg retreated.

KL returned to the room, uncharacteristically pale. "Chris will be here soon. He was already with the family attorney, so he's coming, too, thank god." He looked around. "Where are the girls?" KL shook his head and pulled out his phone. "Where are you two?"

Jenna's voice announced: "I've looked everywhere for her. Becky's car is in the garage, but she's not there. She's not in the studio, either. Studio's a mess, by the way."

"Just come back," KL responded. "You know she probably went out late last night, found some guy and passed out in a hotel room." KL cast a quick look at Rebecca, shaking his head just enough for her to notice. His face was a strange mix of frustration and compassion—one she didn't quite know how to read.

There was silence, then Jenna replied, "Okay," and hung up.

As Jenna returned, a police siren burped once from the street outside the property. Chris White, accompanied by a comparatively pocket-sized and studious-looking man, entered shortly after. Not long after that, the sheriffs walked in. Gradually, Rebecca recognized the officer in charge as the man who'd protected Jenna on stage. Standing in the doorway, he watched with the posture of someone ready to help as Chris White lowered himself into the room's largest chair with KL and the attorney's assistance.

The lead officer straightened his posture and addressed the room: "Thank you all for staying here. I know you all have busy schedules, and we want to get you on your way as soon as possible." His eyes stalled on Rebecca with a look of unfamiliarity. She grew warm. He looked better in the uniform than he had in a suit. "For those of you who don't know me, I'm Patrick Donnelly; I am a sheriff here in Sacramento County. I like to think I'm a friend of the family..." Jenna scoffed at the last part; Sheriff Donnelly either didn't notice or chose not to. "...which makes this an especially difficult visit. A woman was discovered deceased on the outskirts of the property and—."

"Outside the property," Chris interjected. "As our realtor can confirm." He motioned to Rebecca, who froze at the mention. She couldn't confirm anything. As far as she knew, the property line survey hadn't even been completed.

Caroline had been found at the eastern tree line. It was *possibly* public land, but Rebecca wasn't sure. The trees were wild and overgrown, untouched for years if not decades. The last official assessment had been in 2004, and twenty years was plenty of time for visual borders to shift. Either way, she had a feeling she'd be blamed for any lack of clarity.

"Sure, of course," Sheriff Donnelly said, nodding slightly. Rebecca breathed deeply, relieved that she didn't need to defend herself. "She was discovered *near* the property line." Chris White whispered into his attorney's ear, clearly unhappy with the sheriff's half-hearted compromise. "As someone familiar with this family's troubles, and as a friend to Caroline herself," Rebecca thought she heard another bridled snort from Jenna, "I, too, want a swift and complete resolution to this sad event, and I want justice."

Chris and his attorney continued their whispering, with the attorney finally asking Sheriff Donnelly, "We understand that Caroline, a known drug user, showed signs of an overdose." Sheriff Donnelly nodded. "Well, then, where does justice come into play, unless you intend to single-handedly stop the distribution of whatever recreational drug she took?"

The sheriff again nodded, opening his mouth to respond, but he was cut off by the raucous sound of several hard-soled shoes echoing through the front door and into the hall outside the room. "This will be our...missing musician," announced the sheriff.

The cacophonous entry returned Rebecca's hangover to the forefront of her consciousness. Hearing the number of footsteps, Rebecca worried for Becky, imagining that she had been discovered under the influence, or worse, with the previous night's drugs on her person.

Except the expressionless deputies weren't bringing in Becky. Instead, they brought in Ghosted—James Logan—propelling him into the room and toward an open chair. Ghosted scanned the faces of those inside, stopping at Chris's with a chimp-like grin. "Oh, you will do anything to get out of meeting your obligations, won't you. Get off me!" One of the deputies forced him into the seat and stood nearby as the others exited the room. Ghosted winced, massaging a spot much lower on his back than where he had just been manhandled

"James Logan here was discovered in a parked car near the front gate of your property. He tried to drive away when we approached—"

"It's a bright amber corvette. It's the most obvious car I could possibly be driving. Don't let's act like I was trying to hide! I tried to leave because I have no interest embroiling myself in this family's downfall! I simply want what I'm owed so I can get back to my life. It's not illegal to park on a public street."

"I can confirm," Chris admitted, "that this man and I had a business meeting scheduled for this morning. About matters I was already discussing with our attorneys." Ghosted glared at the sheriff, the reveal filling him with righteous indignation. "Not for several hours, mind you, but nonetheless."

In an effort to regain order, Sheriff Donnelly positioned himself in the center of the room. "A woman is dead." All movement in the room stopped. "I'm aware there are many complicated feelings in this room, but Caroline Invers is in a bag waiting to be examined. We can at least show the woman a modicum of respect." He looked at Ghosted. "As for you, you were nearby, and you have a known history with the family, so we're interested in hearing your account." His emphasis on the word 'history' conveyed a menace and a depth of emotion Rebecca couldn't quite decipher.

"Excuse me, Patrick," Chris White said, looking around the room. "We're all struggling right now with the death. But what I want to know is why my daughter is not here with us?" He looked to his attorney and added, "Surely if you were holding her for any reason, we would know that by now." The sheriff's green eyes trained on Chris, but he could not maintain eye contact, and he cleared his throat.

"Yes, well, that is part of why I asked you all to remain here. We are, of course, waiting on toxicology to determine the cause of Ms. Invers's death. It appears to be...well," he took a breath. It looked to Rebecca like he was a little shaken by the confrontation. "To answer Mr. Gutierrez first, yes, an overdose is the most probable cause of death. However, to your question, Mr. White, the answer is: we don't know. Your daughter is missing. What we do know is that she is almost certainly driving Caroline's red Model S." Chris pulled the attorney to his ear and whispered furiously. KL tried to massage Chris's shoulder, but the big man shoved him away with an unnecessary force. The others were silent, all wondering, Rebecca assumed, the same thing she was: had Becky been involved in Caroline's death, and if so, how?

Once Chris and his lawyer completed their discussion, the sheriff said with a hint of exhaustion: "We are keeping the matter private as long as we can," he glanced knowingly at the attorney and Chris White, "not just for your family's sake, but so our investigation is not interrupted by external distractions. However, we all know that, at some point, information will leak, and when it does, we will all be in a better place if we know Becky's whereabouts." Sheriff Donnelly stared hard at Jenna, then at Chris. "If any of you knows *anything*, you are acting in Becky's best interest to let us know now." His gaze moved to Rebecca; they both blushed and looked away.

The room went quiet.

"What about her wrist thing, the GPS tracker?" Faces turned to Rebecca. She stammered, "She has one, doesn't she? Shouldn't that tell you where she is?"

Jenna replied. "I checked. It's somewhere in the woods. She probably threw it out before leaving to wherever she went."

"No," Sheriff Donnelly corrected, "The tracker is currently on its way to the morgue. It was...wrapped around Ms. Invers's wrist."

Chris shot to his feet, faster than Rebecca would have thought possible given his size. "You're not implying that my daughter—" The attorney cut him off before he could finish. As he turned away from the attorney, the transformation in Chris's face told Rebecca that he had hoped bringing in a friendly sheriff would provide a sense of control, forestalling any undesired outcomes; the results thus far were not matching that expectation.

"No one is implying anything," Sheriff Donnelly assured them. "These are the facts, and we are investigating these facts. Not because we think we know what happened but because we know we don't. I'm sharing this with you because, again, it is imperative that anyone here with information should tell us." He waited. "No one? Okay."

He beckoned a deputy who approached obediently. Using a lower voice that was still clear to everyone in the room, he said, "Because that Becky Sweet's wrist tracker was on the deceased, and the fact that both she and the deceased woman's Tesla are unaccounted for, we need an ATL on her and the vehicle. But keep the notice off comms. Internal *only*." The deputy nodded and left.

Chris White cursed at the attorney urging him to do his "job." There seemed to be some disagreement between the two of them, a fact that did not go unnoticed by a smiling Ghosted. KL had moved to the other side of the room and was talking with the doctor in hushed tones while Jenna appeared lost in her phone.

"Hey," the sheriff said, addressing everyone. "All we can do is follow the leads. Wherever they lead."

Rebecca was sifting through remnants of the previous night. Becky had said Caroline would return. It was clear that at some point, in some way, she did. She had also predicted the two of them would "take something and make up." What if that, too, had happened and that "something" they took had been the cause of Caroline's overdose?

The pills in the pool house were gone. Taken. Why? And the guest house, someone had cleaned it out, if the empty trash cans were anything to go by. Rebecca's stomach turned; she had been with them and seen at least part of what happened, but there were no definitive memories. What had she swallowed, or drunk? What had she done? She didn't have the answer. Did anyone?

"The others?" Rebecca asked, feeling everyone's eyes on her.

"Hmm? What 'others?'" the sheriff asked.

Rebecca swallowed. "Yesterday, there were people here."

He shook his head. "We reached out to the event crew and the security team. All guests and laborers were gone and accounted for." Sheriff Donnelly said, "It was only you," he paused, "Becky and those in this room—excluding James Logan—who were present at the time period in question." Ghosted raised an arm in triumph, then winced, checking the same area on his back he'd earlier tended to.

"What about the paparazzi?" Rebecca asked. No one was defending Becky, leading her to feel it was on her to do so. Maybe if she could prove Becky's innocence, she would prove her own, too.

"It was a closed event. There was no outside press." That was KL.

Rebecca shook her head. "No, we saw camera flashes in the trees last night, after everyone was gone." She looked at Jenna, "I don't know if it was your people, but there was someone." She saw that several people, including Chris, were now looking at Jenna. Rebecca added, "The guy with the dollar sign on his hand and the Asian lady."

Jenna rose, opening the drawer of a side table. She pulled out a pen and Post-It. As she wrote, she explained, "That was: Dollar. Bill. Hicks. And...Moneyshot. Karen Fukuhara." She tore off the paper and handed it to the sheriff, shrugging. "I agreed to speak with them about an upcoming project, and they arrived early. They admitted to snapping the odd photograph while they were waiting. They showed me the pictures: nothing inappropriate. I doubt they stayed past our meeting."

Rebecca shook her head. "Okay, but even if it wasn't them, someone was out there." She thought of the man she'd seen from the room. "There was someone in the woods. I showed his picture to Becky. She—I could be wrong, but—she seemed to recognize him." Rebecca stopped. The only images of him were on the iPad. The missing iPad. Plus, if Becky did know the man, and he was the one taking pictures, what did that mean about Becky's involvement? Rebecca worried that she'd made things worse.

"Pictures?" the sheriff asked. Rebecca shook her head. Sheriff Donnelly produced a small notepad and pen from his pocket. "Then, can you describe the man you saw?"

She thought back. "I don't know; he looked like a bald man with a sort of, um, handlebar mustache and—"

The room erupted. Nearly every person reacted to the news—gasps, murmurs, even a growl. Rebecca's stomach tightened. Should she have known who he was? Struggling to remember any news story about B*Sweet that might have shown or described the man she'd seen, she drew blank after blank. Until she didn't: the ex-husband. He had been balding when they married, shaving his hair to compensate. And, in more recent stories about him—many of which referred to his increasing instability and, maybe, a restraining order against him—he had a mustache. How had she not realized it earlier? She struggled to recall the man's name. *Something Sheffield—Mike?*

"Marc is not allowed within 300 yards of her. Nothing good can come from his presence here." The attorney raised his baritone voice to be heard above the commotion.

"We're aware." Sheriff Donnelly plucked his phone from a holster and pulled up an image of Marc Sheffield, B*Sweet's ex-husband, holding it in front of Rebecca's face. "Is this him?"

"He was far away, but" she felt sure it had been the same man in the bushes, "I think so."

"Bastard jumped me last night; must have been around 2 a.m.. He ran away like a coward before I got a chance to—" Ghosted raised his fists, miming a fight. Then he stood, removing his shirt to reveal a large, yellowish–purple bruise on the lower of his back. He spat onto the rug; the mumbling in the room intensified.

"Okay. Okay. HEY!" The sheriff shouted, restoring order. "I need to ask you all questions about last night and this morning." Harshly, he grabbed Ghosted's bare arm. "Let's start with you so you can go your merry way?"

Chapter Ten.

Despite the departure of Ghosted and the sheriff, the room retained an emotional frisson as those remaining acclimated to the new information. Over time, that energy reduced to a state of, not peace, exactly, but homeostatic equilibrium. The doctor was thoughtful and observant, Chris was noisily consulting with his attorney, and he summoned KL back for the conversation. Rebecca couldn't hear what was being said, but she caught several accusatory glances at Jenna and assumed they had something to do with the photographers.

Jenna, for her part, appeared unconcerned by her father's disapproval, tapping on her phone in an almost performative way, loudly enough to be heard from across the room. Rebecca seemed to be the only one, possibly excluding the sheriff, visibly impacted by the dead woman. Any time her mind wandered, it fixated on the image of Caroline huddled under the trees; KL lifted the smooth face, revealing her lifeless eyes. It felt like they were still staring at her.

Rebecca needed to focus her mind elsewhere. The easiest distraction was to look into the property line issue. Although Chris's attempt to involve her had taken her by surprise, she understood his reasoning: a dead body on the property would be a black mark on it. California law requires that a death be reported conspicuously on any listing for the next three years. Despite centuries of advancements in science and medicine, humans remain notoriously superstitious animals, especially concerning death. Say a skydiver's parachute malfunctions, and, as the growing air resistance smothers their cries, blowing them in the direction of two family homes. Though which house they hit is a matter of chance, that thrill seeker's death will affect any future sales of the impacted home, clinging to the property like a curse. Its assessed value will decrease, in some cases, drastically. No one wanted to deal with that, if they could help it.

Admittedly, Caroline's death—how it looked, anyway—was a lot less random than that. If, however, her body hadn't been on the Sweet property, there would be no legal obligation to disclose it. Sure, it might be more ethical to be upfront about such things, but the financial risk often outweighed ethical considerations for most people. Rebecca quickly sent exploratory emails to surveying companies Halcyon Realty had used before. Waiting for a lull in Chris White's conversation with KL and his attorney, she approached them.

"I'm sorry about all this, Mr. White." Even seated, Chris White had to look down at her.

"Don't blame yourself. She goes on these *benders*," KL said. Chris silenced him with a sharp glance.

"Thank you," Chris added, checking the time and adjusting the gold watch on his wrist. "She'll be devastated to learn about Caroline. I believe it will be a wake-up call." Rebecca wondered at his statement, at its ignorance, but she shot straight through to the point. "I know this is probably not the best time, but I've reached out to a couple of folks we know, and we should have the exact property line established by the end of tomorrow. Most likely." Chris nodded but said nothing, and, this time, KL followed suit. The attorney remained as expressionless as ever.

Feeling satisfied for having nipped, at least, this one future problem in the bud, Rebecca returned to her seat and waited a turn with the sheriff. Soon, however, the moment of finding the body began playing on repeat in her mind. Caroline's face, so expressive just hours before, was blank: a silly-putty recreation of what it had been. It was a fragile shell, no longer animated by the spirit that had shielded it from the encroaching wilderness. Wild plants and animals and the universe at large would consume every last person if given the chance.

Our minds are our armor, Rebecca thought. *They protect us from even the most innocuous things. Grass; grasshoppers.* She wanted to purge the image of Caroline's slack face and toneless muscles. *Minds are weapons, too: double-edged and dangerous.*

Rebecca's own mind, in the early stages of compulsively fixating on that face, was fighting a battle against itself. Insidiously, it asked her if things at the house would have played out as they did if she had refused Charles and gone on her trip. Worse, it suggested that she was somehow responsible for the death, though she didn't remember. If nothing else, maybe she could have saved Caroline by rejecting Becky's pill. Rebecca excused herself from the room, pacing the length of the foyer as she waited her turn with the sheriff. Her eyes glanced at the shelf, passing down the pictures and awards, and Rebecca was filled with a sense of growing wrongness.

"Rebecca Ziel, right?"

"Oh!" Rebecca turned to see Dr. Bridgette Lane standing there. "I'm sorry; you startled me."

Rebecca had initially perceived the doctor as younger than her, maybe in her early thirties. But up close—close enough to smell her sophisticated wildberry perfume—it was harder to guess her age. She had wrinkles that appeared natural, but they were few and far between, without artificial smoothing. Her skin had a certain quality—a texture, a color—that was hard to place. Despite her soft features, she could pass either as a hard-living twenty-eight-year-old, or a woman in her fifties who had aged remarkably well. The woman, apparently, had good genes.

Dr. Lane gently rubbed her arm below the shoulder, "You must forgive my earlier impatience. I didn't realize you were with the girls last night. Do you remember Anton Yelchin. He was in Star

Trek." She gazed into the distance. "He was so young. I counseled...his director friend who found him pinned against the car. I won't say the man's name out of respect. He was so grief-stricken that he couldn't talk at first. But talking is what eventually moved him through his grief." She paused for a response, then asked, "Would you like to talk? About what you saw this morning, or last night? How you're feeling after, well, you know?"

None of Rebecca's concerns were worth taking up anyone's time. Rebecca shook her head and said, "Sorry, I don't know. It's all of it. It's overwhelming."

Dr. Lane nodded. "You knew Caroline more than in passing. That must make it especially hard." The doctor's sympathetic eyes probed Rebecca's, who looked away, certain that she could have done something to prevent the death.

"I don't know. I don't really remember much about last night. I had been asleep when Becky asked me to join them, and I," she hesitated. "I took some things I probably shouldn't have." Rebecca shook her head again, ashamed. "I know I know better. I just. Sometimes, I have a hard time saying no to people when they ask me to do something."

Dr. Lane nodded, then shook her head. "Yesterday, I had a meeting about a reality show I'm producing. Celebrity therapy sessions. The working title is 'Chatting with the Stars.' Terrible, right?" She smiled, then shook her head. "Knowing I had that meeting, not knowing when we would be finished, I agreed, nonetheless, to speak at yesterday's event as well. You know how that went. And I also told an associate I would speak with her partners about working together. Did I want to do either of those things after my trip? No, but they asked me, so I said yes." She leaned in. "I've been contemplating all morning what I might have done or said differently that might have helped Becky better or otherwise prevented Caroline's death."

"I've been feeling the same. But, no." It was Rebecca's turn to be comforting. "You helped. She was so angry when he came yesterday." She pointed to the room where Sheriff Donnelly was questioning Ghosted. "But after talking to you, even on the phone, it was like she was a whole different person. There was...peace."

"You're too kind. I heard about what she did: deleting the album, disrupting the fundraiser. She's been abusing her medications." She looked around the room. "This family can be a bit, shall we say *liberal* with their usage. And now she's missing." The woman smiled weakly. "I make as many mistakes as anyone. More, even. But, as my mentor, Tony Robbins, told me over dinner last year, 'Mistakes are part of the process.'" Dr. Lane put her hand to her chest, "I'm not perfect, but I'm perfection *in progress.*" She placed that same hand on Rebecca. "You're not perfect, but you are perfection in progress. I'm not here to tell you what you should or shouldn't do. I'm here to listen. I'm at my best when I'm like a recording played back to them, but in autotune. I listen to my clients, and I repeat back not what they literally sound like, but the notes they're trying to hit. If you're my client, I may see what you're going through as clear as day, but I need you to know that you know what you're going through."

Rebecca was quiet for a minute. "Sorry, that makes sense. I just needed to work out what you meant." Rebecca tilted her head. "But you're not just an echo, are you? You know things normal people don't. You've gone to school. You're a psychiatrist, right, so you know what medicines help with what disorders, for example."

"We all know things someone else doesn't; we all see things other people miss. We all have flaws, and we all make mistakes when trying to do what others find simple," the doctor said. She breathed deeply. "Yesterday was a mistake on my part; I took on too much, and things turned out worse because of it. And you, are you okay if I make an observation about you?" Rebecca blushed and nodded her assent. "You apologize an awful lot."

"I'm sorry," Rebecca said. They both chuckled politely. "I'm only half kidding."

"Right, perfect. That: both halves," Dr. Lane looked authentically pleased, engaging Rebecca in the conversation, "both the apology you mean and the half you're joking about. They're defense mechanisms. There's something in your past, somewhere, where those tactics were employed to defend you from some great pain. That technique worked to stop whatever it was in its tracks, and to redirect it away from you. And that worked. But, if you're like most women, at some point, the act of always apologizing for everything or making light of your feelings lost its protective properties. Those behaviors became less about redirecting the pain and more about just keeping things moving, moving so that whatever it was could just flow past to deal with later." She let that sink in.

"You got all that from just listening to me? Maybe I need to be your patient."

Dr. Bridgette Lane shook her head. "I wish I could, but I'm swamped. The new show is consuming most of my time, and the clinic is booked solid. I need to learn from my own mistakes, and that means not overextending myself. But I do want you to be able to talk about what you're feeling." She pulled out a business card and wrote her personal cell number on it, handing it to Rebecca. "Call me if you get overwhelmed by what you witnessed last night and this morning. I might not always be free, but Becky's my client. I told her to apologize, so I feel responsible for what you're going through. But what about now? Do you feel a bit better?"

Rebecca nodded, smiling. "Thank you," she said, realizing the doctor's approach had not been accidental. She had sensed Rebecca's anxiety, but rather than confronting it directly, she had eased it through distraction. Not an empty distraction, either. She had guided the conversation to actively involve Rebecca instead of letting her remain passive. It worked. She was still uneasy, but no longer obsessively replaying Caroline's death. She felt empowered, like she could actually do something about the situation.

She wasn't sure how to improve things, but talking to the sheriff was a start. Perhaps she would provide the perfect clue that would help find Becky. "I am feeling better now." Rebecca replaced the trophy she'd been absently handling when Dr. Lane first approached. She tried to position each award where they'd been before fidgeting with them, placing Jenna's somewhere in the middle, hoping to satisfy both sisters. Double-checking her arrangement, she noticed only one Grammy on the shelf.

Rebecca twirled, figuring she must have mindlessly set it down. She felt sure she hadn't moved any of them from their shelf; she'd only shuffled them about.

"Are you alright?"

"I'm sorry, I just...I think I've misplaced one of B*Sweet's Grammys." The thought of losing something so valuable made her sick.

"It's alright," Dr. Bridgette Lane reassured her. "Take a breath. It'll come back to you."

Rebecca breathed slowly, thinking back. "No," she said, remembering: the Grammy had been gone from the beginning. She'd felt a vague unease when she first looked at the shelf, but the stress of everything had prevented her from pinpointing the cause. Now, with a calmer mind, the missing Grammy was obvious.

Chapter Eleven.

KL joined them in the foyer, wrapping an arm around Dr. Lane. "Chris and Hernando are in with Patrick. I'd *kill* for a drink right now. How are you two so calm and collected?" The doctor elbowed KL gently in the ribs. Releasing her, he bit a thumbnail and grimaced apologetically at Rebecca. "That was in bad taste."

"It's okay. One of the Grammys you showed me yesterday is missing, I think. At first, I thought—but it was gone when I walked in, I'm sure of it."

"I *see.*" He slipped past her, searching the shelves with a graceful familiarity. He examined the plaque on the remaining award and chuckled thoughtfully. "You're right. It appears the missing award is for *(Not) So Sweet.* The record she made with 'he who shall not be named.'" He tilted his head toward the other room.

"Ghosted?" Rebecca asked, "James Logan?"

KL shushed her and nodded.

Rebecca's eyes danced, focusing on nothing as she processed the news. "It's peculiar that she kept it in the first place, then, isn't it? Given what happened." KL raised an eyebrow. Rebecca elaborated, "I mean, she's willing to scrap the new album because he's involved. Why keep that?"

KL lifted a finger. "*First,* he gave up all rights of ownership of the songs. That was part of Chris's settlement after the assault. Ghosted was never *publicly* credited—you could still hide those things back then—though you *know* he still used them to get work. Second, she's being a drama queen. She loved all the new songs before he showed his face. *Raved* about them for days: 'the best I've ever done,' and the like. She wanted to perform only new material in Vegas, but hotel management said they'd cancel, so she agreed to stick to her hits. Guess which album has the most of those." He cupped his hand to his mouth and whispered, "*(Not) So Sweet.*"

"Sorry, I—uh," she stuttered. Dr. Lane's analysis was echoing in her mind. Shaking her head, she said "I mean, could she have done something with it?"

KL shrugged. "*You* were with her last night, weren't you? What do *you* think?"

Rebecca shook her head. Becky had been adamant about not wanting to have anything to do with Ghosted, her abuser. It was easy to picture her, in a fit of anger, getting rid of something so closely associated with him. In fact, the image came naturally, almost like a memory: Becky at the edge of the property hurling something into the woods. The more she thought about it, the more confident Rebecca became that it *was* a memory.

Closing her eyes, Rebecca tried to recall every detail: warm concrete under her feet, Becky's bright face, twisted in a paroxysm of ecstasy and anger, the...something hurtling through space, gleaming with reflected light. Rebecca took the remaining Grammy, weighing it in her hand. The award wasn't heavy, but it was too heavy to match Becky's easy throw. Assuming she had actually thrown something.

The iPad, though, that might be the right size. And, though it didn't make sense, Rebecca thought she remembered seeing Becky in the dark yard, holding an iPad. Had she been shouting at it? Did Becky see something on it she wanted gone? The pictures of Marc?

Rebecca finally answered KL, her eyes clamped shut, replaying the scene. "I think I remember her throwing something into the trees last night. I can see it. But I'm not sure. It might have been the Grammy. Or something else." She addressed the doctor, "When she talked to me, she was calm, thanks to you. But she wanted Ghosted out of her life. I think getting rid of the Grammy is less extreme than deleting her work."

"So, your memory is returning?" Dr. Lane asked.

Rebecca shook her head. "I don't think so. Pieces. If that. It might be a dream. I just have this image of her throwing something." She sighed, searching the doctor's eyes for something she could be certain of. "For all I know, she threw a rock at the paparazzi in the trees."

Dr. Lane took Rebecca's hand, holding it gently. She studied Rebecca's face. "It's going to be okay. You will get over this. I'm here if you need me."

Rebecca could almost cry. "Thank you."

The doctor nodded and returned to the other room with KL, waiting their turn with the sheriff. After a couple of minutes, Rebecca followed suit, trying to ignore KL tapping his fingers on the wooden armrest and the doctor's compassionate stare.

***

"Ms. Ziel?" Rebecca, mired in her uncertainty, hadn't heard Sheriff Donnelly's percussive steps approach her. He extended his hand. "Will you join me in the other room?"

The study had been designed to resemble an English manor library, filled with rich, raw umber shelves and a dark green, diamond-lattice wallpaper. It was two stories high, with tall, narrow bookshelves accessible by a rolling ladder. It fit perfectly with the overall feeling of the place and would provide excellent pictures. But, of course, her camera was still missing. She'd have to use her personal phone until she could find it.

Sheriff Patrick Donnelly stood behind the antique desk, framed by the curtained windows, and gestured for Rebecca to sit. She felt awkward and small, like she was applying for a job she had no business doing. He handed her a bottle of supermarket water and pulled out the same notepad and a silver pen from earlier. Asking her the basics—her name, residence, employer, and employment—he wrote quickly, occasionally crossing out elements for reasons Rebecca couldn't guess.

As she answered, Rebecca stared at the sheriff's striking emerald eyes. Her focus, though, fell repeatedly onto his hand. He was left-handed, but what fascinated her was the way he held the pen: gripping it between the knuckles of his index and middle finger. It was like watching someone peel a banana from the bottom; it looked like it shouldn't work, but—against all odds—it did. Somehow, it made him seem more approachable and human. He glanced up from the notepad and his cheeks grew red when their eyes momentarily locked.

Rebecca quickly looked at the shelves, reading random book titles and suppressing the smile she hadn't realized was there.

His expression grew serious. "I understand you were with Becky and Caroline last night," he said. He asked for every detail, and she provided them: the surreal jaunt from her room to the pool house, the spat between Becky and Caroline, even the half a Xanax and subsequent blacking out. Though she tried to be thorough, she omitted the hazy memory of Becky throwing something into the woods, unsure if it was real.

"You said you only saw cannabis, alcohol, and prescription pills?" Rebecca nodded. "But you described Caroline as," he flipped through his notes, "'on edge,' using 'exaggerated gestures,' and 'grinding her teeth when Becky spoke dismissively about the book.'"

"Yes."

Sheriff Donnelly probed her; Rebecca maintained eye contact, sensing that to avert her gaze was tantamount to admitting some wrong. "Do you know what that suggests?" She nodded. "Becky's an addict. She surrounds herself with addicts. There have been close calls before." He studied her again, and this time, she looked away, not from guilt, but from uncertainty. If he was right about Becky, what did that say about her? Why had she been chosen to join them at the pool?

"Ms. Ziel." He waited until she looked at him, their eyes meeting. "I don't know what happened between you, Becky, and Caroline last night, but I believe you've been honest with me," he paused for confirmation. When she nodded, he continued. "Becky and I, we grew up together. I knew Elaine. Her mother. She was...heavenly. They both were." He grew distant, and he exhaled a long, slow breath soaked in nostalgia or, possibly, regret.

Rebecca wanted to hold his hand like Dr. Lane had done for her. She wanted to tell him that whatever he was feeling, it was okay; it would be okay. But he was a sheriff, and she was a witness.

"And like any celestial body, Becky pulls you in. It feels natural and...intractable. But she's also being pulled, by forces that are bigger and more powerful than she is." He locked eyes with her, making certain she was listening. "Anyone unwise or...unlucky enough to get caught in her orbit can lose themselves to her and to the gravities that move her."

"Okay," she squeaked.

He stood up, but he halted at the half-open door, turning to watch her eyes. "What are you doing here?"

That caught her off guard; she thought they were done with the baseline questions. "I'm here to help sell the house," she said, trying to steady her voice and the tremor in her chest. She felt like she was still being interrogated. "Researching things, noting details for the disclosures, and—." She desperately wanted to escape the moment, to provide the answer that would end the conversation and fix everything.

"No." The finality of the word snapped her back to attention. "What are you doing in Sacramento? You're not from here, correct?"

She looked away, more embarrassed by this question than any of the others. "I guess I am now. But, uh, you mean..." She hesitated, giving up with a shrug. "It's a cliché, I know. One thing led to another, and I ended up here."

"That's your official statement?" His smile read as an attempt to be playful, but under the circumstances, it came off as a threat.

She wanted to stop there, but he'd pulled on a loose thread, and now it was unraveling. His hand rested warmly on her shoulder. "It's okay, I'm just curious. It's my nature." He shifted his weight and crossed his arms. "But this isn't a sheriff asking. It's me, Patrick. You don't have to answer."

"It was—" She shook her head. "It was my boyfriend. He wanted to go to school up here—the school up here admitted him— and I wanted to, you know, be with him, so I came, too. Enrolled in the same school." That had been so long ago.

"At the time, it felt...not right, exactly, but necessary to keep us together. It sounds ridiculous now, but I thought I'd disappear if he left." She tried coughing, but the lump in her throat didn't budge. "When things didn't work out like they were supposed to, I was here, and so, one thing led to another, and I stayed." She felt a brief elation, like the relief after throwing up, before the sickening urge creeps back. She'd finally articulated her situation and could analyze it. But she knew the feeling was fleeting. The anxiety that had kept her from facing the truth would soon return, and along with it, shame for revealing so much to a stranger.

"I take it, then, the boyfriend's a was and not an is?" Sheriff Donnelly asked her. She reddened. "Sorry, I didn't mean to pry." *He totally meant to pry,* Rebecca thought. "Look, I don't know your plans. "I understand you were going to stay at the house for a few days. I wouldn't blame you for reconsidering after everything. In fact, I probably should advise you against it, but...I know this family. I care about them, but I can't trust them to put the investigation first. Maybe that's unfair of me. Having someone on the inside, someone objective and observant, would be invaluable." His eyes met hers, and Rebecca felt exposed, as if he could see her entire life. "Can I reach out with questions? And can I count on you to call me if anything unusual happens, or if she comes back?"

Though framed as requests, Rebecca understood they were directives. "Of course," she said.

The sheriff asked for her phone and sent himself a text. "This number goes direct to me." As he confirmed the text arrived, another message came in. He read it and excused himself.

The heavy door was old, and though Sheriff Patrick Donnelly pushed it closed when he left, the door crept open. His conversation with the deputy drifted into the room. "So, mass spec found multiple drugs in her blood, particularly a huge amount of ketamine along with...benzos." He ran his hand through his thick brown hair. "We won't know what without more tests, but damn if it looks like the amount is far too high to be an accidental overdose. Either she injected herself with a massive amount, or someone else did." Rebecca felt like she was eavesdropping on something forbidden. She recoiled, her heart racing. She couldn't erase what she'd just heard.

"Homicide?" asked the deputy.

"Or suicide...or both. Any luck with Becky Sweet or Marc Sheffield?" The sheriff paused, long enough for the deputy to shake his head. "We need to keep this quiet for as long as possible, but..." Rebecca's head swam. She needed to sit down.

Chapter Twelve.

Rebecca sensed the dissociative beginnings of an anxiety attack. She mimicked Dr. Lane's mindful breathing techniques, counting the seconds with each breath. Outside, sheriffs and deputies were completing their searches of the property. Chris White's attorney intercepted Sheriff Donnelly at his cruiser, and the two of them exchanged a few words before shaking hands and leaving in their separate vehicles.

Caroline's death had already been traumatizing; she had been right there, near enough to touch. Learning her death wasn't an accident made things much worse. Rebecca didn't remember her seeming particularly suicidal, though she didn't remember much. And if Caroline had been killed, was Becky—or Rebecca herself—at risk? Were they responsible?

To protect herself, she needed to understand what had happened, starting with the clues she had. Massaging knuckles into the sides of her head, Rebecca focused on trying to force her memory to return. Other than abstract impressions, however, the only semi-clear image was Becky tossing the mystery object. She could almost see it, glittering in the air before being, finally, swallowed in the bramble. Although she had work to do—the loss of the iPad meant she would be starting over on so many forms, finding clues from the previous night felt more urgent and immediately achievable. Even if the thrown item was neither the iPad nor the Grammy, finding it could reveal some other truth about Becky and what happened to Caroline.

The storm had been all bark and no bite. By the time Rebecca headed toward the front forest, the sky was a clear blue, and the sun shone bright and hot like an oven, evaporating away any water brazen enough to have fallen on open land. Rebecca followed the edge of the circular driveway, trying to find the location she saw in her mind's eye. The sensory details were the strongest. Closing her eyes, she willed herself to remember: the pad of her big toe scraped against the cracked edge of the driveway; the crack edge audibly crumbled into gritty pebbles and collapsed, causing her to slip and fall onto the spongy turf; Becky's forceful laughter had pierced Rebecca's ears as the object was thrown.

Rebecca was able to find the same dilapidated corner of concrete from her memory. Sure enough, not four feet from the crack, there was the divot her elbow had made in the soft ground. And under the eaves of the house, there was the flood light that had illuminated Becky and the object. She ran to the trees.

Unlike the dryness outside, the dense woods retained their dampness from the rain; hot and humid, the air thrummed with the sounds of insects and small animals hunting for water or food. Unmanicured trees clawed at her, urging her back into daylight. Rebecca brute-forced her way past them, shining her phone flashlight this way and that, trying not to think about the gunk sticking to her. A web stuck to her arm, and she dropped the phone; for several terrifying seconds, she was convinced that the crispy black beetle corpse stuck to her wrist was a venomous spider prepping its fangs and she slapped desperately at her arm, trying to remove it without being bitten.

Finding the phone was simple enough, but the reality of her situation was beginning to set in. She looked above, hoping for a glint of metal tangled around a gnarled twig. Outside the woods, or perhaps hidden in the trees, corvids were cackling. It felt like they were laughing at her. She was lost, wading through bushes and thorns back toward the light to reorient herself with the entry point.

Rebecca's phone buzzed violently, and she nearly dropped it again. Her eyes moved across the face of her phone from the notification to the time. The message was from Sydney; she had probably just landed. Her message was "Look what you're missing!" and included several videos. Perhaps Sydney's adventures could cheer her up.

The first showed off the airport terminal in all its mall-like glory. Sydney flaunted the clean surfaces, open spaces and abundance of English signs, which meant she didn't even need to translate with her phone to understand. Rebecca grimaced, imagining herself walking beside Sydney, mortified by her loud breathing and constant chatter. In the background of the video, Rebecca noticed people Sydney overlooked, disapprovingly watching the tourist.

Sydney turned the phone camera toward her shirt, cutting off the video. But she kept recording as she entered a restroom, hoping to find one of the famous "Japanese robo-toilets." Even in the restroom, she wouldn't stop talking, relying on hushed tones to make it seem like what she was doing was totally natural. She turned the camera back on her face once in the main concourse, rating the latrines a letdown, but heaping praise on the immaculate bathrooms "like they're for the queen of England."

A second video was a silent clip photographed through a taxi window. It showcased the stacked and winding freeways and the slowly rising sun, seemingly frozen in place behind a parade of slim skyscrapers. The video transported her; all her worries melted away, and she was there, holding Sydney's hand in the taxi, ready for an unforgettable experience. Then it ended, and she was back— alone, damp, and scratched—in the dense undergrowth.

Sydney was living her best life while Rebecca was miserable and tired and hot and wet and wasting her time. Half her day was gone, and she hadn't completed a single page of work. All Rebecca had accomplished was adding a few new scratches to her arms and new reasons to feel like a failure. She wiped the sweat from her forehead and tried not to start crying or cursing herself.

Agitated by her exit, a bird chortled and launched into the air, fluttering its black and white wings in a frenzy. Rebecca, startled in return by the sudden magpie, fell backward, snapping sprigs and branches as they scraped her torso. She deserved the scratches, she thought, for wasting her time like that, and she checked them for blood. She winced, but the scratches were shallow. Rebecca shielded her eyes and tracked the magpie's flight across the sky until it blended into the blue. *How nice it must be to fly away like that.*

Where the bird had been pecking, tangled in the grass, a mirrored bronze whatsit reflected bits of sunlight at Rebecca's eyes. Tearing away the sod, she revealed a brushed-metal object shaped a bit like a miniature flip lighter. Engraved on the flat side was the word Zosia. That was the middle name Becky had given her stillborn daughter. Rebecca picked up the object, unsure that it was what Becky had thrown, but fairly certain it belonged to her.

Toying with the seemingly solid item, she discovered that one end pressed inward, releasing a spring-loaded USB-C connector. Rebecca considered texting the sheriff. But what did she really know about the drive? Would turning it in bring clarity to the case, or complicate things further? The most sensible thing to do was check the contents before turning it in.

She went back to the pool house, where she'd left the green iPad sleeve and the electronic notebook that Dr. Lane's patient had lost at the fundraiser. She'd forgotten about it. Rebecca rummaged in her fanny pack to find Dr. Lane's business card. She dialed the office number.

"Hello?" The man answered curtly. Rebecca felt like a nuisance. She nervously rifled through her fanny pack, pulling out a crumpled envelope.

"Hello? Is this Dr. Bridgette Lane's office?" Rebecca uncrumpled the paper, reading Dollar Bill's hand-written contact information. She stuffed it back in her bag.

The man answered with: "Dr. Lane will not be taking any new patients or scheduling any sessions as she develops her new program."

"Oh, okay. I, um, I'm not calling to talk to her. I met one of Dr. Lane's patients at the Sweet's house yesterday. At the charity event. She left her computer, electronic notebooky thing, and I was hoping to get it back to her."

"We can't give out any patient information."

"Oh, no, of course not! I'm not asking for that. I was just hoping to drop it off so you could give it back to her." Rebecca wished she hadn't called. The man sighed, his breath heavy, before replying.

He finally said, "I can't help you over the phone. You'll have to bring it in." Rebecca agreed to stop by after finishing up at the house, despite the man's warning, "I leave at 5:00 sharp."

Finding Dollar Bill's envelope reminded Rebecca of the flashes she'd seen in the woods. If his had been the source, he might have pictures of what had happened to Becky or Caroline.

The phone connected after a single ring. "About time," he said gruffly. "I've been waiting over an hour. They'll be here any minute, and I'm giving them the pictures. If you want them, you better have what I want." He paused, then added, "Is that you or them pulling up?"

"Sorry? No, I-I spoke to you yesterday in front of B*Sweet's house. Big red hair? I wanted to ask you about last night."

He didn't seem to be listening. "...I told you. You didn't know about this house, did you? Do you want..." Dollar Bill's voice faded, lost in the static of wind rushing past the phone; he wasn't holding it to his ear anymore. Rebecca thought she heard another voice in the background. "...I thought it was you—" Bill's voice returned, loud and clear. "Hello?"

"Hi, it's me—" The line went dead. He could've been talking to anyone about anything, but she could only view it through the lens of her recent experiences. His words felt connected somehow. Was that idle hope? She called back. No answer. Her heart pounded. She tried again: straight to voicemail. Connected or not, Dollar Bill wasn't letting her ask.

Chapter Thirteen.

Rebecca tapped the screen of Lucy P's D-Note, thinking she could maybe find her information there, but it required a password. She rubbed her head. Was she really going out of her way to return the property of someone she didn't know? Of course: she'd want someone to do it for her if it had been hers. She stuffed the tablet into her sun-dried green case and moved toward the main house.

When her phone rang, Rebecca answered quickly, expecting Dollar Bill. Instead, it was Dr. Lane; she was breathing heavily. "Rebecca! I was told you called. You caught me in the middle of a run."

"Yes, I found a tablet belonging to one of your patients from the fundraiser, and—" Her phone buzzed. It was Charles; she had to answer. "I, uh, I already spoke to your receptionist and arranged to come by. I'm sorry, I need to take this. It's my boss."

"Anytime," the doctor said, still catching her breath, and she hung up.

"How are you?" Charles asked in a single breath.

"Fine," she answered cautiously.

"Good, good. Hey, Paul and Jason called me; they said you contacted them about surveying the property?" The statement had transformed into a question by the end.

"There was concern about where—"

"Yeah, I canceled that. Look, you need to clear any external contracts with me first, okay?" Charles paused, speaking loudly and clearly to correct the distorted voice on his end: "No cheese, NO CHEESE. I can't—okay, yeah, yeah. Diet Coke. Yeah. Rebecca?" He waited for her to respond. "The Sweets haven't made any payments or signed the contracts, so we can't pay anyone ourselves, okay? You understand?"

"Sorry, got it." So Halcyon didn't have a signed contract with Chris White. That was clearly foolish, but it did explain why Charles had not tasked Rebecca to start on the paperwork earlier. Her experience told her that the wealthier a client was, the less they expected to pay and the more they expected to receive. Riding the line—accomplishing just enough to keep things moving but not so much to risk holding the bill if relations went south—was one of Charles' go-to techniques for reeling in high-value clients. That he was not working on it himself indicated that he was either apprehensive about losing the possible sale or engaged in some sort of weird powerplay.

"Trust me," he continued, "whether she died on the property or not won't really affect this sale. The news will get out anyway, even if we don't have to disclose it, okay? Besides, for buyers in this price range, it's just another bargaining chip. They'll already expect to negotiate down by a few hundred thousand at least, so the news won't change much. And for some, a famous death might even be a selling point!"

"Sure," she responded.

"Okay. Great. Oh! I talked with Chris White; he said he wanted to discuss something with you. Did you say anything to him that I should know about?"

That was news to her. "Only about the property line assessment," she answered.

"Okay, okay, well, whatever it is, if he asks you to do something, do what you can to help, but don't go out of your way without talking to me first, okay? I've got to go." Charles hung up.

Rebecca had no idea what Chris White wanted to talk about or where he was, and she didn't have his contact information. She shielded her eyes and looked at the house. The windows of the upper level gave the edifice a menacing pareidolic appearance, and the idea of re-entering the maw at the base of the window-eyed facade was exhausting.

"You look like you just had a *street fight* with an *alley cat*! And you *lost*! Are you well?" KL, carrying two garbage bags, approached her from the eastern side of the lot.

Rebecca looked down at her scratches and said, "Sorry, yeah, I was looking around the trees for...I don't know. I'm a mess this morning."

"Uh huhhh," KL said slowly, his eyes narrowing. "Come." He set down the bags, tossing his yellow gloves inside, and took Rebecca's upturned wrist. With a dancer's grace, he led her in the direction he'd come: around the back of the house to the recording studio. On the outside, it looked like the three-bedroom servant's quarters it had once been. Entering it filled her with a sense of *déjà vu*.

"It's just past here," he said. As they passed through the living-room-*cum*-lobby to the kitchen, Rebecca glimpsed chaos in a room off to the side: the large tinted window was spiderwebbed with cracks, and the floor was littered with electronic debris. KL pulled her past—avoiding any questions about the disarray—into what was likely a former bedroom, furnished with a mini-fridge, a sofa, and a large, angled TV. The room smelled strongly of cleaning fluid, and a broom leaned against the wall. As Rebecca's eyes scanned the three framed gold and platinum records on the wall, she asked KL, "Yesterday, you were in Mr. White's room; today, this. I thought you were Becky's stylist. Why all the cleaning?"

" '*Becky*.' Huh." His reflection in the large mirror looked at her with a knowing smirk. He said, "We do what we can for the people we care about. Even if they're in the wrong." He tapped her with the back of his hand. "*You* know that."

KL led her to the chair and curtsied, waiting for her to sit. Flipping on the clear glass bulbs dotted around the painted wood frame, he stepped out of the room, returning with a bottle of water, gauze, individual antiseptic wipes, self-adhesive bandages and a bottle of pills.

"Oh, no, I'm fine, thanks."

Rebecca started to get out of the chair, but KL commanded, "Sit," and held her arm. "You're not getting an infection on *my* watch." He cleaned her scratches and applied bandages to the deeper ones. "You really don't remember what happened last night?" She shook her head. He bent over and gently held her head, plucking leaves and God-knows-what out of her hair, dropping the debris into a lined tin trash can. "It's a shame. I hoped you might know where B*Sweet hid the album."

She gawped at him. KL laughed, saying, "That girl may be crazy, but she's *not* stupid. You give her too little credit if you think she'd throw away *all* of her work like it was garbage."

Rebecca wasn't so sure. Becky had sounded so sincere. KL hmmed, and he watched her as she thought. He was clearly convinced there was still a copy somewhere and that Rebecca was obfuscating. He spilled several pills into his palm. Popping one into his mouth, he offered her the remaining two. "The brown one is for the inflammation, and the white one is for the anxiety."

"Oh, no, I'm not—"

"Ms. Ziel, there's panic written *all over* your face. Don't worry," KL assured her. "I get these from my sister, and she knows her stuff. They're pure, they're safe and they'll do the job. I swear." She accepted the pills, and as he reached past her body to the assemblage of creams and sprays arrayed at the base of the mirror, she placed them in her pocket. He eyed her knowingly and spritzed a sweet-smelling mist across her frizz.

"I'll take it later," she promised him.

KL tutted. With a flexible metal brush, he teased her hair from the tips. "You'd have gorgeous hair if you took care of it properly. If you can't run your fingers through your locks without snagging, you have knots, not curls. You need a metal brush like this. Never use plastic, they're *trash*. If I see one, I throw it *out*." His gentle touch nearly lulled her to sleep.

"You're really good at this," she told him, her eyes closed.

He infused his "thanks" with enough sarcasm to bottle up and sell in a high-end boutique.

"Oh, I'm sorry, of course, it's your job."

"Unless you plan on paying, sweetie, it's not a job."

"I'm sorry," she said sleepily. KL smirked and shook his head. He applied multiple creams and scrunched her hair in tight clumps, securing them with elastic bands. "Here," he said, handing her a spray bottle, "this will help you maintain your curls. Use it after you shower."

"I can't—" KL silenced her objection with his stare. She shoved the bottle into her fanny pack. It was getting full. "Thank you," she acquiesced and let loose with a long sigh. "I was supposed to talk to Chris White," she remembered suddenly, her back stiffening.

"Look at you. You're *exhausted*. Why don't you just go home?" Rebecca was confused. KL explained: "You've been through a lot. I think you should just consider this a little adventure—staying in a fancy house, partying late with a pop star, making a mess in the music studio and playing detective in the bushes. It's not worth it," he advised her.

"Oh," Rebecca said, "it's really not that bad. A few scratches won't kill me."

KL grabbed her arm, squeezing it painfully for a moment. He released it and stepped back toward the door as she rubbed her wrist. "I'm sorry," he said, "your vibe is giving '*trauma*,' so I know grabbing you like that doesn't help." He locked his eyes with hers, waiting to ensure she understood where he was coming from. "But, *look*, I know it's exciting to spend time with B*Sweet. She probably makes you feel like something in this world is *finally* going your way. She does that. But she is trou*BLED* with a capital B-L-E-D. We all are, in case you didn't notice. And you don't want that in your life!" He swept his arm like he was removing insects. "Move on to the next thing; you're too innocent for a place like this. Don't give *that* up. I mean, oh my *god*, you found a *dead* woman in the *woods!* Who *does* that?" His shoulders slumped, and he leaned against the wall, drained. "I don't care what people say—and neither should you—naivety is a gift, it needs to be protected at *all costs*. Call your boss and say you need to step away."

"I..." Rebecca felt a strong urge to agree and leave, if only to calm KL down, but she knew she couldn't. As stupid as it felt to admit it, Becky was her friend. She couldn't know whether Becky felt the same way, or whether it was like KL was saying: a feeling she gave everyone. That was probably part of it; meeting Becky finally showed Rebecca that she had never experienced *true* charisma. But it didn't matter. Rebecca might never be friends with B*Sweet, the pop star, but Becky Sweet, the person, *was* her friend, and Rebecca wanted to help her friend. She wasn't going to leave things where they were, which meant she needed to talk to Chris White.

Rebecca bit her cheek to resist KL's plea. "I'm sorry, but, thank you. However, Chris White asked to see me. Sorry."

KL sighed. "Chris's office is in his boat on Folsom Lake," he said, as if that were perfectly normal. "It's peaceful there; he says it helps him think. Can I borrow your phone?" She gave it to him. KL created a contact for her. "If he's not at the dock, you'll have to call the harbor master. They'll either take you to him or call him back by VHF."

"Like the old videotapes."

He smiled sadly and said, "I used to think the same thing. No, it's a type of maritime radio, or something. Boat people and their secret language." Taking her hand, gently this time, he helped her back into the seat and said, "Now let's see how these curls turned out and make you up real nice."

Chapter Fourteen.

It was on the drive to the lake that Rebecca came to recognize the flash of déjà vu she'd had in the studio as another fractured memory. Events from the previous night were returning, but they clarified nothing. She couldn't recall how long she'd been in the studio or piece together any coherent sequence of events to explain what had happened or why. In the shards of memory, she caught glimpses of Becky leading her into the studio's recording booth.

It had been smaller than she expected, missing the giant soundboards she'd always imagined in a studio. Other than the soundproof window looking into the unlit space where the artists would sing or play, the room had only a single ochre table on which were three monitors and a specialized keyboard with a series of rubber dials. Cables snaked from these devices down the table's back, running into a big, black metal box on wheels, along with bundled wires emerging from a small hole in the wall.

The music possessed an eerie familiarity, like something once heard in a dream. She could just about picture herself and Becky, reflected in the glass partition, grinning as they listened. Then, a folding chair hurtling through the air, shattering the window. Metal crashing to the floor. Who had done what? She couldn't recall. Air from the lake blew cool into her window as she entered the parking lot, and any further memories drifted away. Rebecca entered the Ravine, Folsom Lake's most exclusive private marina. The office contacted Chris White and sent a young woman in a white polo shirt and faded denim skirt to direct Rebecca to his boat.

The *Miriam*, named for Becky's late mother and Chris White's only wife, was a large, dull gray cabin cruiser docked at the large vessel pier. Rebecca thanked the marina attendant, bracing herself for the awkward moment when she couldn't tip. Thankfully, her guide departed without a word. The yacht, docked beside a relatively minuscule speedboat named *Miriam II*, was by a wide margin the biggest in the marina. It had two above-water decks and was easily spacious enough for Chris White's considerable bulk.

White exited to the deck. "Ahoy!" Noticing Rebecca's interest in the speedboat, he said, "My daughters'. They don't take it out as much as when they were younger. I should probably sell it." He extended his hand to help Rebecca board. "Thank you for joining me." His enormous frame noticeably dipped the boat, despite its size. Rebecca, already unsteady from the gently swaying dock, felt her nausea worsen with the boat's movement.

"I spoke to Charles. I understand your surveyors won't be coming. That's fine; I've hired my own. He told me I should discuss any paperwork I'll need to sign on behalf of Becky's trust regarding the sale." He waved his hand assuringly, "To be frank, I'm not interested in any of that. I have other priorities. Send any legal documents to my attorneys; they'll review them to their hearts' content. Otherwise, as long as you're my representative in this sale, I'll assume you're acting in my best interest, and we'll leave it at that." The deck cabins had been refitted into an open party room wrapped in windows. Chris led her to the forward cabin, which was now his private office.

Rebecca followed despite a growing unease. He'd just told her he didn't want to talk to her about her job, so what? He gestured for her to sit on a slightly stained loveseat, and she sat obediently. Then lowered himself into a large wooden swivel chair behind a heavy desk wincing as he sat, just as he had at the house. The desk was strewn with papers, as the one in his room had been, though a beige folder and lone key were neatly and conspicuously placed atop the pile. On the cabin wall hung several of the same gold and platinum records she'd seen in the studio, along with many of the same family photographs that Rebecca had seen on the shelf at the house.

Looking at the office accouterments was not helping Rebecca with her seasickness. Nor was Chris White's scrutinizing stare.

Chris swiveled to face the lake and the pine-covered mountains enclosing it. "It's beautiful here, no? I find I can think on the water. Oh, of course, the lack of cell service helps too. I wouldn't carry a phone anyway; they're little more than marketing devices we embed on ourselves. They are specially designed to steal your time and money. God help us when they're chips implanted in our brains."

He swiveled back to her and asked, "Did you know this lake is fed by the American River?" Rebecca shook her head, and Chris nodded his. "No, no. Well, the river played an integral role in the transportation of goods and gold during the rushes of the 19th century. That gold fueled men's dreams, and Samuel Brannan and Joseph Folsom empowered those dreamers. Do you know the names?"

When Rebecca understood that White expected a response, she said, "I've heard of Folsom."

"Folsom, of course: the city, the lake. The prison. Brannan, you may not know his name, but you certainly know his saying: 'In a gold rush,' he said, 'sell shovels.' What's more American than that?!" White chuckled softly, an invitation for her to join. She chirped politely. "In a gold rush, you sell shovels. Of course, he was right; no one remembers that he said it, but he was right. He sold men the tools to dig and the spirits to celebrate, and he grew very wealthy, helping not a few of those miners make it rich in the process. Yet no one remembers him."

"Folsom, on the other hand, he built roads where waterways were insufficient. He surveyed and purchased the land, and it was through his planning that the motley camps of men grew into burgeoning cities. Tools break, dreams fade, but civilization endures. If you want to leave a legacy, you need to build more than just personal wealth."

Rebecca wasn't sure where this was heading. Worse, most of her focus was on not throwing up. She felt detached, watching herself from above, unable to escape. She hoped he'd get to the point soon. The man's poor chair groaned as he stretched his back and smiled; in his smiling face, Rebecca could almost imagine the young man he had once been, filled with dreams of his own. Many of those dreams had surely been realized, but there were bound to be others that had been lost to time. Chris cracked his neck and cast his eyes at the ground.

"I require your assistance, Ms. Ziel. Our family has so much opportunity to contribute in a meaningful way. Had I known when the girls were younger what I know now..." Chris White's head, heavy with regret, made a slow side-to-side motion. "Miriam was always more knowledgeable when it came to how to manage the girls' careers. But when it comes to their fortune, we still have a chance to change the world if the three of us can work together. Yet my daughter actively undermines my efforts."

Rebecca felt a small surge of sick in her throat; she swallowed it. Hiding her discomfort, she suggested, "I'm sure it wasn't personal. Becky seemed angry, but maybe she's just afraid of repeating past mistakes. She said she wants a normal life."

Chris's expression shifted from confusion to minor annoyance. He dismissed her words with a gesture. "Yes, of course, very astute. But I am not talking about my eldest daughter. This disappearance, in all likelihood, this is one of her *rumspringas*. She goes out, does what she does, but she always returns. As long as she is back before her residency, and I am confident she will be, she and I have no problem."

"I'm sorry, I thought you meant her destroying the album. I don't understand."

Chris White rubbed his forehead. "That, that is a setback, but not one that can't be overcome. She knows her place is on the stage and in the studio. She builds her roads on the hearts and minds of the millions who hear her sing, and they, in return, provide her with the love of a multitude. She will make the correct choice in the end, even if it is difficult for her. She has made those difficult choices in the past." He pointed to the ostentatiously-mounted gold and platinum records as though they proved his point. "No, I'm talking about my other daughter. What they don't tell you in Sunday school, Ms. Ziel, is that the prodigal son is the lesser threat. The one who remains close to home—who feels increasingly entitled to it and all it affords—that child is the danger. She is eager for the end, may even hasten it to acquire what she has earned."

Chris spun his chair to open a tall, wooden cabinet. Inside, Rebecca saw bottles of wine alongside a few framed pictures she hadn't seen anywhere else. These showed Chris and KL together. Two included a young girl, maybe six or seven, with them—one at a seafood restaurant, the other at a park—and another depicted KL and Chris alone in what looked like a romantic pose on a tropical beach. He closed the cabinet and presented a TwoSweet Riesling.

"You are familiar with my daughters' wine company? They started it together in 2011. It's grown impressively since then; we are preparing to branch out into rum and tequila by Q4 next year." Rebecca sensed that she was expected to be impressed; she lifted her eyebrows and nodded. "When they began this venture—which was only possible thanks to B*Sweet's funds and face—they would often turn to me for advice. But Jenna has grown power hungry, securing for herself 80% of the company." Chris slammed his fist into the top of the table, then moved aside papers to check whether he had cracked it.

"Furthermore," he said, "Jenna conspired with B*Sweet and Caroline on a memoir, intending to paint me in such a falsely unfavorable light as to forcefully remove me as Becky's caretaker.

Thankfully, I have friends who have received unredacted copies—Jenna has been shopping the book around in L.A."

He poured for them both and took a sip. Rebecca, lips pressed together, gripped the stem of her glass, fearing one sip might come back up and paint the room. Chris continued: "Caroline's master copy was kept on her personal laptop. Her laptop was not with her belongings; it is nowhere. I have reason to believe that Jenna secured the laptop to hurt me, and to drive a wedge between Becky and myself."

Rebecca set the glass on the table, hoping he didn't notice her squirming in her seat. Would he move this conversation ashore if she asked?

"Charles has you with us until Monday, yes?"

Croaking, "I believe, I, uh, yeah," she nodded stiffly.

Chris White put his hands together in a silent clap. "Great. Tomorrow morning, Jenna will be at the farmers market for five hours selling this." Chris held up his glass and swirled the wine contained within. He then took the key that had been patiently sitting on the desk and placed it onto Rebecca's palm. "I would like for you to conduct an inspection of the house tomorrow. This key opens all doors in the house, including the door to Jenna's room. If, during your duties, you are in her room and you find that laptop, or any other incriminating evidence, it's your duty to turn it over to me so I can assess it and give it to the sheriff."

Rebecca stuffed the key into her fanny pack. Her head was spinning. Legally, as Becky's conservator, Chris could probably ask her to search any room. Morally, however, Rebecca was appalled. "I don't know," Rebecca said. "I don't think I'm the right person for this. Can't you hire a private investigator?" She held out the key, but Chris only grinned.

"Don't assume you are the only one helping me to protect Becky's interests. But you're the only one with a legitimate reason to be in that room tomorrow." His expectant smile slowly smoothed into a disappointed frown.

He passed her the folder he'd been guarding with his hands. "This was waiting for me here," he told her. "Whoever delivered them, they knew where I was docked." Rebecca flipped open the unsealed flap. Inside was a small stack of pictures. "And they were not seen."

The first photo was too wide to show details clearly, but it showed Caroline standing over someone on the ground, gesturing angrily. Caroline was wearing the same clothes she'd been wearing when she died. The imaged showed the luminous pool house, placing the photographer at the western edge of the property. The next photo zoomed in on Caroline's target: Rebecca.

Blood drained from her face, and her eyes felt like they were bulging out of her head. The third picture showed Rebecca raising her arm, handing a white blob to Caroline. Rebecca brought the photo to her face and squinted; it looked like Becky's GPS tracker. When did she have it? Why? What were her reasons for giving it to the doomed woman? And where was Becky?

The final image was Caroline walking toward the guest house Rebecca had awakened in. As Rebecca looked through the pictures again, fragments of sound—Caroline's piercing accusations—replayed in Rebecca's mind. She felt the flood of vomit only after it reached her throat, and despite her efforts to hold it in or swallow, it shot through her lips, splashing onto Chris's desk, and soiling her clothes, the photos and the floor.

Thick strings of saliva dangled from Rebecca's face. "I'm so sorry; where's the restroom?" she gasped.

Chris White, disgusted, pointed her to a door labeled "Head."

Rebecca wiped her face and shirt, thinking. It wasn't just the content of the pictures that disturbed her. She wasn't a professional photographer, but she understood composition, and the pictures lacked a coherent perspective. It was like someone had given a toddler a Polaroid and let them go wild.

She wiped as much vomit off the pictures as possible. They were on quality stock—only slightly stained—but the weight and texture of the paper was indistinguishable from the type Becky had used for her signed one-sheets. That implied someone with access to the printer Becky had used delivered them. Could it have been Becky herself? But the pictures connected Rebecca to Caroline and, by extension, her murder. What reason was there to bring something like that to Chris's boat, unless Rebecca *was* involved. Or, was he only showing her what he wanted her to see?

Chris White was waiting for her with water and a towel. He led her to the main deck, saying, "Worry not, if these pictures leak, I will ensure you are represented; I have no doubt that you are innocent of any wrongdoing. Still, without proper context, they may appear incriminating."

"Who?" she asked feebly.

"I would have imagined it was obvious. Jenna has paparazzi in her employ. Caroline is dead, and I receive these photographs, in an effort to misdirect my suspicion on you, no doubt, while she has free rein."

"But why would she do that?" Rebecca asked.

"To stall the sale of the house. To wrest control of her sister's estate." His sturdy shoulder rose in an awkward shrug. "She has already poisoned her sister's opinion of me. I accept that, but I will not stop protecting her."

Rebecca shook her head, "What evidence is there?"

"That is where your investigation comes into play. Please," he pleaded, "during your duties tomorrow, I implore you to investigate Jenna's room. You are a fan of my Becky; I see that in the way you talk about her. Help me help her. Bring to me whatever you find that might help me continue to care for my daughters."

Rebecca offered Chris back the slightly soiled pictures. "Keep them. I made copies." He returned inside, closing the door. His request didn't feel like an assignment; it felt like a setup. A cold gust of the water hit Rebecca, and she shivered.

Legs still trembling, she staggered to her car. Accusations were flying in all directions, and now she had gotten hit with one. It seemed like everyone wanted something. They all had their own version of Becky. Somewhere, the real Becky was drowning under the weight of all these expectations.

Rebecca needed to think.

Chapter Fifteen.

Despite the sheriff's request that Rebecca remain with the Sweets as his eyes and ears, KL's strange behavior in the studio had convinced her to collect her belongings before leaving the house. Chris White's attempt at blackmail confirmed to her that she had been right to do so, and that the house wasn't safe.

Rebecca needed to hurry if she was going to reach Dr. Lane's office before it closed. She weaved between lanes, attempting to get ahead of the rush hour traffic. Instead, she seemed to be falling further back. It mirrored her life, as far back as she could recall. If she tried to stay in her lane and go with the flow, everyone else passed her by. When she tried to chase every potential opening, suddenly the lane was filled with competition, and she was worse off than if she'd simply stayed the course. It was like there was no winning.

Abutting the southern border of the Arden-Arcade suburb of Sacramento, the sprawling three-story rectangular building in which Dr. Lane operated was part of an extensive commercial park on the banks of the American River. The white facade with tall black windows resembled, from a distance, the ebony and ivory keys of a grand piano rising from the earth. The psychiatric office was on the third floor, next to the doctor's own Aegis Clinic, which, at present, appeared to be a series of brightly lit but seemingly empty rooms.

While the clinic retained the building's clean, modern design with subtle touches of naturalistic colors and curves, entering the lobby to Dr. Lane's psychiatric office felt like stepping into another world entirely. The sensation began with the custom doors: wide and green-black, like they had been transported from the gates of Oz's Emerald City. Passing the threshold, patients were thrust into a deceptively large and open room with creamy, marble-colored floors. Inverted Doric columns lined the walls, which shared the same marble texture as the floor. A brushed gold mirror on the ceiling made the room appear twice as tall, creating a subtle sense of spatial distortion. The combined effect left Rebecca with a light case of vertigo that encouraged her to sit as soon as possible on one of the plush chairs set between the columns of the rearmost wall.

From the entrance, the well-groomed man in his 30s seated behind the room's lone desk appeared small and insignificant. Behind him was another set of unusually large doors that almost certainly led into Dr. Lane's inner sanctum. The receptionist was moving his lips as he read from his computer screen, making sure not to move his eyes anywhere that could indicate he was aware of Rebecca. Despite transparently ignoring her presence, his look of concentration drifted increasingly toward annoyance as Rebecca approached. Only the man she'd spoken to on the phone could be that rude.

Rebecca pulled off her backpack to remove the patient's device and stood at the desk. "I'm sorry," he said before she could speak, "I'm afraid she just stepped out. And," he searched the computer screen, "we're near closing time, so she won't be back for the day. If you need to make an appointment, please call back tomorrow." His smile stopped at his lips, and it only barely covered those.

Rebecca looked at the giant analog clock on the wall: it was barely 4:30. She set the found D-Note onto the man's desk and said, "No, I'm here to return this. It belongs to one of Dr. Lane's clients. I spoke to you earlier; you said to bring it in before five."

The man shook his head, letting Rebecca know she'd transgressed one of the unwritten laws he lived by. He extended his hand, expecting Rebecca to place the device in it. "Who's the client?" he asked.

Um, she said her name was Kelli, but I didn't get a last name."
Rebecca shook her head. "She also mentioned Lucy—it says 'Lucy
P.' on the back—so it could be either. I'm sorry, that's all I know,"
she said.

He breathed a deep, uncomfortable breath and typed quickly.
"I can't do anything without a full name, but let me see what I can
do." He cleared his throat and returned it to her, "I'm not seeing any
Lucy or Carrie." He apologized again, with all the sincerity of an ad
for healing crystals.

Rebecca stood there, the device in her hand, speechless. He
lacked concern enough even to listen to the owner's name; what
was the chance he would listen if she corrected him? How did Dr.
Lane retain any patients, especially young ones, with this kind of
receptionist? No way was he this dismissive to her celebrity clients.
It hit her that was likely the point: he was the type to fawn over
wealthy or famous clients while wielding indifference as a weapon
against anyone he deemed unimportant, like her.

Exiting the office, she turned over the tablet; there was the
bookstore name tag. As she walked past the deserted clinic, she
found the bookstore's number online and called.

"Hornet Bookstore, stingers up," the soft male voice answered
like a public radio host.

"Great, you're open," she said.

"Nope, we're closed. Summer hours are 7:30 a.m. to 4:00 p.m.,
Monday to Friday. I'm just here late," the voice replied cheerfully.
"What can I do for you?"

"I know this will probably sound weird, but I found a, um, D-
Note, electronic notebook thing that belongs to someone I think is
named Lucy P. There's a sticker on the back with this store, so I
thought—"

"Oh sure, I know Lucy," the voice said. "She's not here during
the summer, unfortunately. She and her friends are usually

auditioning or recording videos. I can check if she's available, though."

"Okay," Rebecca said, pleased that some progress, at least, was being made.

"Not today," said the voice apologetically.

"Oh, okay. Thank you." Rebecca hung up. What a waste of her time.

It was late when Rebecca descended into the garage beneath her apartment building. As the automatic gate clacked together, sealing her off from the outside, Rebecca paused, needing a few moments to decompress in the car. Her relief was palpable, bordering on joy.

The job wasn't over, and all the uncertainties surrounding the Sweet family and her stay with them were still out there, but they were *out there.* Even the laundry room next to the elevator—with the constantly roaring dryer that always left her clothes a little damp—was a surprise comfort to her, its arid, soapy scent a warm welcome home. She lingered in the hot, sweet-smelling air, waiting for the elevator.

Her key slid into the lock with a familiar metallic click, and she opened the door. Lilith, her neighbor's cat, weaved between her legs, purring low and longingly.

Rebecca poured a small portion of tinkling cat pellets into a shallow porcelain bowl and placed a saucer of cool tap water beside it. After quenching her own thirst, Rebecca set the brushed metal USB drive on her laptop's closed lid. Finally, she stripped off her soiled clothes, tossing them into her overflowing hamper. In the shower's hot streams, she felt a momentary peace as the dirt of the day's events was wash away.

Lilith, sprawled out across the back of the rough couch, mewed and stretched when it saw Rebecca. It stepped leisurely to the front door. Rebecca, spraying her hair with KL's mist, paused to scratch the black cat on its white ear. Then she let it out to return to its home, wherever that would be for the night.

Scrunching her hair in the way KL had showed her, she sat at her laptop and plugged in the Zosia USB device. Two drives mounted on her desktop. The first, labeled "Back4More," made Rebecca's heart race. In the pool house, Becky had given that as the name of the scrapped album. Was KL right? Did Becky keep a copy, unable to destroy it completely?

She stared at the screen. If this was what it looked like—if Becky hadn't been able to bring herself to destroy every copy of her album—then Rebecca was looking at something that wasn't meant to exist.

The "Back4More" drive was unreadable by her computer. The Internet explained that either the partition had been corrupted, or it contained an incompatible format. Rebecca thought about the trashed music studio, and the large black box with all the wires. She wondered, *What would I find if I stuck this USB into that computer?*

The other drive did open, revealing about a hundred scattered root folders and who-knows-how-many subfolders. Rebecca sorted them by name. At the bottom of the list was a folder called "Zosia"; she opened it, revealing a stack of text documents. Opening one at random, Rebecca found a diary entry written when Becky was first pregnant. The writing was so personal, and filled with so much hope and yearning, that Rebecca had to close without finishing it. Thinking about the singer going from that to losing the baby broke Rebecca's heart.

Back in the parent directory, at the top, was a folder also named "Back 4 More". Inside were eight subfolders, including an orange-highlighted one labeled "Pop Scars (DEFINTIE Single)," which she opened. These were lyrics to a song she'd never heard, and it felt like they confirmed her theory that the album was on the drive.

Because checking everything would take forever, Rebecca skimmed the names, looking for the most intriguing ones. Her list ultimately included: "House," "Remembrance of Marc's Past," and "Jenna." She started with the Marc folder.

Immediately, this folder was different from the others; it consisted almost entirely of image files. Sorted by date, the first photo showed Marc Sheffield with a full head of hair and no mustache, likely from when he and Becky first met. In it, Marc was wearing an oversized leather jacket and an equally oversized smile as he manipulated (or pretended to) one of those giant audio boards. The next photos, from the same period, showed Marc and Becky laughing, kissing, and posing outside the Whisky a Go Go, the club Marc managed at the time. In these photos, their age gap was striking: Becky, nearly 30, looked 21, while Marc looked every bit of his 42 years, and then some.

She continued through their Vegas wedding and honeymoon photos, jumping to her feet and slamming shut the laptop when she accidentally opened one showing the sweaty couple mid-coitus. She gave herself a ten-minute break to refill her water and pace around her apartment and try to forget what she had just seen.

When she returned, she skipped ahead, finding pictures where Marc had begun to bald and Becky began to look her age. Some also showed Marc posing with other women, including one with several backup dancers.

Interspersed with these were pregnancy photos—including a series in which a proud Marc and Becky show off the sonogram. Three lines of what Rebecca assumed was cocaine had been sorted on the black and white image of the fetus's head.

As she continued, Rebecca was increasingly confused by the sheer number of remaining photos. Hadn't they separated at some point during Becky's pregnancy? They'd briefly reconciled, but according to reports, it was only for a few months. The quantity suggested years together. She skipped to the final picture, finding an image of Marc and Becky together, lovey-dovey and undeniably intoxicated. Becky looked almost identical to how she had looked in person.

Rebecca checked the metadata: the image had been taken in March...that year. Which didn't make sense. Everyone knew there was a restraining order against Marc; half of the singer's erratic history was tied to him in one way or another. For God's sake, *she* had been arrested for battery against *him* at one point.

She moved through the pictures in reverse, checking the dates. Sure enough, the more recent photos were all clusters; there would be a few days together, and then four, five, even eight months of nothing. Despite the divorce, the restraining order, and whatever had happened before Becky's postpartum hospitalization and loss of financial control, she and Marc Sheffield were trapped in a cycle of reunion and separation. What were the chances Marc was at the house to rekindle that flame yet again?

Ghosted told Sheriff Donnelly that Marc attacked him around 2 a.m. Might he have returned to the house afterward, to pick up his ex-wife? Considering how upset Caroline had been at Rebecca for distracting Becky from the book, how angry would Marc make her? An imagined sound like Caroline screaming at someone bloomed in her head, then vanished: a memory? Would the writer have attacked him? Would he attack her back? Rebecca closed the Marc folder, her mind telling her something was there.

The Jenna folder, like most others, looked to be mostly journal entries or poems, peppered with the occasional photograph. The only thing its contents—including a poem called "Anchor"—told Rebecca was that Becky considered Jenna a source of calm wisdom and guidance. If Marc had done something to Caroline—if Becky had been there—Jenna seemed like the person she would turn to for help.

Yawning, Rebecca checked the time. It was almost 10:00 p.m. She'd been exploring the drive for nearly two hours and considered calling it quits. But she'd promised herself three folders, and "House" was still unread.

It contained a lot of PDFs, some of which Rebecca immediately clocked as legal forms. She opened the first; it was a letter from a law firm. "Based on your request, and in confidence, we have looked back at court filings for your conservatorship," the letter began. It confirmed that Becky's conservatorship allowed for "charitable gifts" and "asset upgrades" that did "not require approval from the conservator, nor must they be disclosed." Later correspondence revealed that, based on Becky's calculations, "the manuscript outlined within could be classified as an asset upgrade, assuming the 1300-square-foot subdivision of the Sweet estate could be assigned a separate lot number."

Which had been accomplished. Becky had succeeded in acquiring a unique parcel number for the guest house, severing it from the rest of the property. Furthermore, she had successfully transferred the lot: "all right, title, and interest in and to the Real Property are conveyed to Caroline Invers in exchange for certain assets as specified in the Property Exchange Agreement executed by the parties concurrently herewith."

Despite the interference by her father, Becky had done it. After Chris stopped the life estate, she persisted, figuring out how to circumvent the conservatorship altogether, making Caroline the legal owner of the property. Almost. The only thing missing were the signatures. A transfer of title wasn't necessarily ironclad, especially given Becky's history, but, once signed, these documents would have made stopping the exchange exponentially more costly and difficult. That, to Rebecca, sounded like motive. It wasn't proof, but a place to start. Both Chris White and Jenna felt they should have ownership of the property. They had reasons to prevent

Caroline from acquiring the guesthouse. If they even knew what Becky had done.

Before closing the computer, Rebecca opened the final document in the folder. It shared much of the verbiage of the others, but this one lacked any mention of Caroline or the book. "The purchase of your home in 95691 has been successful. Escrow closes at the end of March." The cited zip code covered a large chunk of the city, including parts of West Sac, where Becky had lived as a child. Hadn't she said it was there that she thought of as home.

This opened a whole new line of questions. Did she purchase the house she grew up in? Several recent photos in the Marc folder had showed the couple posing in front of the same white facade. She tried reverse-image-searching them, but all that produced was home improvement ads .

She then searched for anything detailing Becky's early life, including where the singer had lived as a child. Though a few fan articles mentioned the city, no one had an address. There would be records, but because the family lived there in the 1980s, none would be readily available: online records didn't go back that far. Any physical copies would require a visit to the county clerk's office which was closed until Monday. She put that on her to-do list.

Whether or not the purchase was of her childhood home, if Becky was trying to remain hidden, a secret house seemed the best place to look. The question was: did Becky fear being connected to Caroline's death, or had she gone there to spend a few days with Marc, pretending to be a normal couple until they reminded each other why they had broken up in the first place?

She couldn't check sales records, and she couldn't trust Chris White to admit whether *he* knew about the transfer. But she could ask Jenna. Becky trusted Jenna. And, thanks to Chris White, Rebecca knew precisely where she would be in the morning.

Chapter Sixteen. Saturday.

Midtown Farmers Market was something Rebecca used to do as an escape on Saturday mornings shortly after she'd first moved to Sacramento, before the breakup with Steve. She hadn't thought of him in years, and the realization that it had been so long scared her; where was the time going? When last she walked the street, she was in her twenties and, it felt like there was still time to turn her life into something wonderful.

The relationship with Steve had not been moving in the right direction. He was somehow content with where they were as a couple, sometimes going so far as to suggest that they actually spent too much time together and needed their individual hobbies. She felt, on the other hand, that somewhere along the way, they had gotten stuck. They weren't kids anymore and their relationship wasn't pretend. She had invested so much into it—they both had—that they deserved progress as a matter of course. Yet, that didn't matter to him.

Going outside, being around people who wanted to improve the world and who were actively participating in their own lives, appealed to the part of Rebecca that had awakened in the earlier days of their courtship when she believed that she not only could be a better version of herself but that the relationship was somehow the key to achieving it.

Her first visit had been with friends from college: an escape from studying for midterms casually suggested as an alternative to spending the morning at another dorm room or studio apartment. But after the first visit, when even the friend that had suggested the excursion found the market boring, Rebecca chose to return. It didn't remind her of her past exactly, but there was something nostalgic about the place that she couldn't explain; perhaps seeing families happily sampling muffins and teas reminded her of what she wished her childhood had been. Eventually, she established relationships with market regulars, growing increasingly closer to these new friends while, at the same time, distancing herself further from her classmates and boyfriend.

On rare occasions, she convinced him to join her there rather than dedicating his weekend to online video games or D&D or feeling sorry for himself. Her new friends were always pleased to see him, and, each time, it felt like their future was becoming a more legitimate thing. But afterward, rather than trying to recreate the good time they'd had, he returned to the same activities as always. It had felt like such a waste of his time and potential.

In retrospect, she concluded that those regular activities had been his personal way of socializing with others and managing his anxieties, just as the farmers market had become hers. With the benefit of hindsight, she could see that his solitary hobbies had not been the catalyst for their separation so much as a retroactive justification for it, and only one of many. In an alternate version of this life, the two of them would have spent more time engaging in the other's avocations, consolidating their bond and maturing together both as a couple and as individuals. Instead, they ceased trying to incorporate each other into their lives and, predictably, they ceased to be in each other's life.

Less than a year after the breakup—perhaps significantly less, it was hard to tell—her enthusiasm for the experience at the farmers market waned, and she slowly slipped out of the lives of the people there like she had her school friends' lives. Though the escapades at Midtown Farmers Market began as an excuse to pursue greater independence from from Steve, after their relationship was over, the Saturdays spent there came to, ironically, feel like an extension of it: a reminder of his absence.

By the time she dropped out of Sacramento State at the start of junior year, the shame of leaving her education unfinished prompted her to withdraw from her peers; she began devoting more time toward work to prove to herself that she still had value. Over time, her job at Starbucks ceased to provide that value: she wanted to do something meaningful, but she felt incapable of taking on too much responsibility, fearing she would abandon it like she had abandoned everything else. It became a self-fulfilling prophecy, repeating for more than seven years. Finally, at an event she was bussing, she met Charles Sprock.

Rebecca inhaled the sweet smell of cookies and candles and crystals. Being back at Midtown Market, she was presented with two realizations: first, she hadn't remembered the crowds feeling so...crowded; second, it appeared that there were a lot fewer families; nearly everyone was alone, moving booth to booth with their phones out. They were taking pictures or comparing prices or chatting with distant friends. Rebecca had been expecting to find that she had changed too much to find comfort in the once-familiar place. Instead, the place had changed almost beyond recognition, losing whatever it was that used to bring her comfort. Or perhaps that idealized version had only ever been in her mind, a snapshot of *her* and not of it.

Sweat trickled down her skin and she could feel her hair drying in the hot sun. Like a novice, she had forgotten to bring a hat. Leading with her shoulders, she tried to avoid making physical contact with these phantoms of her former life. Stopped in a clearing, she consulted the map she'd saved to her phone for the TwoSweet wine pop-up. When she looked up, a bottle of water dripping with condensation was thrust at her chest, stopping Rebecca in her tracks. Was no place safe?

"You look like you could use a drink." Her eyes traveled from the sinister water bottle to the friendly face of Sheriff Donnelly, focusing on his iridescent teeth. What had seemed threatening moments before suddenly felt necessary, and she accepted it eagerly, emptying the bottle in a single draught. "Careful," he said, pointing at his temple. "Brain freeze." She hiccupped; his smile broadened, and he tilted his head.

"I've never seen you here before," he said, his face reddening from a combination of embarrassment and nascent sunburn. "Though I guess we met yesterday, so I probably wouldn't know you even if I had." He offered her a second bottle and drank from his own. "No, I think I would have recognized you." He pointed to his hair and then hers; "You don't really blend in."

Wiping sweat from her cheeks, Rebecca smiled back despite herself. She kept her lips closed, self-conscious about her imperfect teeth. "I used to come here a lot," she explained unbidden, "But it's been a long time. It's different than I remember." Rebecca stuffed her phone into her back pocket, catching him subtly staring at it.

He nodded and pointed toward a stall just over thirty feet away. "I'd assumed you came here for her." Jenna Sweet stood, back straight, beneath the shade of a deep purple pop-up tent stall, speaking emphatically to a familiar woman.

Rebecca nodded. "Yeah, I wanted to talk to Jenna about her sister." Though she found herself enjoying his company, the chance encounter with Sheriff Donnelly suddenly did not feel like chance. Chris White had mentioned that he had others following his daughter. The sheriff would be a safe bet to keep an eye on Jenna while Rebecca was expected to search the room.

Anger flared. The idea that this lawman was working so blatantly for Chris White, following Jenna instead of finding Becky was the definition of injustice. She asked him outright: "Does Chris White have you watching her?"

His smile was so unexpectedly good-natured that Rebecca felt absurd for doubting his intentions. If she could be so wrong about that, she could be wrong about everything, from her taste in music to her understanding of the Big Bang. He shook his head and pointed back toward the booth. Squinting at the sunlight, he said, "I believe that is the woman you saw taking pictures outside the Sweet home." Rebecca turned and watched the woman until she moved her hand. It certainly appeared to be the Asian woman she'd seen in the trees at the Sweet Estate.

Rebecca turned to face him, melting in the heat. Maybe it was his smile. "That's, um, Moneyshot Karen," she said. "I didn't know she was here."

"Yeah, well, we haven't found her partner yet, but all we want is to ask a few questions and get a look at the cameras' memory. Depending on what she says, talking to her may be good enough." He waved to someone near the entrance and explained, "We've got a man who volunteers here on weekends. He saw her enter; he knows I live nearby and that we've been looking for her. When he told me she was talking to Jenna, well...I thought we ought to let them talk." The women appeared calm, especially Jenna. But as Rebecca watched them alongside the sheriff, something about the suddenness of their movement, and their posture made them seem much more tense than either was willing to reveal in such a public place.

"Are you recording them?" Rebecca looked around, "Are you recording me?"

"That wouldn't be legal," the sheriff said with a smile. "No, hopefully she'll cooperate." He shook his head, sweat dripping from his brow. "It seems a little peculiar, I think." To Rebecca, the whole situation seemed peculiar.

"Do you want to grab something? There's a guy down the way who makes the best smoothies. They have excellent strawberries." He pointed in the opposite direction to Jenna's tent, and Rebecca was tempted to go with him, but she shook her head. "Or stone fruits, if you're not a berry girl," he suggested.

"Strawberries aren't actually berries." He raised his eyebrows, and she stopped herself from getting lost in pedantry. "No, I like strawberries, and it sounds good, but—how about a raincheck? I actually am here to talk to Jenna."

Sheriff Donnelly put his hands to his chest. Rebecca assumed he would make an "ouch, my heart" proclamation, but instead, he produced from his chest pocket the small notepad and pen with the Sacramento County Sheriff's ideogram he kept there. He turned the page to face her, and Rebecca read: "Raincheck for smoothies with Ms. Rebecca Ziel!!" The whole exchange felt goofy but pleasant; she snorted involuntarily. Clearing her throat, she said, "It doesn't need to be smoothies."

He grinned again, showing off his teeth and scratched out the word 'smoothies,' replacing it with 'victuals'. "If you mean it, I'd like to hold you to it."

"I'll be seeing you around." She smiled openly, trying to convince herself that it was okay to show him her imperfect teeth. Thankfully, his gaze remained locked on her eyes.

"I certainly hope so, Ms. Rebecca Ziel."

Chapter Seventeen.

The mutual frustration between Jenna and Moneyshot was increasingly apparent the closer Rebecca approached, amplified rather than diminished by their tightly controlled voices and rigid stances. Jenna spotted Rebecca before her companion did and smiled, lifting her hand as an invitation to join them. Moneyshot Karen turned in kind. Lifting her eyebrows, she released the mirrored aviator sunglasses balanced on her forehead to slip down, covering her eyes, and she split her fingers like a peace sign, departing without a word.

Rebecca turned to look for Sheriff Donnelly, but he was gone, and she couldn't find him in the crowd. Moneyshot, too, was nowhere to be seen.

"I thought that was you," Jenna said, straightening the remaining wine bottles. "Talking about me with our friend at the crepe stand."

If Jenna was trying to make Rebecca feel guilty, she was succeeding. Rebecca bit her lip to stifle an apology. Then she apologized anyway. Deciding that honesty was her best option, she affirmed, "You were mentioned, though the sheriff was more interested in who you were talking to. He still hasn't talked to her or the other one. Dollar Bill."

"He won't," Jenna predicted. "Not unless they want to be found. Moneyshot could evade police in a prison cell, if she wanted." She followed Rebecca's look at the crowd. Moneyshot, too, was no longer in sight. Jenna continued, "Dollar Bill is hard to miss. But...he is *missing*, so," she shrugged. "Is that why you wandered over here? To talk to me about the people I employ?"

Rebecca shook her head. "No, I—it's just, I know that's what he wanted to know."

Jenna laughed. "All Patrick cares about is being noticed by Becky. It's not friendship with my father; that is why he's here. Every so often, he comes around signaling how good a guy he is, and every time," she opened her hands, revealing empty palms, "nothing. It will be the same this time. He doesn't realize that she only notices what people *withhold* from her. When your entire existence revolves around giving her what she wants, you might as well be invisible." Jenna shook her head. "I think the only time he actually impressed on her was New Years 2009." She waited for Rebecca to open her mouth to ask. When she didn't, Jenna answered regardless: "He put Marc in the hospital."

"The ex?" Rebecca asked, imagining Sheriff Donnelly beating the blurry image of the man she'd seen at the mansion.

Jenna nodded, then abruptly turned to the middle-aged couple approaching the booth, Rebecca watched the perverse pleasure disappear from her face, replaced by a façade of authentic interest. She treated the wife's questions about the source and vintage of the grapes, what foods paired well and what it was like working with Dean Cain in *Merry Princemas* as though the answers were the most interesting things in the world. She even remained unruffled when the husband asked whether B*Sweet would be making an appearance at the booth in one of her 'cute costumes.' "I don't think so," Jenna answered with a saccharine smile .

At the couple's departure, Jenna was, once again, fully committed to the conversation. "That's the reason you're here? To talk to the sheriff about me and to me about him?"

"Your father asked me to—" Rebecca hesitated, unsure if her distrust of Chris White warranted the potential family fallout of revealing what he'd asked her to do. "He wanted me to arrange and oversee home inspections today. I was asked to pay special attention to your room. There were suggestions that you might know something about where Becky disappeared to, and what had happened to Caroline. He said you took Caroline's laptop to control the memoir and remove him as conservator." She girded herself and asked: "Do you? Did you? Do you?"

"Huh." Jenna stared, momentarily speechless. It was the first time Rebecca had seen the woman caught off guard. Instead of reacting to the accusations, she seemed more interested in Rebecca. "You just put it all out there, don't you?"

"I want to help Becky." If the sheriff who had known Becky since childhood was invisible to her, what did that make Rebecca? Was she an idiot to care about Becky's well-being after so short a time?

Jenna laughed. "You and everyone else." She straightened her sleeves. "Myself included. I want my sister to be healthy and have the opportunity to show the world what she is capable of doing on her own." She reached under the table to restock pamphlets. "And I believe Becky needs to be financially independent from him to do that. I have no desire to control her estate; our business is enough responsibility.

Rebecca hadn't asked if Jenna wanted control of the estate.

Jenna looked Rebecca square in the face and asserted, "As for the book, he's the one who wants to oversee that narrative. He doesn't need me to make it clear he's no longer up to the task of managing her assets—he does that well enough on his own."

Rebecca said, "Becky said you were involved in it until recently, the book. But there was a falling out with Caroline?"

"I'm sensing an unspoken accusation there." Rebecca opened her mouth to explain, but Jenna cut her off: "No, no, it's okay. I was involved early on as a resource. I provided her my perspective for certain events, and I turned Caroline on to people or information I thought might enhance the truth of her narrative. Our falling out had nothing to do with how I am portrayed in the book; it was a disagreement over how to handle the media rights."

"Did you want them? To turn it into a movie?" Rebecca asked, testing Chris White's claim.

"God, this is tedious," was her reply. When Rebecca did not dismiss the question, Jenna added, "It was Caroline's opinion that any licensing deals should wait until after the book was released. She believed it would blow up and raise the value exponentially. I take a more 'one in the hand' approach. I favor stable growth over possible windfalls. I do, however, feel that my sister and I are better equipped to manage the story than the average seventy-year-old man running a movie studio. And if we make less by going our own way," Jenna shrugged. "There's more to life than money." She shuffled a few glossy pamphlets, placing them on the table for the passers-by. "When Caroline and Becky were not convinced by my argument, I washed my hands of the project."

"And what about Becky's transfer of the guest house to Caroline? How did that make you feel?"

Jenna snorted. "Dad stepped in before she could make that mistake. One of his unfortunately-rare good decisions."

Had Becky really not told her sister? Keeping the guesthouse as part of the property was the one thing everyone agreed on. Rebecca was struggling to think of a follow-up question to determine whether Jenna knew more than she was saying.

Jenna Sweet's face twisted as she watched Rebecca; it was like she could read her mind. She asked, "What is it?"

Desperate to change the subject, Rebecca pulled off her backpack and took out the blackmail pictures she'd received from Chris. "What do you know about these?" she asked.

Jenna continued examining Rebecca for another several seconds before casually flipping through the pictures. "These don't mean anything to me."

"Your father believes you hired those paparazzi to blackmail him."

"Does he now?" She took another look and held them like a magician with playing cards for Rebecca to take back. "I hired them to take pictures of *you* to blackmail *him*? That does sound like his sort of logic. And do you share his supposition?"

"I think," Rebecca looked at the top image before returning them to her bag. "I think if you hired professionals to take these, you wasted your money."

Jenna laughed and said, "Right; Dad is upset because he hired them to follow Becky a few months back, and they came back with more than he'd paid for. Bill gave him first right of refusal for the 'special' photos. Dad cried 'extortion' before paying them. He disapproves of my working with them."

"Why did he hire them in the first place?" Rebecca asked.

"Publicity," Jenna answered like it should be evident to even the biggest dunce in the schoolyard. "A person's only real asset is their influence. It's what makes or breaks you. With the record release coming up—or, it *was*—Becky needed to be relevant. Even the memoir was fine with Dad until he heard things about it from Becky's therapist."

"Dr. Lane?"

Jenna nodded. "He hired her. He doesn't pay for anything without expecting a return. Sometimes, those investments pay off."

Caroline had been reluctant to send anything to Becky's regular email, as though it was under surveillance. If Chris was receiving intel from Becky's psychiatrist, was he also monitoring her email?

What did he know? Was there something in the memoir about Becky transferring the guest house to Caroline, maybe as a special thanks? What about the secret house, did he know about that? Did he know that Marc and Becky were still getting together? Did Jenna know?

Rebecca asked, "Becky and Marc have been regularly getting back together for years, haven't they?"

Again, Jenna appeared taken by surprise. Not by the news itself, but by Rebecca's knowledge of it—and her willingness to ask. "Not until recently," she answered cautiously. "I'm surprised Dad told you. That information cost him a lot. He must be desperate."

Rebecca didn't understand at first; then she did: "Those were the photos they threatened to sell, Dollar Bill and Moneyshot, that your father paid for." Dollar Bill had mentioned pictures during their brief call. Pictures that sounded for sale.

Realizing her slip, Jenna suggested, "Dad didn't tell you that. You guessed based on, what: how we all responded to his mention yesterday?"

"So, you knew," Rebecca said. "Are they together? Does your father know? Are they at Becky's other house?"

That caught Jenna off guard again. She asked, "What other house?" She gripped Rebecca's shoulder and leaned in. To observers, the hold probably looked friendly, but it didn't feel friendly. "What aren't you saying?"

Rebecca stepped backward, yanking her arm from Jenna's grasp. "I thought someone mentioned a second house, like her childhood home. Do you know where that is?"

Jenna shook her head no. "Did your mystery source not tell you?"

Rebecca continued her retreat. No longer under the shade of Jenna's stall, sunlight splashed across her face.

"Never do anything halfway," Jenna continued, keeping pace with Rebecca, "If you're going to be honest, be honest all the way. It makes you vulnerable, which is dangerous, but it's a hell of a lot less dangerous than the game you're playing right now." Jenna stopped.

"Rebecca," she called, and Rebecca turned. "If you ever deal with people of influence—the type of people I work with on a daily basis—they won't let you go." Her head dropped and she sighed wearily. "Don't mistake my kindness for the way the world works. I don't need you to tell me whatever it is that you know. I can find it out."

Rebecca hurried away, glancing back to make sure Jenna wasn't following. Jenna was already back at her booth, chatting pleasantly with a couple of women in their twenties. She thought she caught Jenna's eyes dart to her for a moment, but the younger Sweet made no move toward her.

Rebecca slowed as she reached the invisible boundary line separating the farmers market from the outside world. As the adrenaline dissipated, she could think again. To all appearances, Becky—the person everyone deemed incapable of caring for herself—had been able to circumvent the restrictions placed on her. If Becky was anywhere to be found, Rebecca felt increasingly confident it would be in her secret second home, the place where she had grown up. Where she last felt "normal." Her best bet for finding the house was to access Halcyon Realty's suite of real estate subscriptions. To do that, she needed to go to the office.

Chapter Eighteen.

Halcyon Realty comprised two office suites in the downtown area of West Sacramento: the office for show and the office for work. The show office, where Charles met with prospective clients and entertained the city's well-to-do, was on the 18th floor of Park Tower. It comprised two rooms and a bathroom—complete with a shower. The first thing anyone noticed when they entered was the large, lavishly furnished meeting room: a heavy table between brown leather chesterfields and a tufted leather chair, all illuminated by antique copper fixtures and Edison bulbs. The adjoining room acted as Charles' personal office and was where he made calls, filled out paperwork and took naps whenever work kept him busy well into the night.

The work office, located two blocks away (five minutes on average, for Rebecca), was one-and-a-half small rooms in the basement of a three-story building on K Street. Its restroom was on the ground floor and was shared with the building's other tenants. This office was lit by LED tubes mounted in formerly fluorescent fixtures set above two pine student desks and an outdated oak monstrosity, each paired with a used (but surprisingly good) Steelcase chair. All extra office supplies were stored in a narrow closet at the back. Computers—and everything else of value—were each identified by a sticker illustrated with the logo that Rebecca had designed for Charles as her first job with him. Most importantly, however, the space contained Halcyon Realty's network storage server, making access to the company's collection of files, forms and references infinitely faster.

Every so often, agents who hung their license under Charles Sprock—or who were otherwise affiliated—would charter one office or the other as they grabbed documents or conducted research. Generally, however, Rebecca had the entire space to herself. That proved true yet again as she descended into the dim space below K Street.

Rebecca knew it was highly improbable that Becky had used her trust to purchase any property in secret. Yet she also knew that people often sacrifice anonymity for convenience—a fact many overlook when seeking people's secrets. 'Sometimes the answer is right under your nose,' as the saying goes. Because it was a private trust, Rebecca couldn't directly access its financials, but she could search public records to, hopefully, glean the trust's activities. If she looked at the data from just the right angle, the trust's activities might come into focus like dolphins in a Magic Eye.

One bit of interesting information she had already discovered was that Becky's trust had owned at least one property in the zip code she was searching. It turned out to be a commercial property, making it unlikely to be Becky's childhood home, but, interestingly, it had been sold the previous year to a REIT with holdings along the West Coast. A Real Estate Investment Trust was a publicly-traded company whose business model revolves around managing real estate. The one that had purchased the property from B*Sweet was called *Cascadia Subduction Trust.* And that property was not the only one.

Becky's trust had begun investing heavily in commercial property less than a year after Chris White was given control. It, in fact, still owned a handful of commercial properties spread out between Sacramento and the Bay Area. Most of these properties had remained insufficiently occupied for years, and many had liens that put them at risk of foreclosure, making them less desirable. Of the assets that remained solvent, however, two housed organizations with which Rebecca was already familiar: the Galaxy School in Fairfield and a UFU office outside of San Francisco.

Rebecca noted all the addresses: if the secret house was nonexistent or impossible to find, she could still investigate those properties in case Becky had been hiding out in an unleased office space.

Halcyon Realty did not specialize in commercial real estate. Charles was, therefore, very likely unaware of these sales. Though she didn't have experience in it either, Rebecca had heard whispers and rumors among temporary acquaintances who did about the tenuous state of that market. The difficulties had already bankrupted several companies with extensive commercial holdings, leaving behind unfinished skyscrapers scattered all across the globe, rotting like the skeletons of ancient colossi.

Rebecca was no closer to finding Becky's secret house, but she was cobbling together a much better understanding of how Chris managed Becky's trust, and it didn't look good. The situation was teetering between somewhat concerning and *dear-God-no* catastrophic. Chris White had wasted no time in his position using Becky's money to invest in commercial properties, leveraging each purchase to acquire loans for the next one.

At first, it seemed, the investments were paying off. On paper, B*Sweet once owned upwards of 16 commercial properties, some of which were substantial. After a couple of years, presumably when things started going wrong, Chris stopped buying and started selling.

Except, as Rebecca researched further, she learned that all but one of the sold properties had been purchased by the same Cascadia Subduction Trust of the most recent purchase

Despite the "trust" label, REITs are publicly traded, so, unlike Becky's trust which kept its financials private, Cascadia Subduction was required to regularly publish its financials as a way of warning away and/or attracting potential investors. Rebecca found its most recent records, learning that while the REIT was not bankrupt, its value *had* been declining since 2021, with the most recent—and most dramatic—losses having occurred over the past two months. Adding to the 10% losses reported in the most recent account, the total lost value year-over-year could be as high as 20%-25%, putting Cascadia Subduction on the brink of collapse. That was only part of what she was looking for, however. She also wanted to get a look at its investors—

It was right there on the third line: The B*Sweet Trust held 27% of Cascadia Subduction shares. Rebecca looked further back in the records. Beginning in 2019, Becky's estate switched from investing in individual properties to investing in Cascadia Subduction. It had likewise begun liquidating most of its commercial holdings, selling them almost exclusively to the same company, creating a buffer between Becky's wealth and the properties themselves. In theory.

Contrary to Rebecca's initial assumptions that Chris White's property sell-off had meant failure, according to the financials, those years had actually been exponentially profitable. It wasn't until 2021 that the company's value began its steady, sawtooth descent. At that time, Becky, through her father's management of the trust, was actually the largest shareholder, owning 39%.

That wasn't all: TwoSweet Wineries, LLC had been a shareholder until October of that year, when it sold all of its remaining holdings in the company. Looking at when TwoSweet first bought in, its sell-off came before the worst of the depreciation, netting the sisters a tidy profit. Becky's trust had not been so lucky. By the time it started selling, Cascadia was worth less than when Chris White had first invested into it. The way Jenna spoke of her father's financial mismanagement, Rebecca inferred that she knew specifics. She likely saw Cascadia's losses and witnessed her father's delayed exit strategy

In addition to Becky's trust and TwoSweet, Chris White was listed as a shareholder, and his stake had been dropping in large chunks over the past year. That meant that, essentially, Chris White had funneled a portion of his daughter's wealth to himself through the trust he controlled. Rebecca didn't know exactly how illegal that was, but it seemed like a clear conflict of interest. Had Caroline written about that in the memoir? If so, just how important was control of Becky's trust to Chris White?

Rebecca couldn't determine how much of Becky's and Chris's wealth was tied to Cascadia Subduction or their gains and losses. Not without a lot more research. But she could see—based on the dates—that the value of Cascadia at the time of sale was far below what had been spent to buy into it. Jenna had seen the writing on the wall, but hadn't stopped her father's losses, or her sister's. Perhaps that is what she had meant when she said they needed to 'learn for themselves' before it was too late.

Rebecca returned to the investor list, fascinated by its story and intrigued by what else it might tell her. Near the bottom, she saw one last twist: eight months earlier, Ghosted, LLC had acquired 1000 shares. That name seemed like too much of a coincidence. Looking up the corporation, she confirmed that its sole owner was listed as James Fenimore Logan. Additionally, it was on the same day he became a shareholder that the B*Sweet trust and Chris White sold 1200 shares between them.

She didn't know for sure, but eight months seemed long enough to write, record, and produce an album. A new story was emerging, one where Chris White, short on liquid assets, had purchased Logan's services as a music producer using shares of Cascadia Subduction in lieu of cash. Seeing the value of his shares dropping, Ghosted had come to Sacramento demanding that Chris White renegotiate an increasingly worthless paycheck. That he had shown up on the very day that Caroline had died and Becky had disappeared seemed too significant to be coincidence.

According to his own account, Ghosted had encountered a violent Marc Sheffield that same night, and then had been found loitering outside the Sweet estate the following morning. Was he there, as Rebecca suspected, to demand remuneration for the lost value of his shares? Did he know anything about Caroline's death and Becky's disappearance? Only he could say for sure. And he was staying at the Exchange, a hotel less than a mile from where Becky was sitting. In room 742.

Chapter Nineteen.

Based on his behavior at the house and his reported history with Becky, Ghosted was unstable and could not be trusted. *Unless,* Rebecca thought, *I can offer something he wants.* Revealing she knew about his shares and the trust might get her in the door, but to get him to answer her questions, she needed something more. What that was, she hadn't figured out yet, but, as she walked the busy street, Rebecca texted Sydney and Erin her location and who she was going to meet. She double-checked that they could follow her location in real-time, just in case something happened to her.

Not the most expensive hotel in the city, nor anywhere near as ostentatious as the Sweet's large home, the Exchange was, nonetheless, one of the nicer hotels in downtown Sacramento. Reputed to be, at one time, the tallest building west of the Mississippi, its ten stories were now dwarfed by the surrounding skyscrapers.

Rebecca had sketched this part of downtown before and was familiar with the building from the outside, though she had never set a foot inside. It had always looked to Rebecca a little like a white Lego on its side, she found a lot to like in the building's neoclassical, Beaux-Arts style.

Standing outside the glass doors, she craned her neck, gazing up at the building; it made her feel small. She reflected on her life; it wasn't just the Sweets or her recent choices, but the world itself that felt fundamentally off. These thoughts intermingled with inchoate sentiments about the city's history like the idealistic story Chris White had told of Folsom. The vaguely attractive past he so admired was represented in front of her by the simple, yet beautiful image of the former fruit exchange. So much had happened since the building's construction.

Phantom pains of a less complicated past stung Rebecca. She longed for a time when she didn't need a seven-figure job to afford a small house, or to worry that everyone she had ever known was keeping a running tally of her successes or failures online. Of course, any job she could get back then would likely pay next to nothing and put her at risk of some incurable disease. And the reason no one would care about her choices was because she couldn't vote, speak freely to men, or live without a husband. After a second's thought, she felt grateful to have missed that particular past.

She ascended to the seventh floor, still considering what leverage she had. *The USB drive,* she realized, *the one with the album on it.* She didn't need to give it to him straight away—she'd left it in the office anyway—but she could offer it to him in exchange for information. The elevator dinged and the broad doors opened.

Given its age, this was one of those hotels where the rooms did not follow a logical sequence, forcing Rebecca to circle the elevator and a housekeeping cart several times before figuring out the 'system.'

"Can I help you find something?" Rebecca jumped, her heart suddenly racing. The housekeeper had emerged unexpectedly from a nearby room, but her tone was friendly and helpful.

Rebecca pointed down the hall toward where she believed Ghosted's room was. "I came to talk to Mr. Logan, room 742."

The housekeeper scrutinized her. "You older than most his friends. Do you picking up, or...dropping off?"

"Neither," Rebecca shook her head. "I need to discuss business with him on behalf of my client."

"He with someone," the housekeeper warned. "Very young. Come." The woman offered to guide Rebecca to his room. Rebecca politely declined.

A loud commotion inside the room stopped Rebecca at the door. Violent, cracking slaps were followed by groans and the wet, choking gasps of a woman. Rebecca's hair stood on end, and she dialed 911, afraid that Ghosted was in the middle of an assault, but before completing the call, she detected pleasure in the muffled voices. Her alarm melted into embarrassment, and she looked away, ashamed to have heard any of it. It was almost a relief, though: finding herself unable to confront Ghosted about his financial dealings with Chris White. Maybe it was better to go directly to Chris himself—or better yet, to the sheriff. Let him deal with the fallout.

The sounds stopped, replaced by the stamping of feet and a muffled "I know what you need." The door opened, and Rebecca was suddenly face-to-face with Ghosted: flushed and sweaty, nose running. He was holding an ice bucket, his open tiger-pattern kimono not quite concealing the doughy nude underneath. His pinprick pupils stared at her like a puppet. "Excuse me," he blurted.

"Sorry—"

He shoved past her. "Move lady," he muttered, and continued down the hall. Gesturing wildly with his arms, he mumbled to himself: "What's wrong with people? Mind your own damn business."

Through the half-open door, Rebecca caught sight of a small woman with long, straight black hair emerging from a side room. Her makeup was heavy and smeared, especially about one of her eyes—or perhaps it was a bruise. Her petite form, visible through a translucent tiger-pattern kimono matching Ghosted's, appeared malnourished. She snorted something from the top of the brown minifridge then spun to face the door, considering Rebecca with the same dull affect of a child regarding a clothbound dictionary. As the young woman slowly approached, a trail of blood dropped unceremoniously from her nose, staining her face and splattering on the girl's hand, then onto the floor below. She didn't seem to notice, or to care, and Rebecca hoped, as the door slammed shut, that she was older than she looked.

Once outside, breathing in the city air like her life depended on it, Rebecca returned to her car, relaxing the death grip on her phone. Without realizing it, she had missed messages and calls from her sister and Sydney. Rebecca guessed these confirmed that they had received her missive and, probably, chastised her for being so cavalier. She didn't need to read them to realize she had been reckless, but Rebecca missed her friend and sister. She missed the Rebecca of a week ago, the one whose primary concerns were what socks to pack and what to do if she couldn't exchange dollars for yen.

She wanted to talk to Sydney and see what new pictures or videos of food, fashion or festivities she had sent. Doing the math in her head, knowing that Sydney had probably slept in, Rebecca figured her friend must have just awoken when she tried to call. She opened the chat, hoping for some good news or vicarious visions, anything that might distract her from her failed attempt at playing detective. Instead, the message read: "Why didn't you tell me?! CALL!!!!" with a hyperlink ending in "-b-sweet-vanishes.htm."

The proverbial cat had been let out of its bag. Rebecca called Sydney and clicked the article, scanning the text while her friend's phone rang on the other side of the world.

B*Sweet Vanishes

Pop Star's Shocking Disappearance Sparks Frenzy

SACRAMENTO, CA — What happened to B*Sweet? That's the question everyone is asking after the one-time pop princess vanished without a trace following a high-profile fundraiser at her opulent Granite Bay estate.

An anonymous source reported the disturbing disappearance early Saturday morning, June 29, though friends and family have remained tight-lipped. The only official response has come from representatives for her sister, Jenna Sweet (best known for holiday TV hits like *Wishmas* and *A Prince in Denver*), who issued a cryptic request for "privacy as we work to do what's best for B*Sweet."

Meanwhile, authorities have yet to confirm reports that the singer—real name Becky White—was behaving erratically at the event or that an alleged overdose occurred on the premises. The last confirmed sighting of the troubled star was at the fundraiser Thursday night. Since then? Radio silence.

A Rocky Road to Stardom—And Beyond

Once considered America's sweetheart, B*Sweet rose to fame in the late '90s youth-pop craze with dance anthems like 'Back2You' and 'Wanna.' But her fairy-tale career soon turned tragic. At just 19, she lost her mother to ovarian cancer, and in the years that followed, she spiraled into a storm of scandal, drug charges, and disturbing media appearances (*click HERE for videos*)

This downward slide ultimately led to a 2017 conservatorship controlled by her father, Chris White who, at the time, promised to "protect my daughter from herself." But a growing number of devoted fans are dissatisfied with the arrangement, citing its draconian control as "the ultimate injustice." These self-proclaimed "Sweeties" have exploded in recent months, increasingly flooding social media with demands to *#ReleasetheB* and *#BFreeBSweet*.

What Comes Next?

Rumors had been swirling that B*Sweet was on the verge of a long-awaited comeback—an entire album of new material, rumored to be raw, personal, and her best work to date. But now, with her whereabouts unknown, the future of her music—and her independence—hangs in the balance.

As speculation runs rampant, fans and celebrities alike have taken to social media, pleading for answers and hoping their pop idol is safe. The investigation is ongoing, and authorities urge anyone with information to contact the Sacramento County Sheriff's Department.

💬 What do YOU think happened to B*Sweet? Drop your theories in the comments!

(Updated to include the statement from Jenna Sweet's representation.)

Chapter Twenty.

"What is going on?!" Sydney's voice squealed from the receiver, and Rebecca pulled it from her ear, looking around to check whether anyone had heard. "Why didn't you tell me!?"

Rebecca had been so caught up in the investigation that she hadn't shared details about it with anyone. "I'm sorry, I just—"

"Oh, I don't even care about that." When she was excited, Sydney never let Rebecca finish a thought. "Just tell me now!" Rebecca heard a low thrum mix with the high clash of water splashing against a porcelain tub. She smiled; she could picture her friend in the bath—probably surrounded by delicate, Japanese bubbles.

Sydney's insistence was fueled by disappointment, not because Rebecca was missing the Tokyo trip, but because she was missing out on Rebecca's adventure. "I want to hear all of it!"

Rebecca started from the beginning, unsure what she'd already shared: Dollar Bill and Moneyshot at the entrance, Ghosted at the door, Becky's ex-husband lurking in the woods. When Rebecca got to when she'd awakened in the guest house, with no memory of what had happened, Sydney blurted, "OH MY GOD!" Rebecca laughed despite herself. She knew it wasn't funny: one woman was dead, and the other was God-knows-where in who-knows-what condition, but she couldn't help it: Sydney was outside of everything, innocent in a way. To her, bless her heart, these people's lives were not much more than a story.

Contrary to what she had told Erin, the Sweet family was beyond dysfunctional, possibly beyond repair. And yet, sitting there in her car, talking to her best friend since forever, Rebecca felt somehow removed from the situation, like she had been plucked up by giant hands and placed side-by-side with her friend. It was like the two of them were girls in school talking about the crazy things they'd heard their principal had gotten up to with their English teacher. It felt nice. It felt, for lack of a better word, normal.

Rebecca was just getting to the part about searching the contents of the USB drive when her words slowed to a crawl. An amber Corvette convertible stopped at the light facing her, and she recognized Ghosted as the driver. He was alone, his face radiating annoyance and determination. His mouth moved urgently, speaking to either himself or someone on the phone.

Rebecca started her engine.

"What's happening?"

Rebecca didn't register the question. She didn't often act without thinking, but, every so often, something in her gut told her to move and she moved. This was one of those times; she *needed* to follow him.

Pulling into the street, she pursued. Lacking both the opportunity and instinct to filter other cars between them, she drove directly behind him for an entire block. By the time they reached the 5th Street stoplight, she had allowed herself to fall slightly behind, hoping it was enough to go unnoticed. An ambulance screamed from the right, pulling up to a building ahead, cutting off at least one traffic lane.

"What's going on?" Sydney's voice dissolved in the passing siren.

When the light changed, Logan's car squealed left across two lanes, eliciting horn blasts from the cars that weren't driven by maniacs. Rebecca witnessed Ghosted's small hand rise from a partially rolled-down, fully-tinted window and salute the drivers he'd cut off with his middle finger; their incessant honking showed they didn't much care for his actions, but his smooth movement showed he couldn't care less. Cursing under her breath, Rebecca tried to merge left, struggling to keep his car in sight.

"Are you there?" Rebecca finally heard her friend and cursed again, narrowly avoiding a collision with the car in front of . She switched to speaker phone. Sydney's voice was in the middle of asking: "What's going on?"

Grateful to have spotted her quarry ahead in the distance, Rebecca started: "James Logan—"

"Who?!" Sydney interrupted.

"Becky's music producer. Ghosted, or whatever. The one I went to the hotel to talk to. He's driving, and I'm following him." She was following, but Logan was switching lanes at every opportunity, making his own opportunities when they didn't come naturally. He exemplified the worst stereotypes Rebecca had heard about both L.A. drivers and Corvette owners: he was reckless, impatient, and convinced the road belonged exclusively to him.

Fortunately, rush hour traffic was negating his lead. Rebecca's heart drummed, and her peripheral vision dimmed to darkness as she strained to focus on one thing: keeping him in her line of sight.

"Like a car chase?" Sydney sounded impressed.

The ridiculousness of the question was matched only by the ridiculousness of her current reality. It was a car chase, of sorts, and Rebecca could only respond with an honest, "Uh-huh." Ghosted took a quick right turn onto F Street. Rebecca followed, about two blocks away and at risk of losing him altogether.

"So," Sydney left enough space between her words to fill it with a dump truck. Rebecca wanted to explain that now wasn't the time when her friend preempted her with: "You're like on a first-name basis with all of these people?"

"I think he knows I'm tailing him. Do you think, maybe?" Ghosted's car, still swerving between lanes, was edging further out of range. Rebecca cut in front of a gold Prius, barely avoiding impact. "Sorry!" she waved to the driver, hoping she hadn't just ruined someone's day. The Prius driver beeped his horn anyway, flashing his high beams as Rebecca's hand popped out of her window to offer a conciliatory 'thank you' wave. The Prius honked again, longer this time, and probably harder, but Rebecca was already two cars in front of it.

"You're tailing him! If I had known what was happening, I would have just come up for a vacation with you!" Rebecca wished Sydney was sitting there beside her, helping her decide what to do and bearing witness to the insanity.

"Next time," she said.

"There's a *next time?!*" It sounded like Sydney had leaped out of the bath, spilling water all over the tile floor, ready and willing to jump on a plane right then and there.

Ghosted turned abruptly, two-and-a-half blocks ahead of Rebecca, and she thought out loud: "I think I might have lost him. Crap."

"Did he see you? Was he trying to lose you?"

"I don't know." As she rounded the corner onto 19th St, her eyes darted from car to car, hoping she was wrong. "I don't know. I was right behind him, and he cut off a bunch of people, but I don't know if it's because he saw me or because of the ambulance at the accident or because he's an asshole."

"It's the last one!" Sydney crowed. After a brief pause, she asked: "You didn't cause the accident, right?"

No...no," Rebecca said, barely listening as she scanned the road. "Yes!" she yelled, spotting the amber convertible ahead, now driving calmly. She eased through traffic, changing lanes more aggressively than she had ever done before, while also striving to remain, somehow, inconspicuous. "He's there, but he's slowed down. Finally."

"Okay?"

There was silence for a time, or, at least, Rebecca wasn't listening.

"You okay?" Sydney asked again.

Rebecca was physically incapable of answering until she got closer. She had followed him on impulse, but now that she had, she needed to know where he was going.

"I don't know," she said. "I thought maybe he saw me, but he's driving normally now, so I don't know if it's because—"

"Just go with it." Sydney cut in before Rebecca could spiral off into the standard series of reasons to doubt herself. "Tell me, what's going on with the family?"

As traffic crawled, and she kept an eye on the amber Corvette, Rebecca described the rest of the madness from the past two-and-a-half days. Sydney interrupted her at Sheriff Donnelly and the rain check at the farmers market, teasing Rebecca's upcoming "date." Rebecca, momentarily flustered, explained that it was all professional, but Sydney asked, "Oh?" and Rebecca suddenly wasn't so sure.

Ghosted slowed, exiting the freeway. He pulled into one of those strip malls that seem to exist under a perpetually sepia haze, like they reside in a photograph of the world as it was 30 years ago. Rebecca pulled off the main road but waited until Ghosted exited his vehicle—slamming shut his door—before parking in the same lot. She watched him push through the scuffed glass double doors of a cheap laundromat and stand beside a wall of dryers, arms crossed and annoyed.

"The way he's standing," Rebecca said, "he's here to meet someone, but I don't see—" As though on cue, the large man who Ghosted was there to meet entered her periphery. "It's Chris White and KL." Anticipating Sydney's unfamiliarity with the family, she added, "Becky—I mean B*Sweet's dad and stylist." KL, who was carrying a full laundry basket, was leading them.

"Shiiiii—"

"I'm going to get a little closer. See if I can see something." Rebecca turned off the speaker and hazarded exiting her car. Risking exposure, she secreted herself at the glass facade. KL set the slender black and red hamper between Chris and a disdainful Ghosted. A few patrons escaped outside, and each time the door opened, shouted syllables flew out with them, collapsing into a rumble when the door swung shut.

Ghosted dismissed KL who looked to Chris for direction. Chris didn't seem to move one way or another, and so KL shuffled across the room, leaning on a vending machine beside two darkened arcade cabinets.

Sydney's voice squelched unintelligibly from the phone. Rebecca stuffed it into her shirt and snuck inside, sitting on a blue particle board bench, next to a dozing old woman.

Chris White breathed heavily, exuding a conscious calm that made it almost seem like a laundromat in Oak Park was the most natural place in the world for him to be. Ghosted, meanwhile, burrowed into the laundry basket like a vole. He didn't like what he saw inside and made no effort to hide the fact.

"Are you retarded?" Ghosted asked loudly. "This isn't even what you owe me for my work. And you have the *audacity* to demand copies of *my* music?" Ghosted's body wriggled as he struggled to comprehend the large man's idiocy.

"If you want more money, we need the songs," Chris said calmly.

Ghosted clapped, his head wobbling like a top at the end of its spin. "More money, that's brilliant. I want what I'm owed and nothing more."

"My daughter has misplaced the—"

"You," Ghosted interrupted, cackling cruelly. "Your daughter. I wish I could see the look on your face when you realize you've lost her. She's *gone.*" He grabbed the basket and said sardonically, "*All* thanks to me." He spat on the ground and took two steps backward, then pivoted to face the door and leave.

Rebecca's phone rang, and she fumbled, trying to turn it off. She bent her head to her chest, hiding her face behind fluffy red curls, imagining everyone staring at her. "Hold on," she hissed into the phone, cautiously lifting her head.

KL had returned to Chris White and was hugging him, speaking words of comfort only they could hear. They exited, hand in hand. Despite the size difference, KL gave off the impression that he was supporting Chris as they walked, like Atlas bearing the weight of the world.

Rebecca returned to her GTI and watched. Chris opened the passenger door for KL and the two of them spoke.

"What are you going to do now?" Sydney asked from the phone. For the first time that day, Rebecca didn't have a plan. She was watching Chris White's measured return to his side of the black Escalade. He paused as he opened his door and answered his phone. Initial annoyance became concern, and he sat. The bottom of the car scraped against the road bump as it left the parking lot.

"I think," she said, "I need to follow Becky's dad and ask them about what just happened."

"Won't that be dangerous?" Rebecca knew Sydney wasn't trying to discourage her; she was genuinely curious.

"Maybe." Rebecca croaked, leaving the parking lot. "Stay on the phone with me. Can we talk? I feel like it's been a long time. Not about me or any of this. Let's talk about you. Your trip. How are Bethany and Fern handling your mom?"

As Rebecca drove up CA99 onto I–80, following Chris White's steady yet urgent pace, Sydney recounted both what she had gotten up to after arriving and what her plans were for the day. Illuminated headlights became more frequent on the passing cars, and it was disorienting for Rebecca to hear her friend speak about the upcoming day when hers was coming to a close. Sydney would visit the Imperial, then a couple of museums, if she could find the time and energy. She'd end the day with some nightclubs in Roppongi.

Chris passed the exit to the house. He passed the exit to the marina. Rebecca wondered aloud whether he had seen her and was deliberately trying to lead her on a wild sheep chase. When he finally exited the freeway, directing them toward an area of the lake she'd never seen, the burnt orange sun had sunken nearly to the horizon.

A large semi-truck was parked facing away from the lake. From its rear, a telescoping crane winched a steel-cable tow line like an old fisherman who's finally caught the big one. Strobing flashes of red and blue and white and yellow from surrounding emergency vehicles cast dancing shadows onto the hillside and lake. Sheriffs and fire trucks aimed super bright beams of light at the point of the water where the cable unsteadily emerged, dragging something heavy and misshapen up the submerged boat ramp. Helicopters, both police and news, hovered about like carrion birds, shining their spotlights below, bouncing between the water and the congregation of first responders.

The Escalade was flagged past a makeshift perimeter near the water. Rebecca parked with a small crowd of onlookers. Following their lead, she climbed onto the hood of her car to see what was happening. The sun was below the surrounding foothills, making it difficult to see clearly. Slowly, a sunken vehicle emerged from the lake, water gushing from every orifice. Straining her eyes, Rebecca recognized first the candy apple red paint job and, second, the IUD shape of the broken taillights and Tesla symbol.

Chapter Twenty-One.

It was Caroline's car; it had to be. Becky's father had been summoned, which meant there was something—or someone—inside the car that tied it to her. Not just Chris; in a gray BMW, Jenna was being waved through the police barricade. Rebecca itched for a closer look.

"I'm calling the sheriff," Rebecca told Sydney after catching her up. "To see if I can get closer."

"Are you sure that's a good idea?" Sydney asked, "What if she's, you know...inside?"

"She's not," Rebecca said mostly to herself, hoping she was right. "But, even." She breathed. "Whatever is down there, if I can do something, I want to try."

"Just keep me in the loop this time, okay?" Sydney said. Rebecca agreed and hung up, dialing the number Sheriff Donnelly had saved in her phone.

Rebecca scanned the scene below. She spotted a figure pull out his ringing phone, but he didn't answer. The phone rang four times, then five. Rebecca was convinced he would ignore her. Finally, he placed the illuminated screen to his ear, snuffing it out. "Ms. Ziel, this isn't a good time." His voice was heavy with fatigue. "We found...we found the car."

"I know, I'm sorry. I'm up the hill, outside the barricade." The figure of Sheriff Donnelly lowered his phone and turned to face the nearest group of civilian bystanders. Rebecca raised her phone, waving its glowing side like a semaphore. She pulled it back to her ear and asked, "Is she there? Can I come down?"

Rebecca sometimes imagined herself in high-stakes scenarios, perfect words at the ready, able to convince anyone of anything. But in the uncertainty of the moment, she had nothing. She lacked the words to persuade him that she needed to be there, to help in some way. All she could do was hope that he understood intuitively and agreed to invite her down. The shadow of Sheriff Donnelly didn't move.

At last, she heard him expel a long, ragged sigh and roughly clear his throat before saying, "Wait there."

The sheriff guided her past the guards, bringing Rebecca face-to-face with what remained of Caroline's car. She almost wished she had listened to Sydney and stayed away. She could be at home, safe in her shower or in bed instead of there, in cool lake air, chilled by what she saw. The windshield was split and shattered, with a jutting slice of glass hanging there like a strip of flayed skin clinging to its wound. Outside that, the hood was left a torn and gnarled imitation of what it once had been.

Rebecca turned to Sheriff Donnelly. "What happened?"

"It was found by chance: a family on holiday dropped anchor and got caught on what they thought was a submerged tree. After desperately trying to pull it up, they cut their line and called us, and we called Parks and Rec, who called us back when they discovered what it was." His finger traced an imaginary path along the automobile's damaged front end. "Some if not all of this destruction is from the anchor," he said. As he said the word "anchor", Rebecca was suddenly aware of the spiky mass of metal violently lodged into the electric vehicle's empty dashboard. An alloy chain trailed from it, spilling out onto the hood, and from there, a nylon rope snaked out into the water, its severed end bobbing up and down with the waves. "It's possible there was a collision or some other damage prior, but we can't confirm one way or another without further examination. This, for example," he tapped the distended driver door, "is likely unrelated to the anchor incident, but we don't know whether it happened before or after the car was submerged."

Suspended at a harsh angle, Caroline's car released in torrents the lake water it had consumed. The liquid pooled and broke at odd angles in the footwells at the front of the car, littered with drifting flotsam being counted and categorized, plucked and packaged into clear plastic evidence bags by a deputy in rubber waders and exceptionally long gloves. Drifting back and forth in the miniature ocean inside the car, Rebecca spotted a floating key fob supporting a chrome 'VF' keychain that waved in the water. A torn blouse and bra drifted past, followed by a jumbled mess of used condoms and empty orange pill bottles. Castaway on the deformed dashboard, she spotted Becky's hoop earring reflecting police lights.

"Did you find—?" She couldn't finish.

The sheriff fidgeted; he said, "No. We found her phone inside, wrapped in tin foil, but we've yet to discover any...bodies. God-willing, we won't. There are divers trawling the area." He appraised the scene, clearly pained by the possibilities contained within. At last, he broke the silence, "I just don't understand how you're here. Or what you hope to get from this."

"I followed Chris White from a meeting he had with Ghosted. James Logan," she admitted. "I think he gave him money."

Sheriff Donnelly pressed his palm into his forehead, then scratched a knuckle across the five o'clock shadow that wasn't there in the morning. "I, what? Who paid whom?"

She told him about the laundromat, then worked backward to Chris White's suspicious investments. Rebecca couldn't take the sheriff's hard stare and focused on the ground as she spoke.

"You didn't think to tell me any of this, after I explicitly asked you to?" he huffed.

Rebecca opened her mouth but couldn't speak. When could she have told him anything? It all happened so fast—but deep down, she knew that wasn't the truth. There was always time. Maybe Caroline had been right. Maybe Rebecca didn't appreciate the impact of her actions. Perhaps she spent so much time deliberating over her decisions as a way of distancing herself from them. And their consequences.

Her silence felt damning. The sheriff nodded as if confirming his suspicions. He looked back out at the lake. "We were all so happy about so much rain and snow this past winter, but...now it's just making things harder. The boat ramp extends another 50 feet under the water, built during the drought. Caroline's car had a straight, flat path all the way down. I reckon, whoever dumped it here knew that."

He guided her away from the crime scene and stopped, breathing a silent curse. She followed his gaze to a full-size van pulling into the parking lot above. It had a rooftop parabolic dish that slowly rose into the sky, rotating in search of a meaningful connection with its satellite. Two figures burst out of the van, wielding a top-lit camera and microphone like weapons of war. They vantaged themselves from the crowd, ensuring a clear shot of the developing scene. "Is there more that you haven't told me?"

Before she could answer, a deputy wielding an ultraviolet flashlight summoned Sheriff Donnelly to another matter. "If I don't come back, I'll call you. I need to know everything you know," he said, disappearing into darkness.

Rebecca spied another officer transporting several water-logged evidence bags, one of which contained a space gray tablet computer with a thin, white wire emerging from its bottom like a tail. She followed the man, trying to get a good enough look at the back of the tablet to determine if she had seen what she thought she had. There it was: the silhouette of a spread-winged kingfisher soaring between two buildings. Partially covering the Apple logo, peeling at the corners, was her Halcyon Realty logo that adorned all of Charles' belongings.

There was no point trying to access the iPad now. Even if it was ever returned to her, there was no telling whether it would still work. At least now she had something to tell Charles, an explanation for where it had disappeared to. Why it was in the car and what the police might conclude when they learned it was hers, Rebecca could only guess. And then there were the documents she'd been working on. Until that moment, she had been clinging to the prospect of continuing from where she had left off once the device turned up. At least now she knew she'd be starting from scratch. As insignificant as that realization was compared to the mystery surrounding the car, it stung like yet another failure in a long line of them.

"Yo... ..er...tin. She. no. de..." Jenna's unusually nasal voice carried in fragments on the lake's breeze. Rebecca found her, trapped between an empty Parks Service truck and a parked ambulance. Jenna was desperately pleading with Chris White's hunched, unyielding shadow. KL, barely visible, sat facing Chris, clasping the man's hands. Rebecca approached, keeping to the shadows.

"She is," Chris White whimpered. "She's dead, and it's my fault. I pushed her too—No." He gazed down at KL, realization dawning on him. "No, it was Logan. He told me she wasn't coming back." The family patriarch rose, towering above the others. He thrust his clenched fist like a boulder into the side of the ambulance, denting it and drawing the attention of nearby emergency workers. "He said it was thanks to him. He did this."

Jenna jumped back, agitated. "Trust me," she said, her voice wavering despite an apparent attempt to remain calm. "She's not. This—I don't know what this is—but she's not dead. I'm telling you. She's probably with Marc. Like last time."

"You," her father said, turning his body to face his daughter. "If you hadn't pushed me to hire Logan, this never would have happened. You did this."

KL stepped between father and daughter, arms outstretched, calmly pleading, "Please. Chris. Please."

Jenna retreated, shaking her head in denial or disbelief. "I never suggested you hire him," she argued, a tremor in her voice. "I mentioned him, but only as a reference for the album's sound. I never thought you would actually—"

"You said only he could give us exactly what we wanted. You." Chris White's voice bellowed. Officers joined KL between the distraught giant and his daughter. His advance stalled, and his arms dropped like felled trees.

"You are not my daughter," Chris White said, his voice sticky and deep. "I do not want to see you again."

Jenna ran her fingers through her hair, then pulled it like pigtails. A glistening trail of tears scarred her cheek. It was the first time Rebecca had seen the woman not in control of her situation. "You're not—" Jenna turned to her car, a look of fierce determination washing over her face. Chris again sat, KL draped across his shoulders.

Rebecca watched Jenna hurry to her car and focus on her phone. She typed something, then brought it to her ear, speaking with renewed vigor. Though Rebecca wasn't near enough to hear, Jenna enunciated with such a fierce firmness that Rebecca could almost read her lips. Jenna drove away too quickly for Rebecca to follow her, even if she had wanted to. Sheriff Donnelly was beside Chris White and KL, comforting them.

Anxiety coiled inside Rebecca's chest; she froze midstep. The iPad. If the car hadn't been immediately submerged, its location history might show where Becky went, or even where she was now. Rebecca had used that feature to find her own phone before. She'd never used the cloud backups, but as she understood it, any photos or videos should also be accessible—including those from the night Becky went missing. Even the work she'd completed might be saved somewhere.

Charles restricted work account access to the office computers. If she wanted that information, she had to go there. She could return to the office in the morning, but she didn't know how time-sensitive the information might be. If she were very lucky, it was possible to find Becky that very night. This time, she'd text Sheriff Donnelly the moment she learned anything. She sprinted up the hill in the direction of her car.

Chapter Twenty-Two.

"Hey." It was more a hiss than a greeting. "Psst."

Rebecca was not even halfway back to where she had parked. She squinted into the twilight, searching for the voice's source. A petite woman stood alone beneath a tree, tucked away from the crowd watching the chaos unfold.

Caustic fumes curled from the cigarette she held loosely at her waist. Her other arm remained concealed behind her back, tense, as if gripping onto something. She lifted the cigarette to her pursed lips. "You don't want to go that way," she said as Rebecca stepped closer. In the dim orange radiance of the embers, Rebecca saw first the scorpion logo on the body of the cigarette, then the two dollar signs on the back of the woman's hand that briefly glowed, then faded.

"Karen...Fukuhara?" Rebecca asked, tightening her lips.

Casually exhaling in Rebecca's general direction, she spoke matter-of-factly. "Moneyshot," she said, and tilted her head in the direction she wanted to go. The butt fell from her hand, and she grounded it into the dirt with the ball of her foot. Behind her back, held securely in the hand Rebecca hadn't been able to see, was a camera with a long black lens.

"I'm over there," Rebecca protested, despite following the photographer away from her car.

"That's legacy media there." She waved at the van with the antenna. "You don't want to talk to them."

Moneyshot climbed without confirming whether Rebecca was following her. "There's another way to your car. Volkswagen, silver, right?" She quieted a moment, letting Rebecca know she knew.

"This route is private. We can talk." Rebecca unsteadily hurried to catch up.

"Why were you meeting with Jenna Sweet?" Rebecca asked. Moneyshot said nothing.

"Let's pause here." They stopped and settled on a level stretch of land. Moneyshot placed the viewfinder against her eye and fired off a burst of photographs. She dropped it to chest level and scrolled through the images she'd just taken before adjusting her position and doing it again. She repeated the action four more times before snorting a satisfied "hmm" and asking, "Mind if I smoke?"

Rebecca minded, but it didn't seem to matter either way; the cigarette was lit in her lips before asking permission. And she was avoiding Rebecca's questions. The whole trek felt like a diversion. Rebecca turned away.

The hillside and lake shimmered in a deep Yves Klein blue under the fading light, a cold contrast to the sunbaked earth beneath their feet. Along with the constant call of crickets and katydids, the scene was slowly becoming white noise, taking on a surreal form that threatened to pull Rebecca outside of herself, turning her, temporarily, into a passive observer of her own life. She tried to focus on Moneyshot, struggling to repel the growing anxiety.

Walking over, gripping the lens, Moneyshot presented the camera's display to Rebecca. Leaning in, despite the harsh dryness of the smoke, Rebecca examined each image, compliantly progressing to the end of the roll.

They're great," she said, stepping back. Even the misaligned or blurry shots carried an artistic edge, like the flaws were deliberate. "But they're all a bit far, aren't they? I'd have thought, in your profession, you'd want to be nearer to your subject. Like when you were in the trees at the Sweet house."

Moneyshot snorted and pulled the cigarette from her mouth. "I took those," she said. Spinning the dial several complete rotations, she stopped at a shot of the car being pulled from the lake. Even with the long lens, the pictures could not have been taken from outside the police perimeter. The photos weren't exclusively of the salvaged vehicle either: there were shots of Chris, Jenna, KL, the sheriff and even Rebecca herself. It was more evidence that the photos Chris gave her did not come from the paparazzi.

"Can I ask you something now?" Rebecca hazarded, turning to watch as the semi-truck that had pulled out Caroline's car departed the park.

"Shoot," said Moneyshot, the cigarette held in her lips bouncing like a child's sparkler on the fourth of July.

"Were you at the mansion Thursday night? After the event. Was that you taking pictures of the argument between B*Sweet and her friend?"

Moneyshot stared ahead at the horizon in silence, breathing in the smoke. She wasn't going to answer. Rebecca had followed her for nothing but to be shown pictures of the wreck she'd just left.

"We were there," the small woman said eventually, dropping into a squat and erasing the burnt end of her smoke into the earth. "I didn't take any pictures of that night."

"Bill?" Rebecca asked. Moneyshot nodded. "Did he get any pictures of what happened to Caroline?"

Moneyshot stood and stretched her neck front-to-back and side-to-side. She said, "I can't say what he did or didn't shoot. We left when—" she stopped herself. "We left together. He forgot something outside their mansion and went back. I haven't seen or heard from him since then." She shook her head, clearly annoyed at the man's absence. "He's in Mexico for all I know."

"I talked to him Friday," Rebecca told her. "Well, sort of. He answered, but it sounded like he was expecting someone else, and they showed up." Moneyshot's raised eyebrow glowed orange and vanished as she sucked the life from the cigarette. "He said something about photographs and meeting at another house. Does any of that make sense to you?"

Moneyshot leaned her head. She was hard to read in the dark. "We're photographers," she said, "we take them. Sometimes, we meet people about them."

"Becky has another house, doesn't she?" Rebecca pressed, wondering when or if the woman would ever give a straight answer. "Do you know where it is?"

"Come on," Moneyshot continued her climb, unable or unwilling to answer.

Rebecca stopped short, planting her feet. She needed to change tactics. "If I'm going to follow you, I need answers." Moneyshot paused, turning back, flashing a grin. Rebecca asked, "What does Jenna Sweet have you doing? What were you meeting about?"

"We have an arrangement in L.A.," Moneyshot answered. "She uses her contacts to get us into certain celebrity soirees; we use our contacts to get her into others. It's a mutually beneficial arrangement. Now she's leaving Hollywood, giving up acting to focus on the business side of things, is the word around town. You can only play so many quirky best friends before you want to slit your wrists." She stopped, shrugging at Rebecca. "Trades say she sold her house down there a few months ago. I guess she's expecting to spend more time up here. Or in Vegas." Her head titled to the side like a broken pencil. "I've been told her wine business is doing well. It doesn't matter where you are, folks love to get wasted."

She pulled the cigarette box out of her pocket, shook it and tapped her fingers on the top. They stood facing one another, Moneyshot's gaze shifting between Rebecca and the distant specks of light from houses and boats lit by the crescent moon. Rebecca glanced down the hill; the winch truck was long gone, and the few remaining emergency vehicles were pulling away. Moneyshot hadn't answered the question.

"That's why you're up here in Sacramento?"

"The first time she called us up was a surprise. We don't usually come this far north except when the politicians visiting are celebrities: Schwarzeneggar or Obama. She put us in touch with her father. He wanted 'real' pictures of B*Sweet." She placed her fingers to her lips, blowing on them. "He had a very particular definition of 'real': we could shoot her wherever, whenever, but he didn't want anything damaging."

"We charged less than normal," she continued, "but we appreciate Jenna; it was a favor. Of course," Rebecca could hear the change in the woman's voice as she grinned, becoming more nasal and almost predatory. "When we saw some things he didn't want us to see, he grew unhappy and threatened not to pay. But he paid."

"You saw her with Marc Sheffield," Rebecca stated. Moneyshot cleared her throat in a way that said yes without saying it. "And this time? She has you trailing her sister again?"

"In part," she replied. "It's less structured, I'd say. No restrictions: shoot-to-sell." Looking down at the departing vehicles, Moneyshot said, "That's the last of them; let's head back." Moneyshot started back down the same route they'd come.

"Can you tell me where she is? B*Sweet? You've been following her, so you must know."

"I told the cops I don't know where she is. We followed her that night, though Bill turned back like I said. I don't know where she wound up." Moneyshot coughed. "I'll tell you what I didn't tell the cops, though. The pictures were a side job. This time, we came to get in touch with one of her contacts. Even with our resources, without someone like Jenna, someone with an in, you don't get inside. You need that golden ticket." Again, with the grin. "We met that evening, after the event, though we couldn't find any common ground." She sighed, "But we persevere. There are always other ways."

When they were back at the tree where they had begun their journey, she asked, "So we hiked all that way just to end up where we began? That was your 'other' way?"

Moneyshot shrugged. "We got around the media."

But I didn't get around you, Rebecca thought. *Or your camera.*

Moneyshot walked Rebecca back to her GTI. "Well, here you are, safe and sound." The paparazzo hesitated, then asked: "Favor for a favor?"

Rebecca shook her head in confusion. "You need a ride?"

"No," Moneyshot's soft chuckle was somehow both delicate and throaty, like the chirp of a canary with emphysema. "A request."

"Okay," Rebecca cautioned.

"Jenna has been unresponsive since our...disagreement yesterday. I didn't have the opportunity to speak with her just now." Another lit cigarette materialized between her lips, as if by magic. She said, "When our meeting with her friend didn't go so well, she offered us a package as a consolation prize. Now she's ignoring my calls. Next time you see her, will you ask her about it? If acquiring it directly is more convenient for you, she probably still has it in her bedroom." She spread her hands; the cigarette bounced in her fingers as she motioned. "Briefcase. Yay-big. Old-fashioned flip locks." Moneyshot mimed unlocking a suitcase with her thumbs, then brought the butt to her lips.

Rebecca thought of the briefcase she'd seen in Jenna's room. She shook her head. First Chris White, and now Moneyshot. What did Jenna have that everyone wanted so badly? "I'll try to talk to her about it, but I can't do more than that. I'm sorry."

Moneyshot exhaled, studying Rebecca. Kicking at the dirt, she said, "That's fine. We all have our roles to play." From her pocket, she removed a silver case and from that a business card. She offered the card with a practiced formality. "In case you change your mind."

Moneyshot strutted to the only other vehicle in the dirt lot—a sleek gray motorcycle. She slipped on her helmet, revved the quiet engine, and took off, kicking up a spray of pebbles and dust in her wake. Rebecca watched her taillight dissolve into the distance. She wondered where Moneyshot was headed, but it didn't matter. She needed to get downtown.

Chapter Twenty-Three.

The narrow strip of moon did little to illuminate the tops of the buildings not already lit by artificial accent lights or the occasionally occupied windows. Flaming stars bloomed and disintegrated in the sky as eager patriots shot off early fireworks. All her usual parking spots had been taken by weekend revelers out partying with friends or their partners or on the prowl for new ones, forcing Rebecca to park half a mile away, under the looming presence of the Grand Hotel.

Sheriff Donnelly had texted during Rebecca's drive downtown, confirming that he planned to call in the morning to go over "whatever you haven't told me." She replied simply, hoping that when they spoke, she'd have enough good news to offset his disappointment in her.

Despite the intermittent groups of people wandering boisterously down the sidewalk past shuttered stores toward open restaurants and bars that advertised their openness with brightly lit signs, or perhaps because of them, Rebecca strode down the street with a sustained sense of solitude she'd never before experienced. Any time she'd been in the city at night, it had been with friends or boyfriends or, more recently, with Charles Sprock after a late night working in the office. Now, the sense of purpose she felt weighed only on her shoulders, and the world around her reflected that.

As she crossed the street toward the Cathedral of the Blessed Sacrament, its up-lit, sharply-pointed towers making it both menacing and holy, she thought she spotted a silver pickup dented across its left bedside. One had passed her when she first crossed the street, and she worried it might be the same one. Rebecca sheltered under the shadow of the church, and, as the truck pulled to a stop at the traffic light, she memorized its license plate just in case it passed by her again. Was it following her? The past few days had been too weird and unpredictable to completely dismiss the idea. The truck drove away as the light turned green, and she stepped out of the shadows, quickening her pace.

One block over, she saw it for a third time. The truck moved slowly, as if searching for someone. Rebecca was so focused on it that she nearly collided with a drunk who seemed to welcome the physical contact. She darted inside the nearest shop, positioning herself behind the nearest curtained mullion, apologizing to the couple seated at the closest table for interrupting their dinner. She snuck a peek; the truck was still there. Its windows were too tinted to see through at night, but Rebecca felt eyes probing the restaurant.

A hostess offered to help, her way of telling Rebecca that she was upsetting the guests. Rebecca asked for the restroom; she needed to think. The helpful young woman hesitated but ultimately pointed her toward a back corner. Rebecca thanked her, apologized to the couple at the table again, and left.

Seated at a table beside the restrooms, was Ghosted, sawing a well-done steak, enthusiastically chatting up a couple of women sitting across from him. The younger of the two was the same Rebecca had seen in his room, and she had the same dead-eyed stare. The older woman was doing all of the talking, nudging the other without eliciting a response.

Rebecca, not wanting to be seen, about-faced, exiting with a large group of departing patrons. She was out in the open with other normal people; why was she so scared? Paying all her attention to the cars that passed, she didn't realize that the group was cutting through an alleyway until they were well inside. Taking a corner into a dead end, the group coalesced in natural cliques, leaving Rebecca unsure what she was going to do. The group's guide unlocked a back entrance into a luxury condo, ushering them inside. The party drained in through the door like sands in an hourglass, passing the man with the keys. When it was only Rebecca, the man appraised her with an I-don't-know-you-do-I-? stare, then shut the door in her face.

"Sorry," she croaked at the closed door and turned around. Moments before, the conversation was bouncing off the walls. Now, all was quiet and empty.

She repeated to herself: this wasn't the old days. Cities weren't full of laughing hyena men, high on crack and hunting for prey. Still, she kept her back tight and her legs spring-loaded, ready to run. To her left, in the direction of her work, she saw the bedraggled shape of a homeless man muttering to himself in staccato pronouncements beneath a pulsing streetlight. He stopped momentarily, his head rising in her direction. The barest glimmer of light appeared in the shadow of his face where his eyes should be.

Rebecca veered right, abandoning any thoughts of using the office. She would do her research after the sun was up; if finding Becky couldn't wait eight hours, it was probably too late for her, anyway. Behind Rebecca, the homeless man barked something. Rebecca bolted, glancing back. He was still there, alone under the light, separated from her by more than mere physical distance.

Rebecca swiveled her head back forward and was ripped forcefully from her path into another of the alley's closed-off side lanes. She felt black wind on her face, and a pressure she didn't understand cutting off the blood in her arm.

Long, strong appendages wrapped around her bicep, and the moment she tried to shout, something covered her mouth. It was soft and smelled of charred meat. It was a hand.

"Don't struggle," a gristly voice hissed, spraying his hot, sweet-smelling breath and spittle across her cheek. "This will be quick," he said. His tongue slithered along the fold of her ear.

Rebecca strained, twisting her face until her lips felt the folds between the man's fingers. She bit down hard, tasting blood. "Stop," the man commanded, voice higher but still under control. Rather than releasing her, he held her tighter, shifting his hold of her arm to the back of her head, creating a vice with his hands.

"Stop." As the pressure in her head built, and her ability to bite him was compromised, Rebecca swung her limbs, elbowing his ribs and stamping his feet. He pressed her harder against the wall, pulling his hand from the front of her face to secure her arms. Hundreds of microscopically small cavities in the brick cut into her like a cheese grater. The man again took her arm, folding it behind her and pressing it into her back. She could no longer discern whether the blood she tasted was hers, his or a mix of the two. "Stop," he repeated steadily, and the fingers at the back of her head twisted with her hair, pulling it and her head backward, facing her to the sky. The man tackled his entire body weight onto her, fitting his thigh between her legs to control them and pin her whole body.

Rebecca's neck stretched to its limit. Her torso, crushed between the wall and his body, fought for breath, fearing each would be her last. She would never again see Sydney or Erin or her father or daylight. She prayed, refusing the impulse to flee her body or escape into shock. She braced herself to push off the wall and escape the moment he next repositioned himself. Tears or blood, or both, was pooling on her chin, drip-dripping down onto the filthy ground.

"Stop. Stop. Stop! STOP!" Her attacker's demand rang in her ears; the pressure on her body was growing too much to resist, and, despite her determination to maintain a ready awareness of the world around her, a blackness enveloped her perception, irising in from the periphery.

"Good Gawd!" the voice whinged. The man balked, throwing her to the ground. "You covered me in PISS!" he moaned. She hadn't noticed her bladder empty itself, but now, on the ground, it was unmistakable. She shivered as the night air wicked away the heat from the fresh urine.

"It was a JOKE!" The man spat on the ground as he bent over to squeegee his pants with a discarded newspaper. "What's your problem?!" he asked, and Rebecca almost laughed at him. What was her problem? *What was her problem?!*

"You skulk outside my hotel room, stalk me all over the city, then you interrupt my dinner, and now you do this to me!" James Logan—Ghosted—was no longer trying to disguise his voice, overflowing as it was with annoyance. "I think you should apologize to me," he said, standing over her, soiled paper crumpled in his fist. "You should offer to pay for these pants that I know you can't afford. I won't hold you to it, but we both know you owe me at least that much."

Rebecca had to force herself not to do it. The urge to apologize rose in her throat like vomit. It was reflex—muscle memory—but this time, she swallowed it down. "No," she said finally, lifting herself unsteadily from the ground—gripping a fallen brick in her hand.

"These Kitons cost me more than your whole fuckin' life." He said, grinning. "It's okay, I'll just add that to Chris's bill, since he has you following me." There was no doubt in his voice. To him, Rebecca's presence was nothing more than an extension of Chris White's machinations.

"I'm not here for him. I'm here to find Becky." She backed into a parked Subaru, tightening her grip on the brick in case he lunged at her. If she missed him, she thought, she could at least smash the car window and set off the alarm.

Her answer confused him. He analyzed her like she was a baby babbling over a nightmare. "Oh!" he said at last. He laughed, clapping his hands like a trained sea lion. Despite knowing she shouldn't care what he thought of her, his mockery stung. "You think that you mean something to her." He clapped in amazement. "You really are a sad, pathetic little loser."

When he noticed her trembling hand gripping her weapon, he raised his hands in a momentary false surrender. "What a waste of my time you've been." He scrunched his face in—of all things—pity. Tossing the sopping newspaper at her, he said, "Here, clean yourself up." The paper landed with a wet squish. "I've got a playdate in my hotel room, and I need to wash off your filth to get ready."

"Chris White thinks you took Becky. If she turns up dead, you'll be next," Rebecca warned him.

Ghosted swallowed his laughter. "Of course he does, because it's *always* my fault. Let's not hold to account the father who cried in court about my supposed abuses of his daughter, but was eager to use *my* songs just because they took my name off of it?" He stepped forward. "The same man who begged me to labor in secret and not tell the daughter I supposedly raped that I was writing all her new music. He was worried I would upset her, isn't he such a *loving* dad?"

"I-I'll report you. You attacked me." Rebecca wiped her face, thrusting her fingertips at him like a javelin; blood, already starting to coagulate, dripped from them like red wax down a candle. "And you have a history."

"Oh, please. *You* have a history. All of you. You take what you want, then decide you shouldn't have to pay for it. When the bill comes due, you blame the men who made your life possible for wanting a little kindness in return." He spat again. "And you. My *stalker.* You think I'm worried about what *you* might say? Or that *anyone* will care? Go ahead. It didn't work before when it was someone *important.* They tried to murder my legacy and failed; a nobody like you couldn't hurt me if you tried."

Ghosted spread his arms in a Christ pose and shook his head. "I was canceled. The world ghosted me. They spent years trying to pretend I didn't exist." He stepped forward, baring his teeth. "You can't cancel talent. I'll be dead in the ground, and lost girls in their little skirts will still be singing my songs. Praying that I come and rescue them from their banal little lives." He howled like a street corner preacher.

He waved at her dismissively with a force and suddenness meant to frighten her, and his smile grew wide when he saw her flinch. Then he walked away with a level of pride Rebecca had never felt about anything in her life.

She wanted to tell him that she was friends with the police, that Sheriff Donnelly would listen to her and hold him accountable. Donnelly wasn't the sort of man to let Ghosted go unpunished, she wanted to tell him that. She wanted to make him fear for his life as she'd just been afraid for hers. To let him learn just how funny his jokes were when he was the target. But he still had the upper hand. If she could make him feel the fear she wanted, he seemed unstable and psychopathic enough that he might decide she was not worth the risk of leaving alive.

But more than likely, she could make no threat that would pierce through his ego. She was far too low a lifeform for him to worry about. When he'd thought she was there for Chris, someone with power, she'd been something akin to a threat, someone he could play his "joke" on because she, through her employer, had value. Now, she was just another woman in the city. Anger and helplessness overwhelmed her and she wanted to run at him, to bash him in the head with that brick until his teeth were ground to dust. That anger frightened her.

"Oh! I'm going to get you!" Ghosted shouted. For a split second, Rebecca thought he was coming for her, but he bolted to the alley's exit. A moment later, she saw why: another man stood there, blocking his path, poised to fight. As Ghosted made contact, knocking the other man to the earth, she caught sight of the interloper's bald head and handlebar mustache.

Marc Sheffield shoved Ghosted off of him, struggling to his feet. He swayed; either he had been drinking, or he hit his head in the fall. He led the tarnished music producer back through the central alley in the direction of the homeless man Rebecca had earlier worried herself about. Ghosted's voice echoed, rising above the sounds of the city.

The alleyway was empty when she finally reached it some eternity later. Had Ghosted truly meant to attack her, she would have been a goner, another Kitty Genovese among who knows how many. She didn't decide where she was headed, she moved by instinct. And when she was finally there, seated inside her car, finger urgently pressing the lock button over and over again, she couldn't remember a single footstep she'd taken between the alleyway and her automobile. When she saw the silver pickup driving past her on the street, she wasn't sure if she was dreaming or going crazy. Wasn't she parked underground? The window of the pickup was down, and Rebecca saw the driver was Becky, shining like a phantom as she passed.

Rebecca reached for her phone, only then realizing she was still gripping the brick. She forced herself to release it onto the floor, and she began to cry uncontrollably. The tears came not only because the reality of what had just happened had begun to wash over her but because she needed to pay for parking at an automated booth, and her legs and arms were too numb with residual panic to leave her car. She felt safe and trapped all at once, her entire body fluttering like a paper doll in a sandstorm, and she could barely navigate the phone, clicking the wrong contact five times before successfully dialing Sydney. She didn't know the time in Tokyo or if Sydney was able to answer. Consciousness faded as the phone rang endlessly.

Chapter Twenty-Four. Sunday.

"Oh, you are going to get it!" Ghosted's final words echoed endlessly in the darkness of Rebecca's mind.

Arched like an arachnid beneath an enormous blue crescent moon, Ghosted's arms were now giant, articulate fangs tattooed with skulls and Celtic crosses and "This, too, shall pass." He rubbed them together, greedily, taunting Rebecca with sickening laughter. Inching his face toward hers, spumes of acrid breath coated her skin with spittle. He halted with a howl, responding to the emergent *rip ˜rrriiipp* behind him. The sawing vibration grew in intensity, casting ripples onto the moon, exposing the sky above her as nothing more than the reflective surface of a pond.

Rebecca shifted with difficulty, bound still in Ghosted's cocoon, eager to see her savior, knowing it to be Marc Sheffield. But it wasn't. Patrick Donnelly, clad in knight's armor, wielded an enormous handsaw like a sword. With precise strokes, he sawed off Ghosted's legs, one at a time, dropping them into the dark. The predator curdled in agony, teetered on three legs—then two—then one, before plunging into the chasm below.

Rebecca expected the sheriff to see her, to unbind her, to take her into his arms. Instead, a creeping terror rose as he shifted his focus to the misty webs that held her. She saw then that his eyes were like ice, white and frozen. She screamed—or tried to—but her mouth was overflowing with spider's silk, and all she could hear was the gruff rhythm of the saw blade. Ting, ting, ting; the individual strands making up the cords holding her broke, until— ting—the final cord snapped, sending her into a freefall. As the moonlight and the tops of the buildings receded into the black emptiness of the universe, the only sensation became sound, and the only sound was the persistent grind of the saw blade, which followed her, never moving nearer or further but growing steadily outward until it filled everywhere.

Rebecca awoke to the sound of Sydney's snores filling the car. Her phone screen glowed dimly on her lap—still on after seven hours. Blinking away sleep, she did the math: it wasn't even 10:30 p.m. for Sydney. "Hello? Are you sleeping?" she asked, picking up the receiver. "It's so early."

"I'm not asleep," Sydney slurred, soon again snoring. "I'm waiting for you to wake up," she said eventually, smacking her lips.

"I'm awake." Once Sydney's breathing evened out, confirming the claim, Rebecca described the attack in the alleyway. There was silence for a time afterward as Sydney and Rebecca both came to terms with the reality of what happened. Only after Sydney whispered, "I love you. We're going to get through this," was Rebecca comfortable enough to leave her car and pay for parking. She detailed the events leading up to the attack.

"That sounds unlikely." Sydney didn't believe Moneyshot's story. Rebecca nodded, then shook her head.

"She was hiding something, but I don't know what. I need to call the sheriff," Rebecca realized aloud, "tell him about what happened." She paused, then named her attacker: "Ghosted. James Logan; he needs to know. Can I talk to you later?"

"No," Sydney said. "I'll stay on hold while you call, then be here with you until he gets there."

Rebecca drove up from the second basement level. The sun had not yet fully risen, but its developing influence already made the street in front of her feel solid, turning the previous night's happenings incorporeal. It would be so comforting to doubt they had ever happened, she thought.

She parked in a smaller lot closer to her office, and, following the sheriff's instructions, she waited inside her car for his arrival, listening to Sydney gradually fall asleep.

Sheriff Donnelly arrived in loose, Sacramento Sheriff-branded sweatpants and a tight gray short-sleeved t-shirt, sweat-stained from his morning run. His hair was wet and uncombed, tousled like ocean waves on a windy day. His appearance on the scene made her feel safe. But that sense of normalcy evaporated the moment he stiffly invited her into his cruiser. He matter-of-factly asked her to recount the night's attack, including as much detail as possible, then, upon completion, asked her to go over it again, asking questions as she went. After the second retelling, with a minimal delay for consideration, he pulled out his badge and popped open his door.

"That's enough," he said, pausing before adding, "It's plenty to arrest him. If he gets a little banged up resisting," he let the statement lie there. He drove to the base of the hotel, parking in the emergency lane, setting the car's roof lights to flash but leaving the siren turned off. Pulling the radio transceiver to his mouth, he announced to the station where he was and what he was doing and why, abbreviating Rebecca's story to the operator as "245".

Rebecca followed his lead, exiting the vehicle. "I want to go with you." He shook his head no, but she insisted. "I want to look at him in the daylight, see who he is when there are no shadows to hide in." She wanted to look him in the eyes when the sheriff cuffed him and walked him past her. Even if he couldn't accept it as an 'L,' he would know she hadn't been bluffing when she told him her word meant something.

Sheriff Donnelly watched her for a moment, then he clenched his jaw and nodded curtly. "Okay, but you stay in the hallway until I give you leave to enter," he said, and Rebecca agreed. As he informed hotel management of their intentions, Rebecca caught sight of the housemaid she'd seen the day before, sitting in a back room weeping into her hands as a manager-type listened to her speak. Sheriff Donnelly and Rebecca followed an overworked hotel representative into the elevator and up to the seventh floor.

Back to the wall, Sheriff Donnelly reached his right arm across the door, banging it with the bottom of his closed fist. "James Logan." His duty belt was on over the sweatpants, and he wore his sidearm holstered in the belt, leaving the thumb break securely fastened across the grip. Though hovering about the gun, his left hand remained still and steady. "James Logan," he blurted again, "this is the sheriff's department. Open up!" He leaned his head toward the door, listening for movement.

"He's probably not—" the hotel employee was interrupted by the sheriff's open hand; Patrick Donnelly was trying to hear inside Ghosted's room, and Rebecca, intrigued, did likewise. It was much quieter than when she'd visited the day before; he and the women he'd been with were probably passed out across the room's king-size bed. "He comes and goes all hours of the night," the employee whispered to Rebecca, shutting up and placing his index finger to his lips when Sheriff Donnelly turned his head to look at him.

"If you do not open up, we will enter by force," the sheriff warned, wielding the key card he'd been given and sliding it across the reader. He grappled the knob. Nothing. The card reader flashed red three times; Sheriff Donnelly glared at the hotel rep, who shriveled in silent shame. Finally, it turned green, and the lawman quietly pushed the door in. He leaned around the door jamb for a quick scan of the scene, and he cursed. Then, he readied his gun and announced, "If anyone is in here, I am entering with my weapon drawn." Taking a deep breath, he disappeared into the room.

Thinking about it later, Rebecca would admit she had been waiting for a minute or two at most. In the moment, however, anxiety building, watching from the niche of a nearby door, time lost its meaning. Had she been waiting for five minutes? Ten? A lifetime? She had expected to hear shouted orders or screeching slurs, but the floor was uncannily silent. She crept toward the open door of room 742.

The hotel representative clawed and hissed at her to stay and wait with him, but once he accepted she was going, he followed after her, just as curious, if not more so. As they neared the doorway, a trail of scattered belongings told a story: one of struggle and panic, of violence. She edged nearer, then froze. A hand lay splayed on the floor, its stiff fingers covered in the rust-colored flakes of dried blood. A cold weight pressed on her chest. Whatever had happened was worse than a simple fight.

The body was facedown, its skull caved in. Beside it, blood-stained and bent lay a broken Grammy award smeared with spongy bits of brain.

Chapter Twenty-Five.

Sheriff Donnelly returned from the adjoining room, holding a walkie-talkie to his face. Though his lips moved—first into the radio, then at her—Rebecca heard nothing but the high whistle of a desert wind and the thrumming of blood in her ears. She didn't feel the sheriff wrap his arm across her chest and shoulders as he swept her out of the room.

The hotel employee had vanished. In his place stood a nosy woman in a white bathrobe. Rebecca was vaguely aware of being directed into the elevator and through the lobby, but, like a balloon on a string, she drifted through the corridors, always a second or two behind.

It was not the first time Rebecca had witnessed death. She was 5 when her mother's mother died, though that memory had been scrubbed of all emotion by time. When she was 14, a boy she barely knew from school was shot by his friends with a pellet gun. She and Sydney had buried their weeping faces in their pillows, not understanding why it felt like such a loss. When she walked into the only class they shared and sat at the black Formica counter topped with a stoppered flask, she felt his absence more acutely than she had ever felt his presence.

As with everything, she got over her grandmother and the boy whose name she'd forgotten, and death as a concept moved to the edges of her perception. That was until two days ago when Caroline's corpse stared through her like she was nothing. But with Caroline, it had been stormy and dark, and—despite the horrific emptiness—the woman's face had contained a peaceful indifference, as though, when death came, her body had surrendered willingly.

In the hotel room, on the other hand, the curtains were splayed open; harsh white sunlight laid bare the entire bloody scene. James Logan's expression—when Rebecca had finally been able to differentiate it from the clumps of hair and splintered bone—was a blend of fury and terror. Rebecca comprehended with certainty that, as Ghosted's consciousness fled his detestable body through the split in his skull, it had done so unwillingly. Until the very end, a volatile awareness clinging to life, energized by a hatred of himself and the world around him.

When Ghosted discarded her in the alley to chase Marc Sheffield, Rebecca had wished to make him afraid, to see his eyes fill with the same helpless horror that she—and who knew how many others—had felt. She envisioned herself shattering his head with a brick. If she could only see him face justice, she thought, that would set things right. But the frozen fear in his broken face, the chaos of the room, filled Rebecca with sadness. It was all so pointless.

Whatever had happened to him, Ghosted earned it, she had no doubt. But that didn't bring her peace. Was Ghosted's death in that room justice? Maybe. But, if so, then achieving it had required decades of abuse. If justice could only be achieved after something terrible had occurred, what right was there in celebrating it? Didn't that mean it was nothing more than an extension of the original evil? What was it, ultimately, that made things not merely *just,* but *right?*

Was there a version of the world where James Logan—sans narcissism or sociopathy or whatever flaws separated him from others—not only created beautiful music, but made the world itself beautiful? Or was his destructive nature essential to who he was and what he created?

Life, she saw, was itself the ultimate predator. Ghosted, James Logan, despite his abhorrent actions, had been a victim of it as much as Caroline or Becky or Rebecca's mother. Seeing the man's dead body did not satisfy Rebecca because it was a vivid reminder that what was wrong with the world could not be fixed by something as simple as a brutal bash to a bad man's head.

On-duty officers arrived quickly, allowing Sheriff Donnelly to personally guide Rebecca back downstairs to his vehicle, where he tried briefly to comfort her with platitudes before realizing that she needed to process her feelings before any explanations or rationalizations could motivate her toward recovery. "There are people who can talk to you about this. What you're feeling." He pulled out his notepad and scribbled. "These first two volunteer with the department; they specialize in trauma. This last one," he tore out the paper and slid it into her folded hands, "is someone I've spoken to when...things were tough."

Rebecca glanced at the names, immediately forgetting them. Sheriff Donnelly was right. She was going to need to discuss whatever it was she was going through: the tangle of physical sensations, emotional reactions and mental explanations that defined her current state. But it wouldn't be the people on the sheriff's paper. She appreciated the gesture, but it would be Sydney, or another friend or family member—someone she knew and knew cared for her. If they weren't enough, she'd call Becky's doctor, Bridgette Lane. She had shown compassion after Caroline's death, bringing comfort. And she had offered to continue the conversation if things got bad.

"I shouldn't have let you go up with me," he said. "I know better." Then he reached over her into his glove compartment. "I wanted to give you this." He pulled out a small black metal canister with a button on top and a small, pointed spout. "I should have given it sooner, but—" He squeezed the container, turning his knuckles white. "This OC spray is not what you get at a pharmacy; it's police grade. You understand? You need to be careful. Don't take it out unless you plan to use it. But I want you to be able to protect yourself." Rebecca accepted the gift, letting it sit in her palm as she looked at it. She gripped it reflexively when another sheriff tapped on the glass.

Sheriff Donnelly exited the vehicle, closing his door so she couldn't hear. The new sheriff, who looked to be in his sixties, thumbed his mustache and gestured at Rebecca. Sheriff Donnelly pulled their conversation to the curb, farther away from her. The new sheriff stuck his thumbs in his belt, glancing on occasion at Rebecca. He looked almost bored by their discussion. They approached the car from the passenger side. He invited her out, introducing the older officer as "Sheriff Walter Hines, he has a couple of questions for you."

Sheriff Hines tipped his head at her and said, "Ma'am. I understand you had previous interactions with the body upstairs?" She nodded, and he mirrored her. "Including what you would describe as assault and battery this past evening?"

"I." She shook her head. He had called it a joke, but she didn't know what the legal term was for what he had done. "He attacked me."

Sheriff Hines' mouth twitched, and he bobbed his head. "Of course, forgive me. Why don't you just tell me what you experienced last night." She told him, distracted at times by Sheriff Donnelly's fidgeting; she wasn't sure whether his discomfort came from hearing the story again or from watching her be interrogated. When she finished, Sheriff Hines turned to Donnelly and asked, "This is what she reported to you before the two of you found him?"

Sheriff Donnelly tried to disguise his distaste at the question and said, "That's what she told me, yes."

Hines nodded and asked Rebecca, "And that was the last time you saw Mr. Logan before seeing him in the room?"

"You don't have to answer that." Patrick Donnelly interjected, eliciting raised eyebrows and another mouth twitch from Sheriff

Hines. Donnelly tried to recover, "She's been through too much. She needs time to process it." He turned to her and said, "Write it down. Maybe talk it over with a friend." He was clearly trying to protect her, but from what, exactly?

Oh, she realized, *I'm a suspect.* And why shouldn't she be? She had been one of the last people to see him alive, and she had reason to want him to suffer. Not only that: she had been in the vicinity before and after the murder. She had assumed the killer was Marc Sheffield, but Ghosted had probably made enemies of scores, if not hundreds of people, over the course of his career. Besides that, he had been attacked from behind. Under no reasonable circumstances would he have allowed Marc into the room, or exposed his back to him.

"He's right," Sheriff Hines confirmed, "anything you say, if you've done anything wrong, can and will be used as evidence of your guilt in court. If you have any reason to fear that scenario, it is in your best interest to consult an attorney before speaking to us. I'm sure Sheriff Donnelly here can recommend any number of them." Sheriff Hines concluded, effectively saying the quiet part out loud, and casting Sheriff Donnelly a chastening glare. "We have no reason to believe that you have done anything wrong, of course. We simply appreciate any help you can give us in bringing whoever murdered a man to justice."

"I don't know." She shook her head. "All I can say is that the Grammy in there is probably B*Sweet's, that it came from her house, and that it was last seen some time on Thursday."

Sheriff Hines nodded his head. "You don't have any plans out of town, do you? Nothing that might make you inaccessible if we have future questions?"

"I was supposed to be going out of the country, but this," she made a circle with her hand meant to encompass everything she'd experienced since taking the job. "This delayed that. I was hoping I could still make the trip, but other than that, I don't have anything coming up."

"I want to strongly advise you to delay those trip plans indefinitely, okay? Well, thank you, ma'am." He again tipped his head at her. "Oh, and, uh, Sheriff, do you think I might have a word with you?"

Sheriff Donnelly stiffened, avoiding eye contact. "I'll talk to you later," he told Rebecca. "You'll be okay?" Rebecca gripped the pepper spray he'd gifted her and nodded. Both sheriffs returned to the hotel, leaving her alone in the street.

Rebecca headed back toward her car. She had come downtown to do research, but with all that had happened, the thought of doing anything except submerging herself completely in the bath was impossible. She probably should have listened to KL and dropped the job altogether. That would have been the smart thing to do. Part of her still wanted to head into the office, try to find Becky's second house—if it even existed. Becky might need her help. But there were so many rooms in the office, so many places for people to hide. Being alone in there wasn't an option. She needed to go home, and that's what she was going to do. Whether she would be inclined to help after resting was for later-Rebecca to decide. She pulled out her keys and unlocked her car.

"Hey, RB." Erin opened the door of a rose-gold Toyota and exited it. She approached Rebecca and hugged her sister tightly.

Chapter Twenty-Six.

Rebecca fully left her body during their embrace. She hadn't seen Erin since going home at Christmas, even though she had visited Sydney several times since then, and Erin was only one town over. The last time she'd spent appreciable time with her sister had been the year before that, when they'd gone to Las Vegas to celebrate Erin's engagement. What started as a trip with Erin's closest friends—plus Rebecca—had, by the end of the week, dwindled to just the two of them as the others left for work or family obligations. By the final day, the sisters had fallen into familiar patterns of annoying each other and being annoyed.

As far back as Rebecca could remember, Erin had been the sister with strong opinions. She wanted things a particular way, the right way, and woe to those who disagreed. Whenever she was eventually proven wrong, Rebecca's sister simply adopted the new stance, ignoring that she had once believed differently. The military had smoothed out those edges in public, but with family, they came back with a vengeance.

Their largest disagreement came the penultimate night, and it revolved around their plan to see Harry Ivans, a stand-up both sisters had enjoyed for years. Erin had decided it would be better to—instead of seeing the show she had suggested—go to the Bellagio and watch the Cirque du Soleil because that show was being replaced with something new in a week.

Erin had arranged the comedy show because of the history they and their father had with the comic, a fact Rebecca brought up at least twice. They'd never seen him live, but Ivans's Comedy Central special had played about three times a week for what seemed like a six-month period during her senior year at high school. She couldn't count how many times she'd come into the living room to find their father, a dumb smile glued to his red cheeks, watching the show, nor how many times the three of them had sat on the sofa, watching it together and laughing at each joke all over again.

Erin characterized Rebecca's desire to stick with the original plan as a rejection of her as a person. It was her engagement party that brought them there, so Rebecca was being disrespectful by arguing, and she was trying to "guilt trip" her sister by bringing up their father. Erin magnanimously forgave Rebecca for her selfishness, explaining that it was better to see a show that would be ending forever than to watch a resident comedian retell jokes they already knew.

Rebecca ended up enjoying the show more than she'd expected, but that enjoyment was lessened by her sister's weaponization of guilt. She also didn't understand how Erin didn't see that because they were unlikely to see either show later—seeing as they both lived in Northern California—which show ended first was irrelevant. From far enough away, little differences like that didn't matter. It was like arguing about the probability of seeing a T-Rex versus a Neanderthal; though one had vanished millions of years before the other, neither was coming back.

"Sydney called me," Erin said as they separated, looping her arm into Rebecca's. She pulled her sister away from the parking lot. "I'm pretty sure she fell asleep before she told me everything, but she said you were attacked, so I came. I brought a bat." She revealed the scuffed bat.

"I was attacked, but...he's dead," Rebecca said stoically.

"Good for you," Erin replied. Rebecca couldn't tell whether Erin's expression was meant to be mock-cheerfulness or mock-pride. Erin hugged her, holding her tight. "I'm sorry that you went through that." They continued walking, going nowhere in particular. "I haven't eaten. Are you hungry? You should probably get something in you; it'll make you feel better, don't you think?"

Rebecca hadn't eaten, but she wasn't hungry. The emptiness in her stomach felt appropriate. But it wasn't worth arguing with Erin. She followed her sister into a diner, letting her order for them both.

"In the space of a week, you've seen more dead bodies than I did during my four years of service."

"I'm sorry," Rebecca replied.

"For what?" Erin was smiling, recognizing her sister's habit. "You didn't do it."

"I know. I don't know. I'm surprised to see you. Not upset, just surprised."

Erin nodded. "I didn't mean to get in the way of your work. Like I said, Sydney called, and I left before she'd finished telling me what had happened. I know you don't need me here, but if it had happened to me, I'd want you to come comfort me, and I like to think you would do that." Rebecca wasn't sure she would have. If Erin didn't say to come, Rebecca would assume she wanted to be alone. "I love you. I want you to be okay." Erin shoved a breakfast sandwich overflowing with egg and bacon into her mouth.

"I want you to be good, too," Rebecca responded, picking at the sandwich on her own plate.

"You know, as I was driving up here, trying to think about what you must be going through, you know what popped into my head?" Rebecca shook her head lamely. "You remember when we spent the week at your friend Danni's house? When dad went out of town for his conference?"

Rebecca never had any friends called Danni, as far as she remembered. She suggested: "Dana? The one whose dog disappeared while we were there?"

"Yeah, that's her," Erin said. "That's what initially brought it to mind. Do you remember?"

Rebecca nodded. She didn't remember much of the sleepover beyond the dog. She'd seen the dog's collar in the trash, then found its dog tags on Dana's parents' dresser when she'd needed to use their en suite bathroom. She'd realized then that the dog had probably died, and that Dana's parents had stretched the truth when they said it was missing. She never said anything to Dana, even after the girl showed her true colors later that year, and their friendship ended.

She also remembered her father's trip. It had not taken an entire week; maybe Erin was conflating two different memories. Erin continued, "I was so excited because her dad had the tapes for all three Star Wars movies—the originals, before he changed them— and I wanted to watch them back-to-back-to-back-to-back-to-back. But then, when we got there, we could only find Empire in the box, and I was disappointed because Jedi was always my favorite, and I wanted to watch all of them. I know it's only because I kept annoying you about it, but you spent the first couple of days fully searching for them. You looked in all their VHS boxes in case they accidentally mixed them up. Then you checked all the drawers and closets, and the trash. You even looked outside for a while. You finally found them under your friend's bed. And when the music started—" She sang the first few notes of the opening fanfare. "Da-da, da-da-da-da-da! It was that much sweeter."

The event was a hazy memory, something Rebecca had not really thought of for years. It was clearly less significant to her than to Erin. Regardless, Rebecca thought her sister had misremembered a couple of details. "Dad's conferences were always on the weekends," she said, "so I think we were only there for a couple of days at most. The entire search lasted a few hours, tops. Also, I don't think I looked for the tapes because you were annoying me about it; I looked for them because I could see in the way Dana looked at you when you grabbed the box set, before you even saw they were missing, that she was pleased about something, and not in a nice way. There was something about that smile. It came out a lot when we were at school, and there was a girl she didn't like who just so happened to have an embarrassing secret traveling around the class. I don't remember why we were even friends." Rebecca reflected on the girl with the long black hair and pink princess dresses, how she'd wanted so much to be liked by her. "If they were under the bed, I was an idiot for not looking there first. I think I only found them in the first place because I figured that she took them. They'd have to be somewhere she would think to hide them. She wasn't the most creative person, if I remember right."

Erin, swallowing the last of her sandwich, looked at Rebecca, who had given up playing with her food. "I don't even know why you would say that. You found them, we watched them. It doesn't matter whether Dana or Danni or whoever hid them deliberately or not; they were lost, and then they weren't. That doesn't make you stupid." She smiled absently, reminiscing on the past.

"And I think that's also why I was reminded of that." Erin continued. "Sydney told me the things you haven't bothered telling me. What you've been doing up here: you've been finding things. People. It's what you do, what you've always done. Even in your drawings, when I look closely at a picture of myself or at the high school, or at Dad's glasses on the refrigerator, I see the details that I miss when I'm just looking at the person or the place or the thing. I don't know how you do it, but you do."

"Sometimes," Rebecca said. "Sometimes I look at what I've drawn and realize it bears no resemblance to reality."

"Sometimes," Erin agreed. "But I can't make something that looks so bad look so good."

Rebecca passed her plate to Erin, who had been eyeing it. They sat there, silent except for the sound of Erin chewing. It was funny, Rebecca thought, how memories worked. Even in their shared experiences, they'd lived different lives. Not only had she not thought about the sleepover in a long time, but her primary recollection had been, first, that Dana's parents were lying to their daughter about the dog and, second, that that had been the weekend that she had realized both that Dana didn't really like her as a friend and that she didn't really want to be Dana's friend, either. Though their actual separation had taken several more months and had, ultimately, coincided with a rumor that Rebecca had stolen something or another from Dana's parents, it was that weekend that ended their friendship, as she remembered it. She never would have guessed that Erin even remembered the sleepover or search for the missing tapes, let alone valued the memory, especially because Rebecca didn't.

"What were you working on? Before the dead guy attacked you, I mean. Why were you out here?" Rebecca told Erin about the car and the damaged iPad the cops pulled from it. She had been attacked after having the "stupid" idea to check its history and iCloud contents in case they revealed the location of a second house, and with any luck, Becky herself.

"Should we go there, do you think? Check it out?" Erin asked. "It's around the corner, right?"

Rebecca shook her head. She said, "You came all this way. We should do something you want to do. Go to a movie or something." Erin rolled her eyes. Rebecca began bouncing her leg, then forced herself to stop, knowing it bothered her sister. She tried what Dr. Lane had shown her, counting the seconds as she breathed. Erin was examining her. Rebecca wondered what her sister was seeing, and how it was wrong.

Rebecca said, "Look, I just spent the last two days trying to help these people, and all I've done is make things worse. For them and for me. I—it's just not worth it."

Erin nodded slowly. "If you don't want to do it, okay, we won't do it. But if you're saying we should do what I want to do, I'd like to go to your office and help you look for B*Sweet's house. You wouldn't have spent the past couple of days doing what you're doing unless you felt it was important, and if it's important to you, it's important to me. However it turns out."

Rebecca sighed. She did want to know where Becky was and to make sure she was safe. But something inside warned her to stay away, to let it all go. She was right to be afraid, after what she'd been through. She felt around for the pepper spray, resting her hand on the solid container when she found it. But if something happened to Becky because she had been too afraid to do anything, she wouldn't be able to look at herself in the mirror without seeing a coward. Besides, Erin was with her. She was annoying sometimes, but she was a soldier.

Rebecca scooched out of the vinyl booth. "Okay, sure," she said, standing, "we can take a look."

"All right, RB!" Erin leapt to her feet and stretched. She said, "Let's find that house!"

Chapter Twenty-Seven.

"Forgive the mess," Rebecca said as they descended into the office.

"I work with sixth graders," Erin replied. "Unless your walls are covered in feces, I promise you I've seen worse. Even then, probably."

Rebecca turned on the light and led them to the obscenely heavy oak table atop which sat a brushed-silver unibody computer monitor. She leaned into the desk, trying to push it out so they could sit behind it together, but even with Erin's help, it wouldn't budge. She rolled the only chair at the table around to the other side, inviting Erin to sit. Then, she gathered the scattered papers near the monitor, stacked them at the other end, and rotated the screen 180 degrees.

"I take it all back," Erin said. She sat, then reached to a neighboring table for a chair to give Rebecca. "You should be really ashamed of the state of things."

The computer was already logged into the business account, which meant that once Rebecca found the right device, she could track its location history. The task was momentarily complicated by the discovery of a second Halcyon iPad she wasn't aware of. Since neither had a unique name, they were identified by serial numbers that meant nothing to Rebecca. The first one she checked was active and located in Santa Barbara, indicating it was likely with Charles Sprock, who must have been, at that time, socializing with someone north of L.A.

The second device—her iPad—was inactive and had, predictably, most recently been detected at Folsom Lake as of Friday night. Before that, it had spent a day in and around West Sac.

Whoever dumped the car had waited until nightfall. That made sense, but it didn't explain who had abandoned it—or *why.*

Using the iPad's history, Rebecca compared its zip code with the one detailed in the document mentioning the secret house; they matched. She zoomed in on the West Sac location and said, "This has got to be it. Becky lived in the area as a kid. If she wanted to buy a house that reminded of her life before music or fame, it's somewhere here." The iPad, and thus Caroline's car, had been parked on or around a small street called Manzanita Way. Rebecca trembled with excitement.

Moving to a computer at another table, Rebecca plugged in the Zosia USB drive. Finding the series of pictures of Becky and Marc at the suspected second house, she compared those to the street view of the neighborhood where the iPad had spent its final day.

Whoa, is this their house?" Erin asked from the main desk.

"What are you doing?" Rebecca asked. Her sister was browsing the listing photos from the cloud.

"I just figured I'd enjoy your pictures while you were looking for whatever. I might find something." Erin answered, adding, "It's a literal castle, isn't it?"

"Mmmm, not *literally*," Rebecca replied, watching Erin scroll through the photos. "Wait, wait, wait," Rebecca said, "go back." Erin backed through the images one by one until Rebecca took control, stopping her at the picture of the empty foyer after Ghosted had run everyone off. "Look there." Rebecca zoomed in on the gilded shelf.

"Oh," Erin said, not immediately grasping the significance. Then, after Rebecca pointed out the discrepancy, her expression shifted; she looked even more confused. "Ohhh..."

"It was already gone. Hold on." There was only one Grammy on the shelf. Clicking back to a shot taken before Becky's arrival, she pointed at the same spot: both Grammys were present.

"Ohhhhhh," Erin said.

"Becky or Caroline would have made a big deal of taking it, I think. KL, maybe, but—" Then she remembered. "Ghosted. When he came in, he sort of had his jacket on his shoulder. But, when he left, he was cradling it..." She picked up her backpack, hugging it to her chest, "...like a baby." She looked at Erin, expecting her to be just as excited. She paced the narrow space between desks and continued: "He took it. It was the award he felt he should have received; he lost any claim to it when they sued him for abuse. He took it. Which means it was already there in his hotel room!"

Rebecca hadn't realized how worried she was that Becky, in rage, had been the one to take the Grammy. That she had been the one who attacked Ghosted. Knowing that he had it the whole time freed her of that worry, for the moment.

"So, what does that mean?" Erin asked.

Rebecca shook her head, slowly deflating. "Only that it could have been anyone who killed him, and not necessarily someone from the house."

Erin advanced past the pictures Rebecca recognized to those taken during the night's blackout. There was a picture of Becky, hands on her legs, back arched in a classic B*Sweet pose, followed by one of Rebecca, holding a full wine glass, looking much less coordinated as she attempted the same position. "Okay; work it," Erin said in a sort of sing-song voice, scrolling through more images of the two women modeling. Rebecca took over, skipping past pictures showing her drinking or otherwise atypically enjoying herself. There were pictures of the studio—already a mess—and even of the Zosia USB drive plugged into the box by the desk; there were pictures of pill bottles and paraphernalia and there were pictures of Rebecca snoozing near the pool. But the final image was a video.

"It's gone Dad." Words flowed from Becky in a torrent. The camera was fixed on pixelated black. "I deleted every copy of every song, and I threw away the master record where no one will ever find it." A sudden bright blue-white swept across the trees, and Becky temporarily tilted the camera to the driveway. Caroline's red Tesla had returned. Its headlamps went black. Becky continued: "You wanted to trap me into working with that *animal.* And so, this is what you get: nothing. I will not allow *him* to profit off of my pain. And I will not let *you* make light of me or my trauma. It doesn't make me unstable because I don't—"

"Becky, Becky," Caroline stepped into view. In response to the interruption, the video image swept down past the grass, settling on an upside-down vertical frame of the pool house, which showed Blackout-Rebecca as she noticed Caroline and took interest in the interaction. She stood from the concrete, head rising to the bottom of the frame, and watched. "Look, I have something you need to hear. After our quarrel, I called your doctor; she's coming. Our book, your story, it's important. You *need* to talk to her. To listen what she has to say."

"I'm not. I don't need to talk to anyone. I know what I'm doing, and I mean to be doing it! He destroyed my—" The video vibrated with Becky's anger.

"No, no, just listen, you need to talk to her. It's important," Caroline insisted.

Becky's hold on the image shook. "I can't, I'm seeing him tonight. You don't know what he did, but—I was going to tell you, but you were gone. I don't know when I'll be back." The frame lifted and spun, showing the grass. The floating video triggered Rebecca's motion sensitivity. She forced herself to focus on the edges of the screen hoping to lessen her disorientation.

"I gave her my GPS because I'm leaving." The camera shifted again, and Becky's voice said: "I'm sorry. Don't be mad. You mean too much to me." After a pause, she asked: "Can I take your car? Hers is ghetto."

"Okay, whatever, sure." Caroline acquiesced. Keys jangled as they were handed, then pulled away. "You know what, never mind. I'm done. Take your *new best friend's* car. I'm gone, okay? Out. We'll see how long you survive without me. I'll grab my things and—"

"No, wait; I did it. I got the title. The house is yours I swear, okay? I have the paperwork." Caroline scrutinized Becky.

From the safety of her office, Rebecca knew that Becky was telling the truth. She had seen the documents. What did Caroline know? How many times had Becky made promises that she hadn't kept. Caroline asked, "You did it? How?"

"It doesn't matter but I swear I'll sign it over when I'm back tomorrow. Monday at the latest, and I'll talk to my doctor about whatever you want," Becky pleaded.

"Tomorrow," Caroline insisted. "We sign with a notary tomorrow."

"I.... Okay. Tomorrow. Sunday at the latest."

Caroline hesitated, then nodded, handing over her key fob. Then she traveled across the wall of grass toward the pool house. Becky's face filled the frame. "What was I saying? Oh yeah: you're going to be SORRY for thinking that was a good idea." In the background, Caroline was wrestling with Blackout-Rebecca, speaking unintelligibly. Becky turned, pointing the camera at the altercation.

Erin looked at her sister, visibly impressed at the physical altercation. Rebecca paused the playback, rewinding it several frames. "What?" Erin asked.

From her fanny pack, Rebecca procured the vomit-stained pictures Chris White had given her. She unrolled them on the table. The first one, though cropped, rotated and sharpened, matched the frame on the screen exactly. She arrowed ahead, finding the remaining shots. Astonished, Rebecca said, "He told me someone left these for him. I knew there was something wrong with them, but he made them. Printed them out to scare me."

"Because?"

"He wanted me to do something." Rebecca continued playing the video. It showed Becky rushing to stop the argument. "Stop, guys; stop."

In the video, Blackout-Rebecca was on the ground. Slurring, she protested, "Carrerline took the freship bracet you gave me so they think I'm you if you're gone."

"I told her she could take it," Becky said.

"Oh." Blackout-Rebecca passed out. She couldn't handle listening to herself on a good day. Seeing herself humiliated like that in front of Becky and Caroline—and her sister—was physically painful.

Becky asked, "How do I send this? Rebecca?"

"She's passed out," Caroline's voice offered. Recorded Rebecca, sprawled in the grass, had begun to snore. "Let me look at it." The iPad was handed off, and the video ended.

"That's it?" Erin asked. There was no additional media associated with the device.

"This is a lot," Rebecca said, still reeling from seeing herself intoxicated. But it wasn't only that: "Chris must have received this tape. There's no other reason for him to have those stills. That means he knew he failed to stop the house transfer."

"That's your motive right there," Erin suggested.

It sounded plausible, but something didn't fit. The timing was off. Rebecca rewatched the video, confirming there was no mention of where Becky had planned to meet 'him.' She downloaded a copy of all relevant files and emailed them to Sheriff Donnelly. Back at the computer where she had been searching for Becky's secret house, she typed the house she'd found on street view into the MLS records: its title was held by 'Miriam Zosia.' She realized: *Becky purchased the house under the name of her dead daughter.*

"This is it," Rebecca said.

Erin jumped from her chair. "I'm driving!"

Chapter Twenty-Eight.

The white two-story house was badly in need of a fresh coat of paint. Its roof, long and sloping, reminded Rebecca of an Andrew Wyeth barn: charming but a little drab. Other than that commonplace detail, nothing about the house matched the "small family home" Becky had described. At 2,500 square feet, it was larger and nicer than any home that she, Erin, or any of their friends had lived in as children—or as adults. Compared to the massive home the Sweet family now occupied, however, it *could* be described as *quaint*, she supposed. In the end, it was all relative.

Tall wooden privacy fences stretched to the sidewalk on either side, blocking the neighbors' view, though the sizable front yard was left accessible. Despite an empty driveway, the sisters parked on the street, reasoning that doing so would avoid arousing suspicion. Since there was no online record of B*Sweet sightings in the area, either the neighbors kept to themselves, or they were unusually secretive. Or no one cared anymore; but you could never be too careful.

The sisters approached the door with forced nonchalance. A few lights were on inside, but the entire property exuded an uncanny feeling of vacancy. Erin and Rebecca stepped onto the raised concrete block outside the front screen door and pressed the doorbell.

"I don't think anyone is home," Erin said and immediately bent into a squat. She gently but firmly maneuvered Rebecca off the welcome mat, which she lifted and replaced in a practiced move, like a magician pulling off a tablecloth. She then moved to several conspicuous rocks around the entryway and picked them up, shaking them.

"What are you doing?" Rebecca hissed, searching the street and neighboring houses for evidence of unseen eyes.

"I'm checking for hide-a-keys," Erin answered, feeling around the porch light.

"I know, but I mean, why?!" Rebecca tugged at her shoulder straps, shrinking into her backpack as if it could make her invisible, or at least absolve her of guilt if they got caught. "It's a dead end," she said, "they're not here. We'll find her another way. We'll find her." They'd come so far, locating the house, identifying it as a motive. They were resourceful enough to figure out another way of finding her.

Erin, not listening to her sister, trotted back toward the street. To Rebecca's horror, she reached into the mailbox and pulled out the crumpled collection of mail. Rebecca ran to intercept, and Erin willingly handed the mail to her as she grumbled, "There's nothing." Rebecca collected the grocery store circulars, cable flyers, utility bills, and what looked like a neighbor's fan letter—an unaddressed white envelope with "B*Sweet" scrawled on it and something hard inside. Compressing them into a small mass, she shoved it back into the mailbox just as her sister was hopping over the fence into the backyard.

With Erin breaking in, Rebecca's plan to call Sheriff Donnelly now seemed too risky. If he came now, what were the chances they'd be arrested? The front door opened, and Erin said, "The back door was ajar. The whole house is a disaster zone; I think someone broke in."

Yeah, Rebecca thought, *us.*

"Come on."

Upon entering, Rebecca was buffeted by the harsh smell of cigarette smoke and old sweat. "Becky?" she called, pulling her collar to cover her nose. The entryway was stuck in the 1980s: the upper half of both walls were fitted with mirrors that reflected

Rebecca and Erin infinitely. Below the mirrors was a border of brass or faux-brass trim and wood paneling. A small table on one side supported two spider plants caked in dust and a weird, possibly handmade clay vase. On the other side was a cushioned bench, and under that, a pair of toppled high heels and a single basketball sneaker. The plants and shoes appeared fresh, but Rebecca wondered how much of the decor had been installed to simulate Becky's memories of the house versus what had been there when she was a child.

In the living room, a stale and sickly-sweet smell, like hidden vomit or old sex, was added to the mix. The long, turquoise sectional sofa inside was covered in abandoned and sometimes torn articles of clothing. On the shaggy brown floor, she spotted the missing sneaker from the front room and a silver top—one Rebecca was almost certain Becky had worn that night at the pool house. A used condom hung from the fold of the couch like a kitten on a motivational poster. Rebecca gagged, overcome with disappointment in what she saw. The disorder inside didn't look like the aftermath of an invasion, it looked like what happens when you don't care—or can't care—about your surroundings. Was the state of the house Marc's fault, or was it what Becky honestly saw as normal?

In one wall was a large fist-sized hole in the drywall that left the surrounding floor coated in a fine white dust. All of which is to say, the house, while it retained enough order to appear lived in, appeared better suited for squatters than for a family. Erin picked up a turquoise plastic teasing comb from the counter, using the pointed end to sort through the scattered refuse.

"I may have something." Erin showed Rebecca a ripped corner of glossy paper with a portion of a blue circle encasing a date, time and name written in blue permanent marker:

Chapter Twenty-Eight

Katie Frost
7/29 — 12pm
Marjorie Heinz

"That's," she looked at the date on her phone. "That's tomorrow. Maybe we can look up the names in your databases at work?"

"We don't need to." Tapping the top name, Rebecca explained: "She works for a special needs school." Rebecca removed her backpack and pulled out the one sheet she'd received from the fundraiser. Rebecca turned the paper over to the side describing the three organizations. Erin snatched the paper, comparing it to the scrap piece. It was the same. The appointment details were in Becky's script. If so, the scrap proved that Becky had recently been in the house, and it showed them where she would be tomorrow, and when.

Marjorie Heinz, the supervising director of the Galaxy School, had spoken at the event. To the extent Rebecca had paid attention to her time on stage, the older woman had come off as tight and to the point. Based on Rebecca's research, she knew that Becky's trust—through Chris White's management—owned the property on which the Galaxy School was housed. How was it all connected? Was Becky exerting more control, meeting behind her father's back to discuss the property? Or did it have something to do with the fundraiser? And *who*, Rebecca wondered, *was Katie Frost?* Could she be somehow tied to Cascadia Subduction?

Erin returned the papers to her sister and continued rifling through the shelves and countertops of the connected living room and kitchen. "There must be something here that will tell us where she is," she said.

Rebecca hesitated. "We know where she'll be," she said, "that's good enough."

Erin looked at her, an unexamined statue in her hand. Slowly, she lowered it back to the shelf. "Okay," she responded, shaking her head. "I have to be back by tomorrow. We have meetings all week. I thought; no, never mind."

Rebecca could now see Erin's FOMO. She wanted to help. "We have the school's number. If they set up an appointment, as this suggests, maybe we can get in contact with her through them. You're a teacher; maybe you can say something that'll convince them."

Erin hmphed and left for the front door. When Rebecca moved to the rear of the house, she asked, "Where are you going?"

"To close the back door."

"It was open when we got here!" Erin retorted, obviously annoyed.

Rebecca didn't care. If they had gotten in, someone else could too. Maybe someone already had. The thought rattled her, and she tightened her grip on the pepper spray. She peeked out the door and looked around, worried she might see someone. The image in her head was of Ghosted, hidden in the shadows of the back neighbor's tree, sprinting at her full speed. Of course, he was dead; he couldn't be there. But *somebody* was.

Rebecca called to her sister, and together they inched toward the slumped figure. The man was large, but the way he was positioned felt familiar. Like Caroline. His hands were locked in a death grip around...something: a camera

"Who is it?" Erin asked rhetorically. She was remarkably calm.

Rebecca yelped when she saw the man's face—calm, like Caroline's—and the trail of ants swarming his dry nostrils and hollow right eye. "It's him," Rebecca retched, and Erin reached to her, patting her on the back. "Dollar Bill."

"Who?" Erin kneeled, examining the man's camera. Careful not to touch it with her fingers, she used the comb to wiggle the open compartment on the camera's side, revealing that its memory card had been removed. Once that was confirmed, she used the same comb to brush away the ants. "He doesn't deserve this," she said, knowing nothing about the man other than that he was—or had been—a man.

"A paparazzi," Rebecca said. "He was following Becky. Taking pictures."

Erin, now kicking the hungry ants into the dirt, quipped, "I guess he got a little too close."

But to what, Rebecca wondered. Moneyshot said she hadn't heard from him since Thursday night. This solved the mystery of his whereabouts, but, by doing so, it opened a whole new one. "I have to call his partner, Moneyshot, and let her know. But I have to call the sheriff first." Her heart thrummed up, lodging itself in her throat; she felt a rising panic. "I might be in trouble."

"We." Erin corrected, using the comb to tease a piece of cloth lodged behind the camera grip in Dollar Bill's hand. "We broke in together. We found him together. I'm sorry I made you do this. It's my fault, really."

"Not just that." Rebecca's head bobbed, feeling like it was full of water. "I didn't say anything because...I'm scared. They think I might have had something to do with the people who died. I found Caroline, Becky's dead friend and the man in the hotel. And now—" She turned to her sister, her eyes begging for the one thing she didn't have: certainty. "I blacked out the night Caroline died. I don't remember doing anything we saw in that video." Rebecca closed her eyes and wagged her head. "I want to say I had nothing to do with any of this, but I don't know."

Erin stared into Rebecca's eyes and grabbed her hand. She squeezed it—a little too hard. "I know." Erin spoke conclusively. "I know you; you would never do anything to hurt anyone. You can't think that way."

Though Rebecca could not share her sister's confidence, she was grateful for Erin's unwavering belief.

Erin returned to the body of Dollar Bill. Rebecca's gaze followed her to the man she'd met only once in person and spoken to briefly over the phone. Neither encounter had revealed much about him. Erin tugged at the fabric caught in the man's clenched fist—a clue perhaps.

"Stop!" Rebecca blurted as her sister worked it free; she *recognized* it. Erin, uncharacteristically, obeyed. Hanging limply from the dead man's hand was black silk, its hard-to-read red embroidery unmistakable.

Chapter Twenty-Nine.

"We need to leave it," Rebecca said, thinking the scarf looked just like the one KL had been wearing. Erin, kneeling at the body, looked up. "We need to call the sheriff. We need to tell him what's happened."

"Of course," Erin said, rising to her feet and following Rebecca as she backed away from the body. Unsteadily pulling out her phone, Rebecca dialed Patrick Donnelly. He asked her where and how she was and instructed the sisters to remain at the scene, seated in their car, doors locked. Noises on his end—rushing air and clapping footsteps, keys jingling—evinced that he was moving and with urgency. The loud 'pop' and growl of an engine meant he was in his car and on his way.

"I'm about thirty minutes away," he said. "Other officers will get there first. They'll ask you what happened—how you found the body, what you did after. Tell me now, so I know what I'm walking into." She told him, including as much detail as possible. Erin occasionally tapped Rebecca's leg, as if trying to remind her of a missed detail or encouraging a better explanation. Rebecca swatted away Erin's 'help.'

He tried to be sympathetic, Rebecca thought once she had explained how they had found the house and why she'd gone. He asked her why she hadn't called him. After all, that was why he had given her his number, "...exactly for this situation, this type of situation," he said, and then "No, don't...don't feel bad." She gripped Erin's bat, tapping it lightly against her knee. She didn't need him to tell her how idiotic she'd been; that inner voice had been saying as much since she had sat in Erin's car to search the second house. Of course, she should have called him; of course, she shouldn't have broken in. She was forever making avoidable mistakes; maybe jail time would finally convince her to stop.

Sheriff Donnelly had told her he would contact Galaxy School to check if the blue scribbles meant what they seemed to mean. She had already tried calling them, but the line was busy.

Her mind went, then, to poor Dollar Bill Hicks, and his partner. Moneyshot initially assumed Rebecca was calling about the briefcase. After hearing about Dollar Bill's fate, she responded stoically, almost as if she'd expected it. She asked where he had been found. Rebecca hesitated.

"The woods?" Moneyshot asked. When told no, she deduced, "It wouldn't be somewhere random...Manzanita Way?" Rebecca gasped and the photographer hmmed. "I take that as a yes."

"So you knew about it," Rebecca said after a moment's thought.

Erin mouthed: "Knew about what? Let me hear."

"Becky's secret house," Rebecca clarified, turning on the speakerphone. A long pause followed. Erin and Rebecca watched each other, waiting.

Instead of answering, Moneyshot asked, "Who did it, do we know?"

Erin announced, "We found a black handkerchief with large red embellishments."

"Letters," Rebecca added, wishing her sister wouldn't blurt out information. She had noticed flourishes this time she hadn't when he showed it to her earlier, but she could still find his initials.

"That son of a bitch." After a moment, almost to herself, Moneyshot said, "He wouldn't have had the photos on him."

"We think they were removed by the killer. Unless: do you know where they might be?" Rebecca suggested.

"He didn't mail them to me," Moneyshot said with a mild annoyance, and then, "Thank you." She hung up.

Rebecca and Erin looked at one another, equally unsure of what they were missing, but both convinced it was something. Gradually, the ambient city sounds morphed seamlessly into distantly approaching sirens, which became the sheriffs' vehicles and an ambulance. Rebecca saw only a single neighborhood family come out to watch the proceedings; they had returned inside by the time Sheriff Donnelly arrived.

Rebecca popped out of the car. The tension in her stomach melted, and before she could stop herself, she went in for a hug.

Sheriff Donnelly jerked back like she'd just brandished a weapon. She realized she was still holding the bat. He instead offered her his hand.

"I'm her sister." With the strength and confidence Rebecca had always envied, Erin stepped between them, taking the sheriff's hand. He glanced at Rebecca and, after the greeting was finished, he stretched and swung his hand like a pitcher on the mound. Erin had a crushing grip when she wanted to. Erin added, "I found the open door. The instant I saw it, I was concerned about the immediate safety of my sister's friend, so I convinced her that we needed to investigate." The ease with which Erin injected plausibility into her behaviors was another characteristic Rebecca sometimes wished she possessed, even as it annoyed her endlessly when her sister directed the skill at her.

He nodded. "I called the school. They confirmed the appointment. From the sound of it, they considered canceling; Becky has been trying to expedite things. They claim she stopped by the school this morning...behaving erratically."

"Did you get the number Becky was using?" Rebecca asked. Sheriff Donnelly shook his head.

"The woman who runs the place is a...stickler. She wouldn't give out that information over the phone." He watched the sisters look at one another. "Look," he said, "I know you're going to want to go down there tomorrow. Don't make the same mistakes you've been making." Rebecca's head dropped, and she nodded; she knew he was right to tell her to stay away. She shouldn't be roving around, reaching for things outside her grasp. "Let me go with you this time."

She peered at him, unsure if she'd heard him correctly. Sheriff Donnelly was looking away from her toward the house; he scrunched his face like he was holding in a fart. "Yeah," she said, "please come." He nodded and then strolled to a group of officers on the front lawn to join their discussion.

It was Erin's turn to look disappointed. "At least I helped out a little this time."

Rebecca thrust her arms around Erin. "Don't be modest. You always help. Come with us."

Erin, still embracing her sister, shook her head. Rebecca felt what might have been tears dripping on her shoulder. Erin sighed. "Can't. I work in the morning. In fact," she pulled away and looked at her phone. "I should probably be heading back now." Erin locked her car when Rebecca reached for the handle. "No, stay. Get as much as you can from him. He'll give you a ride home, I'm sure."

"I doubt it."

"Oh please," Erin smirked. "It's written all over both of your faces. You may be better than me at finding things, but I'm better at reading people." Rebecca wasn't sure she agreed with Erin about that, but she let it go.

"Oh," Erin remembered, rolling down her window. "Did you know Dad got a letter from Mom? Not recently, back when we were still kids." Rebecca's jaw hung open. "Yeah, he brought it up in a conversation, and he sailed past it like he hadn't just blown my mind. I was like, 'Whoa, slow down!'"

"What did the letter say?"

Erin thought about that for a while. She had a look like she was trying to condense the nature of life and the universe into a few choice words. "I'll text it to you. A copy of it. I'll get it from Dad when I see him." They lingered, neither willing to end the moment. Things felt different between them. Finally, Erin mouthed "Bye," and drove away.

Chapter Thirty.

Sheriff Donnelly was acting a little dazed, or lost in thought, when Rebecca asked if he would drive her to her car. He nodded mindlessly and opened a back door. Rebecca watched through the plexiglass partition as he circled the car and slid into the driver's seat. In the rearview mirror, she saw him biting the inside of his cheek as he stared at nothing in particular. She knew he was disappointed in her, but the way he was avoiding her gaze felt like something more.

Needing air, she groped for the window control. When she couldn't feel it, she looked, but there was no button. That's when she became aware of her position in the back of the cruiser. She tested the door; it was locked. A wave of unease prickled her skin. Was this protocol, or was she under arrest? And why wasn't he saying anything? He started the engine and left the neighborhood. Rebecca exhaled sharply and, in the calmest voice she could manage, said, "I know I did wrong. I thought I was helping Becky."

He looked at her, his eyes showing relief and concern by turns. He wasn't upset with her, she realized; he was conflicted. He said, "I know you did. I did, too. But...." The car made several more turns before he continued: "Three bodies; this doesn't look good for her. For any of them." More silence, then, "I received your email, by the way, with the video and the financials. I don't want to encourage more reckless behavior, but you do good work. You're wasted as a personal assistant." He looked flustered. "I'm sorry, I didn't mean; that was rude."

Rebecca shrugged. He was probably right. Putting her hand to her neck, she told him: "That scarf in Dollar Bill's hand, we think it's KL's. I've seen him wearing it." He nodded, unsurprised. "I mean, I guess," she said, trying to fill the emptiness she felt growing between them, "Someone else might have one that looks just like it, but that doesn't seem likely. Does it?" He was watching her in the rearview mirror, and Rebecca felt like a child explaining an impossible story about a giant caterpillar smoking a hookah while the adult in the room decided whether to be impressed or deeply concerned.

The sheriff's phone chimed, providing an escape from her embarrassment. He inserted a white earpiece, responding with occasional monosyllabic affirmations. He shifted in his seat, glancing nervously in the rearview mirror at Rebecca. She wanted to know what they were talking about; to distract herself, she looked out the window to the street and pieced together what she knew.

Caroline had been trying to finish the memoir for some time, but Becky was stalling. On the night of Becky's disappearance, they had argued about it. When Caroline returned, fed up and ready to leave, she urged Becky to talk to her doctor, but Becky had already planned to liaise with Marc Sheffield. Becky only barely convinced Caroline to stay by telling her about the loophole she'd found enabling her to transfer the guest house and a small piece of surrounding land to Caroline.

That information came to Chris White in the video where Becky gloated about destroying the record. Through a series of poor investments, Chris had positioned Becky to lose everything, and the three things he was banking on to save the estate—Becky's six-month residency in Vegas, the new album, and the sale of her house—had been compromised in one night.

KL had been with the family for over fifteen years; his love for Chris White bordered on devotion. Rebecca thought he might do anything for the man. It was he who had been with Rebecca when she found Caroline's body; heck, he'd even tried to discourage her from searching the grounds in the first place. And now his lucky scarf had been found in the hands of a dead photographer who had likely taken pictures of the original crime scene.

An unbearable shriek filled the air, and Rebecca could think of nothing other than how much she wanted it to stop. Hands pressed to her ears, she watched as the cars ahead of them parted, and she realized that the screech was the siren. Somehow, knowing that made the sound more bearable. "What's happening," she asked, trying to remain calm.

The car stopped with a jerk, and Sheriff Donnelly jumped out, opening the door and ushering Rebecca onto the street. "We got the confirmation: KL was recorded entering the Exchange last night. He was in disguise, but a porter identified him heading up to the seventh floor."

"You think: Ghosted?" Rebecca asked.

Sheriff Donnelly nodded. "His DNA was all over Caroline, but so was everyone's...including yours. That wasn't enough. The initial report is that Bill Hicks was drugged. I'm willing to bet he shows the same drug cocktail that killed Caroline. With KL's scarf in the dead man's hand and video evidence placing him at the hotel around James Logan's time of death..." he was back in his seat and buckling up before Rebecca realized he had dropped her off outside her office building. "We have to bring him in." He sped away, leaving Rebecca in a daze as she struggled with what had just happened.

She reached for her phone to text Erin and Sydney—then it was gone. A hand snatched it from her grip.

"*Just* keep walking," a voice murmured. Fingers pinched her triceps, steering her forward. She didn't need to turn to recognize the man as KL. "Do you have it on you?"

Rebecca stumbled, and he held her, preventing a fall. "What?" she asked, "The camera? The memory card?"

"If *that's* where it *is.*" He attempted a growl, but it sounded more like an old cat yawning.

"I assumed you took it," she said. "Is that why you killed him? Because he didn't have it on him?"

KL stumbled, catching himself on Rebecca to stop his fall. "What do you *mean*?" He asked. "I watched *you* searching the trees where she threw it away. Get in!" He pushed her at an open door into the black Escalade she'd seen at the laundromat.

Ghosted had gotten the jump on Rebecca, reducing her to a quaking mess. She wasn't going to let it happen again. She twisted out of KL's hold, ramming her shoulder into his chest. He stumbled back, cursing.

"Hey!" she shouted to anyone and everyone, "help!" She ran from the vehicle. KL seized her arm. With a strength she didn't expect, he forced her into the back seat of the black SUV and jumped in on top of her, slamming shut the door behind them. He wrapped his arms and legs around her, but Rebecca fought back, cracking into his chin with her head. He let go with a grunt, and she drove her elbow into his cheek, forcing him to scurry backward. Before she had a chance to fall on him again, KL climbed into the front seat and started the car. Rebecca reached for the door and yanked desperately on the lever...to no avail. She scrambled to the other door, but it wouldn't open either.

"Child safety lock," KL announced triumphantly. Rebecca didn't hesitate—she lunged over him, frantically pressing every button on the driver-side door. The car swerved as he wrestled her away. "It's not on the door!" he screeched, pulling the car to the side of the road.

Locked together in the car, the two caught their breath and stared. KL extended his hand slowly, treating her like an unruly dog that he was trying to tame. "I don't want to hurt you, Ms. Ziel. I only want the album you *stole*."

Rebecca didn't care; she stretched her legs and locked her knees, pinning him to the driver-side door. She was prepared to kick him in the face, repeatedly, if necessary, at any indication he was reaching for a syringe or some other weapon.

So, he wanted the Zosia drive; too bad for him, she'd left it plugged into the office computer. "Is that what you told them before you did it?" She asked. KL didn't answer. She bared her teeth at him and said, "You were seen on *camera*. They know it was you at the hotel."

KL shook his head—or did the best he could with her foot on his face. "He was dead when I got there. There was a tweaker girl in a bloody nightgown running down the hallway. I passed her on my way to his room." The young girl she'd seen in Ghosted's room flashed in Rebecca's mind.

"You're saying you didn't kill him?" she asked.

"Of *course* not!" he insisted. "Chris was a mess when they found the car. He believed his daughter was *dead*. And that James Logan had something to do with it. How would *you* feel? I went to *force* Logan to tell me what happened. And, if he *didn't*...." Rebecca couldn't imagine KL forcing anyone to do anything. "But when I got to his room, the door was open. There was blood and..." KL screwed up his face thinking about it. "He was scratching at a hole in his skull, fingering bits of brain. Moaning." His body shivered.

"Ghosted was alive?!" Rebecca was aghast.

"No." KL's face turned scornful. "I once saw a cat get hit by a car. The driver slowed down, as if they could help. They didn't even roll down their window; when they saw what they'd done, they gunned it. There were skid marks when they left."

He shook his head. "The cat sort of growled as it twisted in circles, clawing at the pavement. It was trying to escape, but all it did was leave a red spiral on the asphalt." He bit his lip, trying not to picture the body. "The cat was dead the moment that car crushed its head, though its body needed time to realize it. Ghosted was dead, too, when I found him. He just didn't know it yet."

Rebecca shook her head. "But when we got there, the door was closed and locked."

KL straightened himself in the seat, licking at the split she'd put in his lip. To Rebecca's horror, he glowed with pride. "I wiped that girl's bloody handprint off the door and shut it. That girl who killed him, I'm sure she left evidence somewhere in the room, but she's innocent of any crime as far as I'm concerned. She deserved to get as far away as possible."

Rebecca's head spun. "And the others; did they deserve it?"

KL was defiant. "I don't know what you're talking about."

"I found your scarf on the body. He pulled it off you when you killed him." KL's hand went to his heart; he stuck his fingers inside the breast pocket. Something inside of it—something dark—shifted. Rebecca added, "And your DNA was all over Caroline's body."

KL shook his head, frantic. "I moved Caroline. I moved her, *moved* her. She couldn't be on the property. It would ruin the sale. You know. But she was already dead. She *overdosed!*"

So it was about the money, Rebecca thought. "And the paparazzi? Dollar Bill Hicks?" she asked.

"I, I, I don't—" KL struggled to find his words.

"He was holding your lucky scarf," she exclaimed. KL still didn't understand. "The Italian one with the red initials no one can read. Unless you can explain how he got it—"

KL's eyes widened in a momentary recognition, then he lost all expression. "I guess...that's it, then. They know I did it." His nose whistled as he exhaled. "You say they're looking for me. Where are they?"

"At the estate." Rebecca spoke slowly, expecting trickery.

KL nodded and slowly scooted into the driver's seat. He pressed a button, snapping open all the doors' locks. He reached past Rebecca, opened her door and said, almost to himself, "I told you to leave. I wish—" His fingers tightened on the wheel.

"I wish *any*one listened to me," he finished, slamming the door and driving away.

Rebecca collected herself. The unfamiliar voice of an unknown pedestrian asked her if she needed any help. She shook her head and walked back to her car. Her phone had flown out of KL's hand during their altercation and landed face down on the asphalt. Hard. The screen was too shattered to effectively text without glass splinters piercing her thumbs. She carefully called the sheriff.

"He was just here. He tried to pull me into his car. KL. I think he's headed to the estate."

"I'm on my way."

Saying it out loud, saying it to someone who listened and took action, it was a relief somehow. Things weren't fixed, but they felt better. "I think, will you stay with me tonight?" she asked, "Or can I stay with you? I just, I don't want to be alone."

***

When Sheriff Donnelly arrived, he informed her that KL was in custody. He had turned himself in, though he refused to say anything until he spoke to an attorney. Rebecca nodded wordlessly, trying to keep hold of even one of the myriad emotions circling around her like a tornado. They left her car in the lot, and he drove her home.

By the time she opened her door, letting the sheriff step inside first to check for intruders, she was exhausted. She collapsed onto the couch. "Take the bed," she mumbled. "I'll be fine here."

She barely registered movement until warm arms lifted her into the air. Her eyes flew open, panic seizing her chest. The world had dropped away and she was falling. She clawed at him like a cat dropped in water trying to climb up a person. But that didn't affect him. He held her firmly, carrying her to the room.

When she saw it was him, she relaxed again. Her breath released all at once and her head rested on his shoulder. "It's okay," she mumbled, half–asleep. "You can hold me. I won't be mad." Then, sleep took her, soft and absolute.

Chapter Thirty-One. Monday.

She awoke to the smell of coffee and a slightly burned cinnamon muffin. Sheriff Donnelly was seated on her sofa, arms crossed, his chin buried in his chest. His soft snoring stuttered.

"I'm just resting my eyes." He stood up and stretched. Walking into the kitchen, he poured her a cup of coffee and handed it to her. She accepted with a nod, looking up into his eyes; they were red and puffy, glistening from a sleepless night. "How are you feeling?" he asked.

"Thank you for staying," she said. "I don't think I could have slept. I know it's...there's no reason to feel—"

"Nope." He touched her hand. "We're not going to do this. You are right to feel everything you are. I didn't go through what you did and even I feel everything is...off." Rebecca nodded and sipped the coffee. Though no longer hot, it tasted lovely. "What did he say to you? KL, when he...went for you?"

She told him that KL wanted the album and what he'd admitted to doing: moving Caroline's body and leaving Ghosted to die.

"And Bill Hicks?" he asked.

"He didn't deny it. But," Rebecca shook her head. "He looked, you know, confused when I mentioned it."

Sheriff Donnelly chewed on his lip, his expression tight with concern. Something didn't make sense; he'd gotten something wrong. Or maybe she was projecting. Either way, it was a feeling Rebecca knew well. She reached for his forearm and tapped it, saying, "You'll figure this out. Whoever did what." He nodded, and the two prepared to depart.

A silent solemnity blanketed Rebecca and the sheriff as they drove away from the city. There was an unnatural rigidness in their posture, like they were refugees at a border crossing, and a single misstep might ruin everything.

For Rebecca, the prospect of finding Becky was as appealing as it was terrifying. She'd dedicated the past several days to finding her, and she didn't know what she'd find. When they met again, would she still be Becky, the friend, or would she be back to B*Sweet, the pop diva? If she had misinterpreted niceness as something more substantial, would the time she'd spent, and the scars she'd earned, be worth that temporary feeling that she, Rebecca, had been friends with a celebrity?

"There was a time," Rebecca said. "A long time ago, when Becky—uh, B*Sweet—was all I listened to. On MTV, it seemed like her videos played every other song. I sang them in my head even when I was at school, or trying to sleep." She rubbed the window, looking out at the passing hills. "It felt like there was truth in them, something I was too young to understand. So, I kept singing, like I was immersing myself in a foreign language; I imagined that the scales of childhood would fall from my eyes, and I would, at last..." Rebecca, arms crossed, slapped her elbow for emphasis, "...understand what it meant to be a woman."

Silence returned to the car. Sheriff Donnelly eventually suggested, "I think we all have those people as kids."

"Sure," she continued, "but if I, *today*-me, could meet *kid*-me, I'd seem ancient to the kid-me. I'd think, 'She's a grown-up. She knows everything I don't.' Except, if anything, I feel like I had a clearer picture of the world back then."

Rebecca clicked her tongue. "I thought I was above all that fangirl stuff, but after meeting Becky in person, I might be more of a fan now than I was then. The difference is, I know she's not perfect. She needs *a lot* of therapy, but I like her *because* she's not perfect.

She's human, and I feel more connected to her now, as a *person*, than I ever did when she was...a voice I heard in music videos. Does that make sense?"

"Of course. She's very personable. And charismatic." Rebecca felt in the sheriff's reply a hint of his earlier words about Becky's gravitational pull.

"But I feel like I'm a bad fan. I've listened to her music more in the past week than I have in years. It's catchy still, but simplistic. And some of the songs make me cringe. The lyrics I relate to now are from the songs that don't get stuck in my head; they almost dare me to remember the melodies. I don't know if that says more about them or me." She took a few breaths, then turned to Sheriff Donnelly and asked: "How can I call myself a fan if I feel that way?"

"I think..." he paused, clearly considering her words. "You're putting too much into the idea of being a fan. Or a friend, for that matter. There's no such thing as a 'bad' fan. Even a bad friend is just someone who's grown in a different direction. When you notice that happening, the growing apart, you have to let it go. For both your sakes."

Rebecca was annoyed with herself. She couldn't articulate what she meant. "You've been in love, right?" Sheriff Donnelly mm-hmmed. "There's that feeling, especially early on, when you want to just blast your love at them, like a fire hose. It's not—you're not doing it because you want to; you can't help it. It's all-consuming. But, for me at least, eventually I can't focus so intently on that single person. Life comes in and says, 'there's this thing I need you to do, and this and this and this....' And it just gets lost."

On the eastbound side of I-80, a pair of crumpled Sprinter vans had stopped traffic. Sheriff Donnelly slowed the car; whether his interest was professional or if it was the same morbid curiosity as the other drivers, Rebecca wasn't sure. Once they passed, she continued: "I think that's what I mean when I say, 'I feel like a bad fan.' I care about Becky more as a person than I ever did about B*Sweet. I want her to be happy and healthy and whole. But I don't have that same all-consuming desire inside of me that I had as a kid. I don't know that I can offer anything of substance to help her be those things."

"That doesn't sound like a bad thing," Sheriff Donnelly replied, "it sounds like a healthy thing. Look...what you're describing, I've felt it. I even felt it for Becky, once upon a time. But the truth of it is, while you're projecting that love outward, what you're really experiencing is, ultimately, the passion you're directing at yourself. 'I like the way this person makes me feel...about *me*." He let her think about that before adding, "I like that I feel like I can finally be more than I thought was possible.' It's a drug. But like all drugs, we acquire a tolerance to its effects. That we're able to maintain our love for others despite the cycle of highs and withdrawals, that's what makes it profound."

Rebecca nodded. He was right, but he still wasn't grasping her. Probably because, until that moment, she wasn't sure what she was trying to say. Since finding the secret house, Rebecca had been wondering who Becky really was. Superficially, the home had been designed to look like a typical 1980s residence. The kind you'd see on TV and wonder if it ever existed. But Becky had treated the inside like she was an unruly rock star and that was her hotel room. Perhaps Marc's reappearance had been a relapse. Before his return, maybe the floors were swept, and you could sit on the sofa without catching an STI. But, if it was a relapse, it wasn't her first.

Suppose the family plot from which the Sweet sisters had sprouted was as diseased as it appeared to be. Was it reasonable to expect that Becky did not carry some of that poison inside her? If those who loved her accepted her as she was, letting her do what came naturally to her, would that acceptance eventually heal her, or would it merely enable her to continue her maladaptive behaviors? Were those the only two options?

"You're right," Rebecca said. "That's kind of what I think I mean. I was talking about being the one in love, but it's really when you're on the receiving end, the one who's loved. When it disappears, it hurts so much you just want to end everything. You *pray* for oblivion. And that's when it's one person. Now imagine you have millions of people, all across the world, pointing their love directly at you. When *that* stops, when you wake up and it's gone, what kind of abyss does it leave behind? That's what she had, I think. And I am one of the people who, for a brief time, blasted my love straight at her, and now," she shrugged, "I don't."

"I don't know," he said after several minutes of quiet reflection. He looked at Rebecca, his cheeks red and said, "I don't think I've ever talked to anyone like you."

Rebecca might have blushed, but she wasn't paying attention to Sheriff Donnelly's words. She was thinking about Becky. Could anyone ever really recover from being adored so much by so many?

***

Fairfield, California sat halfway between the state capital and the bayside metropolises of San Francisco and Oakland. Average in size, as far as cities go, it was surrounded by the aesthetically pleasant rolling hills that define much of Northern California. When winter ended, the hills washed over with vivid green curves; by early autumn, they erupted in a cascade of fiercely golden grasses. Despite an increasing population, for anyone visiting from the surrounding cities, Fairfield felt small, almost rural. The Galaxy School was on the southern edge of town, not quite at the marshlands, but in a flatter and more humid part of town.

Marjorie Heinz, a primly dressed woman with round spectacles and a white pixie haircut, offered them a curt handshake upon their arrival. Sheriff Donnelly showed her a picture of Becky on his phone, and the supervisor confirmed that Becky had come by earlier in the day to visit with one of the kids.

"She was relentless," Ms. Heinz complained. "Fifty calls, I swear. I tell her Monday, and she agrees. Then it's, 'What about Sunday? No, Saturday. Actually, I want to do it today.' That was on Friday. I had to tell her, 'Sorry, ma'am, but our rules for new guests don't allow weekend visits.' I had to block her number. So then, guess what? Then she calls from a completely different number. I was tempted to cancel it all. One of the girls urged me not to. Said she's famous. What does that matter?" The woman scoffed. "I had to tell her, 'I don't care if it's the *governor*, rules are rules.'"

"I'm sorry to interrupt," Sheriff Donnelly said. Rebecca smirked: he wasn't sorry, and she knew it. "On that note, you said I couldn't get those phone numbers without showing you my credentials in person." He pulled out his badge and laid it on the table for her to examine. "I'd appreciate you presenting those now."

The older woman spent several minutes reading the badge and comparing the picture with the man's face. She returned it to him and said, "Yes, well, I have to find them. They're out right now with Katie."

"Who's Katie?" the sheriff asked as Ms. Heinz searched recent callers, noting them on a yellow sticky note. "Did Becky explain why she was so interested in Katie specifically?"

Marjorie shook her head. "Nothing specific, no, but she asked for the girl by name and case number. It was a little unusual. Katie is a gorgeous little girl, one of the few children who's been with us since birth. She was born with microcephaly—her brain was too big for her little head. Her mother died during childbirth. She was an addict." She clicked her tongue. "Such a waste. Katie is a little slow, but not so bad that she couldn't have had a normal life if she'd been raised in a healthy family. We probably would have sent her to a foster home once that was apparent, if it wasn't for the donations."

"Donations?" The sheriff stuck the yellow note into his notepad and scribbled her answers on the opposite page.

"Oh yes, we get all sorts. Usually, it's from churches or rich men on their deathbeds looking to improve their image. Occasionally, the donations are allotted for certain children." She leaned in, "You know, parents who feel guilty later on. They feel bad about giving them up but are too ashamed to take them back." She squished her face like a skunk had just entered the room.

"So, you believe Katie's...parents donated to keep her with you?" the sheriff asked. Marjorie Heinz shook her head. "Then who, exactly?"

"Oh, it was anonymous. Usually is. But I suspect I met them. Large man. Huge, like a brick wall come to life. He came by a few times with his son—I thought it was his daughter at first, pretty as he was. I'd say the young man was the father, but he doesn't look anything like her, so, if anything, Katie's mother was probably the son's sister. All I know is he looked into adopting her. They got pretty far into it, but something happened, and they haven't come back for a couple of years."

"But the donations continued?" the sheriff asked.

She waved her hand impatiently. "Oh, we couldn't have kept her if they didn't. Like I said, I *suspect*. But I'm never usually wrong about those things."

Sheriff Donnelly found a picture of Chris White and KL. Marjorie Heinz squinted, examining it. "Yes, that's them." She removed her readers and her mouth approximated a smirk. Looking from the sheriff to Rebecca, she asked, "Can you imagine being that big?"

Sheriff Donnelly pressed his lips together. "I surely can't. Do you mind directing us to Katie and her visitor?"

Chapter Thirty-Two.

Becky Sweet was alive. She was more than alive: in her rainbow-colored flat-brimmed cap and massive red sunglasses, she was radiant. Squatting beneath a tree to remain at eye level with the blonde child facing her, Becky beamed. Rebecca touched her own cheeks as if feeling the strain.

Marc was nowhere to be seen, but Becky and the girl were in a small park near the school, accompanied by a short, round woman clutching a CD case. When Becky noticed the pair's arrival, she directed the young girl to turn and say hello. The pretty child was equally as expressive as Becky, and the two skipped over to welcome the newcomers. Becky pulled them in for quick, one-armed hugs—first, "Patrick, hi!" then, "Rebecca!" She introduced the familiar-looking child as, "This is my daughter."

Sheriff Donnelly bent down to shake the girl's delicate hand. "Hi, I'm Patrick. You have a lovely smile." He looked up at Becky and back. "What's your name?"

The girl struck a pose and said, "Katie," utterly confident. Donnelly chuckled as he straightened up.

Rebecca suddenly understood why Katie looked familiar—she had seen her before. Among Chris White's secret photos, hidden in a cabinet on his boat, were a couple that included this girl. She looked at least two or three years older than in the photos, but it was definitely her.

Your daughter?" Sheriff Donnelly's voice lifted incredulously.

Becky sat on the grass, nestling the girl between her legs. "Have you ever seen anything so precious?" Katie vogued, and

Becky clapped. Rebecca joined them on the ground, watching the girl, infected by her easy happiness.

Sheriff Donnelly remained upright, biting his lip. "She's definitely got your gregariousness. Still, can you clarify what you mean? You're adopting her?"

Becky shook her head vigorously, determination carved on her face. "She's mine—the daughter they stole from me. My own blood." She wouldn't give Katie up—no matter what.

"Huh." Sheriff Donnelly grunted. Rebecca knew what he must be thinking. When Becky last insisted her daughter was alive, it had resulted in forced hospitalization and, eventually, the conservatorship. She had been given no proof, but fueled by a cocktail of drugs, mental illness and Marc Sheffield, she'd driven for hours to learn the supposed daughter was another man's son. Rebecca and the sheriff suspected Becky had been using at least two of those substances as recently as the day before. Her wide-eyed euphoria and boundless energy made it seem she might still be.

Rebecca examined the girl's face. Whatever physical difficulties she'd had at birth, she seemed to have grown out of them. The longer she looked, the more she saw a younger version of Becky. Had KL not broken her phone, she could have searched for images of a younger Becky in *Mighty Ducks 3* or *Hocus Pocus* or any number of small roles from that time. She felt certain Katie could pass for Becky's characters in any of them. The girl's smile—a smattering of empty spaces between baby and full-grown teeth—reflected the shape of the older woman's, and they shared the same contour around their cheeks and eyes.

"What makes you say that?" Sheriff Donnelly asked her. Becky didn't answer.

"How?" Rebecca asked.

Becky's smile widened as she lifted her sunglasses, revealing bright eyes and dilated pupils. "I don't know. A miracle." She wiped away her tears and kissed the girl's head. "We thought she was dead. We all did, but the doctors must have revived her at the hospital. Because I wasn't there, I guess, they...I don't know." Becky pulled back down her sunglasses and wrapped her arms around her daughter. A rivulet of water ran down her chin, spilling onto the young girl's head. Becky kissed the spot.

"How did you find out about her?" Sheriff Donnelly asked, finally kneeling to meet her eye level.

"I don't know. It was Marc, he figured it out; said it was someone he had on the case. There was proof this time. He'd never given up hope. I didn't, but—" Becky's voice wavered.

Marc had fueled Becky's past delusions about her daughter being alive. Sheriff Donnelly winced at the man's mention. "What proof?" he asked.

"Does it matter?" Becky asked, fussing with the hem of Katie's shirt, refusing to look the sheriff in the eyes. "I can tell just by looking at her, she's perfect. You're perfect, aren't you?" She cooed into the girl's ear.

"Where's Marc now?" Sheriff Donnelly asked.

"Oh, you know. He wanted to give us space, so he went to grab some food. He's somewhere." She kept stroking the girl's hair, her fingers lingering near her ears.

"We're going to have a picnic!" Katie's exclamation sang with perfect pitch and endless joy. She raised her arms, jubilant.

"That's right! As soon as he gets back. And if he takes too long, we'll get something ourselves!"

Sheriff Donnelly stood, stretched his legs, and shifted his questioning to the chaperone, who had maintained a respectful distance. "Did he tell you where he was going?"

Valerie shook her head. "He said he was leaving to eat. This is the first I'm hearing of a picnic."

Sheriff Donnelly nodded, looking first at Rebecca, then at the Galaxy School chaperone. "Can I speak to you over here?" He pulled out his pen and notebook and led the woman away.

Rebecca's gaze went from Katie to Becky, and she realized the latter had been watching her watch them. Becky croaked, "She's more beautiful than you could ever imagine, right?" Rebecca nodded.

"I'm sorry for leaving you there," Becky said. "I'm sorry for what happened with Caroline. That you had to deal with that. I was; I sometimes; I just, I get swept away when Marc comes around. He knows how to get me going." Becky wiped away more tears concealed behind the sunglasses. "I know he's not the best influence. But I'm weak. Sometimes. Not anymore." She leaned close to Rebecca, her low whisper thick with saliva. "It's over between us; it has to be. For her: for Katie. I can't be that same person. I have to be better. I won't be the reason she hurts inside, or hurts herself."

In the sting of her sinuses, Rebecca felt the foreshadowing of tears. "You won't be," she said, worried that her promise was a lie: if Becky remained in Katie's life, there would be pain. But there would be joy, too. She hoped there would be infinitely more of the latter.

"What's wrong?" Katie's innocent question bypassed Rebecca's defenses, and tears spilled down her face as she joined Becky in a mostly silent sob.

"Nothing," Becky smiled and kissed her daughter's head. "We're talking about someone Mommy used to know. She's gone, and we miss her, that's all."

"It's okay," the child assured the two crying women.

"Yeah, it is," Becky agreed.

Rebecca reached into her fanny pack and pulled out the USB drive with the album. "I found this outside. Dropped by a magpie, if you can believe it. I know you wanted the music destroyed, but it looked like there was so much more on it, and I couldn't bear to get rid of it."

Becky weighed it in her hands. To herself, she quoted, "'I found, outside, a magpie's nest, a glittering, beautiful sight.' And I thought it best to burn the nest, for want of greater light."

"What?"

"Nothing," was Becky's answer. "Thank you. I said and did any number of selfish things." She hugged the child and said, "But it's different now."

Rebecca nodded, hopeful, but not entirely convinced.

"That feels so long ago," Becky said, "doesn't it?" Rebecca nodded. "Our night under the stars. So much happened. Don't go too far." Katie had risen from Becky's lap and was dancing. "I was so mad about James Logan. When you told me you'd seen Marc, I just remembered that he's always been there for me. I called him. Told him about what happened. Marc didn't hesitate. He located Ghosted and kicked his ass. Texted me pictures. I couldn't turn him down after he did that for me, you know? He tried again on Saturday. I think he was jealous because all I could think about was our little girl."

The way Becky talked about Marc reminded Rebecca of the men Sydney had dated. They, too, had often been intense and exciting, though with violent streaks. And Sydney had also been convinced to ignore her own well-being for their sakes. But, if she was honest, as terrible as they had been, each of them provided Sydney what she craved at those various points in her life. With some it was affection or security, while others gave her a twisted sort of validation. Occasionally, Sydney put up with the man just to have a warm body in bed beside her.

Like Becky had done with Marc, Sydney had often returned to those men when her needs returned. Rebecca, like most girls, had fantasized about marriage and a family. She'd wanted them more than anything, once upon a time. But she had never been willing to sacrifice her safety or selfhood to achieve those dreams. Sydney—and, it seemed, Becky—were built differently. They clung to the dream of being a part of a family, even if it meant sacrificing themselves to the whims of their men.

Maybe their drive was stronger than hers, enabling them to persist through the abuse. But—Rebecca offered Becky a hug and it was accepted—she didn't think so. Were those dreams worth achieving if the only pathway to achieving them was by enduring a perpetual hell? If you regularly did yourself harm in your quest to feel you were succeeding, was that manifesting an aspiration or feeding an addiction?

Rebecca asked: "So you met with him at your childhood home?"

Becky seemed surprised. "You found out about that, huh." She plucked at the grass. "It was only a matter of time. Eventually, we all leave childhood behind. At least," she pointed at Katie, who was rolling around on the grass. "It was worth it."

"How did you find her?" Rebecca asked.

"I don't know. Like I said, Marc found her." Becky stared at the sky, breathing through the pinhole of her pursed lips. "He can be a miracle worker, sometimes. In business; in the bedroom. We were...doing what we do when we get together, and he kept getting texts. I asked him who it was," laughter tinkled from her. "I like to tease him about his other women, sometimes. It annoys him. He checked his phone, but that seemed to annoy him even more. I asked who it was, but he wouldn't let me see. He said Caroline had been found dead. OD'd. I didn't believe him at first."

She stood, and Rebecca followed. Together, they circled a nearby tree. "Then he went into a frenzy, saying we needed to dump the car because it tied me to her. He was going crazy. He checked ten, fifteen times that the car's tracking had been disabled. I tried to calm him down, but nothing worked. I think it was during one of those times he found out because he came back all quiet. He told me about Katie, and we made the appointment. Then he drove me down. It all happened so quickly. He came back up to dump the car that night. I was so happy when he came back, I tried to make Katie a sister."

Rebecca turned away, disgusted despite her desire to care for this woman. She thought aloud, "So he was at the house after the photographer had been there." *Was Marc involved in what happened,* she wondered, *or had he not seen the dead body in his backyard?* She and Erin had almost missed it, couldn't he have?

"What?" Becky chuckled, "What are you talking about?"

Rebecca told her about Dollar Bill and KL's scarf. She mentioned Ghosted's death in the hotel and KL's connection to Caroline.

"No. Nuh-uh," Becky replied immediately. "KL has all the boldness of a mouse in daylight. Don't get me wrong, he can be fierce when you threaten someone he cares about, but it's all talk with him. I can't see him doing any of that unless his back was up against the wall. Besides," she said, rubbing her face, "he didn't know about the house. Nobody did. Oh, wait."

Becky clapped her hands, lifting her sunglasses to look Rebecca in the eyes. Hers were puffy and red. "Marc said there was a motorcycle following us. I didn't see it, so I assumed it was him being paranoid, but.... Do you think it could have been KL? No, that doesn't make sense. I called KL after I left. I told him you were passed out and asked him to help you inside. That's when Marc took my phone and wrapped it in foil to make sure we weren't being followed. But I'm sure he was asleep when I called."

Moneyshot, Rebecca thought. Moneyshot said she and Dollar Bill had followed Becky, but that he had turned back. She must have followed Becky to the secret house and given Dollar Bill the address. Then, he had used the house as a location to sell whatever pictures he'd taken. Rebecca could imagine the sketchy photographer taunting KL with the photos, using the house the family didn't know about as another burn on them.

"Can you help me with something?" Becky interrupted Rebecca's train of thought.

"I don't know. What do you need?"

Becky took Rebecca's hand and said, "Katie is my daughter. But they're not going to just give her to me. Too much time has gone by. I will need to adopt her. I need to have full custody. I can't let Marc—" she shivered. "I need to convince them that I am capable of providing a safe and loving environment. Step one is no more Marc, I know that. It's done. I've decided. But on top of that, I need professional approval. Will you stop by Dr. Lane's office and talk to her about it for me? Tell her I'll do whatever she wants, even guest star on her idiotic show." She pulled a mini blue Sharpie from her pocket, tearing off the plastic cap with her perfect teeth. "I don't know where my phone is, and I don't yet know where I'm gonna be staying; if you give me your number, I can call you tonight once I get a hotel room. I leave for Vegas this weekend, and I'd like to get this figured out before then. Please."

Sheriff Donnelly returned to them, Katie perched on his shoulder, giggling. He delivered the laughing child to her maybe mother, then hugged her, whispering something Rebecca couldn't hear. To Becky, he said, "It was great seeing you. I'm glad you're safe. We all are. We were really worried." Becky took one of his hands and massaged it. She stretched her lips to his face, but he turned his head, letting the kiss land on his cheek. From the sidewalk, Rebecca watched as Becky and the sheriff smiled at each other like the old friends they were.

Chapter Thirty-Three.

Rebecca withdrew her head from the open window once the girls were out of view. She was filled with a profound peace. The wounds from Rebecca's time with the Sweet family were fresh and still very sensitive, but seeing Becky's joy had been a soothing balm. The singer's reunion with her daughter had come after a decade of agonizing loss; witnessing it instilled Rebecca with a sense of vicarious triumph and hope. They couldn't change what had happened or the despair they had felt, but they could strengthen their relationship and, through that, begin to heal.

Sheriff Donnelly's dubious gaze snapped Rebecca back to the present. His expression soured. "She's convinced it's her kid, huh?"

Rebecca nodded. "I believe her," she said. The sheriff pressed his lips together and gave a curt nod. "Did you see her? They've got the same smile."

"Yeah...a lot of people have that smile. You have that smile." His eyes flickered with hope that she might agree, but she couldn't. "Look, I'm glad she's happy," he said. "But happiness built on lies never lasts. When the bottom drops out—and it will—there's nothing to catch you. Nothing."

Rebecca placed her hand on the sheriff's chair. "I get that you're skeptical—"

"This isn't skepticism. I know Marc. He'd steal from his own mother just to get in a picture with Angelina Jolie. Which he did, by the way."

"Okay," she said, "but I saw pictures of that girl in Chris White's boat. She was with him and KL. And you saw Ms. Heinz identify Chris. Even if it's not Becky's kid, they are connected." He veered across two lanes and made a sharp left turn. She needed to stop. Her arguments were only agitating him. It wasn't safe.

"Are you hungry? I'm hungry." The sheriff pulled into the parking lot of a Mediterranean restaurant and stopped abruptly beside a silver pickup. He asked, "Tell me what you want, I'll bring it out."

"I know that truck," Rebecca said, popping open her door. It was the truck she'd seen downtown, the one she thought was following her. But after her talk with Becky, she knew that its driver had actually been looking for Ghosted. "It's Marc Sheffield's, right?"

Sheriff Donnelly nodded. "I need to talk to him alone. You don't know what he's like."

Rebecca shook her head. "Jenna told me what happened in 2009." The sheriff looked away, and Rebecca touched his arm. When he turned back to her, he carried heavy guilt in his eyes. "Whatever you did," she said, "I trust that it was warranted. *Then.* But I'm going in with you because I need to hear what he has to say, too." After a brief pause, the sheriff nodded, and they entered together.

Marc was leaning forward, elbows braced against the counter and his chin resting in his hands like a man without a care in the world. His wide, goofy grin told the woman in the apron that she was doing much better at imitating Mariah Carey than she actually was. He applauded when she finished the song; the darkly tanned woman's cheeks flushed, and she twirled, flaring out her glossy black curls.

"That's perfect," he said. "I will have to bring her back to experience your voice firsthand. She needs background singers in Vegas. Have you ever been to Las Vegas?" The woman behind the counter shook her head. Marc took her hand and said, "We must fix that."

A noise in the kitchen cued him to release her hand and return quickly to a table filled with half-eaten appetizers.

"What'd I tell you, *huh?* An *angel*, yes?" A man with a groomed white beard strode from the back, carrying plates of lamb and shrimp.

"I didn't believe you about her singing, but—and I mean this with the utmost respect—her voice surpasses your skills in the kitchen." Marc's grin momentarily became a grimace when he noticed Rebecca and the sheriff at the glass door. "Patrick," Marc said, "and...a friend."

The cook's baritone laughter subsided, and he looked at the approaching pair. "I'll be right with you."

"That's okay," Sheriff Donnelly said, taking a chair at Marc's table, "We're associates with..."

"B*Sweet's manager." Marc sniffed. "Thank you, Yoshun."

Sheriff Donnelly thanked the restaurateur and asked for time alone with "Mr. Sheffield." The man graciously withdrew to the kitchen.

"Enjoy, it's on the house." Marc grabbed something wrapped in a leaf and shoved it into his mouth; "You have to try the mezze—"

"I'm not interested." Sheriff Donnelly shoved his chair forward with a piercing scrape. Marc flinched, then smirked. The sheriff said evenly, "You need to tell her the truth, Marc." He leaned in. "Becky can't take another disappointment of this magnitude."

Marc shot Rebecca a look that asked, "Do you believe this guy?" He said, "You know, when I told her the hospital stole her baby, everyone called her crazy for listening to me." He turned his stony stare back at the sheriff. "It feels great to be vindicated."

The sheriff sat forward, unclipping handcuffs from his belt. Holding them firmly, he smacked his hand onto the table. "You broke the restraining order. You violently confronted a murdered man, in public, mere hours before he died. If I checked your truck right now, what's the chance that I find enough heroin to get you arrested for a very long time?"

Looking at Rebecca, Marc said, "You see this: his first impulse is always to threaten me." His head twitched; the facade was falling fast. "She called me, okay? She called me. Begged me to come to her. She showed you all again and again that the restraining order was illegally obtained through procedures rigged by her Nazi father and his deep state contacts." Marc hit his palm on the table, clinking the plates. "Just because she chose me does not give you the right to plant drugs in my truck. I tried to forgive you—hooooh." He was shaking now, and he stood. Sheriff Donnelly was instantly on his feet, silent, ready to pounce.

Bracing himself with the chair he'd sat in moments before, Marc declared, "You can't arrest a man for telling the truth. Everyone here:" the three of them, and the two employees watching from the kitchen door were the only ones inside the restaurant. "You all saw him come at me, threatening to frame me and throw me in a dark cell without any consideration of my First Amendment rights."

"Marc," Sheriff Donnelly raised his hands in a conciliatory gesture. "I don't want to hurt you—"

"And now, more threats of violence," Marc shrieked.

"Marc!" Sheriff Donnelly shot Rebecca a momentary glance; '*See?*' it seemed to ask. "All I want is for you and I to go back to Becky and for you to tell her you made this all up. I don't care if she keeps the kid. But if she's going to adopt her, it can't be under false pretenses." The sheriff looked at Rebecca now, and said, "If she goes through the process of adopting that girl and finds out after the fact that she's not her daughter, it's too late. They're both doomed."

"Then it's too bad that she *is* our daughter," Marc spat back.

"No, Marc—"

"Who told you about her?" Rebecca interrupted. The men turned to look at her; the room was silent. "Your source. Was it Chris?"

Marc scoffed, "What, no. I wouldn't trust a word out of that man's mouth. I found her."

"Was it Jenna?" Rebecca asked, and Marc's arrogance faltered.

"What, no, it—"

"It was," Rebecca stood. It suddenly made sense. At the lake, when Chris was so certain Becky was dead, Jenna knew she wasn't. Because she had been in contact with Marc. Had he been who she was texting in the foyer before the family interrogation? "It was Jenna," Rebecca repeated. "And she also told you Caroline had died, didn't she? That's why you dumped the car, because you knew it would tie you to her death." She looked at the ceiling and asked, "But why tell you about Katie now?" *And what else,* Rebecca wondered, *does she know?*

Marc shook his head, "No, no. No, I figured it out. I knew it ten years ago. Okay, so she suggested where I could look, but *I* found her."

Sheriff Donnelly looked at Rebecca, confused and a little hurt. She wasn't helping him convince Marc to recant his claims to Becky. But she didn't want Marc anywhere near Becky. Even in small doses, they were toxic to one another. With her eyes, Rebecca tried to tell the sheriff that he needed to stop insisting he knew what happened and listen to what Marc was saying.

"Tell him." Rebecca assured Marc, "Tell him what happened, and we'll leave. You won't see her again, but you won't see him again, either."

"Rebecca, stop." Sheriff Donnelly placed his hand on her wrist, his grip tight. She didn't budge, but she didn't fight. She waited.

Marc examined his interrogators with a flicker of amusement. He scoffed, then sat down, inviting them to do likewise. "She texted me," he admitted, spinning one of the plates on the table. "She asked if I was with her sister. I told her to screw herself, but she didn't stop. She said Beck's friend overdosed, and like, so what? She was a barnacle on Becky. Sucking her dry. It was only a matter of time before she overdid it." He paused, smirking as the sheriff tilted his stiff neck and shifted in his seat.

"She said this time they might accuse Beck of being involved," he continued. "Because of the car, it looked like she was involved. I can get rid of a car, no problem. I told her. I'd already disabled its tracking because we didn't want anyone knowing where we were. But Jenna said it wasn't enough; we needed to get out of town. I told her to:" he flipped both middle fingers at the sheriff. "We were safe and sound, and I knew it." Marc gave the sheriff a Kubrick stare. He grinned. "It was when she told me about Chris White spending time with a kid our daughter's age that I grew interested. I asked her for information, and she gave me the name and the case number, so I looked into it. I looked into it. On my own. And there was something there." He raised his head in triumph. "Turns out it was our daughter."

"Becky mentioned you have proof?" Rebecca asked.

Marc straightened in the chair. "Yeah, well, I haven't gotten it yet. She said there were blood tests, but we haven't seen them. We will," he asserted.

Rebecca and the sheriff quietly exchanged glances. He asked Marc, "Then how can you know she's yours?"

Marc smiled amiably. "Because I'm not an idiot. Chris White was paying for her. He doesn't care about anyone but himself, so why would he spend time with her if she wasn't something he could use for control? That girl was delivered to the hospital the morning after our daughter supposedly died."

"Katie's mother died," Sheriff Donnelly countered.

"Please," Marc scoffed. "You of all people know about falsifying evidence. Faking a death certificate is almost as easy as faking a death. For all I know, you're the one who did it." He looked at Rebecca as though he'd discovered some obscure truth, and she was supposed to be impressed. All she could offer was a consoling smile.

Sheriff Donnelly stood, clipping the handcuffs back onto his belt. "Okay. I don't believe—but okay." He looked at Rebecca and then at Marc. "You will not be seeing Becky again."

"Of course not," Marc said unconvincingly.

As Rebecca and the sheriff pushed open the glass door, jingling the attached bells, Marc said to the pretty woman behind the counter, "You're going to love Vegas. I'll show you all the best places." Sheriff Donnelly almost turned back to tackle him, but Rebecca caught his wrist and looked him in the eyes. They walked together into the burning air outside.

Once they were back on the road, Sheriff Donnelly said, "Thank you. For going in with me. I'm not who I was when I...in '09. I wouldn't have hit him, but I wouldn't have been able to get the information from him without you." He shook his head: "But I still don't trust him. It doesn't make sense that Katie is their daughter— their daughter is dead. I'm sure of that. Marc...he uses people. He will do whatever he can, say whatever he can to take whatever he can from her." His nose whistled. "If it was Becky's sister who told him about the girl, it's because she wanted the two of them out of town, and she knew a girl of that age who had connections to Chris would be irresistible to Marc and his...delusions." He clenched his fists around the steering wheel. "And believe me when I say I will talk to her about this."

"Good," Rebecca replied peaceably. "Look, you don't have to believe it, but will you look into the death certificates: Katie's mother and Becky's daughter. Look into the mother. Prove him wrong. I don't want my friend believing something that isn't true."

"Okay," Sheriff Donnelly agreed, sighing. "I'll do it first thing in the morning."

Chapter Thirty-Four. Tuesday.

Rebecca awoke dreading what lay ahead. Becky had asked her to talk to Dr. Lane, but that meant getting through that insufferable receptionist. Just the thought of that made her want to pull the blanket over her head and sleep another four hours. One of these days, she'd need to learn to say 'no.'

In that regard, the confrontation with KL was almost a blessing—her shattered phone meant she had to get the screen replaced, buying her a couple of hours before she had to deal with Dr. Lane's office. By the time the repair was done, Sheriff Donnelly had sent three texts imploring her to "call me."

"I hate to admit it," he began immediately, "but you may be right." He sent her two images. "The first one is—"

"One sec, one sec." Another call was coming in. It was the Hornet Bookstore, probably about Lucy P's tablet. She let it go to voicemail. "I'm back."

"The first document is Miriam Zosia White's death certificate. That second one is from the Galaxy School Records; it shows both Katie *Frost's* birth certificate and her mother *Laura Frost's* death cert. The first thing you'll notice is that all three were issued from the same hospital, the second—"

"The signatures," Rebecca finished, "they were signed by the same doctor."

"Same doctor, same date. The handwriting is difficult to read, no surprise there. Eltan or Ellen or maybe Elroy Batridge. I haven't been able to find the doctor yet."

"So, they're fake?"

"It is...increasingly likely," he admitted.

"Well, that's good news, isn't it? For Becky, I mean." The moment she said it, she realized the irony. The good news was that someone had faked her child's death and lied about it for years. And that her own father was almost certainly involved. Yeah, *great* news.

"If..." He hesitated, reluctant to accept the facts. "I've got a call with the hospital in about an hour. Oh," he exclaimed. "Tell no one, okay?"

Rebecca waited for him to continue. She realized he was waiting for her to confirm she wouldn't share. "Yeah, no, I won't."

"Not even your family. We still don't know where the earlier leak came from, but your friend did post about your involvement online."

That felt a little like a low blow—but also true. "Okay," she promised.

"Toxicology for Bill Hicks says he died of the same mix of drugs as Caroline. And the same manner of injection." He let her munch on that, then said, "Yeah. There's little doubt about it: they were killed by the same person. And there's a maid at the hotel who may have seen something; I've got a call with her...crap, now. I have to go."

Sheriff Donnelly hung up, and Rebecca listened to the Hornet Bookstore voicemail. The man to whom she'd previously spoken (Craig, he called himself in the message) had gotten a hold of "Lucy Povich," who was eager to have her tablet back. Then, he provided Lucy's address. Rebecca checked it on the map; the bookstore would take her a little off course, but it was basically between where she was and Dr. Lane's office. Hoping to bypass the secretary, she dialed the doctor's personal number. It went to voicemail.

"Hey, you probably don't remember me, but we met at Becky Sweet's house the day that...Caroline.... Anyway, I'm calling because, um, we found her. Becky. She believes she found her daughter and she needs you to help her adopt. I agreed to stop by and talk to you while she figures things out. I'm Rebecca, by the way. Sorr—I should have said that first." The second tone, indicating she was out of time, sounded before she finished the last bit, but Rebecca let it be and headed in the direction of Lucy Povich.

Being back around the university after so many years away incited forgotten feelings of insecurity that Rebecca thought she had overcome. Despite moving to Sacramento for school, she had never graduated. In each student she passed, all of whom looked too young to be in college, she saw visions of who she might have been had she stayed.

Lucy Povich lived with a group of other students off campus in a brick, two-story Colonial Revival home. Rebecca was disoriented right off the bat when she recognized the housemate who opened the door as another of Dr. Lane's patients from the event. He looked her up and down with a sense of familiarity. He pointed at her waist. "I like the bag," he said, circling to show her his rhinestone-encrusted fanny pack. "Loose!" the young man called, barely turning his head, and a soft voice answered from upstairs. "All right," he said, abandoning Rebecca to the open door.

Inside, an eclectic collection of landline phones had been repurposed as kitschy wall-mounted coat hooks. Only one of them actually wore a coat; the rest were either empty or carried purses and backpacks. Beneath the phone-coat hooks was a table covered with unclaimed boxes, junk mail, keys, a white envelope with hand-written phone numbers, and multiple half-empty Starbucks cups. As she waited for Lucy, Rebecca read the names and numbers scattered across the table. One of the phone numbers looked familiar, but the young woman she'd come to see was downstairs before she could identify whose number it was.

"Hi," Rebecca waved.

Lucy approached Rebecca slowly. She pointed at her. "You were? Hmm." The young woman picked at her ear. "I saw you at the Comedy Spot, right? No, that's not it. Where do I—oh, you were at the thing last week! At the mansion." Rebecca nodded, opening her mouth to speak, and was immediately interrupted. "Why are you here?" Rebecca slid off her backpack and removed the missing D-Note, and Lucy's eyes grew three sizes. She snatched her device from Rebecca's hand and said, "Oh my god, thank you! I was looking everywhere for that. Oh, yeah; you're the lady who helped me look for it at the table, I remember you now. I should have remembered the hair." She planted her hand on her waist. "That gig was crazy! It was so last minute, I had to improvise everything. Well, thanks."

"What do you mean?" Rebecca asked, placing her hand on the doorjamb. "You had to improvise what?"

"Oh. My character. She was a—" Lucy turned on her device and read from her notes, "recovering sex addict whose air fryer was an abusive childhood. Oh, right, her *mother* was the abuser. Wild; I forgot the most interesting part!"

"Her *air fryer*?" Rebecca asked.

Lucy laughed. "You know, like in a divorce. They fight over who gets the air fryer, but they don't really care about *that.* It's like: the air fryer represents what they really want. *Inside.* It's their *underlining* motivations."

Lucy turned the device so Rebecca could read it. She presented her with a page littered with handwritten notes titled: 'Kelli Parsons.' "I had borderline, and mild bipolar: I'm all over the map. My name was Kelli, but I couldn't remember her last name, so I called her Kelli Preston, like the mom in Sky High."

"You're not one of Dr. Lane's patients," Rebecca stated.

"Who?" She referred to her notes. "Oh, yeah, of course. Dr. Bridgette Lane was my psychologist. 'She helped me to get where I am today. Not healed, but in the process. Heal-*ing*. Yeah, she's great.'" She looked up from the notes with a childish grin.

Rebecca was speechless. Being seated at a table full of model lookalikes had seemed unusual, but she accepted it as a rich people thing. Beautiful people need therapy, too. Taking a moment to collect herself, she said, "You're an actor. And the guy who just opened the door: he was there, is he an actor, too?"

Lucy nodded. "Yeah, he is. We all were, us at the table. Oh, and the guy that jumped on stage."

"He was *fake?!*" Rebecca asked. Had *anyone* at the fundraiser been who they said they were?

"I wouldn't say 'fake,'" Lucy corrected, "I mean, he wasn't literally *crazy*, but Jerrod *is* method, and that was disproved, like, decades ago, so he is a little:" Lucy tilted her head and made a face.

"Why would they want him to do that?"

Lucy shrugged. "We were given a little tour of the grounds when we arrived, and a chance to rehearse with each other. Jerrod was going to be with us at the table, but they pulled him out last minute and changed his backstory." She fanned herself with the tablet. "I think they added the attack for the drama. Did you see how everyone reacted? I've waited at a bunch of events like that, and they're usually snoozefests."

Rebecca asked, "Is he here? Jerrod...?" She dragged out his name, hoping Lucy would volunteer his last name.

"Allen. No, I think he lives in LA, doing those Netflix Hallmark movies. You know, *A Prince in Denver*. He played the prince's assistant; his...retainer. He had his own romantic subplot and, like, fifteen lines of dialogue in the final cut. Jerrod used to be with our improv group, but that was before my time. He called someone last week, I'm not sure who. Asked if we wanted the gig."

Rebecca was struggling to understand how—or if—this connected to everything else surrounding the Sweets. "Who hired you?"

Lucy shook her head, "I got paid in cash, so I don't know who the client was. The fundraiser? The guy that showed us around before it started was thin and pretty, like *real* pretty. I think he talked to you, actually; he pulled you away from the table?"

KL. So he knew they were actors. He may have even hired them. Was that why he was so adamant about removing her from that table: to prevent her from talking to the 'patients?' Did Caroline know? Was it possible she had been killed for threatening to reveal that the family was deceiving its donors?

"Well, thanks for finding this. By-ee." Lucy tilted her head and closed the door.

Before she could, Rebecca shoved her arm inside and blurted, "Wait!" Lucy stopped just before closing the door on her arm. Rebecca pointed at the table under the phone hooks. She remembered where she remembered the familiar number from. Lucy turned and stared at the mess, nonplussed. From her bag, Rebecca pulled out the crumpled envelope Dollar Bill had handed her on which he'd written his number. "Can I see that?" Lucy passed her the envelope, and Rebecca compared it to her own.

"Someone got that at the gig. A list of all the photographers that were there. That one," Lucy pointed to the circled number, "says he'll shoot a short we're workshopping."

Rebecca wasn't interested in the circled number; it was the top one, the only one written in Dollar Bill's precise hand that interested her. The number had been crossed out, likely because he had never answered—due to his being dead.

The reason it was so interesting was that she had seen that handwriting on a *third* envelope: the one she'd mistaken as fan mail shoved in with the rest of Becky's mail at the secret house. The one labeled 'B*Sweet.' Why had he put it there?

Dollar Bill had mentioned pictures on the phone. If he had gotten pictures of the fake patients, that would have been proof of the family's fraud. Certainly, someone at the fundraiser—KL, perhaps—would have been willing to pay for something like that. Would Bill have hidden the memory card with those pictures in the mailbox as a contingency, in case something went wrong? If KL paid him for the pictures, no problem. But there hadn't been any payment; there had been a murder.

"Okaay." Lucy droned, waiting for Rebecca to leave.

"Sorry," Rebecca said, returning the paper. "Good luck with the headshots." Rebecca ran to her car; she needed to get that envelope.

She was about halfway to Becky's secret house when Dr. Lane called.

"Rebecca! I just saw your message. I was on the phone with Guillermo—you've probably seen him on TV. He's an alcoholic—and a little into meth—and he's very excited about being on my show. So, I'm free for," she paused, "another hour. There's a meeting I can't miss, so if you can't make it before then—"

"I'll be there," Rebecca said, unconsciously depressing the ignition and passing the blue Honda Fit in front of her. "I've got to pick something up, but I'm on my way."

"Oh, okay, well—"

Sorry," Rebecca interrupted. She couldn't focus on driving and talking at the same time. "I can't focus on driving and talking at the same time," she explained.

"All right, well, I will see you soon." *Click.*

Rebecca was still holding the phone to her face when she turned onto Manzanita Way twelve minutes later. When she saw the police tape at the front door, she silently cursed herself for not considering that the police might have already confiscated the mail. *Well,* she thought, *if they have it, they have it. But, if they don't...*

She jumped out of the car and opened the mailbox. The mail was still there, except for the one piece she wanted. She dumped the pile onto the ground and sorted through it repeatedly, sure she must have missed it.

It was during her third search that she noticed the cigarette butt on the ground. It had a scorpion on the side. Moneyshot. What had she said, something like 'He didn't mail .' Had that been her telling Rebecca where to look? The evidence had literally been right under her nose, and Rebecca was too oblivious to realize it.

She looked at the time. Dr. Lane was leaving in forty minutes. Rebecca shoved the mail back into the box and returned to her car. She called Moneyshot, half-expecting the woman to ignore her call. It clicked after two rings, but there was no voice, only the raspy sound of a woman's breath.

"Karen?" she asked, "Moneyshot?" She waited. "It's Reb—"

"I know who this is," she replied.

I, um, I just left Becky's house. The one where Bill was." Moneyshot didn't say anything, but neither did she hang up. "The backup memory card. Bill put it in with the mail, didn't he? And you have it, don't you?"

Moneyshot said simply, "That does sound like something he would do."

"Please, you have to turn it over to the police. I believe it shows who killed the woman at Becky's house. And, most likely, whoever that was also killed your friend."

"I hear it was the slender man who clings to B*Sweet's father."

"Maybe," Rebecca said, "but the evidence is all circumstantial. Probably. If they had that card, they could prove it."

"If I had such a memory card, who's to say I didn't already format it to take new pictures? We can't be precious with our data;

if the photos aren't going to sell—or will compromise our ability to work—they're not worth keeping."

"I think you'd tell me outright if you'd done that," Rebecca hazarded. "Am I right?" There was no answer. Rebecca exhaled slowly, trying to calm herself. "What do you want for it? I might be able to convince the sheriff to pay."

"You know what I want," Moneyshot said quickly.

"The briefcase," Rebecca said, "in Jenna Sweet's room. The one with your 'property' inside. The one you asked me to get for you."

"That would be a fair trade, I reckon."

Rebecca bit her lip. Was she willing to break into Jenna's room if it meant getting the evidence of who killed Caroline? "Okay," she said. She wasn't sure if she'd go through with it—but as long as Moneyshot still had the card, there was a chance it could end up in the right hands. "Okay. I'll meet you at the estate in an hour." The call ended. That, then, it seemed, was that.

Rebecca looked at the map: it estimated twenty-five more minutes to the Aegis Clinic. She was going to make it in fifteen.

Chapter Thirty-Five.

Rebecca burst through the doors and sprinted toward the stairwell—there was no time to wait on an elevator. Despite the rush, she noted the passing clinic rooms were again brilliantly lit but absent of life. Entering the main office, she could virtually hear the man at the small desk rolling his eyes.

Wasting no time, Rebecca said, "Dr. Lane is expecting me," and walked past the receptionist, knocking on the door behind him.

"Um, no, excuse me." The man placed himself between Rebecca and the door, extending his arms like a windmill, slowly pushing her back toward the chairs. "That's not how we do things here—"

"Ah, Ms. Ziel. You're just in time." Dr. Bridgette Lane opened the door, broadcasting excited satisfaction with whatever she'd been working on. "Excuse me," she said, passing the man and shaking Rebecca's hand. "Come in, let's discuss." The receptionist's narrow eyes followed Rebecca's every step as she followed Dr. Lane deeper inside.

Dr. Lane's suite continued the Classic Revivalism of the outer office, but its dark walls and full wall bookshelves created a more claustrophobic feeling than the lobby, inspiring in Rebecca a more introspective mood. Dr. Lane shut the door and offered Rebecca a seat, then rounded her rosewood desk and hastily closed the laptop she'd left open. The hard leather cushion of Rebecca's high-backed chair didn't budge, and she shifted in the seat, trying but failing to get comfortable.

The desk behind which Dr. Lane sat was ornate and obviously well-built, featuring a matte black corded phone and brass folder niche. An elaborate frame at the front of the desk showcased a photo from an event where she posed with several well-known actors and musicians, none of whose names Rebecca could think of. A wireless mouse rested on a designer leather mouse pad, and a large computer monitor was connected by cable to a second laptop underneath the one that had just been shut. "It's a beautiful office," she said.

"Isn't it?" Dr. Lane asked. "You should see it on camera. I thought we should film here, but they say it's cheaper to do that on a soundstage. No one on a day rate wants to fly to Sacramento for a show's first season. Next year, maybe." The doctor smiled, crossing her fingers for luck. Rebecca could hear Dr. Lane's leg bobbing under the desk. "Now, before we begin," the doctor said, "I have to ask how you're feeling? Are you still struggling with the shock of finding that poor woman's body?" Rebecca shook her head. "Good. Have you had any new memories from that night?" Rebecca shook her head again.

"Great. So," Dr. Lane tapped her fingernails on the desk. "As Becky's doctor, I want to say, first and foremost, thank you for being here for her. She needs the healthy influence of people who care. So many of her previous friendships have been entirely *transactional.*" She sighed. "Now, to the hard part. I have to ask, how did she come across to you? Did she seem mentally stable?"

Rebecca wasn't sure how to answer. She wasn't trained in human psychology like Dr. Lane. Not only that, but she had agreed to talk to the doctor not because she had contemplated what was best for everyone involved but because she believed Becky that Katie was her daughter. How do you deny a mother her child? Sure, Becky was troubled, but everyone has problems; isn't the key to success pushing through despite those problems? That's what they always say, anyway.

Placing a child in Becky's care was potentially reckless, but was it any more reckless than leaving Katie in the hands of the state? Becky, at least, had the resources to ensure her daughter was cared for. "She seemed happy or, I don't know, relieved. No," Rebecca clarified, "she was *overjoyed.* She found the daughter she thought was dead."

"So, you sense she's been convinced the child is the one she lost at birth?" Dr. Lane's question hung in the air.

"I think *I'm* convinced," Rebecca said. Dr. Lane's eyes narrowed, and she pursed her lips in curious disbelief. Rebecca described the girl's resemblance to Becky and explained Chris White's suspicious activities linking him to the girl. "And the death certificates were all faked. Including the one for Becky's daughter," she finished.

The doctor looked stunned; she croaked, "Wow, that's—oh," she was interrupted by her phone. Confirming the caller's importance, she excused herself to the private washroom.

Rebecca sat there uncomfortably for what felt like minutes until the numbness growing in her butt became too much. She stood and stretched and looked around the room remaining in arm's length of the chair. On the desk was a yellow notepad with the hand-written title "Ideas:" and list of possible guests, possible themes and possible crossover events.

Her eyes moved to the computer, fixing on the 'VF' promotional sticker covering the Apple logo. "'VF': Vanity Fair," Rebecca thought out loud, repeating the name to work out why it felt so familiar. "Caroline," she whispered. Caroline had been proud of writing for them. She even had the same logo on her empty laptop case and on her keyring.

Rebecca was frozen; she watched the washroom door for signs that Dr. Lane might exit. She slowed her breath and listened: the doctor's hushed speech carried just barely through the door. Her eyes moved back to the laptop. Was it Caroline's?

That seemed so improbable, but less improbable than Dr. Lane having the same sticker on her own computer. And why did the doctor have two laptops? As far as Rebecca knew, the memoir laptop was still missing. Her chest tightened. Asking herself what she was doing, castigating herself for doing it, Rebecca, nonetheless, rounded the desk and opened the screen. The username read: 'CInvers.' It was the missing laptop.

An error text below the login informed the user: "Password incorrect; try again."

Rebecca closed the screen. She wasn't sure what to do. If she took the computer, and it had been given to Dr. Lane legitimately, she would be stealing possible evidence from a medical professional. If the laptop was there because Dr. Lane had herself stolen it, and if that meant that she'd had something to do with Caroline's death, someone needed to act. Rebecca returned to her seat and pulled out her phone to call Sheriff Donnelly. She needed to tell him about the computer, to let him decide what to do. The line was busy. She tried again. Still busy. She had to choose. Rebecca reached across the desk for the laptop. Before she could change her mind, she stuffed it into her backpack. She prayed that Dr. Lane would not immediately notice the computer was gone. She hurried to the door.

"Oh, I'm sorry about that," Dr. Lane sighed, exiting the adjoining room. Catching Rebecca reaching for the exit door, the doctor asked, "Are you well?"

"I told someone I'd meet them, and I'm late. I didn't know how long you might be, and since you have your other meeting—"

"Absolutely," Dr. Lane said, closing the distance and placing her arm on Rebecca's shoulder, touching the backpack's strap. Rebecca flinched, but the doctor didn't seem to notice. "They gave me the wrong time to meet with my brother and his lawyer. Family, right? I'll walk out with you."

"You don't need to go out of your way." Rebecca was trying hard to sound casual.

"It's no problem at all," the doctor chirped. "Robert, I will be out for the day. The pharma rep assures me that he will be here today with the new shipment of Esketamine for the clinic. I need you to stay a little late and square that away."

"Happily." The receptionist's eyes scowled as the corners of his mouth rose in a mirthless smile.

"I considered what you said, and I think you may be right about this child being good for Becky. She's ravenous for consistency. Having someone she can project her love onto may be just what she needs. This fantasy, though, about it being hers is the wrong direction. We'll need to deemphasize that—all of us. When Becky learns that it's not her child, the attachment may break like a spell, stranding the both of them in deeper despair than before. Do you need to get that?"

Rebecca's phone was ringing, and though she had silenced it, the flashing light and illuminated screen showed clearly that the caller was still calling.

"Sheriff Donnelly," the doctor said, bending her neck slightly to read the screen. "That seems pretty important."

Rebecca answered it. "Hello?"

"I just got off the phone with UC Davis Medical School; they have no record of the doctor who signed the documents. Nor of the death of Katie's mother, or Katie's birth, for that matter. As for Becky's daughter, there's no record of her death, either, though there were a few possible unnamed infants from around then who match the daughter's prognosis, all of whom survived. The certificates: they're all fake. I'm on my way to discuss the situation with Chris White. See what he knows."

"I need to talk to you about something. I can meet you there after I finish working on it."

Chapter Thirty-Five

"Sounds great; just let me know when you're on your way. Bye."

"Bye."

Dr. Lane looked at Rebecca expectantly as they exited the elevator. "It sounds like you two are getting a little close." She nudged Rebecca's shoulder with her own. "I'm happy for you. Both."

"He's at Chris White's boat, talking about Becky's daughter. I'm meeting him there right after...I do another thing."

"Huh." Dr. Lane inquired, "What's that?"

"I'm seeing an associate to discuss a property transfer," Rebecca was being deliberately vague. "I'm going straight from her to talk to the sheriff. This is me." She pointed to the dingy, silver car.

"Okay, well, I'll see you."

"Yup." Rebecca slipped into her car and started it with a swiftness that even she found suspicious. The psychiatrist waved to her as she left.

As long as she drove fast enough to the Sweet Estate, and negotiated well enough with Moneyshot for the memory card, Rebecca could still make it to Chris White's boat with the evidence before he and Sheriff Donnelly finished their discussion. There was no guarantee it would work, but she had to try.

Chapter Thirty-Six.

As Rebecca passed through the familiar tree line surrounding the Sweet Estate, it struck her how empty and sterile the grounds now appeared. The large house, denuded of its mysterious grandness after her experiences with the family, felt like a giant husk: hollow and sad. She stopped in the same spot along the driveway she had parked five days earlier. Neither Moneyshot nor her motorcycle was visible anywhere. Rebecca called, eager to get this over with.

"You have it?" Moneyshot asked brusquely.

"Not yet, I—" the line went dead.

When Rebecca called again, she heard the hint of an engine and wind. Moneyshot's voice sounded muted. "I'm close enough that when you have my package, I'll be there." Somewhere distant, Rebecca heard the loud rattle of a revving motor. She couldn't tell which direction it came from. "If you want the envelope, you will get me the box."

Before the line could be dropped again, Rebecca rushed, "Is the memory card in the envelope?" She waited for an answer, but none came. "I know what you want. You know what I want. If I get you the case—and I'm not saying I will—but if I do, it's only right that I am getting what I need."

Moneyshot remained silent, but she didn't hang up. Finally, she answered: "The envelope contains Dollar Bill's memory card. I won't promise that it has the evidence you want, but whatever photos he took, they're there."

"Okay." Rebecca figured that was about as good a chance as she was going to get. She hung up, still unsure if she was going to get the box. In her pocket, she gripped the master key Chris White had given her and walked inside.

The lights inside were off, flooding the entryway with shadow, and the darkness followed Rebecca up the stairs and through the halls to Jenna's honey-colored door. Rebecca weighed the key in her palm; it was heavy for such a small object. Was possible proof of Caroline's murder worth trespassing and theft? What if, her mind warned, there were no pictures?

But if there were, and if those pictures showed the murder and helped put the killer in prison, what then? She struck the key into the lock. She had to be willing to suffer the consequences either way, and Rebecca decided that she would accept responsibility, be it good or bad. It was better to apologize after a sincere decision made with good intentions than to wonder what would have happened had she followed her gut. She twisted the key, feeling the mechanism unlock, and opened the door.

"Hello?" Jenna, who had been lounging on a long chair, sat upright and said into her phone, "I'm sorry, Mr. Berman, can I call you back? I have a...guest. No, no, I have it under control." Rebecca watched Jenna listen and nod and tell her caller, "Thank you."

Jenna stood up; she strutted to the door with a casual menace. "What's this?" She moved Rebecca's hand from the doorknob and removed the key. "So, you've decided to snoop for him after all."

"No," Rebecca responded, steeling herself against the desire to flee. She reminded herself that she chose this. "In there," she pointed at the large, locked cabinet in the back of the room, the one in which she had seen the keys and briefcase, "is a locked case that Moneyshot Karen says is meant for her."

"And you figure, as reputable as she is, it's your duty to kindly break into my room and fetch it for her."

"Is it hers?"

"Excuse me?"

Rebecca checked the time; she needed to hurry. "Your father sent me here claiming you had Caroline's laptop. You didn't," she said before Jenna could deny it. "I know you didn't because I have it. Here, in my backpack." That got Jenna's attention. "I found it in Dr. Lane's office. She was trying to guess the password."

"So...you stole that from Becky's doctor, and now you're trying to steal from me. Next, you'll be taking our father's boat."

"Jenna," Rebecca closed her fingers for emphasis. "I don't know what you do or don't know. We found Becky. We know it was you who told her that Caroline was dead, and that Katie was her child. But none of that matters." Jenna denied nothing; Rebecca was on a roll. "The photographers you hired were here the night Caroline died. I think they took pictures of her murder. One of them arranged to exchange pictures for something valuable enough to get him killed." She suddenly wondered whether whatever was in the locked box might be valuable enough to kill for.

Rebecca swallowed hard, slowing down. "Those pictures have been found; I can get them. But only if you let me take what's in there and deliver it to Moneyshot. So," she caught her breath. "If you owe her that briefcase, let me deliver it to her and find out who killed Caroline."

Jenna didn't move. Rebecca wondered if she hadn't misunderstood everything. Her theory, since finding the laptop, had been that Dr. Lane was guilty and that her crime would be confirmed by the pictures. What if Chris had been correct about Jenna this whole time? Rebecca might be about to join Caroline and Dollar Bill and Ghosted James Logan in whatever came after life.

"If," Jenna began, "I let you deliver Moneyshot the parcel, will you leave the laptop with me?"

That surprised Rebecca. "I don't understand."

"I admit that I am curious about the memoir. It's been months since I read a draft, and I'd like to preview it before my sister publishes it. I'm sure she'd want my perspective, anyway." When Rebecca didn't answer immediately, Jenna offered: "If you're worried that I'll turn on you, claiming you stole it from me, let's record a video right now. I will acknowledge that I am giving you the case in exchange for the laptop. I'll even claim that I asked you to steal it from Bridgette's office."

"Okay," Rebecca agreed, though she was again unnerved by Jenna's ability to not only perceive her concerns, but to be ahead of them. "But only the truth," Rebecca clarified, "I did what I did, not you."

Jenna shrugged, then stretched her face and straightened her hair. She recorded herself admitting to the trade. Sending the video, she asked, "Does that work?"

Rebecca watched it and nodded.

"Good," Jenna said. "Send it to someone you trust. Someone who will use it if you end up missing or dead." She watched Rebecca for a response. "That is what you're thinking, yes?"

She emailed a copy of the video to Sydney and Erin, telling them it was "just in case." Then, hesitantly, she removed the computer from her backpack and handed it to Jenna. Jenna opened it, nodded, and opened the heavy wooden cabinet. She pulled out the locked briefcase. Where it had sat in the cabinet, she placed the laptop. Then, she locked the cabinet and handed the case to Rebecca. It was lighter than she expected and produced a soft shuffling sound as its contents shifted.

"Open it if you want. The locks are not engaged." Rebecca shook her head. She was willing to deliver it if it meant getting the evidence, but she didn't want to know what was inside. Jenna grinned, nodding, "No, of course not." Her head tilted to the side. "So, off to Patrick, I assume?"

Rebecca nodded. "He's with your father on the lake."

Jenna squinted, scrutinizing Rebecca with an intense curiosity that made her feel like she'd done something wrong.

Rebecca turned to exit and stopped. Something had been bothering her since learning about the actors at the fundraiser. Lucy had said one of the actors had been in a movie that Jenna was also in. There might not be another chance to ask: "Do you know Jerrod Allen?"

Jenna tilted her head and raised an eyebrow. "I worked with Jerrod once or twice."

"Did you recognize him on Thursday, when he jumped on stage?" Jenna pressed her lips together—Rebecca thought she saw the hint of a smile—and she shut the door. Rebecca heard the bolt locking as she pulled out her phone to text Moneyshot.

Removing her helmet, Moneyshot greeted Rebecca with a quick bow of the head. She had been waiting on her motorcycle, parked in front of the GTI. She looked from the briefcase to Rebecca's face, then reached into her jacket, pulling out the white envelope addressed to "B*Sweet" in Dollar Bill's hurried hand. In a show of faith, she offered the envelope before accepting the briefcase. They checked their respective packages.

"This does have the pictures, right? Showing the murder?"

Moneyshot tilted her head in lieu of a shrug. "I can't say I checked. Plug it into any computer and you'll know double quick." Rebecca looked back at the house; had she kept the computer, she could have checked then and there. Her shoulders slumped. "But," Moneyshot offered, "if I know Dollar Bill, he would not risk his life unless it was worth it. He may have been a son-of-a-bitch who went around my back to make a few bucks, but he was a professional when it came to doing the job."

"And you were going to just delete it?"

"No," Moneyshot answered. "It would have found its way to the police." She shrugged. Patting the briefcase, she said, "Things rarely ever travel a straight path, but they always end up where they're meant to be."

Rebecca exhaled, slowly shaking her head. It had been a long day. With the memory card in her hand, she and the sheriff would soon find out what happened to Caroline. She hoped. Jenna had the computer now, so whatever was on there was as good as lost to her. Whatever tied it to Dr. Lane, too, was out of reach. Why did the doctor have it? Rebecca wondered.

She asked, "Was it Dr. Lane? The contact Jenna was supposed to introduce you to? She knows people in Hollywood, too, right?"

Moneyshot didn't answer immediately. Instead, she shifted her head in what might have been a subtle nod, and she gave Rebecca a long, knowing look before pulling on her helmet. It was answer enough. Moneyshot flashed a gloved peace sign, then the Sweet Estate thundered with the sound of her motor. Before Rebecca had covered her ears with her hands, the photographer and her bike were gone.

Chapter Thirty-Seven.

Rebecca texted Sheriff Donnelly her ETA with the following message: "Beckys dr had carolines laptop. Got the memory card from dead photographer's camera. Could drane be involved in the deaths? Headed to you now," followed by "Dr. Lane, not drane". And she raced to the marina, hoping to catch him and Chris White up on what she'd found.

Something like an electric charge buzzed in the breezy air as Rebecca trotted across the crunchy asphalt and onto the springy wooden dock of the marina. Her skin bristled, the light hairs on her arms and neck standing at attention.

Ever since he let her go, KL's guilt had seemed less than convincing. And if he was guilty, she felt it almost certainly was on someone else's behalf. She had assumed Chris, the man KL loved, was the force behind KL's actions. But if it had been Chris, why was Caroline's laptop in the doctor's possession?

Rebecca reasoned that Dr. Lane must have something on KL. Maybe he was an addict, and she supplied him drugs in exchange for access to the family. Maybe she was the person he'd called his 'sister' in the studio when he'd given Rebecca the pills. Or maybe there was some deeper dependence. But either way, Rebecca suspected Dr. Lane was the mastermind, and—given the clear-cut case law enforcement had with KL—she anticipated pushback from the sheriff for suggesting as much.

The strength of her conviction was a new feeling; it made her nervous. Her chest fluttered with excitement as she hopped up onto the boat, oblivious to the stillness aboard. She stopped. Taped to the inside of the deck cabin window was a glossy sheet of paper inviting her inside, assuring her, "We will be back in five. Wait in the office." Hurrying past, moving with familiarity toward the room Chris had previously shown her.

Like the rest of the boat, the office was eerily empty, though the lights had been left on. She knocked out of habit, entering despite no response. The horizon shifted, and she turned, thinking—no, hoping—that it might be the men boarding. But there was no one. The waves, she guessed, were growing restless. No longer entangled so entirely in her own thoughts, Rebecca's body reminded her how much it hated the water: her stomach clenched, warning her of sickness with a sour burp. If they didn't return soon, she was going to have to wait in her car. She pulled out her phone to text Sheriff Donnelly, but the 'X' in the corner of her screen showed no cell service on the lake.

She sat in the center of Chris's chair—a mouse seated on a throne—and saw in the rubbish bin crumpled-up copies of the pictures he'd given her, along with a failed print of the 'wait in the office' message with 'ofice' misspelled. His laptop was open and already logged in. She pulled out the memory card, stabbing it into the patriarch's computer. As long as she had the time, she wanted to confirm that what she had traded for Caroline's laptop had been worth it.

Rebecca clicked through the thumbnails. She enlarged one she recognized as herself from her first day with the Sweets. Did she always look so tired? She scrolled down until the pictures were generally dark, and she glanced quickly at these. There were candid shots of her and Becky both in and out of the pool house. She hadn't realized they'd swum that night. There were pictures of Becky snorting and swallowing and smoking. These saddened Rebecca, but they weren't what she was looking for. She scrolled forward until she saw a new figure emerge in the images, arguing with Caroline. These images were darker and grainier; a flash hadn't been used. *To remain hidden?* But as the figure approached the light of the glass edifice, Rebecca saw—the killer wasn't KL on behalf of Chris or Dr. Lane, it was the doctor herself.

Dr. Bridgette Lane was on the ground, in one photo, Caroline looming over her like an indignant gargoyle. Rebecca could almost hear the two of them arguing, unsure if it was a memory— something she had heard during her incapacitation—or a fantasy her brain filled in to better understand the picture.

Unlike Rebecca in the iPad video, who had remained grounded after Caroline's aggression, the doctor rose to her feet. She was holding something in her hand; it glinted in the moonlight. Caroline, walking to her house, was oblivious to the doctor's approach until the moment before Bridgette Lane jammed the sharp, metal object into Caroline's arm. In the next photo, she had collapsed. Rebecca moved through the images faster. Horrifically, Caroline had tried to crawl away, but Dr. Lane returned to the purse she had dropped and pulled out another object. The doctor returned to Caroline and bent into her, apparently injecting her with another dose of something, then another. The pictures ended.

Rebecca heard tapping from above, like footsteps. She looked to the dock, but it was again empty. The boat tilted hard to starboard, gaining a sudden momentum as the engine roared. Rebecca stood as her stomach evacuated its contents and she fell sideways, cracking her knee against the seat of a permanently installed chair. She heard the crunch in her leg before feeling the pain.

"Stop!" Rebecca shouted wetly at the ceiling. She was in pain and covered in vomit. Where were Chris and Patrick? Why were they taking the boat out?

The boat's movement stalled, and the engine quit with a watery bluster; momentum continued to propel the craft further into the open water, slowly coming to a stop. Rebecca again heard footfalls above her and reached into her fanny pack for the pepper spray Sheriff Donnelly had gifted her, gripping its wide canister with her white-knuckled hand. Rebecca saw first the slender legs wrapped in black stockings, then the fitted suit of Dr. Bridgette Lane descending the stairs from the bridge above. She was carrying the black leather purse she'd seen in Dollar Bill's pictures. The one with the syringes.

"Oh, you've hurt yourself." Dr. Lane's face spread into the perfect approximation of compassion as she stood in the doorway. "I have something here to help you. First aid. Stay right there." She set down the bag and reached inside.

"No, I'm okay." Rebecca lifted herself to her feet using her free arm, trying to keep the canister she held in her other obscured. Her stomach bubbled, eager to spill more of its contents, but Rebecca's fear and leg pain were just about keeping the nausea at bay. She steadied herself against a wall. "Where is Sheriff Donnelly? I am supposed to meet him here with Chris White."

Dr. Lane pulled her empty hand from the bag. A mask of confusion twisted into mock recognition. "Oh, I see where you're mixed up. I mentioned at the clinic that my brother—Kyle—was in some legal trouble. Well, Chris White is my brother's boyfriend, and he has kindly loaned him the family attorneys to represent him against the state's baseless accusations. You can imagine how much that means to us. If Sheriff Donnelly planned to speak privately with Chris White, I assume they would meet there, at the jail. I was supposed to meet with them as well, as I told you. But they gave me the wrong time, so there was no reason for me to go. Once I realized that you were under the misapprehension that they were here on this boat, however, I felt obligated to come and explain your error."

KL. Kyle *Lane.* Dr. Bridgette Lane was his literal sister. The little differences she thought she'd imagined on the scarf, they weren't her faulty memory, they were actual differences, because it was *her* scarf, from the same childhood trip.

It made sense: KL cleaned up after the Sweets—a family he wished to be a part of, though they'd never accept him—why *wouldn't* he clean up after his biological sister? Maybe he dragged Caroline's body off the property to save Chris from losing money on the sale, like he said, but he took the blame for Caroline's murder to save his sister from prison.

Rebecca limped slowly along the wall, touching anything that might be wielded as a weapon, but everything heavy and edged was bolted down. "So, you would let your brother take the blame for what you did? Why?" Rebecca asked. That wasn't even the real question. "I understand why you'd kill Bill; he had evidence of you killing Caroline. But why her?"

Dr. Lane, who had yet to move from the cabin's only exit, considered Rebecca's movements curiously. "Bill? I don't believe— oh, the *paparazzo*. He was a blackmailer. Even if I still needed a proxy in LA, I couldn't trust him. I told him and his oriental girlfriend I wouldn't need their assistance. I have my own means to gain access." She opened her hands palms down and lowered them synchronously parallel to the ground. "As for Kyle, I don't control what my brother says or does. If he claims to be involved in the tragic but accidental overdose of an unscrupulous photographer and an addict journalist, well, I don't believe it, but I'm sure he has his reasons."

"I saw the pictures," Rebecca spat back. "I saw you...attack her."

"Now, Rebecca, you're clearly injured, and your anxiety is putting ideas into your head. There are no pictures. So, let's calm ourselves and sit for a talk."

Dr. Lane gave her a sympathetic look before locking the exit. She stood there, blocking the door.

"You're making me nervous," Rebecca said, doing what she could to increase her distance. Maybe if she played along, the doctor would let her go.

"The first thing we must accept, if we're going to make progress, is that we are the only ones who can control our emotions. I can't make you feel anything, okay? But, since you have these feelings about my presence, what do you believe might calm you down?"

"If you take us back to the dock, I can get off and maybe get my leg looked at. That might calm me down. If you stay the hell away from me, that would calm me down."

"That's good," Dr. Lane said, reaching back into her bag and pulling out a large syringe that would be comical under other circumstances. She wasn't going to let Rebecca leave. "You've been making progress. The old Rebecca, the one I met last week, shaking like a leaf, she would have begged forgiveness and hoped for the best. Look at you!" Dr. Lane seemed genuinely proud, "Calling out what you want, not apologizing for wanting it, and doubling down when it doesn't come. That's progress!"

Rebecca felt her way toward the corner of the room. There was no more space to put between them, unless she went into the office, but then she'd be trapped. Identifying Rebecca's predicament, the doctor moved inside, leaving the exit unguarded. If Rebecca tried to run around the doctor, as injured as she was, she could be easily tackled. If she tried to bum-rush the doctor, spraying her in the face, she would risk being injected with whatever was inside that needle.

The only viable direction was to move toward the dining table. If she was very lucky, the table would afford her a way around the doctor to the exit, but even if it didn't, it, at least, provided enough space between them that she could pepper spray the doctor's eyes without immediate retaliation. Once Dr. Lane was incapacitated, Rebecca could navigate to the door.

"What I have right here is just what you need for the pain. I don't just mean in your leg; in your *life.* It will also feel really, really good. I spoke to Rogan about it two weeks ago—or to the guy who books his show—opening your mind to what lies beyond is mandatory for a fulfilled, purposeful life." She moved slowly toward Rebecca, embodying the benevolence of a bobbing sphere of light in the darkest depths of the ocean.

"Is it because she knew you were dealing?" Rebecca inched toward the table; it was taking so long. "I know about the fake patients. Let me guess, you've been inflating your numbers to get your hands on drugs for your celebrity clients. Celebrity in air quotes. Caroline found out about that, didn't she? And she was going to expose you?"

Dr. Lane looked insulted. "Caroline was a client. And a friend. Anything she wanted to say, she could say it to my face. If there was anything illegal about our transactions, it was for the benefit of her and Becky."

"What then? I have her laptop," she lied (*half-truthed,* she assured herself). "I took it from your office. It's only a matter of time before I find the password and learn what she has on you."

"Rebecca," the doctor slowed, smiling softly, losing the facade of friendliness, "Your leg does not look good. I'm a doctor; if you don't let me look at it, I don't think you'll last long enough to figure out any passwords."

"You're a medical doctor," Rebecca realized. "You have access to medical forms—death certificates." The puzzle pieces were falling into place. "Somehow, Caroline found out it was you who took Becky's child. She was going to include it in Becky's memoir because, how can you not. And there goes your license."

"Your leg," Dr. Lane said, and Rebecca looked down.

Dr. Lane lunged at her. Rebecca could barely get away, half-jumping, half-falling behind the large dining table she had been approaching, successfully positioning it between herself and the doctor.

The pain that shot through her body when she landed confirmed that Dr. Lane hadn't been lying about the state of her leg. During the quick peek, Rebecca was mortified by the increasingly inflamed dark purplish green sac that was growing from the place her knee was supposed to be. It was the size of a cantaloupe, and it throbbed like an earthquake. And, though Dr. Lane couldn't hear it, Rebecca felt a gritty clicking in the joint and a holy hellfire whenever she tried to bend it.

She no longer had confidence that she could reach the door. Rebecca could keep circling the table, maintaining the distance between them, but eventually, she would pass out from exhaustion or pain. Her only hope was for Dr. Lane to approach the table near enough to be sprayed, but the doctor had regained her composure, and the upper hand, planting herself between the table and the only exit, inviting Rebecca to make the decisive move.

Rebecca cursed herself for allowing the woman to bait her into letting her guard down. If only she could bait the doctor. Concentrating was difficult, but she struggled, organizing in her mind everything she knew about the woman; it didn't amount to much. Dr. Lane took enormous pride in being B*Sweet's therapist. From the way she spoke, she was exceedingly proud of her celebrity contacts. Everything about her—from the names she dropped to the way her office was laid out—was designed to broadcast her success.

But it was all a pantomime. The clinic rooms were all empty. The ornate office was a thin layer of cheap decor disguising banal office walls. The clients were all fakes, and every celebrity "friend" came with a caveat. That's why she had killed Caroline, Rebecca reasoned: not because she'd lose her license, but because she'd lose the appearance of being someone important. Without the drugs, why would any of those famous "friends" stay friends?

Chris White had complained about Dr. Lane being a 'nobody from Orangevale' without his intervention, *and,* Rebecca thought, *underneath all her manufactured confidence, that's how she sees herself, too.* She warned: "Whether or not you kill me, it's over for you."

The doctor narrowed her eyes a moment, then smiled. "Oh?"

"They have your scarf, the one you got from Italy when you were a kid. Dollar Bill grabbed it when you attacked him. I told the sheriff that it was KL's scarf, but that's only because I didn't realize you were his sister. 'B' and 'K' look so similar." Dr. Lane raised the syringe. Rebecca said, "That puts you at the scene of his crime."

Dr. Lane took another step forward and grinned, showing only a trace of her bright white teeth. *Good,* Rebecca thought. The longer she could keep the doctor moving, the longer Rebecca controlled their flow around the room. "That leech stole it from me," Dr. Lane claimed, "after the fundraiser, when we met."

"But it's all circumstantial with him—unless you left something more personal there. Caroline is the big one: I found the memory card. It *shows* you injecting her." *Not quite clear as day,* she thought, *but clear enough for a conviction. I hope.* "Once those go public, and people learn *why* you killed her, you're out. *Persona non grata.*"

Dr. Lane twirled the syringe playfully. "I admire the bluff."

"Believe what you want. I saw you stab Caroline with that needle. Soon enough, everyone will look at you with the same disdain you look at yourself." Rebecca gripped the canister, willing the doctor closer.

"They won't find you." She advanced toward the table; a few more steps and Rebecca could aim the spray directly at her eyes and make a run* (**limp*) for the door. "You will, sadly, sink to the bottom of the lake. No one will know where you disappeared to. They'll assume that yet another sad, lonely woman has had enough." The doctor was no longer trying to feign friendliness. "Spineless women like yourself die long before they stop breathing. Sometimes before they even reach adulthood. We all know a few who would evaporate from this world, if only they had the courage, don't we? Becky is one; she'd have done it long ago if it wasn't for me keeping her sane." The doctor's grin widened, exposing her predatory teeth. "She told me about your mother when we spoke. Your mother, leaving you all like that. She was a courageous one. Are you ready to be courageous, too?"

Rebecca's leg was on fire. She wanted to cry. She felt the urge to vomit. But, more than any of that, she needed to make things right. To stop Dr. Lane and then step out onto the deck and shout that, no, she was not one of those people. She would not abandon those who depended on her. She was not like her mother. Rebecca tried her best to blank her face, to prevent this woman from seeing her response. But she couldn't. And that was okay. Rebecca was who she was; she felt the way she felt, she would react the way she would react, and she would say what she would say. She let herself cry a little, and the doctor inched forward.

"Maybe you're right," Rebecca said, finally. "Maybe they won't find me, and maybe I'll be forgotten. Maybe everyone I love, in ten years' time, won't even be able to remember my face or my voice or who I was. But I have seen the pictures. I know what you did to Caroline. And whatever Caroline found out about you, someone else will, too. They will learn about the deaths you faked. And how you promised treatment but sold addiction." Rebecca was risking it all, hurling facts alongside guesses. "Worse than any of that, they'll learn about how you kidnapped an infant. Stole it from her mother. And when that comes out, it's over. People can accept a lot of things, but no one likes a person who harms children. Every one of those fancy customers you cling to for validation, even those you helped with a little extra Xanax or Ketamine or who knows what else, they'll all leave you like you're broken because all you are for them is a conduit, a chute. They push a button, and you dispense whatever it is they're craving at the moment. To them, you're a vending machine."

Rebecca shook her head, more tears spilling from her eyes. She said, "The sad thing is, you're not. You're more than that. You helped me. I think, even, you helped Becky. You could have been the real deal, helping millions if you weren't so insecure."

Dr. Lane's mouth did not change expression, but her eyes lost all reason. Feral, she leaped forward like a monkey in a Tarzan serial. Rebecca waited until just the right moment and raised her arm, spraying the doctor directly in her eyes, nostrils and mouth with the burning spume. The doctor howled. Rebecca hobbled to the door as quickly as she could, wincing, crying with every step, refusing to look behind her lest that lack of focus cause her to miss a step and fall again.

She unlocked and opened the exit, and, as she passed through, a sharp pain stung her shoulder. The feral Dr. Lane—face blinded by thick blankets of slimy snot and viscous tears—depressed the plunger, but Rebecca sprayed the last of her canister onto the woman's hand and face. As the doctor shrank back, Rebecca dropped the pepper spray and pulled the partially injected needle out of her muscle. She stabbed the doctor, trying for the heart or lungs, and pressed the remainder of the clear fluid into the doctor's breast.

Outside the door, Rebecca searched frantically for something in arm's reach that she might use as a weapon. She grabbed a small fire extinguisher and limped to the steps leading to the bridge. Still blind, but determined, Dr. Lane groped her way out onto the deck, the long needle hanging from her like a harpoon. Rebecca crawled up the steps, seeing the steering wheel and controls she hoped she could use to navigate back to the shore.

Next to them, she saw, was the radio's coiled black cable. Even if she couldn't steer, which the growing darkness implied might be the case, maybe she could use the radio to call for help.

She heard the clang of metal, and she flinched, thinking it was the doctor attacking her. Instead, she realized it was the fire extinguisher. She had dropped it, and it was rolling down the stairs toward the deck where the doctor, covered in a dripping slime, swung her glistening hand like a tentacle, trying to use her sense of touch to replace her lost sense of sight. Rebecca wasn't worried. There were so many steps between them, and more were being added every second. She looked back up toward the controls, and she panicked: the stairs leading to the bridge, too, had multiplied exponentially, and she could no longer see her salvation. Rebecca tilted her head and felt herself sinking into the stairs, faintly fearing that if that continued, she might slip between the spaces of the wood, falling down into the infinite ocean below.

Chapter Thirty-Eight. ???

Rebecca could no longer see the slimy mass that had once been Dr. Bridgette Lane; the stairs had telescoped upward like a fireman's ladder, and the deck below was too distant to make out anything beyond its gooey gray floor. Rebecca attempted to lift her arm, but the fat and flesh that made it up were dripping from the arm. Not just her arm—her whole body was sloughing off of her, slurping like jelly in smacking waves as it fell onto the stairway, sliding down, down, down. Free of the heaviness of her form, Rebecca slithered upward, victorious.

The victory was short-lived. Her ascent was halted by a pulsating hand-like thing that was coiling itself around the part of her lower half that had once been her ankle. The hand thing was covered in a viscous ooze that burned, burrowing into Rebecca's pores, pulsing as it filled them. She and the sentient slime had begun to merge.

Rebecca wanted to scream, but the thick fluid that had entered her was snaking its way up her throat, and no sound could escape. Her neck was expanding, the fluid collecting inside inflating it until it throbbed with an obscene tension. She struggled to scratch at the expanding membrane, desperate to release its contents before they destroyed her. A stream of oil and saltwater and every person she'd ever known shot out from her open mouth, propelling her up, past the ladder, splashing into a layer of watercolor clouds.

Now free from her body—though still connected by delicate tendrils that affixed themselves to the formless thing she had called Rebecca, weighing her down—her non-being undulated violently, like a frenzy of fish at spawn, and the slime which had been rising drained back down her throat, past her stomach, down, down and out through the holes in her ankle. The goop hit the ladder's upper rung, splashing against each below it, breaking apart and reforming again and again as it fell. The slime made a sound like words filtered through an infinitely long tube, and she tried to respond, but language had long since ceased to be anything more than the simplest form of communication; words were the trails of the psyche, left behind like the chemical paths ants used to find a source of sustenance. She was beyond that now.

She was in the air, but she was not flying. Flight necessitated individuality. To fly was to impose on reality the burden of recognizing one's distinction from it, to assert that one possessed will enough to wrest control of swirling air pockets and to use those recursive spirals of disparate matter as a ladder into the sky. She was not flying, for there was no longer a clear separation between her and the space surrounding her. She flowed as a part of the everything that she was and was becoming.

Eternity was darkness—not as in an absence of light, but as in an absence of division—where this from that was as meaningless as sfumato on a flat Vantablack body. She flowed out of the darkness, simultaneously at the beginning and end of existence, because she was time and space and the bonding agent between them. She was existence itself. No; all of existence was she. Exhilaration in the form of being and nothingness.

Singularities hung and vibrated from the eternal darkness in spirals, harmonizing in twelve dimensions simultaneously, popping into and out of existence. She longed to join them, to move beyond the event horizon, to glow and spin and sing with creation. But she couldn't move and hadn't been able to for an eternity. She looked down, through the expanse, following a wisp of consciousness to Rebecca's hand, her hand, squeezed around the small black metal cylinder. She longed for release, flailing and fluttering, hurling herself against the closed fist, frantically focusing all energy to force the hand's release.

It was too late. The very act of focusing her self on a task was a declaration of independence. By seeking to join the infinite and evacuate the body, she had inadvertently identified herself as the Rebecca she'd left behind on the water, fastening herself to the decomposing pile of spongy meat. Sound was returning, great crashing vibrations that bellowed and hissed, distended by hubris, vying with the infinite for attention. With it came flashes of white fire, bright and hot and so, so depressing.

Sensations bored into her, relentless as a swarm of blind, ravenous creatures, following the remains of her consciousness toward the cache, the vault wherein Rebecca herself resided, bound by moonlight to the little girl lying alone in her bed, paralyzed as her mother abandoned her. And beside that one, the Rebecca who had worked three jobs while trying to finish university, only to drop out because she couldn't satisfy both her needs and the needs of her employers. There was an endless array of Rebeccas—stretching from before time began into the infinite future—each was boxed up and frozen at different moments in her existence, and each was certain that it was the only real Rebecca. Somewhere in the middle of them was the box containing the 'her' of that moment: writhing on the stairs of Chris White's boat.

Among the swiftly approaching sensations were bursts of sound that defined, to all the world, her: Rebecca Ziel. The names, the pulsing lights, the bitter taste of being folded and shoved and fitted back into the body she'd fled, it overwhelmed her. Time was returning. Her mouth was dry.

Chapter Thirty-Nine. Tuesday (the Following Week).

The room was all clouds, and Rebecca felt oh so cold inside the mist. She pulled up the blanket, clutching it to her chest, trying to banish the chill enveloping her. There was movement in the mist, an excited clucking that, as she blinked, revealed itself to be her sister Erin. Beside her was Hank, their father. He had clearly been sleeping until minutes before, and he blinked at her with swollen eyes, speaking her name with the heaviness of being newly awake.

Erin, on the other hand, was fully alert and smiling. She pointed her phone at Rebecca: it was Sydney on Facetime, in the middle of talking.

"I'd be too good," Sydney concluded.

"Huh?" Rebecca smacked her lips. "Can I have some water?" Her words whistled like a desert breeze, raspy and fleeting. It hurt to swallow, but Hank held the plastic cup at chin level, manually placing the straw in her mouth so that she could siphon up the water in uneven spurts.

"Do you really not remember what we were talking about?" Sydney asked from across the world.

"I told you she wasn't awake yet," Erin scolded.

Rebecca shook her head, "I don't know," she whispered.

"You were telling me," Sydney started, "about our boat trip through the universe. You said we were listening to B*Sweet's new album, but you had paperwork that you needed to do."

Rebecca was struggling to make sense of anything.

"You were dreaming," Erin explained. "Talking in your sleep."

"You still have a little drool," Sydney added. Using the towel already in her hand, Erin wiped Rebecca's mouth.

Rebecca nodded. She wasn't sure what was happening, and agreeing was all that her brain would allow for the moment. Still holding the plastic cup, though no longer at her mouth, Hank petted Rebecca's shoulder with his knuckle as though he was afraid to lose touch of her lest she disappear. He'd regained more awareness since standing, and there was a concern underlying his comforting expression that Rebecca hadn't noticed before. Her eyes widened. "I think I just peed in my bed."

"It's okay," Erin assured her.

"You've got one of those things that suck it all up," Sydney explained enthusiastically. "You're looking good!"

"One of those things? A catheter?!" Rebecca tried to lift herself, but her muscles were sore, and there were tubes sticking out of her from all over her body. Fear overtook her: she was hyperventilating. She didn't know where she was, or why. Her whole body vibrated with pain, but there was a deeper pulsation in her leg.

Hank, with the steadiness of a mountain stream, shushed Rebecca repeatedly, stroking her shoulder with an openness she hadn't felt from him in such a long time.

Erin rose and took Rebecca's hand. "Hey, you're safe. It's okay. We're here."

"I'm not sure," Rebecca began, "where 'here' is." She shook her head and shut her eyes, spilling a single fearful tear from each eye. "I know," she spoke slowly, looking around, "I'm in a hospital, but I don't remember coming here or why. Is there something wrong with me?" Rebecca's head threatened more tears, and her voice trembled. "Do I have Alzheimer's? Is this one of my lucid moments?"

Erin snorted; she couldn't help herself. "Yup," she said. "Surprise, you've got dementia."

"Stop that," her father chided. He looked Rebecca deeply in the eyes. "You were attacked and drugged," Hank spoke softly and earnestly. "They found you on the lake." 'On the lake,' what did that mean? "Your friend, the singer's sister, found you; you're a little sunburnt." At the mention of the boat, the scene gradually pieced itself together before her. The girl's father began to cry, "You almost died. If you had any more of that stuff in your system—" he couldn't finish. Erin set the phone on Rebecca's lap, rubbing her now free hand along her father's arm.

"Dr. Lane." In fragments, she could remember the doctor cornering her, holding a syringe that couldn't possibly have been as large as the image in her head. "Dr. Lane, what happened to her?"

"I've heard she's alive, but barely. She's here." Erin said.

"She tried to kill me. Out there." Rebecca erupted in a string of hoarse coughs, and her father brought the water back to her lips. "Thank you. She stabbed me with the needle, but," she halted. Her memory of what had happened was returning, and, along with it, a deluge of emotions tied to the event. "I took it out and stabbed her back; I injected her with...I don't know."

No one spoke. Rebecca looked around the room, from her father to her sister to the unusually quiet Sydney on the phone. Rebecca was vulnerable to each of these people, and each was vulnerable to her. They all, in their own ways, exploited that sensitivity from time to time, but they were family, and those breaches, as awful as they might sometimes be, were ultimately worth it because of the human connection that resulted from them.

Her father and sister were family by blood, but, like Sydney, they were also family by choice. At some point in her life, possibly in everybody's life, blood relation lost some of its significance. From that point on, she had elected to not merely keep them in her life, but to foster and feed her relationship with them. Sometimes she faltered, but she loved them, and she never wanted to lose that love. The arrangement carried obligation, certainly, but what was any relationship—even to one's self—except a series of obligations and acting upon them?

She thought, too, of Becky and of her family. Their vulnerabilities, and breaches of each others' vulnerabilities. What was Becky's threshold? At what point was the pain quotient of any relationship more profound than the sense of human connection it offered?

"Can you hear me?" Sydney asked from the phone. "Oh my God, I was on mute this whole time."

Sheriff Patrick Donnelly knocked softly and entered. "I thought I heard some talking," he said, reaching to Rebecca's foot, touching her toe as if to convince himself she was actually there. "We're all relieved that you are...you know." She knew. "I'm sorry to ask this of you, all of you, but I need some time alone with Rebecca."

Hank stood and walked a few steps to the door, but Erin did not move. "Erin," her father said.

"I think I'm fine where I am."

"Erin," Hank repeated.

"She's impaired. She might make claims without thinking about who she's talking to." Erin's eyes met Rebecca's. Even in her state—a growing clarity intertwined with cloudy swirls of grogginess—Rebecca understood Erin was talking about her admission of injecting Dr. Lane.

Rebecca tried as best as she could to assure Erin with her eyes that she would be careful about what she said. "It's okay," she croaked. "I want to talk to Patrick alone." Erin was a statue. Then, all at once, she shot up and walked past their father out of the room.

From the hallway, Hank sent Rebecca his familiar, sad smile. He closed the door.

Sheriff Donnelly turned his head from the door to the bed. His face brightened with a mischievous grin. "Patrick?" he said.

"Sorry. Sheriff." The sheriff opened his mouth to correct her or apologize or say whatever, but before he was able to get a word out, Rebecca added, "Dr. Lane tried to murder me."

Sheriff Donnelly looked at the window. "Yeah. We found the memory card you left in Chris's computer on the boat. We don't have why, yet, maybe we never will, the way it's looking. But, thanks to you, we know the what and the when and the how."

"It was fear, I think," Rebecca's voice eroded with each word; her throat itched. The sheriff proffered her the cup of water and straw. "Funneling drugs, faking patients. And she helped kidnap Becky's baby. What did Chris White have to say about that?"

Sheriff Donnelly shrugged. "His counsel made sure he said nothing."

"And KL?" Rebecca asked.

"KL maintained that it was him who killed Caroline and James Logan and Bill, until we found you...and his sister. He hasn't spoken to anyone but Chris since then. And he's been tight-lipped about what was said. Fortunately for KL—or unfortunately, I don't really know—all the evidence points to his innocence. Other than moving Caroline's body. His scarf was found stuffed in a seat of Chris White's SUV; it wasn't his in Bill's deathgrip." He breathed through his nose; it whistled. "There's concern he might...self-harm is what they say. He's been hospitalized. To prevent it."

"What about Dr. Lane? Has she said anything?" Rebecca coughed and the sheriff helped her with more water.

"They don't think she's going to make it. Her blood was full of the same cocktail in Caroline's and Bill's...and yours. Though, she received more than three times the dosage that you did."

"She stabbed me with the thing, but I was able to stop her because—" she remembered the pepper spray. "It was you. Your gift. If it hadn't been for that, I'd—" she felt herself tearing up. I'd be dead, she thought, like the others, if it wasn't for you. And what about the others, she wondered. Where were the people who could have protected them?

Patrick shook his head. "You wouldn't have survived if that's all it was. Besides, the..." he mimed hitting himself in the head with his fist. "...fire extinguisher did a lot of damage."

Rebecca remembered reaching for the fire extinguisher, but that was right as things got weird. Had she used it as a weapon, or did it fall and hit the doctor's head? She might never know. And there was the escape.

"What about Jenna? My family says she found me."

The sheriff nodded. "She radioed the marina and brought you back. She was so focused on keeping you alive that she didn't even know the doctor was inside the cabin."

"But how did she find me?" Rebecca asked. The question, And why did she, remained stuck in Rebecca's throat. She'd always look a gift horse in the mouth, but she rarely voiced what she found there. Why would Jenna have come?

"She says the two of you spoke before you headed to the lake. Said that you had mentioned your suspicions of the doctor and she wanted to make sure you were looked after. Does that sound right?"

He waited for Rebecca to explain; Rebecca wasn't sure she could. Jenna wasn't that selfless, to all appearances, but Rebecca had made a bargain with her; perhaps Jenna had wanted to make sure that investment was protected? She'd have to think about it.

"My deputy confirmed that she called around the same time and he told her Dr. Lane cancelled her meeting with KL. Anyway," Sheriff Donnelly continued, "she says she worried you were in danger and used their speedboat to search for you. Thankfully Chris's boat isn't any more difficult to see than he is."

That same misunderstanding about Patrick's location, and her transparency about it had been how Dr. Lane knew to go to the boat as well. Rebecca's head hurt. She wished, sometimes, that she would just keep her mouth shut. She supposed she should be grateful for being alive—and she was—but her mind was going over everything she'd done wrong, and everything she'd gotten wrong. She should have noticed the similarities in KL and his sister, in their appearance, in their speech, in all the ways they were alike. She should have asked Patrick where he was meeting Chris White instead of just assuming. She should have looked inside the case she gave Moneyshot—perhaps the trade had been the best choice at the time, to get the photographs—but if she knew what was inside, she might be able to report to Patrick and the sheriff's office what had been loosed on the world. What she had helped let loose.

It was too much. Rebecca found herself wishing that Dr. Lane was there in that room, that she had not been the killer and could help her not focus on what she had done wrong. But, then, Dr. Lane, too, had focused on the negative. Even with all her celebrity friends and all her successes, Dr. Lane was, at the end of the day, Bridgette: a woman who, like Rebecca, couldn't seem to believe in herself no matter how much evidence was laid before her. 'You're a lot like my sister,' KL had told Rebecca. Was she? Put in a desperate enough situation, would she, too, take a person's life? From the sounds of things, she had, and though attacking Bridgette Lane had been self-defense, if the doctor died, would that count?

Rebecca noticed Patrick Donnelly watching her, and his scrutiny pulled from her reverie. "What?" she asked, feeling her lips curl.

"I'm just...what's it like in there?" He tapped his head.

"Probably not as glamorous as it looks." Her grin blossomed into a full smile. He laughed. They remained quiet for a time, just to take it all in. It was so much that thinking about it made Rebecca realize how tired she was. But she was also happy to be there in the hospital with her family and this man who made her feel safe.

"I told you it was more than professional interest," Sydney's voice sounded from somewhere in the room. Sheriff Donnelly scanned the windowsill, then the cabinets before zeroing in on Erin's chair. There, face down, was the phone with Sydney's animated face still watching and listening. "Oh," she declared, seeing Patrick through the camera, "if things don't work out between you two, maybe give him my number." He laughed.

Erin, who had clearly been listening outside the door, re-entered with her arm outstretched. "There it is," she said, "I was looking for that; I needed to make a call. Thank you." She waited for him to place the phone in her hand.

Rebecca tried shaking her head and she winced. She loved Sydney. She loved Erin and her father. She was grateful they were there, but sometimes, she thought, sometimes they're all a bit much.

"I'm feeling sleepy," she said.

"That's okay, we'll be quiet," Sydney promised from the phone.

Hank, who had barely sat down, stood and said, "Actually, ladies, I'm feeling hungry. What's say we go get something to eat and let Rebecca here rest?"

"Do you think I could join you?" Patrick asked. Hank nodded.

"I'm fine." Erin attempted to stay, but her father stared at her until she grew exasperated and stood, exiting the room behind the sheriff.

"I love you," Rebecca said to her father. "Tell her I love her, too."

"She knows," he replied, "we both do. I love you." He kissed her on the forehead; he hadn't done that since she was a child— possibly not since before her mother had left. After he departed the room, Rebecca cried until she was asleep, dreaming of a time when she had both parents, a sister who looked up to her and her whole life ahead of her.

Chapter Forty. Wednesday (Another Week Later).

Rebecca hadn't expected an invitation to Caroline Invers's funeral. She hadn't seen or heard from Chris White or the Sweets since winding up in the hospital.

Dr. Lane had died there. Rebecca, before being released, tried to visit. She didn't really know what she wanted to say; maybe she wanted to forgive her—or to be forgiven. Maybe she just wanted to understand how such a strong woman could still be so weak. It didn't matter anyway: the doctor's room was guarded, and they weren't allowing anyone inside. All Rebecca could see through the door was a frail, intubated body that no longer resembled the vibrant woman that had tried to murder her. To date, no information about the cause of Dr. Lane's death—or her involvement in...anything—had been revealed to the public; though some fringe outlets had begun to speculate based on her disappearance and her brother's arrest. Though the deaths of Caroline and Dollar Bill were publicly classified as 'under investigation', Charles Sprock said he had on good authority that the doctor's role in them was being withheld out of respect to her family, and that it would be announced in a month or two— coincidentally coinciding with the memoir's release. Sheriff Donnelly had confirmed the delay, though he stopped short of admitting the timing was deliberate.

Back at the office, Charles had purchased her a wheelchair and insisted she use it while at work, but after two days of being restricted to the main building, she decided she needed to be able to move between the offices, even if very slowly.

"You're alright though, yeah?" Charles Sprock had been seated at his desk when he saw her climb to her crutches. "What about your leg?" He pointed to the brace around her knee.

"The doctors said I need to stay active, even if it hurts a little." They had prescribed oxycodone for the pain, but she didn't like the way it muddled her thoughts.

Charles nodded, acquiescing. "Maybe I should try to consolidate everything into a single office. I just need to find the right place. Hmm."

"Maybe," Rebecca said noncommittally. It would probably be better for Halcyon Realty to move everything together, but, in a way, Rebecca hoped he never would. The separate office gave her a place to escape from Charles, sometimes, and prevented his particular brand of crazy from overwhelming her. She didn't know that she'd be able to keep working for him if he was always hovering over her shoulder. Maybe she needed that, though, to move on in her life.

Rebecca had enrolled in classes to get her agent's license. They started in the fall; if he could just keep both spaces until then, she'd have a quiet place to study for the state exam between all the meetings and paperwork. "I'm going to check the mail," she said, hobbling through the office as he watched, trying to think of any solution except grabbing the mail himself.

The formal invitation—printed on a stiff, glossy paper—had been sent to the office, and only she had been mentioned by name, though Charles took it for granted that he, too, was expected to attend.

Chris White's mismanagement of Becky's Trust and his participation in what the tabloids dubbed the "Not-so-Sweet Tot Plot" came to light the day after Rebecca had been found on the boat. Several outlets promised "more information in B*Sweet's forthcoming biography." The way they all seemed to mention the book, to Rebecca, sounded suspiciously like paid advertisement. Becky's conservatorship had been put on a probationary hold, but every expert on television agreed that Chris's temporary removal would be made permanent, with many also predicting that autonomy would most likely be returned to Becky in the coming weeks.

Until then, a neutral group appointed by the state would evaluate the degree of mismanagement, as well as Becky's current state of mind. Included in that group was a new psychiatrist. Jenna also was on the team overseeing the conservatorship until its status was made official. All of which was to ensure consistency with what had come before, they claimed. Because Chris had always been the primary voice advocating to sell the Sweet estate, his ousting ended that.

"He was a liar anyway," Charles had told her. "Kept saying he was going to sign the contract, but there was always something else he wanted done. I shouldn't have sent you over there." Charles got a distant look in his eyes: "The commission would have been nice, though."

Charles had nothing critical to say about anyone at the funeral. Instead, when he spoke to Chris White, who was surrounded on one side by Jenna Sweet and on the other by Katie— in the process of being adopted—he spoke only of the fabulous things Chris had done for his family, and lamented the difficulties that Becky's father was facing, including being outed by CNN during their coverage of Ghosted's murder, when KL was still the lead suspect.

After one of the hotel's maids had come forward with new evidence, and news anchors caught wind that the murderer might actually be a drug-fueled teenage prostitute, even networks that hadn't been covering the news jumped on it. Then, a curious thing happened: a woman in Nebraska, a local singer with dreams of fame, spoke about being raped by James Logan. More voices followed, and, soon, everyone was talking about Ghosted's misdeeds. Most of the country, by that point, agreed that 'Candi,' who claimed that she had attacked him in self-defense, was a hero. No one anymore asked why, if it was self-defense, she had hit him multiple times in the back of his head, or why she had been found with his leather jacket and wallet in her possession. No one needed to: the world had decided it was a better place with him gone. But Rebecca still heard his songs on the radio.

Though Jenna—who had gone to Vegas with her sister to help her adjust to the new normal—was in town for the funeral, Becky was said to be contractually obligated to remain there. Instead of attending the funeral service in person, the family hired a company to provide a 75" television on which her emotional responses were broadcast live. Most photos of the event included, or even prioritized the TV in the frame, focusing on Becky's tragic expression as a symbol of the love Caroline had inspired through her charitable personality and undeniable talent.

Rebecca, seated between Charles and Patrick Donnelly, listened as Caroline's family and friends described a woman little like who she'd met: patient, kind and possessing a personality that lit up every room she entered. But who was Caroline, anyway? Was she the jealous woman who insulted Rebecca every chance in order to keep Becky to herself? The energetic addict who partied with Becky at all hours of the night? The loving daughter and sister? Or was she the diligent journalist who sought the truth, even when it cost her life? She was all of them, Rebecca decided, and more. There were facets to Caroline—to all people, including Rebecca—that even they themselves would never know.

She excused herself to the restroom.

Passing by an open door on her way back to the sanctuary, she saw Chris White outside with Katie, who had seemed unaware that she was meant to be somber. He noticed Rebecca watching and beckoned her to join them.

"I suggested you might not be an ideal guest, but Jenna felt otherwise. And she calls the shots now." Despite the joy on his face when he watched Katie dancing—performing the same moves Rebecca had watched in Fairfield—something about how Chris carried himself had changed. Like a support column that has cracked and can no longer bear the load, he occupied the same space as before, but there was a subliminal feeling that he was no longer essential.

"Why did you do it?" Rebecca asked, her eyes on Katie. "Why'd you take her from Becky? This could have been your life the whole time."

"Becky was an addict. She still is at times, but that was her at her worst. The prenatal tests suggested Katie was not developing normally and would be severely handicapped. But in her impaired state, Becky was unable to consider the child's—or the family's—well-being. Someone needed to do what was best for everyone, so I made the choice on her behalf. By the time it was clear the baby wasn't going to be....." He shook his head. "It was too late to stop."

Rebecca grew warm, angry. Chris White and the Sweets—all of them, even Becky—they course-corrected when it would get them something they wanted. But when the outcome didn't really matter to them, they acted as though they had no choice, like they were slaves to misfortune. Still, Rebecca had to wonder, would Katie's life have been better if she had been raised from birth in the Sweet home, with a famous mother, a controlling grandfather and a scheming aunt? And what about Dr. Lane, or people like Ghosted, what would their impact be? If it wasn't them, it'd be others, Rebecca thought. There's always people like that. Even Rebecca had known a few.

"No, that's not it." Chris shook his head, tired. "When Katie is finally a White and can leave the state, Becky will be laser focused on her job in Vegas; performing for fans is her life, as it always has been. She'll come back from work, and they'll hug, but Katie will spend the majority of her time with a nanny. Or Jenna," he sighed, his face disfigured by disappointed frustration. "Katie will grow up knowing almost as little about her mother as if she had remained an orphan."

Katie had begun waving at her grandfather, hungry for his attention; he waved back. Continuing, he said, "I thought that we could, KL and I," his voice broke faintly as he spoke his partner's name, "But when the investments turned into losses, I had to focus on staunching the hemorrhage before adding complexity."

"Cascadia Subduction," Rebecca murmured. "I read they're selling everything to settle debts."

Chris grunted. "Yes, a catastrophe. A catastrophe." He turned again to his granddaughter. "But, from the ashes, growth is inevitable. How many times has London been burned to the ground? Yet it has always risen bigger and better than before, and now it is the center of the world." He looked at Rebecca one last time. "That can still be her future, if we do it right, this time."

Chris, ever hopeful, chuckled as Katie aborted a somersault. He waddled to her, helping her to her feet and supporting her weight as she attempted another.

Rebecca returned inside. She hoped Chris was wrong. Becky had sworn that she would do things differently, that she would stay sober and focus on Katie's welfare. But she had already been involved in a collision on the strip, which mainstream news sources stopped short of citing as alcohol-related. The tabloids, however, hadn't been so forgiving in their reports.

Rebecca reminded herself that 'better' did not always mean 'perfect,' that, no matter what, by the time Katie reached adulthood, she'd know disappointment and pain, regardless of where she grew up, and with whom. Katie might not have a perfect life with Becky, but if she was loved—in whatever way the Sweets were capable of loving—that foundation, no matter how wobbly, would carry the girl through, providing her the opportunity to fix what had been broken.

Following the ceremony, Jenna Sweet texted Rebecca, asking her to join her in the church's back office.

"I didn't get a chance to thank you," Rebecca said upon entering. "For saving my life." She still didn't understand why Jenna had gone out of her way to save her, though she had suspicions.

Jenna shook her head and pulled out an envelope , handing it to Rebecca. "It's what anyone would do. Anyway, I should be thanking you. This is what you are owed."

Rebecca opened the unsealed envelope; inside were two all-access passes for the duration of B*Sweet's time in Las Vegas. Under the tickets was a check for $350,000. It was made out to Rebecca Ziel. A sharp pulse of anxiety surged through her head, leaving behind the throb of a growing headache. She wavered a moment, then asked, "What's this about?"

Jenna smiled amiably. "Becky asked me to give you the tickets and to tell you to come by anytime with anyone you'd like. She wants to make sure you know to visit her after the shows. As for the check, I'm aware my father never made any official agreement with your company, but I want to make good on what he should have done."

"I don't understand," Rebecca shook her head. "The house never sold. And, from what I hear, Caroline's family is suing for the guest house Becky promised her." When Charles had spoken about the development, he had been both satisfied by the news—"it's only right"—and disappointed that he wasn't involved.

Jenna shook her head, and she smiled. "The Invers family situation has been handled. The paperwork transferring the house was never filed, so there was no legal agreement. Still, I wanted to do right: they agreed to take a lump sum in exchange for renouncing any potential deal that might ever come to light. If any such arrangement is found, however, of course the agreement won't hold. But, by then, the property will have sold and be beyond their greed."

Rebecca looked surprised and Jenna seemed pleased by that. "You see," she continued, "Becky really couldn't afford to keep the home, thanks to our father. But while he was looking for a buyer outside the family, I looked within. I have agreed to purchase the house through our winery. As a symbol of its growth. The deal has not been approved, nor will it be until the conservatorship is rescinded completely. I wanted to give you the good news. And the check. You did the work, and you deserve to be paid." Jenna's smile felt like the evening sun on a cold winter's day: not nearly as warm as one might expect.

Rebecca removed the tickets but placed the check back in the envelope and returned it. "I can't accept this. Legally, I mean. It must be made to the brokerage. Whatever I make will have to come through Mr. Sprock." She wanted to throw up; why was she willingly letting this opportunity slip through her fingers? *It's not a real opportunity*, she told herself. *It's a noose around my neck that Jenna will be able to pull whenever she wants.*

Knowing that was almost enough to convince Rebecca that she was making the correct decision.

Jenna regarded her. "Most people I know would kill for that amount of money."

"Don't get me wrong," Rebecca said, "I could use it, but," she shook her head again, "unfortunately, I would be doing a disservice to Becky, to you and to my broker if I accepted it. And it could land me in a lot of trouble with the state."

She added, "If you want me to earn anything from the sale, you'll need to take it to Charles. Do you know him?"

Jenna nodded. After waiting for Rebecca to come to her senses for a moment, she moved to the exit.

"Jenna," Rebecca announced. "I am grateful that you saved me, but I have to know: how are you able to do that?"

"What do you mean?"

Rebecca tightened then released her fist several times. She examined the indentations her fingernails had made in her palm, touching them with a finger. An inner voice was telling her to let it go; she hated confrontation, and yet she was being confrontational. With her savior, no less. But a person's actions aren't alchemy: a single good deed—if the rescue had been that—doesn't transmogrify a history of wrongs.

She was shaking as she answered: "The drugs, the deaths? Your sister might be forever alienated from her father, and she missed ten years of her daughter's life."

Jenna turned away. She shut the door, locking both of them inside. "I believe you're confused. I'm not responsible for any—"

Rebecca cut her off, in a race with her pulse to see who would give in first. "I wondered for a long time why you wanted Caroline's laptop. What was in her book that you didn't want to see the light of day? I finally realized it wasn't about what was in the book. It was about how what was in it got there. You knew about Katie. Marc told us that you were the one who told him. I don't know when you knew, but at some point, with all your poking and prodding into your father's management of the estate, you saw his donations to the Galaxy school, his purchase of the organization's property, and whatever other actions he took, and you connected it to her. But you didn't immediately tell your sister that her daughter was alive. You waited until you saw a moment the revelation could benefit you."

"You think I waited until Becky was wanted by police in connection with a murder?" Jenna asked incredulously.

"I think you told Caroline about it first. For the book. If I were to read Caroline's notes—before you got a hold of her manuscript—

I am willing to bet you would be identified as the original source of that information. Whether you knew it was Dr. Lane who falsified the death certificates or not—whether you knew anything about the death certificates—I think that wasn't important. You knew Caroline, as a journalist, would investigate all the angles, which she did, and you didn't care what came from that so long as it stripped your father of his control. And so, Caroline was murdered to prevent that information from leaking, and Bill Hicks was murdered to prevent her murder from coming to light."

Jenna considered that. "You gave me the laptop," she said finally. "If you wanted the truth." She shrugged.

Rebecca nodded. "I did. And I gave Becky back her album, the one with Ghosted's stink that she wanted so badly to never see again. But you're the reason for that, too." She limped to the other side of the table, leaning on it. "I overheard your father at the lake. He said you suggested that Ghosted produce the album."

Jenna opened her mouth to object, but Rebecca couldn't be interrupted. She had been holding in her theories and now she needed to expel them. "Okay, maybe you never suggested it outright, but that's because it's not how you operate. You probably only mentioned him, right? You knew your father was desperate enough to find the idea appealing, if not irresistible. If he found someone else to produce, it wouldn't matter, but if he hired Ghosted, that would create another rift between your sister and him, bringing the two of you closer together. Which it did, but it also resulted in James Logan's death, because he would not have come to Sacramento if you hadn't convinced your father to hire him."

"Interesting," Jenna acknowledged. "And I suppose you would say a charity is responsible when its donations are intercepted by a warlord, and children die as a result."

"If the charity knows the risk, yet takes no precautions, then yes, they share in the responsibility." Rebecca answered. She closed her eyes. Her mind was telling her she needed to give voice to the truth, but looking Jenna in the face while doing so was painful. It was like sunlight, necessary , but it burned. "I'm not trying to say you don't have good intentions. I don't—I don't know. But even if you can ignore the downstream effects, what about your direct actions? What was in the case you owed Moneyshot?"

"The briefcase that you gave her?" Jenna asked.

That stopped Rebecca. The contents of the suitcase were tied to her now, too: good, bad or indifferent. Like Jenna, Rebecca dwelled in the shadow of a mountain littered with unintended consequences; any of them could avalanche down on her without warning. And it would be her own doing.

Rebecca said slowly, "I think it was drugs. Moneyshot called it a 'golden ticket:' the special pass into parties and places you'd otherwise never access. Something you could share, sometimes, to get others in as well. That would justify setting up a meeting with the paparazzi and Dr. Lane when you left Hollywood, to transfer the connection." Rebecca watched Jenna for a response. All the woman did was raise her eyebrows, inviting Rebecca to continue.

"Dr. Lane was illegally obtaining the drugs. No one may be saying it outright, but why else the empty office and fake patients? And how is it everyone in your family has access to every medication known to man? It was her getting the drugs, but it was you who distributed them, wasn't it? You bridged the gap between her practice and the rich and famous. You were her golden ticket. But then your winery took off and you didn't need illegal drugs to be profitable. Lucky for her, she suddenly had a show that put her in direct contact with celebrity addicts. One produced and provided for by you and your sister. Lucky for you, too, if I'm right."

"You've constructed an interesting narrative there," Jenna admitted.

"Dr. Lane died in the hospital," Rebecca said, "Patrick said she received triple the dosage I did." It had finally come to this: the lake rescue. It was both the part of the confrontation that Rebecca was dreading, and also the whole reason for doing it. "I might have been out of my mind on whatever she gave me, but I know that there wasn't that much left in the syringe after what she stuck in me. And I couldn't have hit her with the fire extinguisher."

"You 'know'?" Jenna asked. "Couldn't you have?"

Rebecca shook her head. Did she really know how much had been left in the syringe? Or what her body had been doing while her mind was out of it? Did she know anything about what happened on the boat? Would she ever? She shook off the questions. "What would Bridgette Lane have said if she had survived? Who would she have implicated? Did you find me to save me, or to silence her?"

Rebecca followed Jenna's gaze: In the distant sky outside the window, a bird flying in the sky was joined by another. The two shapes darted at and away from one another in a strangely violent ritual. Whether they were dancing or fighting, Rebecca couldn't say.

"It's hard to accept what we've done, sometimes," Jenna spoke solemnly. "Especially when it can't be easily identified as right or wrong. The only way to live with our guilt is to place the blame on someone else." Looking into Rebecca's eyes—making certain that Rebecca was looking into hers—Jenna said, "If you need me to be that for you, I will." She released a worn-out exhalation. "You've done a lot for my family." Again the envelope was offered, and, again, Rebecca declined it. "Are you sure? You do deserve it, all the work you put in."

"How are you able to stay so calm?" Rebecca asked, feeling hot and angry and helpless.

"I'm a businesswoman," Jenna answered evenly. "In my world, you can't show weakness if you want to survive." She ran her hand through her hair and looked at the hand; several strands stuck between her fingers. "Before that, I was an actress. A good one, if you listen to my sister. Always will be, I suppose." She pulled out an alcohol wipe and cleaned her hands. "Do I make the check out to Charles Sprock or Halcyon Realty?"

"Halcyon," Rebecca said, exhausted. She felt like she should cry, but the well was dry.

She watched Jenna open the door to rejoin the remaining mourners and Becky, frozen on the 75-inch TV, in the sanctuary. There were already tears spilling from Jenna's eyes and dripping from her chin as she took the hands of Caroline's mother and uttered something that triggered an emotional embrace from the grieving parent. Rebecca, unable to take any more, turned to the back door, and she left them there to mourn.

Epilogue. Saturday (Five Weeks Later).

Rebecca sat in sunlight, scraping her fingernail against piping on the cloth seat at the Indian restaurant where she and Patrick Donnelly had just finished their meal. She wasn't a huge fan of Indian food, mostly because it tended to upset her stomach, but Patrick had told her it was the best in the city, and she owed him a rain check meal. To be fair, it was the best she'd ever had, though she still would not go back on her own. Maybe if he invited her again.

Against all protestations of friends and family, she had decided to take her trip to Tokyo. Sydney was the most vocal, warning her about the tight seats on the plane, the overcrowded trains, and the rather punishing walking requirements. If her doctor hadn't given her the green light, she would have listened, but he told her she was physically able to travel if she felt up to it, and, boy, did she. It was something she'd wanted to do for a very long time, but other people's needs had always gotten in the way. It was about time she did what she wanted.

Charles hadn't bought the tickets, but not for lack of trying. In the end, Rebecca didn't need him to. Becky called Rebecca two weeks after the funeral. She talked about how much of a hellhole Las Vegas was, "Except the people," she said, "they're all so lovely. They know all the words, even to songs I thought people hated. And the nightlife is honestly not that bad. Let me know when you stop by, I'll show you around." The main reason she had called, however, had been to discuss Rebecca's art. After all the sturm und drang, Becky had decided to release her new B*Sweet album as *Pop Scars* after Jenna suggested the original title was too retro. Becky asked Rebecca to do the cover art. "They don't really do physical covers anymore, of course—or records, for that matter—but art is still vital to branding. And you were there. You saw what I went through. There's no one else who can do this."

While the commission didn't bring in as much as she had hoped, it—along with what had trickled down to her from Jenna's payment to Halcyon—was enough to cover her travel expenses and leave a comfortable buffer in her bank account. But more than the financial aspect, it was the thought of her art being seen on screens and devices around the world that filled her with a sense of achievement. It felt like, finally, she was moving in the right direction.

Patrick Donnelly had agreed to drive her down to the San Jose airport, ostensibly to ensure she arrived safely and without spending too much on Uber or parking. She had chosen that airport because she wanted to see Sydney in person before leaving, so flying out of the airport nearest San Martin made that possible. That Patrick was taking her—meaning they would be spending half a day together—was a bonus.

The assault by Ghosted, and the attempted kidnapping by KL over such a short span of time had deeply unsettled her. As much as she tried to act like nothing had changed, and she was just as willing to go outside as before, she had remained almost exclusively indoors since the accident. Her injury was only partially to blame. She wanted to challenge that anxiety by immersing herself in an unfamiliar place surrounded by unfamiliar people. The fact that Sydney had done all right in Tokyo by herself was a part of that comfort. If Rebecca only stayed in the hotel the whole time, at least she would have tried. She knew she wouldn't forgive herself so easily if she did, actually, end up staying inside, but she changed the subject whenever her brain tried to tell her as much.

Patrick, at first, implied that he might be willing to go with her. He spoke about the paid time off he'd accrued, and about the things he'd like to see there one day. He stopped talking about it a week earlier. He had been assigned mandatory classes for his continued education. Sheriff Hines, seemingly, felt Patrick needed a refresher.

Rebecca felt relief when she heard the news. Then she felt guilty for feeling relieved. Truth was, she had spent so much time, since her last relationship, identifying as single that she hadn't realized that, by doing so, she was still defining herself according to who she was or wasn't dating. She had decided that, no, she wasn't a single woman, she was just a woman, one who was still figuring things out. She was Rebecca. And before she even thought about getting into another relationship, or whatever you called it these days, she wanted to figure out, at least, who Rebecca was when she wasn't trying to do everything for everybody else.

Sydney called during the drive, explaining again why she had not been able to visit after flying back from Japan. Her absence had created a backlog. "They don't know how to do anything without me there," she said. "What I really need is someone like you."

Rebecca understood that what Sydney actually meant was: "I want you to leave your life in Sacramento and come move in with me and help me do my job." Rebecca knew she could do the job if she chose to. She'd done it for a few months before going full time with Charles. But Rebecca knew also that, as much as she loved Sydney and wanted her to succeed, she would be miserable if she tried to define her own life by what Sydney told her she needed to do.

"Yeah," Rebecca laughed, giving Patrick a look that said, 'My friend, the comedian.'

"I'm serious!" Sydney insisted.

"I know you are. That's why it's funny." Rebecca retorted, and Sydney joined in the laughter.

After they had all met and were saying their goodbyes at a diner near the airport, Bethany, Sydney's eldest daughter—who Rebecca still couldn't believe was going to be a high school senior in a couple of weeks—had called up crying. She and her long-term boyfriend—the one Bethany knew she would marry after graduation—had broken up.

After the call, knowing Sydney would be driving home immediately to comfort her grieving daughter, Rebecca tried to change the subject. "Are you ready to see B*Sweet in October?"

"You have no idea. I ordered three dresses and two skirts—all of them are so cute—that I'm going to need your advice on which is the cutest. Or maybe I could bring all three. We can go as many times as possible, right?"

"Do you really think you'd want to see the same show more than once?" Rebecca asked.

"Are you kidding? The girls are so excited."

Rebecca looked at her friend, hoping she had misheard. "I only have two tickets," she said.

"Oh, well, I'm sure they'll let you get more. You're good friends with the singer!"

It didn't sit right with Rebecca—it felt like taking advantage of a friend, and Becky had too many people doing that already. But she also didn't feel like arguing with Sydney about how realistic or fair the request was. Whatever: they'd figure things out when the time came. Worst-case scenario, they had to buy two extra tickets.

"Have you heard the new single?" Sydney asked. "They released it yesterday." She found the song on YouTube, and Rebecca smiled, seeing her artwork shining from her friend's phone. The song had 24 million plays, which seemed promising, Rebecca thought, though she didn't really know. The three of them listened to the song. It wasn't bad. It didn't spark the same magic that B*Sweet's songs had when Rebecca was a girl, but it was catchy, and she suspected she'd be humming the chorus on the plane.

Her phone rang. It was Charles Sprock.

"Don't answer it!" Sydney cautioned. "If he asks why you missed it, just act like you'd already put your phone in airplane mode and didn't hear it."

Rebecca could've done that—but she wasn't going to. "Hello?" she listened.

"Oh my god, I'm so glad I caught you before you left!" Charles sounded extremely excited. "Look, I know you're leaving today, but I need your help. It's an emergency. We—are you ready? There's the possibility of listing a $32 million house in Santa Barbara. I'm already on my way down, but I need you to meet me here. I'll text you the address." Charles's voice was replaced by the vibration of a text message with an address. "Did you get that?" he asked.

"Mmm-hmm," Rebecca answered, trying to acknowledge she'd received the message without agreeing to anything.

"Look, I'm already in the process of buying you a new ticket. I mean, I will once I get down there. I only need you for a couple of days, you can leave from LA. How do you feel about first class? A flight that long is a lot better in first class, believe me."

She did believe him. And, truth be told, the offer was tempting. After all, the last time she'd canceled her trip to help Charles on one of his crazy sales, she'd become friends with one of the biggest pop stars in the world during her youth. She'd almost been killed a couple of times, too, but, except at those times when she was alone in the dark and she remembered Ghosted's tongue on her ear or the feeling of the needle in her shoulder, the bad memories were slowly but surely fading. She hoped, anyway. And while she had a little extra cash in her bank, it wasn't enough to pay for life as she looked for more work. Plus, her ticket was coach, and if Sydney's complaints about flying coach for twenty hours were anything to go by, it wouldn't be the most pleasant time of her life.

"I'm sorry," Rebecca said into the microphone. "I want to go on this vacation. I deserve it."

"Of course you do, and you will still go. It's just a couple days later," Charles insisted. "Here, I'm pulling over, I'll buy the ticket right now. Hold on." Rebecca could hear the sound of the wind dying away, and there was a muffled squeal as Charles stopped the car a little too quickly.

"No, thank you," Rebecca said. "I'm leaving today."

The phone went silent, and Rebecca checked to make sure that it had not disconnected or been put on hold. She heard Charles' breath, and he said sadly: "Okay." Then he added, his excitement returning, "Okay, I'll send you the documentation. You can look at it when you land. This is great. I can work during the day, and you can work at night. When you have time, of course. It works out both ways!"

"I'm not going to do that," Rebecca said firmly. "I know you're busy, but you'll make it work out. I believe in you. We're almost at the terminal, I have to go, Charles."

"Bye," he said weakly. "If you have any time, take a look at them. Okay?"

"Bye," she said, and she hung up.

***

Rebecca fastened her seatbelt. The sign wasn't on yet, but her row was full and she wanted to be ready for takeoff. She pulled out the water she'd purchased from Hudson News and drank it. The kid in the seat behind her was lightly kicking her seat. She hoped he would tire sooner rather than later.

Her phone buzzed and was followed shortly after by two more buzzes. Rebecca couldn't believe Charles was trying again. It was kind of infuriating, when she thought about it. But the texts weren't from Charles; they were from Erin.

"Hey RB. Sorry it took so long. With everything that happened I forgot to ask dad for mom's letter."

The second message read: "I remembered yesterday, but only got the copy from dad today. Here you go."

The next text was an attachment. Finally, Erin sent: "Have fun in Tokyo! Love you!"

Rebecca texted Erin her love, then opened the attachment. It was a photo of an old sheet of notebook paper lying carefully on her father's brown comforter. In that image was the final message anyone in her family had received from her mother. Rebecca braced herself for tears, and, expanding the image with a pinch, she began to read.

Liner Notes (Taken from the physical release of B*Sweet's brand-new album, Pop Scars)

Foreword

> "Success is not final, failure is not fatal: It is
> the courage to continue that counts."
>   - Winston Churchill

The first time I appeared on people's screens was in 1987
when I was six and I appeared in a commercial for battered
fish sticks. I don't remember much about what happened on the
day we shot, but I do remember how I felt. My face was
burning, my extremities felt frozen, and I was worried sick
that I would forget my one and only line. I practiced
everywhere: in bed, in the car and at the dinner table. I
knew I knew it, and yet I feared that I would forget the
words as soon as the man behind the camera yelled "Action!" I
didn't, and I still don't. I said, "Mom, Zach's stomach
growled at me! Did so!"

I can so confidently describe how I felt then because it is
the way I still feel every time I stand up on stage or speak
to a journalist or stand behind a hot guy on line at a deli.
Like a ton of feathers weighed against a ton of bricks, I
over-prepare and over-worry in equal measure. But in both, I
know I am exactly where I'm meant to be.

This release marks 38 years since I sat in a fake car in
Burbank, California and complained about my fake brother's
hunger for 18 takes. Not once did I flub the words. 38 years
is a long time to be in the public consciousness, and over
those years I have become more known for my mistakes than my
triumphs, and I have experienced more losses in my life than
I have gains. But I have also been wildly, undeservingly
successful.

In a way, I no longer belong to only myself. The moment my
image beamed to thousands of screens across the country, I
stopped being a normal little girl who got to decide who I
was. Suddenly, people on the street—and they weren't all kids
my age—could walk up to me like we were old friends. As I

grew in age and in influence, this public ownership over my identity increased. Today, I take all the risks, and yet the fruit of my labors are spread out among the millions who hear my songs.

That I am beholden to more than my immediate circle is hard truth to swallow. It's a responsibility I have actively tried to avoid for much of my life. But now, as I release this new record, a record that I nearly destroyed in an effort to ignore the contributions of an evil man, I am forced to accept both that I don't belong to only myself and that I am, nonetheless, responsible for who I am and what I do. In the end, I am not who I am because I have always over-worried and over-prepared, I have always over-worried and over-prepared because of who I am. And it is up to me to continue redefining who that is.

Becky Sweet (B*Sweet), August 22, 2024

Open Secrets [from *B*Sweet*, 1997]

Mmm mmm (mmm mmm) | Oh oh oh (oh oh oh) | Mmm mmm (mmm mmm) | Oh oh oh (oh oh oh)

Head down | Eyes on the ground | I see my place | On all their faces

I hide | But in your eyes | I know you see | Inside of me

I write my pages my heart sings | It's silent songs a symphony | I cannot open up to you | My secret here forever true | And on and on and on | I write at home alone

Mmm mmm (mmm mmm)

They can't know | This hidden glow | Blind to the light | Awash in night

Unique | I cannot speak | These new feelings | From my mind springing

I write my pages my heart sings | It's silent songs a symphony | I cannot open up to you | My secret here forever true | And on and on and on | I think of you alone

Mmm mmm (mmm mmm) | Oh oh oh (oh oh oh) | Mmm mmm (mmm mmm) | Oh oh oh (oh oh oh)

One day | I dream I'll say | That I love you | Then you will too

At home | Though no one knows | Here where we belong | We sing our song

Upon my pages my heart sings | It's silent songs a symphony | I cannot open up to you | My secret here forever true | And on and on and on | And you and me alone

An open secret | An open secret (an open secret) | Inside my pocket | My heart in a locket (unlock it) | An open secret | An open secret

Two strong | It can't be wrong | If it feels this right | It's worth the fight

Upon my pages my heart sings | It's silent songs a symphony | I cannot open up to you | My secret here forever true | And on and on and on | And you and me become

An open secret | An open secret (an open secret) | Inside your pocket | My heart you got it (you got it) | An open secret | An open secret

I write my pages my heart sings | It's silent songs a symphony | I cannot open up to you | My secret here forever true | And on and on and on | And you and me are one |

An open secret (an open secret) | An open secret (an open secret)

Artist's Note

When my self-titled debut album released in 1997, no one had any idea how successful its first single, 'Open Secrets', would end up being. I should say, no one but me. I was a hopeful girl who had only known success to that point, what else could I imagine? The song was my first of several times making it onto Billboard's top 100, peaking at number 16. It was also my first experience working with James Logan. Up to that point, he seemed like the coolest, most talented musician I had ever met, and I looked up to him immensely. He and the other writers on the album took my naive insights and worries and they crafted an anthem for the anxious dreamer I was at 14.

Wanna (Kiss Me) [From *(Not) So Sweet*, 1999]

Hold my hand | Before you leave | Stand closer and | Let's wait and see

Oh, oh, oh (oh) | In the night | By (by) your side | Would we end it all...

Oh, oh, oh! | In the night | By your side | Would it end it all | If we kissed

My senses have been achin' | My body shook and shakin' | My lips and legs are quakin' | 'cuz I miss you | And I wanna . . .

It's harder than I ever knew | To keep myself away from you | I never knew a love so true | Before (never before)

I know we say we're only friends | I don't want that to ever end | I close my eyes and count to ten | And breathe (calm down and breathe)

Oh, oh, oh | In the night | By your side | Would it end it all | If we kissed

Oh, hold my hand!

My senses have been achin' | My body shook and shakin' | My lips and legs are quakin' | 'cuz I miss you | And I wanna . . .

I wanna be a stronger girl | An oyster with a perfect pearl | But my defenses, they unfurl | To you (must come to you)

I don't know why we stay apart | These obstacles just make it hard | I never wanna be so far | Again (never again)

Must come to you!

Oh, oh | In the night | By your side | Could we end it all | Just a kiss

My senses have been achin' | My body shook and shakin' | My lips and legs are quakin' | 'cuz I miss you | And I wanna . . .

Forbidden, but I miss you bad | I'm holding back, it drives me mad | They say you're just a passing fad | You're not (I know you're not)

Our friendship is too strong to fail | Expanding it will fill our sails | Denying you I fall and flail | Let's try (oh please, let's try)

Please let us try!

Oh, oh | In the night | By your side | Would we end it all | For a kiss?

My senses have been achin' | My body shook and shakin' | My lips and legs are quakin' | 'cuz I miss you | And I wanna . . .

Kiss you | Feel you | Hold you | In the night

Oh, oh, oh | In the night (night) | By your side | Would we end it all | It's just a kiss | Only a kiss

And I wanna . . .

Kiss you | Feel you | Hold you | In the night

And I wanna . . .

Oh, oh | In the night | By your side | Would we end it all | For a kiss

My senses have been achin' | My body shook and shakin' | My lips and legs are quakin' | 'cuz I miss you | And I wanna . . .

Hold my hand | Before you leave | Come close, I want | For you to kiss me

Artist's Note

'Wanna (Kiss Me)' remains the most successful single of my entire career. When we released the single in February of 1999, it was only moderately successful, cracking the top ten. However, when the record was released, that song went to number one, and it stayed there for 31 weeks straight and won me my first Grammy.

Yet, that song, along with the entire album is a bittersweet memory for me. As some may know, James Logan produced every song on the album, but one. And it was during the recording sessions that he sexually assaulted me. Though I considered myself an adult at the time—I was 16 and he was 28—and I thought what we were doing was consensual, I later realized that he had been grooming me since we worked together on the previous album when I was 14. I am disgusted, not only by what he did, but by myself and what I allowed him to do to me. I carry that guilt, as senseless as it may be, and I believe I always will.

More significantly, while the rest of the world was enjoying these songs, my mother was growing increasingly sick. She died the month after this song lost the top spot, throwing my life into an even greater disarray than it had been put in by Logan. I don't know if I have ever felt as hopeless as I did in the early months of 2000.

I did not realize when I began recording the new songs that Logan had orchestrated the music and that he would be producing and mixing the songs. When I learned about it, I vowed to destroy the record, feeling that, by doing so, I was destroying what he did to me. It was through my experiences with my own daughter, however, that I realized destruction was not the answer. The answer was bringing the truth to light. And so, it was with that in mind that I decided to append to this album these songs from my earlier records. Each of them was the biggest hit of their respective album, but, more importantly, each of them represented who I was at the time.

'Wanna' had begun as a poem I had written for a boy I hadn't gotten over. The intro and second verse are all that remain of the original verse, though both were modified by Logan. I did not recognize how sexualized the rest of the song had been made until years later. And it is only thanks to years of therapy that I can look at the song and recognize that there is still a part of me who dwells in this song as an innocent teenager unaware of how dark the world can be.

Back 2 You [From *Alone @ Night*, **2003**]

No | No, no | No, no, please, no

I push you out, you break back in | A history of sick and sin | Apart I need to feel your skin | On me | All over me

Your ghost it haunts my memory | A silhouette of you and me | Our dances, fights and finally | Our love | Eternal love

We race away and now toward | Aware we can't continue this | Across the nation and the world | Try to escape | I must escape | Into your kiss

When you are running, I give chase | I try to flee, and right on cue | A stalking presence, track and trace | Your fingers | Your touch lingers | I come back to you

You tremble, terrified of love | I know I cannot get enough | I search the dark for traces of | Your body | All over me

We know an end is for the best | Our suicide, but one last kiss | We'll say goodbye right after this | And then

We race away and now toward | Aware we can't continue this | Across the nation and the world | Try to escape | I must escape | Into your kiss

When you are running, I give chase | I try to flee, and right on cue | A stalking presence, track and trace | Your fingers | Your touch lingers | I come back to you

Oh! | Oh, no!

We race away and now toward | Aware we can't continue this | Across the nation and the world | Try to escape | I must escape | Into your kiss

When you are running, I give chase | I try to flee, and right on cue | A stalking presence, track and trace | Your fingers | Your touch lingers | I come back to you

No (no) | No, no, no, no | Not back to you | No

I toss and turn in bed alone | A struggle not to snatch my phone | To call, invite you in my home | Inside | So deep inside

And seeking shelter with my friends | These broken pieces, I try to mend | Belief it's not all just pretend | It's over | Forever

We race away and now toward | Aware we can't continue this | Across the nation and the world | Try to escape | I must escape | Into your kiss

When you are running, I give chase | I try to flee, and right on cue | A stalking presence, track and trace | Your fingers | Your touch lingers | I come back to you

No (no) | No, no, no, no | Not back to you | No | Please, no

Artist's Note

I thought I was being so clever when I wrote this song, couching my drug addiction in a song about a toxic relationship. I also thought I was writing fiction.

Mothers Are Daughters [From *Mothers Are Daughters*, 2014]

Carelessly we roamed those days | On trails paved with endless now | An innocence, unearned in ways | When living was a form of play | And love did not ask how

From darkness we came into light | A frigid world awaiting us | Of tears and wonders, lonely nights | When angered, frightened, lost, contrite | Escape to mother's love

Mother gave the structure to be free | Daughter, a chance to be better | But mother, you too were a daughter | And you sacrificed you to save me

Daughter, no, I never can know you | Mother, forgive me my shame | I can't live up to the name | I won't ever know what you went through | I keep you with me everyday

Celestial, from heaven sent | And for a season down below | Your grace and beauty, to us, lent | And back to paradise you went | Leaving us in tow

Mother gave the structure to be free | Daughter, a chance to be better | But mother, you too were a daughter | And you sacrificed you to save me

Daughter, no, I never can know you | Mother, forgive me my shame | I can't live up to the name | I won't ever know what you went through | I keep you with me everyday |

Our paths, one day, will reconverge | On misty roads that roll and wend | Out from the past you'll reemerge | Reunified through our rebirth | As mothers, daughters, sisters, friends

Mother gave the structure to be free | Daughter, a chance to be better | But mother, you too were a daughter | And you sacrificed you to save me

Daughter, no, I never can know you | Mother, forgive me my shame | I can't live up to the name | I won't ever know what you went through | You both are with me to this day

Mother gives the structure to be free | Daughter, a chance to be better | Our mothers were daughters and so we | Are daughters and mothers together

Artist's Note

In some ways, 'Mothers Are Daughters' is the only song I have ever written that means anything to me. I had begun writing a poem in memory of Miriam Sweet White, my mother, while she was still in the hospital. It was my way of coming to terms with the ineffable grief I felt. The song's first verse is nearly word-for-word from that poem, though I never completed it. For years, I thought it was impossible to top the sadness that her death put me through, or to articulate it in any meaningful way.

What changed that was the loss of my pregnancy in 2014. When I saw my father on the ground, mourning as I had not even seen him do for my mother, I knew that the child that had been growing inside me for nine months was no more. That moment of clarity was so clear, and yet so dark, and I don't think I will ever again know as much despair as I did then.

And yet, that loss revealed to me something about the loss of my mother I had not previously understood. It showed me that I was not mourning only the person I had lost, I was mourning an entire world of which I was a part and a future that would never be. The version of me who existed prior to my mother's death in 2000, or my child's death in 2014 had also died. But the flipside of that realization was that the connection between us also changed. Despite their physical deaths, they both live on through me and the many others whose lives they touched.

I took the old poem I had written for my mother, and now I viewed it from the lens of being a mother myself, even if that motherhood was momentary. In a matter of hours, I had rewritten all the remaining verses. To make it a song, all I needed was the chorus, and that came together when I read an essay by Ann Patchett where she wrote about her own loss. It was there I saw how the same line drawn between my mother and me had also been drawn between me and my daughter and between all mothers and daughters. The Grammy I won for this song remains my greatest professional accomplishment, and I see it as my way to ensure both my mother and my daughter are never forgotten.

I love you mom. I love you Miriam Zosia White, my sweet baby girl. I will see you both before the sun's final set.

Bold Lines

Oh, oh, oh, oh | Oh, oh, oh | Oh, oh, oh, oh | Oh, oh, oh, oh...

Bright lights disguise the tears | Late nights, forgotten years | Whispers in the hallways | Echoes (Echoes) | My life's become a maze

Glitz and glamor fade away | In the mirror now, I look so strange | Pressure cracks on the surface | Suppose (Suppose) | I break free from this circus |

No more chains to hold me down | I'm rising up from under the ground | Cast down judgments, never tried | I choose to choose the me I hide | I'll carry on no matter how | Finally make good on | This fragile smile

Paparazzi chase the woe | They don't see the inner glow | Underneath the bold façade | So close (So close) | Heals a heart that was marred

Public wants the masks I wear | Society of will not care | I won't let me stay confined | Oh, no (no) | I'll live my life in bold lines

No more chains to hold me down | I'm rising up from under the ground | Cast down judgments, never tried | I choose to love the me inside | I'll carry on no matter how | Finally make good on | This fragile smile

Oh, oh, oh

I know someday I'll believe | I'm not the wreck that I used to be | It's step by step and day to day | So slow (I know) | But I will fight 'til I can say |

No more chains to hold me down | I'm rising up from under the ground | Cast down judgments, never tried | I choose to love the me inside | I'll carry on no matter how | Finally make good on | This fragile smile

Oh, oh, oh, oh | Oh, oh, oh | Oh, oh, oh, oh | Oh...

You frame me as a broken girl | And hang me in your twisted world | I'm a canvas that's been painted on | And every stroke was forced upon | But I'm the one who now decides | To paint again in bold lines

Yeah! | Oh...

No more chains to hold me down | I'm rising up from under the ground | Cast down judgments, never tried | I choose to love the me inside | I'll carry on no matter how | Finally make good on | This fragile smile

I live my life in bold lines! (bold lines, bold lines) | I live my life in bold lines! (bold lines, bold lines) | I live my life in bold lines! (bold lines, bold lines)

I make my pledge (I make my pledge) | Declare right now (declare right now) | No matter how | No matter how (no matter how) | I (I, I) choose to live in | Bold lines

Bold Lines

Artist's Note

Originally this was the second song on the new album. It wasn't until a conversation with my sister that I came to realize this song contains the thesis under which the rest of the album falls. Once I understood that, the decision to include earlier songs made even more sense because, suddenly, 'Bold Lines' was a delineation between what came before and what comes from now on.

Back for More

Hey | Hey, yeah! | Let's fight fire with fire (fight fire with fire!)

Risking damnation to make it to heaven | I stare down at death just to feel alive | Tell them they can't, they will want to, you let 'em | We show it in semaphores for the blind | They see it all the time (all the time) | The blind

We say we're mining love from hate | And making peace through war | Fight destiny for better fate (fire with fire!) | Leave early, come fashionably late | Forbid then go in back for more | Audaciously enter through the back door

Surviving this life means we suffer together | Reminder to y'all that we're cruel to be kind | A schadenfreude, break it to build back better | The kingdom of cataracts leading the blind | They say what's yours is mine (yours is mine) | You're fine, you're fine

We say we're mining love from hate | And making peace through war | Fight destiny for better fate (fire with fire!) | Leave early, come fashionably late | Forbid then go in back for more | Audaciously enter through the back door

Love to hate | Peace through war | Never sated | Less is more

Fight fire with fire!

We say we're mining love from hate | And making peace through war | Fight destiny for better fate (fight fire with fire!) | Leave early, come fashionably late | Forbid then go in back for more | Audaciously enter through the back door

Everyone's equal, but some more than others | Move further ahead leaves you lagging behind | Freedom to carry the burden of betters | Servants responsible for masters' crimes | They say what's yours is mine (yours is mine) | We're cruel to be kind

We say we're mining love from hate | And making peace through war | Fight destiny for better fate (fire with fire!) | Leave early, come fashionably late | Forbid then go in back for more | Audaciously enter through the back door

Fight fire with fire!

We say we're mining love from hate | And making peace through war | Fight destiny for better fate (fire with fire!) | Leave early, come fashionably late | Forbid then go in back for more | Audaciously enter through the back door

Love to hate | Peace through war | Never sated | Back for more

Truthful liars | Never tire | Fighting fire | With more fire

Artist's Note

'Back For More' predates most songs on this album, having
been written somewhere around 2007, and it was initially to
be released as the lone new song on my dance remix album.
Originally titled with the number 4 ('Back 4 More'), I
thought it would both act as an incentive to returning fans
and as a callback to my earlier song 'Back 2 You'. When it
was ultimately decided that *Look 2 Me* should consist only of
my greatest hits, this song was shelved with the plan for it
to be used on my follow-up which, of course, ended up being
dedicated to my mother and daughter.

When I was first working on this new album, I knew I wanted
to finally include this song, which was really me expressing
my anger, and it was intended as both the title and the
opening track. I am not in the same place I was when I wrote
it originally, but I appreciate how I was able to express my
rage in such a playful way.

Pop Scars

Fame came creeping in the dark | Promised secrets, left a mark | Lost myself along the way | In the shadows I remain

Flashing bulbs, they blind my view | Fill my sight with black and blue | Memories still cut so deep | Through my mind they crawl and creep

Pop scars upon me | They never warned me | They brought me in | Seeking sin | Pop scars of glory | Tell my story | I'll rise above | Seeking love

Stolen moments never bought | Sublimated into nought | Ashes of the girl I was | Scattered never far enough

Words they twisted into chains | Wrapped in coils around my veins | Innocence lost, stained and torn | From the wreckage I'm reborn

Pop scars upon me | They never warned me | They brought me in | Seeking sin | Pop scars of glory | Tell my story | I'll rise above | Seeking love

Faces fade but the pain lasts | Haunted by my broken past | Love will guide me | Lead me on | Through the night I find my dawn

Pop scars upon me | They never warned me | They brought me in | Seeking sin | Pop scars of glory | Tell my story | I'll rise above | Seeking love (seeking love!)

Pop scars upon me (pop scars!) | They never warned me | They brought me in | Seeking sin | Pop scars of glory (pop scars!) | Tell my story | I'll rise above | Seeking love (seeking love!)

These scars inside me | They won't define me

Artist's Note

Like 'Bold Lines', 'Pop Scars' really felt like it
encapsulated the message of the album, which is that I have
endured a lot of painful experiences, and they have left me
with scars, only a few of which are physical. However, I
refuse to let those wounds define who I am or what I can
become. We went back and forth on which should be the title

track—this or 'Bold Lines'—and after much deliberation, I decided that the other would make the better opening track and this made the better title.

Life's a Stage

They say life's a stage and I hear people clapping | Sometimes they're booing, I'm not sure what's happ'ning | 'Cause all I can see is the lights from the trusses | We're here then we're gone carried off in black busses

The next town, the next one, it's intoxicating | The feeling of knowing it's for me you're waiting | The rush of the cheers in a rising crescendo | No drug can compare, not a lover or friend, oh!

They'll tell you it's lonely when you're at your highest | And, sure, it gets harder to understand, I guess | The feeling of being a part of the masses | Who watch us on stage as we make of ourselves asses

They say life's a stage and that everyone's watching | But I can't see faces, or even the bodies | No, all I can see is the lights staring at me | Stumbling blindly, I smile to the world and sing

Where, o where are you all? | Why am I up here so tall? | Who am I even to think | That I, of all people, won't fall? | How do I get my next drink? | When does the fear start to shrink? | What will I do when you all | See who I am deep underneath?

At the end of the day when I lie down to sleep | And I can't so I get up and pace or I creep | Look up bad decisions and people I hated | The friends I've abandoned, and assholes I dated

The regrets and mistakes and people I'm hurting | Some I love, some I don't, innocent or deserving | They say it's a stage and this won't be forever | They think they are helping or else being clever

But what if I wish this life never would finish? | What's the pathology identified in this? | If life's just a stage and soon this one is ending, | Can I make suggestions before it's the next one?
They say life's a stage and that everyone's watching | But I can't see faces, or even the bodies | No, all I can see is the lights staring at me | Stumbling blindly, I smile at the world and sing

Where, o where are you all? | Why am I up here so tall? | Who am I even to think | That I, of all people, won't fall? | How do I get my next drink? | When does the fear start to shrink? | What will I do when you all | See who I am deep underneath?

Where, o where are you all? | Why am I up here so tall? | Who am I even to think | That I, of all people, won't fall? | How do I get my next drink? | When does the fear start to shrink? | What will I do when you all | See who I am deep underneath?

Artist's Note

When does the fear start to shrink?

ex nihilo

I just climbed the highest mountain | I have ever climbed before | From the peak I looked and shouted | To my echo down below

No, it's not as high as you've climbed | There are higher mountains, yes | But this joy right now that I have | At this moment is the best

And I ask myself | Once the moment passes | 'cause I just can't tell | Did it really happen?

Did something come from nothing? | Yeah, something came from nothing | And if it's back to nothing | It's back where it had begun

All these pathways I am walking | Where I'm headed, where I've gone | All these songs and words I'm talking | Assume that life after goes on

It's not just me, it's all who've lived here | And we all ask what remains | If the darkness at which we stare | Shows us to its grave domain?

And I ask myself | Once the moment passes | 'cause I just can't tell | Did it really happen?

Did something come from nothing? | Yeah, something came from nothing | And if it's back to nothing | It's back where it once began

If that darkness I see is good | Not the evil I suppose | Does that make it much less dreadful | When I ponder in repose?

So I search through what I'm thinking | Seeking thoughts to make things right | Like a tree that I am kicking | Make the birds inside take flight

And I ask myself | Once the moment passes | 'cause I just can't tell | Did it ever really happen?

Did something come from nothing? | Yeah, something came from nothing | And if it's back to nothing | It's at where it had begun

Does it matter in the long run | If I kick the tree just right | After all, the birds, the words sung | Are regardless taking flight

And just 'cause we had connection | And learned we don't get along | Doesn't mean I'm mad I met'cha | Or I want your mem'ry gone

And I ask myself | Once the moment passes | 'cause I just can't tell | Did it ever really happen?

Did something come from nothing? | Yeah, something came from nothing | And if it's back to nothing | It's at where it had begun

And if something came from nothing | Just 'cause now it is a was | Should I give up on a something | Manifesting from this love?

And I ask myself | Once the moment passes | 'cause I just can't tell | Did it ever really happen?

Did something come from nothing? | Yeah, something came from nothing | And if it's back to nothing | It's back where it had begun

Artist's Note

Maybe I flatter myself by suggesting this is the most complex song I have ever written, but I do believe that to be the case. Maybe it has something to do with the fact that this, along with 'Phantoms', was the last song I recorded, and almost all of James Logan's fingerprints were removed in the mix. Maybe it is because I was reading a lot when I wrote it, and I was in a very philosophical mood. Whatever the reason, it is my favorite new song, even if no one else seems to agree.

Bēst (featuring THK)

[*B*SWEET*]
Ooooooooooh (ooooooooooh) Ooooooooooh | Ooooooooooh
(ooooooooooh) Ooooooooooh (ooooooooooh) | Ooooooooooh
(ooooooooooh) Ooooooooooh (ooooooooooh) |

You try your best | And it just isn't good enough | To make me less | And feel like I should just give up | If you could just | Try to accept and give some love | Your loss, I guess | 'Cause I'm not the same girl I was

I won't collapse | Just because you tell me I must | It wasn't chance | That you chose to prey on this one | I must confess | I believed when you called me dumb | Your song and dance | Might have moved me when I was young

But nothing lasts | And you and your lies are done

Ooooooooooh (ooooooooooh) Ooooooooooh (ooooooooooh) |
Ooooooooooh (ooooooooooh) Ooooooooooh (ooooooooooh)

[*T H K*]
Yeah! | T H K | Uh!

You think you destroyed me you ain't | I'm a monster you helped to create | Tryna attack me I fuck up your gait | I'ma make sure you can't procreate | Say your prayers to your god or a saint | Tell yourself that it isn't too late

Yeah! | Ooh!

Boy you just messed with the beast | You a morsel an' I want a feast | I'm a one-woman army, police | Gonna wish you were lost or deceased | Got my bitches beside me so please | Try and test me if you want to see

[*B*SWEET*]
Ooooooooooh (ooooooooooh) Ooooooooooh (ooooooooooh)

Find someone else | I'm finished playing the chump | Or better yet | Do good for the world for once | Don't be a pest | Meditate on the pain you brung | Don't let your death | Be the best thing that you ever done

And don't suspect | That to you I'll ever return

Oooh Ooooooooooh (ooooooooooh)

[*T H K*]
Boy you just messed with the beast | You a morsel an' I want a feast | I'm a one-woman army, police | Gonna wish you were lost or deceased | Got my bitches beside me so please | Try and test me if you want to see

Hoo!

[*BOTH*]
You think you destroyed me you ain't | (You try your best) | Tryna attack me I fuck up your gait | (And it just isn't good enough) | Tell yourself that it isn't too late | Tell yourself that it isn't too late | Say your prayers to your god or a saint | Try your best, but boy, it's too late!

[*B*SWEET*]
Ooooooooooh (ooooooooooh) Ooooooooooh (ooooooooooh) | Ooooooooooh (ooooooooooh) Ooooooooooh (ooooooooooh)

You try your best | And it just isn't good enough | Girl, try again! | Don't you ever be giving up | It's not a mess | If you take out the spray and gloves | And you progress | Even an incremental plus!

Ooooooooooh (ooooooooooh) Ooooooooooh (ooooooooooh) | Ooooooooooh (ooooooooooh) Ooooooooooh (ooooooooooh)

I try my best | And it just isn't good enough (ooooooooooh) | I decompress | Try to accept it's sometimes tough (ooooooooooh) | I've got my friends | And the people I know and trust (ooooooooooh) | But better yet | I am learning to show myself love! |

Ooooooooooh (ooooooooooh) Ooooooooooh (ooooooooooh) | Ooooooooooh (ooooooooooh) Ooooooooooh (ooooooooooh) | (You try your best)

Ooooooooooh (ooooooooooh) Ooooooooooh (ooooooooooh) | Ooooooooooh (ooooooooooh) Ooooooooooh | (I try my best)

Ooooooooooh (ooooooooooh) Ooooooooooh (ooooooooooh) | Ooooooooooh (ooooooooooh) | (Try our best)

Ooooooooooh (ooooooooooh) Ooooooooooh (ooooooooooh)

Artist's Note

This was one of the earlier songs written for the album, and
the inclusion of THK on the track should have been the one
that made me realize James Logan was involved, but I remained
none the wiser. It is fitting, however, in retrospect that it
calls out all the bēasts who try to tie us down and hold us
back.

I have immense respect for THK, both as an artist and as a
woman. She has overcome a lot to come to this country and
make it in a genre traditionally dominated by men. As a
lyricist, I find myself envying her facility with language (I
especially love her lyrics to 'Man8R'), but she has a well-
known history with Logan. As Ghosted, James Logan produced
all of her albums to date, and the two of them were
supposedly dated at the start of her career. Knowing James
Logan, I have sympathy for the experiences she may have had.
It says something about her strength as a woman that she can
come through that and remain such a powerful force in this
industry. I do not understand how she can support Logan, but
I will continue to appreciate her wordplay.

As for the song itself, when I started it, I wanted to
include daily affirmations, but I ended up focusing on the
feeling of them rather than the actual words. And I could
have dismissed THK's contributions, but, regardless of
everything else, her contributions elevate the song, and I
must be willing to accept better wherever it comes from.

Queens

Oh... | Oh...

All rise (All rise) | All rise (All rise)

Bra top | Stiletto heels | She walks | The bitches kneel

When she stops | The heart rates quicken | Then she talks | Everyone listens

And (and) | And (and) | And | Yeah

And she says: | "I am the queen (queen) | Of all England (of all England) | Bow before me (me) | Thou shalt listen

Look out upon my works and | Look out upon my works and | (Look out upon my works and) | Look out upon my works and | Despair"

(Look out upon my works and | Despair) | Then she walks past

And I | And my friends | And our men | Can't but condescend | In the end | We wish we were all her | Confident and cock sure

Wanna be | Wanna be with | (I wanna be with Her)

Maybe if I were | A little taller | My cheek bones and waist | A little smaller | Bigger tits and ass | A money baller

Maybe if I had | A better father | Born in South of France | A fancy collar | Maybe I might be | Okay I'm not her

That I'm only me | I'm only (only) | Only (only) | I'm only (only) | Only (only) | I'm only (only) | Only (only)

Yeah | Me | I'm me! | Hell yeah! | I'm me!

(Look out upon my works and) | (Look out upon my works and) | (All rise) | (All rise)

Tank top | Sensible shoes | Bun knot | Nothing to lose

So I'm not | Grabbing attention | I look hot | Without perfection

And (and) | And (and) | And (and)

Then I say: | "I am the queen (queen) | Of all England (of all England) | Maybe in jeans (jeans) | But, god, we stun (stun)

My fellow queens (queens) | Our time is begun (yeah, yeah!)

Look out upon my works and | Look out upon my works and | (Look out upon my works and | Be glad!)

Look out upon my works and | Be glad" | (Be glad!)

(All rise) | (All rise) | (All rise) | (All rise)

Artist's Note

'Queens' was my effort to write in the style of my earlier songs, capturing the energy and almost stream-of-consciousness that I associate with my millennial lyrics. It was also an effort to close out the album with an anthem declaring that we, as women, will not be pitted against one another. We will all come together and rise as one.

Phantoms

Ooooh (ooooh) | Ooooh (ooooh) | Ooooh (ooooh)

There's a groove in the pillow | Where you used to sleep | A chair at the table | Where we used to eat | A stain on my shoulder | Where you used to weep | A phantom in daylight | I walk down the street

Ooooh (ooooh) | Ooooh (ooooh) | Ooooh (ooooh) | Ooooh (ooooh)

Photos on my phone | We're smiling there, sometimes | But there's an undertone | I can't help but see in your eyes | Something I didn't know | You were hiding it inside

There's a groove in the pillow | Where you used to sleep | A chair at the table | Where we used to eat | A stain on my shoulder | Where you used to weep | A phantom in daylight | I walk down the street

Ooooh (ooooh) | Ooooh (ooooh) | Ooooh (ooooh) | Ooooh (ooooh)

Will I love again? | Do I even want to? | Is it worth it to dream | That I will find somebody new | Who makes me feel seen | And I don't compare to you?

There's a groove in the pillow | Where you used to sleep | A chair at the table | Where we used to eat | A stain on my shoulder | Where you used to weep | A phantom in daylight | I walk down the street

Ooooh (ooooh) | Ooooh (ooooh) | Ooooh (ooooh) | Ooooh (ooooh)

Morning jogs alone | You're drifting in my mind | Through the day I roam | Searching meaning I can't find | Our futures left unknown | Does it make more sense in time?

There's a groove in the pillow | Where you used to sleep | A chair at the table | Where we used to eat | A stain on my shoulder | Where you used to weep | A phantom in daylight | I walk down the street

Ooooh (ooooh) | Ooooh (ooooh) | Ooooh (ooooh) | Ooooh (ooooh)

Will I love again? | Do I even want to | Because of all the pain | Whenever I think about you? | But I am moving on | Whether or not I want to

There's a groove in the pillow | Where you used to sleep | A chair at the table | Where we used to eat | A stain on my shoulder | Where you used to weep | A phantom in daylight | I walk down the street

Ooooh (ooooh) | Ooooh (ooooh) | Ooooh (ooooh) | Ooooh (ooooh)

Artist's Note

As many will already know, 'Phantoms' is the one song on the album for which I did not write the original lyrics—mostly. I heard Shaine Timms' soul-inspired performance live and I asked him if he wouldn't mind me covering it. He not only agreed to the cover, but gave me his blessing to add two new verses of my own.

Though the original song was written from the male perspective, I feel that transposing the traditional roles of, for example, being a shoulder to cry on highlights the many shifting dynamics of our modern world. I also felt that, despite the somber mood of the song making some feel that I was ending the album on a down note, it carries an inherent hopefulness that both reiterates the broadly triumphal message of the album and frames it within a reality where, sometimes, life does not go the way we want it to, even when we're at our peaks.

Acknowledgments

I wish to thank and acknowledge the many writers who have not only built the foundation upon which neophytes like myself can construct our meager imitations, but who have inspired me and many others, future and past, to put pencil to paper.

In addition to the authors, artists and musicians mentioned or referenced within the text, I must acknowledge the profound influence of Raymond Chandler whose works I tried, and failed, to evoke, and of Britney Spears whose music was the soundtrack for the early draft of the book.